A #1 Amazon Charts Bestseller
A *Wall Street Journal,* Publishers Weekly, and *USA Today* Bestseller
A Goodreads Best Book of the Month
A Goodreads Choice Awards 2017 Finalist, Historical Fiction

"A captivating read . . ."

—*RT Book Reviews*

"Highly recommended."

—Historical Novel Society

"Exciting . . . taut thriller . . . *Beneath a Scarlet Sky* tells the true story of one young Italian's efforts to thwart the Nazis."

—Shelf Awareness

"An incredible story, beautifully written, and a fine and noble book."

—James Patterson, *New York Times* bestselling author

"Sprawling, stirring, like the richest of stories, and played out on a canvas of heroism and tragedy, *Beneath a Scarlet Sky* is like one of those iconic World War II black-and-white photos: a face of hope and tears, the story of a small life that ended up mattering in a big way."

—Andrew Gross, *New York Times* bestselling author of *The One Man*

"Action, adventure, love, war, and an epic hero—all set against the backdrop of one of history's darkest moments—Mark Sullivan's *Beneath a Scarlet Sky* has everything one can ask for in an exceptional World War II novel."

—Tess Gerritsen, *New York Times* bestselling author of *Playing with Fire*

"This is full-force Mark Sullivan—muscular, soulful prose evincing an artist's touch and a journalist's eye. *Beneath a Scarlet Sky* conjures an era with a magician's ease, weaving the rich tapestry of a wartime epic. World War II Italy has never been more alive to me."

—Gregg Hurwitz, *New York Times* bestselling author of *The Nowhere Man*

"*Beneath a Scarlet Sky* has everything—heroism, courage, terror, true love, revenge, compassion in the face of the worst human evils. Sullivan shows us war as it really is, with all its complexities, conflicting loyalties, and unresolved questions, but most of all, he brings us the extraordinary figure of Pino Lella, whose determination to live *con smania*—with passion—saved him."

—Joseph Finder, *New York Times* bestselling author of *Suspicion* and *The Switch*

BENEATH A SCARLET SKY

ALSO BY MARK SULLIVAN

Thief

Outlaw

Rogue

The Escape Artist

The Art of Rendition

Brotherhood

Triple Cross

The Second Woman

Labyrinth

Ghost Dance

The Purification Ceremony

Hard News

The Fall Line

With James Patterson

The Games

Private Paris

Private L.A.

Private Berlin

Private Games

BENEATH A SCARLET SKY

A NOVEL

MARK SULLIVAN

LAKE UNION
PUBLISHING

Though based on a true story and real characters, this is a work of fiction and of the author's imagination.

Published by Lake Union Publishing, Seattle

www.apub.com

Amazon, the Amazon logo, and Lake Union Publishing are trademarks of Amazon.com, Inc., or its affiliates.

ISBN-13: 9781503943377 (paperback)
ISBN-10: 1503943372 (paperback)
ISBN-13: 9781503902374 (hardcover)
ISBN-10: 1503902374 (hardcover)

Cover design by Shasti O'Leary Soudant

Printed in the United States of America

For the eight thousand Italian Jews who could not be saved.

For the millions taken slave by the Nazi war machine, and the countless who did not make it home.

And for Robert Dehlendorf, who heard the tale first, and rescued me.

Love conquers all things.

—Virgil

PREFACE

In early February 2006, I was forty-seven and at the lowest point of my life.

My younger brother, who was also my best friend, had drunk himself to death the summer before. I'd written a novel no one liked, was embroiled in a business dispute, and stood on the brink of personal bankruptcy.

Driving alone on a Montana highway at dusk, I started thinking about my insurance policies and realized that I was worth much more to my family dead than alive. I contemplated driving into a freeway abutment. It was snowy, and the light was low. No one would have suspected suicide.

But then, in my mind's eye, I saw my wife and sons in the swirling snow and had a change of heart. When I pulled off the highway, I was shaking uncontrollably. On the verge of a breakdown, I bowed my head and begged God and the Universe for help. I prayed for a story, something greater than myself, a project I could get lost in.

Believe it or not, that very same evening, at a dinner party in Bozeman, Montana—of all places—I heard the snippets of an extraordinary, untold tale of World War II with a seventeen-year-old Italian boy as its hero.

My first reaction was that the story of Pino Lella's life in the last twenty-three months of the war could not possibly be true. We would have heard it before. But then I learned that Pino—pronounced *pea-no*—was still alive some six decades later and back in Italy after nearly thirty years in Beverly Hills and Mammoth Lakes, California.

I called him. Mr. Lella was very reluctant to talk to me at first. He said he was no hero, more a coward, which only intrigued me further. Finally, after several more phone calls, he agreed to see me if I came to Italy.

I flew to Italy and spent three weeks with Pino in an old villa in the town of Lesa on Lake Maggiore, north of Milan. At the time, Pino was seventy-nine but big, strong, handsome, charming, funny, and often evasive. I listened to him for hours on end while he summoned up the past.

Some of Pino's memories were so vivid they appeared in the air in front of me. Others were more dimly lit and had to be coaxed into clarity through repeated questioning. Certain events and characters he clearly avoided, and others he seemed to dread talking about at all. When I pressed the old man about these painful times, he recounted tragedies that reduced us both to sobbing.

During that first trip, I also talked to Holocaust historians in Milan and interviewed Catholic priests and members of the partisan resistance. I visited every major scene with Pino. I skied and climbed in the Alps to better understand the escape routes. I held the old man when he collapsed in grief in the Piazzale Loreto, and I watched the agony of his loss ripple through him in the streets around the Castello Sforzesco. He showed me where he last saw Benito Mussolini. In the great cathedral of Milan, the Duomo, I saw his shaking hand as he lit a candle for the dead and the martyred.

Through it all, I listened to a man looking back at two years of his extraordinary life, growing up at seventeen, growing old at eighteen, the ups and downs, the trials and triumphs, the love and the heartbreak. My personal problems, and my life in general, seemed small and insignificant in comparison to what he'd endured at an unfathomably young age. And his insight into life's tragedies gave me a new perspective. I began to heal, and Pino and I became fast friends. When I returned home, I felt better than I had in years.

That trip led to four more over the course of the following decade, allowing me to do research on Pino's tale between the writing of other books. I consulted with staff at Yad Vashem, Israel's main Holocaust remembrance and education center, and with historians in Italy, Germany, and the United States. I spent weeks in the war archives in those three countries and in the United Kingdom.

I interviewed the surviving eyewitnesses—at least those I could find—to corroborate various events in Pino's story, as well as the descendants and friends of those long dead, including Ingrid Bruck, the daughter of the mysterious Nazi general who complicates the heart of the tale.

Wherever possible, I have stuck to the facts gleaned from those archives, interviews, and testimonies. But I learned quickly that due to the widespread burning of Nazi documents as World War II ground to a close, the paper trail surrounding Pino's past was scattered at best.

I was also hampered by a kind of collective amnesia concerning Italy and Italians after the war. Legions of books have been written about D-day, the Allied campaigns across western Europe, and the efforts of brave souls who risked their lives to save Jews in other European countries. But the Nazi occupation of Italy and the Catholic underground railroad, which was formed to save the Italian Jews, have received scant attention. Some 60,000 Allied soldiers died fighting to free Italy. Some 140,000 Italians died during Nazi occupation. And still, so little has been written about the battle for Italy, historians have taken to calling it the "Forgotten Front."

Much of the amnesia was caused by Italians who'd survived. As one old partisan fighter told me, "We were still young and wanted to forget. We wanted to put the terrible things we'd experienced behind us. No one talks about World War Two in Italy, so no one remembers."

Due to the document burning, the collective amnesia, and the death of so many characters by the time I learned of the story, I have been forced in places to construct scenes and dialogue based solely on Pino's memory decades later, the scant physical evidence that remains, and my imagination fueled by my research and informed suspicions. In certain instances, I have also comingled or compressed events and characters for the sake of narrative coherence and have fully dramatized incidents that were described to me in much more truncated forms.

As a result, then, the story you are about to read is not a work of narrative nonfiction, but a novel of biographical and historical fiction that hews closely to what happened to Pino Lella between June 1943 and May 1945.

PART ONE
NONE SHALL SLEEP

Chapter One

June 9, 1943
Milan, Italy

Like all the pharaohs, emperors, and tyrants before him, Il Duce had seen his empire rise only to crumble. Indeed, by that late-spring afternoon, power was bleeding from Benito Mussolini's grasp like joy from a young widowed heart.

The Fascist dictator's battered armies had retreated from North Africa. Allied forces were poised off Sicily. And every day, Adolf Hitler was sending more troops and supplies south to fortify the boot of Italy.

Pino Lella knew all this from BBC reports he listened to on his shortwave radio nightly. He'd seen with his own eyes the rising numbers of Nazis everywhere he went. But as he strolled through the medieval streets of Milan, Pino was blissfully ignoring the forces of conflict spiraling his way. World War II was a news dispatch, nothing more, listened to and gone in the very next moment—replaced by thoughts of his three favorite subjects: girls and music and food.

He was only seventeen after all, 1.85 meters tall, seventy-five kilograms, long and gangly, with big hands and feet, hair that defied taming, and enough acne and awkwardness that none of the girls he'd asked to the movies had agreed to accompany him. And yet, as was his nature, Pino remained undeterred.

He strode confidently with his friends onto the piazza in front of the Duomo, the Basilica di Santa Maria Nascente, the grand Gothic cathedral that lies at the very center of Milan.

"I am going to meet a beautiful girl today," Pino said, wagging his finger at the scarlet, threatening sky. "And we are going to fall in mad, tragic love and go on grand adventures with music and food and wine and intrigue every day, all day long."

"You live in a fantasy," said Carletto Beltramini, Pino's best friend.

"I do not," Pino sniffed.

"Sure you do," said Pino's brother, Mimo, who was two years younger. "You fall in love with every pretty girl you see."

"But none of them loves Pino back," said Carletto. A moon-faced kid with a slight frame, he was much shorter than Pino.

Mimo, who was shorter still, said, "It's true."

Pino dismissed them both. "You are clearly not romantics."

"What are they doing over there?" Carletto asked, pointing at crews of men working outside the Duomo.

Some were placing wooden cutouts in the cavities where the cathedral's stained-glass windows normally hung. Others were transferring sandbags from lorries to a growing wall around the base of the cathedral. Still more were erecting spotlights under the watchful eyes of a knot of priests who stood near the cathedral's central double doors.

"I'll go find out," Pino said.

"Not before I do," his little brother said, and took off toward the workers.

"Everything's a competition with Mimo," Carletto said. "He needs to learn to calm down."

Pino laughed, then said over his shoulder, "If you know how he can do that, tell my mother."

Looping past the laborers, Pino went straight to the priests and tapped one on the shoulder. "Excuse me, Father."

The cleric, in his midtwenties, was as tall as Pino but heavier. He turned, looked at the teen from the ground up—seeing his new shoes, the gray linen pants, the crisp white shirt, and a green foulard tie his mother had given him for his birthday—and then stared intently into Pino's eyes as if he could look inside his head and know his sinful teenage thoughts.

He said, "I'm in seminary. Not ordained. No collar."

"Oh, oh, I'm sorry," Pino said, intimidated. "We just wanted to know why you're putting up the lights."

Before the young seminarian could answer, a knobby hand appeared at his right elbow. He moved aside to reveal a short, lean priest in his fifties wearing white robes and a red skullcap. Pino knew him in an instant and felt his stomach fall as he dropped to one knee before the cardinal of Milan.

"My Lord Cardinal," Pino said, head bowed.

The seminarian said sternly, "You address him as 'Your Eminence.'"

Pino looked up, confused. "My British nanny taught me to say 'My Lord Cardinal' if I ever met a cardinal."

The severe younger man's face turned positively stony, but Ildefonso Cardinal Schuster laughed softly and said, "I think he's right, Barbareschi. In England, I'd be addressed as 'Lord Cardinal.'"

Cardinal Schuster was both famous and powerful in Milan. As the Catholic leader of northern Italy, and as a man who had the ear of Pope Pius XII, the cardinal was in the newspapers often. Pino thought Schuster's expression the most indelible thing about him; his smiling face spoke of kindness, but his eyes held the threat of damnation.

Clearly miffed, the seminarian said, "We're in Milan, Your Eminence, not London."

"It doesn't matter," Schuster said. He put his hand on Pino's shoulder and told him to rise. "What's your name, young man?"

"Pino Lella."

"Pino?"

"My mother used to call me Giuseppino," Pino said, struggling to his feet. "The 'Pino' part stuck."

Cardinal Schuster looked up at "Little Joseph" and laughed. "Pino Lella. That is a name to remember."

Why someone like the cardinal would say something like that confused Pino.

In the silence that followed, Pino blurted out, "I've met you before, My Lord Cardinal."

That surprised Schuster. "Where was that?"

"At Casa Alpina, Father Re's camp above Madesimo. Years ago."

Cardinal Schuster smiled. "I remember that visit. I told Father Re that he was the only priest in Italy with a cathedral grander than the Duomo and St. Peter's. Young Barbareschi here is going up to work with Father Re next week."

"You'll like him and Casa Alpina," Pino said. "The climbing is very good there."

Barbareschi actually smiled.

Pino bowed uncertainly and started to back away, which seemed to amuse Cardinal Schuster all the more. He said, "I thought you were interested in the lights?"

Pino stopped. "Yes?"

"They're my idea," Schuster said. "The blackout begins tonight. Only the Duomo will be lit from now on. I pray that the bomber pilots will see it and be so awed by its beauty that they choose to spare it. This magnificent church took almost five hundred years to build. It would be a tragedy to see it gone in a night."

Pino peered up the elaborate face of the massive cathedral. Built of pale pinkish Candoglia marble, with scores of spires, balconies, and pinnacles, the Duomo seemed as frosted, grand, and illusory as the Alps in winter. He adored skiing and climbing in the mountains almost as much as music and girls, and seeing the church always took him to high country in his mind.

But now the cardinal believed the cathedral and Milan were threatened. For the first time, the possibility of an aerial attack seemed real to Pino.

He said, "So we will be bombed?"

"I pray it does not happen," Cardinal Schuster said, "but a prudent man always prepares for the worst. Good-bye, and may your faith in God keep you safe in the days ahead, Pino."

⟞⟝

The cardinal of Milan walked away, leaving Pino feeling awed when he returned to Carletto and Mimo, each of whom looked equally thunderstruck.

"That was Cardinal Schuster," Carletto said.

"I know," Pino said.

"You were talking to him a long time."

"Was I?"

"Yes," his little brother said. "What did he tell you?"

"That he'd remember my name, and that the lights are to keep the bombers from blowing up the cathedral."

"See?" Mimo said to Carletto. "I told you."

Carletto eyed Pino suspiciously. "Why would Cardinal Schuster remember *your* name?"

Pino shrugged. "Maybe he liked the sound of it. *Pino Lella*."

Mimo snorted. "You *do* live in a fantasy world."

They heard thunder as they left Piazza Duomo, crossed the street, and walked beneath the grand archway into the Galleria, the world's first covered shopping mall—two wide, intersecting walkways lined with shops and ordinarily covered with an iron-and-glass dome. By the time the three boys went in that day, the glass plates had been removed, leaving only the superstructure, which threw a web of rectangular shadows across the market scene.

As the thunder got closer, Pino saw worry in many faces on the streets of the Galleria, but he did not share their concern. Thunder was thunder, not a bomb exploding.

"Flowers?" called a woman at a cart of freshly cut roses. "For your girlfriend?"

Pino said, "When I find her, I will come back."

"You might wait years for that to happen, *signora*," Mimo said.

Pino took a swing at his little brother. Mimo dodged it and took off, leaving the Galleria and emerging into a piazza graced by a statue of Leonardo da Vinci. Beyond the statue, on the other side of the street and trolley tracks, the doors to the Teatro alla Scala had been flung open to air out the famous opera hall. The strains of violins and cellos being tuned and a tenor practicing scales floated out.

Pino kept up the chase, but then he noticed a pretty girl—black hair, creamy skin, and flashing dark eyes. She was making her way across the piazza, heading toward the Galleria. He skidded to a halt and watched her. Flooded with longing, he was unable to speak.

After she passed, Pino said, "I think I'm falling in love."

"Falling on your face maybe," said Carletto, who'd walked up behind him.

Mimo circled back to them. "Someone just said the Allies will be here by Christmas."

"I want the Americans to come to Milan sooner than that," Carletto said.

"Me, too," Pino agreed. "More jazz! Less opera!"

Taking off in a sprint, he leaped over a vacant bench and onto a curved metal railing that protected the statue of da Vinci. He slid neatly on the smooth surface for a short distance before jumping off the other side and landing like a cat.

11

Never to be outdone, Mimo tried the same trick, but he crashed to the ground in front of a dark-haired, heavyset woman in a floral print dress. She looked to be in her late thirties, early forties. She carried a violin case and wore a broad blue straw hat against the sun.

⚜

The woman was so startled she almost dropped her violin case. She clutched it to her bosom angrily as Mimo moaned and held his ribs.

"This is Piazza Della Scala!" she scolded. "Honoring the great Leonardo! Have you no respect? Go and play your childish games somewhere else."

"You think we're children?" Mimo said, puffing out his chest. "Little boys?"

The woman looked beyond him and said, "Little boys who do not understand the real games played around them."

Dark clouds had begun to roll in, dimming the scene. Pino twisted and saw a large black Daimler-Benz staff car rolling down the street that separated the piazza from the opera house. Red Nazi flags flew on either fender. A general's flag fluttered on the radio antenna. Pino saw the silhouette of the general, sitting ramrod straight in the backseat. For some reason the image gave him the chills.

When Pino turned around, the violinist was already moving away, head up, defiant as she crossed the street behind the Nazi staff car and marched into the opera house.

As the boys moved on, Mimo limped along while rubbing his right hip and complaining. But Pino was barely listening. A tawny-blond woman with slate-blue eyes was coming down the sidewalk right at them. He guessed her to be in her early twenties. She was beautifully put together, with a gentle nose, high cheekbones, and lips that curled naturally into an easy smile. Svelte and of medium height, she wore a yellow summer dress and carried a canvas shopping bag. She turned off the sidewalk and entered a bakery just ahead.

"I'm in love again," Pino said, both palms over his heart. "Did you see her?"

Carletto snorted. "Don't you give up?"

"Never," Pino said, trotting to the bakery window and looking inside.

The woman was stuffing loaves of bread into her bag. He saw she wasn't wearing a ring on her left hand, so he waited for her to pay and come out.

When she did, he stepped in front of her, put his hand over his heart, and said, "I'm sorry, *signorina*. I was overcome by your beauty and had to meet you."

"Listen to you," she scoffed as she maneuvered around him and kept walking.

As she'd passed, Pino smelled her female-and-jasmine scent. It was intoxicating, like nothing he'd ever smelled before.

He hurried after her, saying, "It is true. I see many beautiful ladies, *signorina*. I live in the fashion district, San Babila. Many models."

She gave him a sidelong glance. "San Babila is a very fine place to live."

"My parents own Le Borsette di Lella, the purse store. Do you know it?"

"My—my employer bought a purse there just last week."

"Yes?" Pino said, delighted. "So you see I come from a reputable family. Would you like to see a movie with me tonight? *You Were Never Lovelier* is playing. Fred Astaire. Rita Hayworth. Dancing. Singing. So elegant. Like you, *signorina*."

She finally turned her head to look over at him with those piercing eyes. "How old are you?"

"Almost eighteen."

She laughed. "You're kind of young for me."

"It's just a movie. We go as friends. I am not too young for that, am I?"

She didn't say anything, just kept on walking.

"Yes? No?" Pino said.

"There's a blackout tonight."

"It will still be light when the show starts, and afterward I will walk you home safe and sound," Pino assured her. "I can see like a cat at night."

She said nothing for several steps, and Pino's heart sank.

"Where is this movie playing?" she asked.

Pino gave her the address and said, "You will meet me there, yes? Seven thirty outside the ticket booth?"

"You are kind of funny, and life is short. Why not?"

Pino grinned, put his hand to his chest, and said, "Until then."

"Until then," she said. She smiled, then crossed the street.

Pino watched her go, feeling triumphant and breathless until he realized something when she turned to wait for the oncoming street trolley and looked back at him in amusement.

"*Signorina*, forgive me," he yelled to her, "but what is your name?"

"Anna," she called back.

"I am Pino!" he cried. "Pino Lella!"

The trolley screeched to a halt, drowning out his last name and blocking her from his view. When the trolley rolled on, Anna was gone.

"She'll never come," said Mimo, who'd been hustling along behind them the entire time. "She just said it to get you to stop following her."

"Of course she will come," Pino said, before looking to Carletto, who had also followed them. "You saw it in her eyes, Anna's eyes, didn't you?"

Before his brother and his friend could respond, lightning flashed, and the first drops of rain fell, plump and growing fatter. They all began to run.

"I'm going home!" Carletto cried, and veered off.

Chapter Two

The skies opened up. The deluge began. Pino followed Mimo, sprinting toward the fashion district, getting drenched and not caring. Anna was going to the movies with him. She'd said yes. It made him almost delirious.

The brothers were soaked, and lightning was striking by the time they dodged into Valigeria Albanese, Albanese Luggage, their uncle's store and factory in a rust-colored building at #7 Via Pietro Verri.

Dripping wet, the boys went into the long, narrow shop, which enveloped them with the rich smell of new leather. The shelves were stacked with fine attaché cases, handbags and satchels, suitcases and trunks. The glass displays featured woven leather wallets and beautifully tooled cigarette cases and portfolios. There were two customers in the shop, one an older woman close to the door, and beyond her at the far end, a Nazi officer in a black and gray uniform.

Pino watched him, but heard the older woman say, "Which one, Albert?"

"Go with your heart," said the man waiting on her behind the counter. Big, barrel-chested, and mustached, he wore a beautiful mouse-gray suit, starched white shirt, and a jaunty blue polka-dot bow tie.

"But I love them both," his customer complained.

Stroking his mustache and chuckling, he said, "Then buy them both!"

She hesitated, giggled. "Maybe I will, then!"

"Excellent! Excellent!" he said, rubbing his hands. "Greta, can you get me boxes for this magnificent lady with such impeccable taste?"

"I'm busy at the moment, Albert," replied Pino's Austrian aunt Greta, who was waiting on the Nazi. She was a tall, thin woman with short brown hair and an easy smile. The German was smoking and examining a leather-wrapped cigarette case.

Pino said, "I'll get the boxes for you, Uncle Albert."

Uncle Albert shot Pino a look. "Dry off before you handle them."

Thinking about Anna, Pino headed toward the factory door beyond his aunt and the German. The officer pivoted to watch Pino as he passed, revealing oak leaves on his lapels that identified him as a colonel. The flat front of his officer's cap bore a *Totenkopf*, a small skull-and-bones emblem below an eagle that clutched a swastika. Pino knew he was Geheime Staatspolizei, Gestapo, a high-ranking officer in Hitler's secret police. Medium in height and build, with a narrow nose and joyless lips, the Nazi had flat dark eyes that gave away nothing.

Feeling rattled, Pino went through the door and into the factory, a much larger space with a higher ceiling. Seamstresses and cutters were putting away their work for the day. He found some rags and dried his hands. Then he grabbed two cardboard boxes embossed with the Albanese logo and started back toward the shop, his thoughts happily returning to Anna.

She was beautiful, and older, and . . .

He hesitated before pushing through the door. The Gestapo colonel was just leaving, walking out into the rain. Pino's aunt stood at the door, watching the colonel go and nodding.

Pino felt better the instant she shut the door.

He helped his uncle pack the two purses. When the last customer left, Uncle Albert told Mimo to lock the front door and to put a "Closed" sign in the window.

When Mimo had done so, Uncle Albert said, "Did you get his name?"

"Standartenführer Walter Rauff," Aunt Greta replied. "The new Gestapo chief for northern Italy. He came in from Tunisia. Tullio's keeping an eye on him."

"Tullio's back?" Pino said, surprised and happy. Tullio Galimberti was five years older, his idol, and a close family friend.

"Yesterday," Uncle Albert said.

Aunt Greta said, "Rauff said the Gestapo is taking over the Hotel Regina."

Her husband grumbled. "Who does Italy belong to—Mussolini or Hitler?"

"It doesn't matter," Pino said, trying to convince himself. "The war will be over soon, and the Americans will come, and there will be jazz everywhere!"

Uncle Albert shook his head. "That depends on the Germans and Il Duce."

Aunt Greta said, "Have you looked at the time, Pino? Your mother expected you two home an hour ago to help prepare for their party."

Pino's stomach fell. His mother was not someone to disappoint.

"I'll see you later?" he asked, heading for the door, with Mimo following.

"We wouldn't miss it," Uncle Albert said.

⁂

By the time the boys made it to #3 Via Monte Napoleone, Le Borsette di Lella, his parents' purse shop, was closed. Thinking of his mother, Pino grew fearful. He hoped his father would be around to tame the human hurricane. Savory odors wafted to them as they climbed the stairs: lamb and garlic simmering, freshly shredded basil, and bread warm from the oven.

They opened the door into the family's opulent flat, which was abuzz with activity. The regular maid and a temporary hire bustled about the dining room, setting out cut crystal, silverware, and china for the buffet. In the drawing room, a tall, thin, stoop-shouldered man stood with his back to the hall holding a violin and bow and playing a piece Pino didn't recognize. The man hit a sour note and stopped, shaking his head.

"Papa?" Pino called quietly. "Are we in trouble?"

Michele Lella lowered his violin and turned, chewing the inside of his cheek. Before he could answer, a six-year-old girl came storming down the hall from the kitchen. Pino's little sister, Cicci, halted in front of him and demanded, "Where have you been, Pino? Mama is not happy with you. Or you, Mimo."

Pino ignored her, focusing instead on the locomotive in an apron chugging out of the kitchen. He swore he could see steam coming out his mother's ears. Porzia Lella was at least thirty centimeters shorter than her elder son, and at least twenty kilograms lighter. But she marched up to Pino, tore off her glasses, and shook them at him.

"I asked you to be home at four, and here it is five fifteen," she said. "You act like a child. I can rely on more from your sister."

Cicci turned up her nose and nodded.

For a moment, Pino did not know what to say. But then he was inspired to adopt a forlorn look and hunch over and clutch his belly.

"I'm sorry, Mama," he said. "I ate some street food. It gave me the distress. And then we were caught in the lightning and forced to wait at Uncle Albert's."

Porzia crossed her arms and eyed him. Cicci adopted the same skeptical pose.

Their mother looked to Mimo. "Is that true, Domenico?"

Pino glanced warily at his brother.

Mimo bobbed his head. "I told him the sausage didn't look right, but he would not listen. Pino had to stop in three cafés to use the toilet. And there was a Gestapo colonel at Uncle Albert's shop. He said the Nazis are taking over the Hotel Regina."

His mother paled. "What?"

Pino grimaced and bent over even more. "I need to go right now."

Cicci still looked suspicious, but Pino's mother's anger had moved on to worry. "Go. Go! And wash your hands afterward."

Pino hurried down the hall.

Behind him, Porzia said, "Where are you going, Mimo? You're not sick."

"Mama," Mimo complained, "Pino gets out of everything."

Pino did not wait to hear his mother's reply. He rushed past the kitchen and the incredible smells and climbed the staircase that led to the second floor of the apartment and the water closet. He went inside for a respectable ten minutes and spent it thinking about every moment he'd had with Anna, especially how she'd looked back at him in amusement from across the trolley tracks. He flushed, lit a match to cover the lack of foul odor, and lay on his bed, the shortwave tuned to the BBC and a jazz show that Pino almost never missed.

Duke Ellington's band was playing "Cotton Tail," one of his recent favorites, and he closed his eyes to marvel at Ben Webster's tenor sax solo. Pino had loved jazz from the first time he heard a recording of Billie Holiday and Lester Young performing "I Can't Get Started." As heretical as it was to say so in the Lella household—where opera and classical music reigned supreme—from that moment forward, Pino believed jazz was the greatest musical art form. Because of that belief, he longed to go to the United States, where jazz was born. It was his fondest dream.

Pino wondered what life in America would be like. The language wasn't a problem. He'd grown up with two nannies, one from London and another from Paris. He'd spoken all three languages almost from birth. Was there jazz everywhere in America? Was it like this cool curtain of sound behind every moment? And what about the American girls? Were any of them as beautiful as Anna?

"Cotton Tail" wound down. Benny Goodman's "Roll 'Em" began with a boogie-woogie beat that wound up into a clarinet solo. Pino jumped up off the bed, kicked off his shoes, and started dancing, seeing himself with beautiful Anna doing a crazy Lindy Hop—no war, no Nazis, only music, and food, and wine, and love.

Then he realized how loud the music was, turned it down, and stopped dancing. He didn't want to bring his father upstairs for another argument about music. Michele despised jazz. The week before, he caught Pino practicing Meade Lux Lewis's boogie tune "Low Down Dog" on the family Steinway, and it was as though he'd desecrated a saint.

Pino took a shower and changed clothes. Several minutes after the cathedral bells tolled 6:00 p.m., Pino crawled back on the bed and looked out the open window. With the thunder clouds a memory, familiar sounds echoed up from the streets of San Babila. The last shops were closing. The wealthy and fashionable of Milan hurried toward home. He could hear their animated voices as one, a chorus of the street—women laughing at some small joy, children crying at some minor tragedy, men arguing over nothing but the sheer Italian love of verbal battle and mock outrage.

Pino startled at the apartment bell ringing downstairs. He heard voices bidding hellos and welcomes. He glanced at the clock. It was 6:15 p.m. The movie started at seven thirty, and it was a long walk to the theater and Anna.

Pino had one leg out the window and was feeling for a ledge that led to a fire escape when he heard a sharp laugh behind him.

"She won't be there," Mimo said.

"Of course she will," Pino said, making it out the window.

It was a solid nine meters to the ground, and the ledge was not very wide. He had to smear his back to the wall and shuffle sideways to another window that he climbed through to gain access to a back staircase. A minute later, though, he was on the ground, outside, and moving.

The cinema's marquee was unlit due to the new blackout rules. But Pino's heart swelled when he saw the names of Fred Astaire and Rita Hayworth on the poster. He loved Hollywood musicals, especially those with swing music. And he'd had dreams about Rita Hayworth that . . . well . . .

Pino bought two tickets. As other patrons filed into the theater, he stood searching the street and sidewalks for Anna. He waited until he started to suffer the empty, devastating knowledge that she was not coming.

"I told you," Mimo said, sliding up beside him.

Pino wanted to be angry but couldn't. Deep down, he loved his younger brother's guts and bullishness, his brains and street smarts. He handed Mimo a ticket.

The boys went inside and found seats.

"Pino?" Mimo said quietly. "When did you start to grow? Fifteen?"

Pino fought a smile. His brother was always fretting that he was so short.

"Not until I was sixteen, really."

"But it could be earlier?"

"Could be."

The houselights went down and a Fascist propaganda newsreel began. Pino was still depressed by Anna's standing him up when Il Duce appeared on the screen. Dressed the part of the commanding general in a medal-strewn jacket with waist belt, tunic, breeches, and gleaming black knee-high riding boots, Benito Mussolini walked with one of his field commanders on a bluff above the Ligurian Sea.

The narrator said the Italian dictator was inspecting fortifications. On-screen, Il Duce's hands were clasped behind his back as he walked. The emperor's chin pointed at the horizon. His back was arched. His chest puffed toward the sky.

"He looks like a little rooster," Pino said.

"Shhhh!" Mimo whispered. "Not so loud."

"Why? Every time you see him, he looks like he wants to go, 'Cock-a-doodle-doo.'"

His brother sniggered while the newsreel went on to boast of Italy's defenses and of Mussolini's growing stature on the world stage. It was pure propaganda. Pino listened to the BBC every night. He knew what he was watching wasn't true, and he was happy when the newsreel ended and the movie began.

Pino was soon swept up in the film's comic plot and loving every scene where Hayworth danced with Astaire.

"Rita," Pino said with a sigh after a series of spiral moves had swept Hayworth's dress about her legs like a matador's cape. "She's so elegant, just like Anna."

Mimo's face screwed up. "She stood you up."

"But she was so beautiful," Pino whispered.

An air raid siren wailed. People began to yell and jump up from their seats.

The screen froze in close-up on Astaire and Hayworth dancing cheek to cheek, their lips and smiles to the panicking crowd.

As the film melted up on the screen, antiaircraft guns cracked outside the theater, and the first unseen Allied bombers cleared their bays, releasing an overture of fire and destruction that played down on Milan.

Chapter Three

Screaming, the audience stampeded and charged the theater doors. Pino and Mimo were terrified and stuck in the surging mob when, with a deafening roar, a bomb exploded and blew out the theater's back wall, hurling chunks of debris that ripped the screen to shreds. The lights died.

Something hit Pino hard on the cheek, gashed him open. He felt the wound pulsing and blood dripping over his jaw. In shock now more than in a panic, he choked on smoke and dust and fought his way forward. Grit got in his eyes and up his nostrils, which burned as he and Mimo made their way from the theater, bent over and hacking.

Outside, the sirens wailed on and the bombs kept falling, still far from the crescendo. Fires raged in buildings up and down the street from the theater. Antiaircraft guns rattled. Tracer rounds scrawled red arcs across the sky. Their loads blew so brightly that Pino could see the silhouettes of the Lancaster bombers above him, wingtip to wingtip in a V-formation, like so many dark geese migrating in the night.

More bombs fell with a collective sound like buzzing hornets that erupted one after the other, sending plumes of flame and oily smoke into the sky. Several went off so close to the fleeing Lella boys that they felt the blast waves pound through them and almost lost their balance.

"Where are we going, Pino?" Mimo cried.

For a moment he was too frightened to think, but then said, "The Duomo."

Pino led his brother toward the only thing in Milan lit by anything but fire. In the distance, the spotlights made the cathedral look unearthly, almost heaven-sent. As they ran, the hornets in the sky and the explosions dwindled and stopped. No more bombers. No more cannon fire.

Just sirens and people crying and shouting. A desperate father dug through brick rubble with a lantern in his hand. His wife wept nearby, hanging on to her dead son. Other crying people with lanterns were gathered around a girl who'd lost her arm and died there in the streets, her eyes glazed open.

Pino had never seen dead people before, and began to cry himself. *Nothing will ever be the same.* The teenager could feel that as plain as the hornets still buzzing and the explosions still ringing in his ears. *Nothing will ever be the same.*

At last they were alongside the Duomo itself. There were no bomb craters here by the cathedral. No rubble. No fire. It was as if the attack had never happened but for the wailing grief in the distance.

Pino smiled weakly. "Cardinal Schuster's plan worked."

Mimo frowned and said, "Home's close to the cathedral, but not that close."

The boys ran through a maze of dark streets that led them back to #3 Via Monte Napoleone. The purse shop and their apartment above it looked normal. It seemed a miracle after what they'd been through.

Mimo opened the front door and started up the stairs. Pino followed, hearing the sighing of violins, a piano playing, and a tenor in song. For some reason, the music made Pino furious. He pushed by Mimo and pounded on the apartment door.

The music stopped. His mother opened the door.

"The city's on fire and you're playing music?" Pino shouted at Porzia, who took an alarmed step back. "People are dying and you're playing music?"

Several people came into the hallway behind his mother, including his aunt, uncle, and father.

Michele said, "Music is how we survive such times, Pino."

Pino saw others in the crowded apartment nodding. Among them was that female violinist Mimo had almost knocked over earlier in the day.

"You're hurt, Pino," Porzia said. "You're bleeding."

"There are others who are far worse," Pino said, tears welling in his eyes. "I'm sorry, Mama. It was . . . awful."

Porzia melted, threw out her arms, and hugged her filthy, bleeding boys.

"It's okay, now," she said, kissing them each in turn. "I don't want to know where you were or how you got there. I'm just happy you got home."

She told her sons to go upstairs and get cleaned up before a doctor, a guest at the party, could look at Pino's wound. As she spoke to them, Pino saw something he'd never seen before in his mother. It was fear—fear that the next time the bombers came they might not be so lucky.

Fear was still on her face as the doctor sewed shut the gash on his cheek. When he was done, Porzia cast a judgmental gaze on her older son. "You and I will have a talk about all this tomorrow," she said.

Pino lowered his eyes and nodded. "Yes, Mama."

"Get something to eat. If you're not too sick to your stomach, that is."

He looked up and saw his mother looking at him archly. He should have kept up the act that he was ill, telling her he'd go to bed without eating. But he was starving.

"I feel better than before," he said.

"I think you feel worse than before," Porzia said, and left the room.

Pino followed her morosely down the hall to the dining room. Mimo had already piled his plate and was relating an animated version of their adventure to several of his parents' friends.

"Sounds like quite the night, Pino," someone said behind him.

Pino turned to find a handsome, impeccably dressed man in his twenties. A stunningly beautiful woman held on to his arm. Pino broke into a grin.

"Tullio!" he said. "I heard you were back!"

Tullio said, "Pino, this is my friend Cristina."

Pino nodded to her politely. Cristina looked bored and excused herself.

"When did you meet her?" Pino asked.

"Yesterday," Tullio said. "On the train. She wants to be a model."

Pino shook his head. It was always like this with Tullio Galimberti. A successful dress salesman, Tullio was a magician when it came to attractive women.

"How do you do it?" Pino asked. "All the pretty girls."

"You don't know?" Tullio said, cutting some cheese.

Pino wanted to say something boastful, but he remembered that Anna had stood him up. She had accepted his invitation just to get rid of him. "Evidently, I don't. No."

"Teaching you could take years," Tullio said, fighting a smile.

"C'mon, Tullio," Pino said. "There's got to be some trick I'm—"

"There is no trick," Tullio said, sobering. "Number one thing? Listen."

"Listen?"

"To the girl," Tullio said, exasperated. "Most guys don't listen. They just start blabbing on about themselves. Women need to be understood. So listen to what they say and compliment them on how they look, or sing, or whatever. Right there—listening and complimenting—you're ahead of eighty percent of every guy on the face of the earth."

"But what if they're not talking a lot?"

"Then be funny. Or flattering. Or both."

Pino thought he'd been funny and flattering to Anna, but maybe not enough. Then he thought of something else. "So where did Colonel Rauff go today?"

Tullio's affable demeanor evaporated. He grabbed Pino hard by the upper arm and hissed, "We don't talk about people like Rauff in places like this. Understand?"

Pino was upset and humiliated at his friend's reaction, but before he could reply, Tullio's date reappeared. She slid up alongside Tullio, whispered something in his ear.

Tullio laughed, let go of Pino, and said, "Sure, sweet thing. We can do that."

Tullio shifted his attention back to Pino. "I'd probably wait until your face doesn't look like a split sausage before you go around being all funny and listening."

Pino cocked his head, smiled uncertainly, and then gritted his teeth when the stitches tugged in his cheek. He watched Tullio and his date leave, thinking once again how much he wanted to be like him. Everything about the guy was perfect, elegant. Good guy. Great dresser. Better friend. Genuine laugh. And yet, Tullio was mysterious enough to be following around a Gestapo colonel.

It hurt to chew, but Pino was so hungry he piled a second plate. While he did, he heard three of his parents' musician friends talking, two men and the violinist.

"There are more Nazis in Milan every day," said the heavier-set man, who played the French horn at La Scala.

"Worse," the percussionist said. "The Waffen-SS."

The violinist said, "My husband says there are rumors of pogroms being planned. Rabbi Zolli is telling our friends in Rome to flee. We're thinking of going to Portugal."

"When?" the percussionist asked.

"Sooner than later."

"Pino, it's time for bed," his mother said sharply.

Pino took the plate with him up to his room. Sitting on his bed while eating, he thought about what he'd just overheard. He knew that the three musicians were Jewish, and he knew Hitler and the Nazis hated the Jews, though he really didn't understand why. His parents had lots of Jewish friends, mostly musicians or people in the fashion business. All in all, Pino thought Jews were smart, funny, and kind. But what was a pogrom? And why would a rabbi tell all the Jews in Rome to run?

He finished eating, looked at his bandage again, and then got into bed. With the light off, he drew back the curtains and looked out into the darkness. Here, in San Babila, there were no fires, nothing to suggest the devastation he'd witnessed. He tried not to think of Anna, but when he rested his head on his pillow and closed his eyes, snippets of their encounter circled in his head along with the image of Fred Astaire frozen cheek to cheek with Rita Hayworth. And the explosion of the theater's back wall. And the armless dead girl.

He couldn't sleep. He couldn't forget any of it. He finally turned on the radio, fiddled with the dial, and found a station playing a violin piece he recognized because his father was always trying to play it: Niccolo Paganini's Caprice no. 24 in A Minor.

Pino lay there in the dark, listening to the frenetic pace of the violin playing, and felt the wild mood swings of the piece as if they were his own. When it was over, he was wrung out and empty of thought. At long last, the boy slept.

⇒⇐

Around one o'clock the next afternoon, Pino went to find Carletto. He rode the trams, seeing some neighborhoods in smoking ruins and others untouched. The randomness of what had been destroyed and what had survived bothered him nearly as much as the destruction itself.

He got off the trolley at Piazzale Loreto, a large traffic rotary with a city park at its center and thriving shops and businesses around its perimeter. He looked across the rotary at Via Andrea Costa, seeing war elephants in his mind. Hannibal had driven armored elephants over the Alps and down that road on his way to conquer Rome twenty-one centuries before. Pino's father said that all conquering armies had come into Milan on that route ever since.

He passed an Esso petrol station with an iron girder system that rose three meters above the pumps and tanks. Diagonally across the rotary from the petrol station, he saw the white-and-green awning of Beltramini's Fresh Fruits and Vegetables.

Beltramini's was open for business. No damage that he could see.

Carletto's father was outside, weighing fruit. Pino grinned and quickened his pace.

"Don't worry. We have bomb-proof secret gardens out by the Po," Mr. Beltramini was saying to an older woman as Pino approached. "And because of this, Beltramini's will always have the best produce in Milan."

"I don't believe you, but I love that you make me laugh," she said.

"Love and laughter," Mr. Beltramini said. "They are always the best medicine, even on a day like today."

The woman was still smiling as she walked away. A short, plump bear of a man, Carletto's father noticed Pino and turned even more delighted.

"Pino Lella! Where have you been? Where is your mother?"

"At home," Pino said, shaking his hand.

"Bless her." Mr. Beltramini peered up at him. "You're not going to grow any more, are you?"

Pino smiled and shrugged. "I don't know."

"You do, you'll start walking into tree branches." He pointed at the bandage on Pino's cheek. "Oh, I see you already did."

"I got bombed."

Mr. Beltramini's state of perpetual bemusement evaporated. "No. Is this true?"

Pino told him the whole story, from the time he climbed out his window, until he got back home and found everybody playing music and having a good time.

"I think they were smart," Mr. Beltramini said. "If a bomb's coming at you, it's coming at you. You can't go around worrying about it. Just go on doing what you love, and go on enjoying your life. Am I right?"

"I guess so. Is Carletto here?"

Mr. Beltramini gestured over his shoulder. "Working inside."

Pino started toward the shop door.

"Pino," Mr. Beltramini called after him.

He looked back, seeing concern on the fruit vendor's face. "Yes?"

"You and Carletto, you take care of each other, right? Like brothers, right?"

"Always, Mr. B."

The fruitmonger brightened. "You're a good boy. A good friend."

Pino went inside the shop and found Carletto lugging sacks of dates.

"You been out?" Pino said. "Seen what happened?"

Carletto shook his head. "I've been working. You've heard of that, right?"

"I've heard stories about it, so I came to see for myself."

Carletto didn't think that was funny. He hoisted another sack of dried fruit onto his shoulder and started down a wooden ladder and through a hole in the floor.

"She didn't show up," Pino said. "Anna."

Carletto looked up from the dirt-floored basement. "You were out last night?"

Pino smiled. "I almost got blown up when the bombs hit the theater."

"You're full of it."

"I am not," Pino said. "Where do you think I got this?"

He peeled off the bandage, and Carletto's lip rose in disgust. "That's nasty."

⚔

With Mr. Beltramini's permission, they went to see the theater in the light of day. As they walked, Pino told the story all over again, watching his friend's reaction and feeding off it, dancing around when he described Fred and Rita, and making booming noises as he related how he and Mimo ran through the city.

He was feeling pretty good until they reached the cinema. Smoke still curled from the ruins, and with it a harsh, foul stench that Pino would come to identify instantly as spent explosives. Some people in the streets around the theater seemed to wander aimlessly. Others still dug through the bricks and beams, hoping to find loved ones alive.

Shaken by the destruction, Carletto said, "I could never have done any of what you and Mimo did."

"Sure you could. When you're scared enough, you just do it."

"Bombs falling on me? I would have hit the floor and curled up with my hands over my head."

There was silence between them as they contemplated the theater's charred and blown-out back wall. Fred and Rita had been right there, nine meters high, and then—

"Think the planes will come back tonight?" Carletto asked.

"We won't know until we hear the hornets."

Chapter Four

Allied planes came for Milan almost every night the rest of June and on into July of 1943. Building upon building crumpled and threw dust that billowed down the streets and lingered in the air long after the sun rose bloodred and cast down merciless heat to deepen the misery of those first few weeks of the bombardment.

Pino and Carletto wandered the streets of Milan almost every day, seeing the random carnage, witnessing the loss, and sensing the pain that seemed to be everywhere. After a while, it all made Pino feel numb and small. Sometimes he just wanted to follow Carletto's instincts, to curl into a ball and hide from life.

Almost every day, however, he thought of Anna. He knew it was stupid, but he frequented the bakery where he'd seen her first, hoping to run into her again. He never saw her, and the baker's wife had no idea whom he was talking about when he asked.

On June 23, Pino's father sent Mimo to Casa Alpina in the rugged Alps north of Lake Como for the rest of the summer. He tried to send Pino as well, but his older son refused. As a boy and a young teenager, Pino had loved Father Re's camp. He'd spent three months up at Casa Alpina every year since the age of six, two full months in the summer climbing in the mountains, and a cumulative month skiing in the winter. Being at Father Re's was great fun. But the boys up there now would be so young. He wanted to be in Milan, out in the streets with Carletto, and looking for Anna.

The bombing intensified. On July 9, the BBC described the Allied landing on the shores of Sicily and fierce fighting against the German and Fascist forces. Ten days later, Rome was bombed. News of that raid sent a shudder through Italy, and the Lella household.

"If Rome can be bombed, then Mussolini and the Fascists are finished," Pino's father proclaimed. "The Allies are driving the Germans from Sicily. They'll attack southern Italy, too. It will soon be over."

In late July, Pino's parents put a record on the phonograph and danced in the middle of the day. King Vittorio Emanuele III had arrested Benito Mussolini and imprisoned him in a fortress on Gran Sasso Mountain north of Rome.

By August, though, entire blocks of Milan lay in ruins. And the Germans were everywhere, installing antiaircraft guns, checkpoints, and machine gun nests. A block from La Scala, a garish Nazi flag fluttered over the Hotel Regina.

Gestapo Colonel Walter Rauff established curfews. If you were caught out after hours, you were arrested. If you were caught breaking curfew without papers, you could be shot. Having a shortwave would also get you shot.

Pino didn't care. At night, he hid in his closet to listen to music and the news. And during the day, he began to adapt to the new order in Milan. The trolleys ran only intermittently. You walked, rode a bike, or hitched a ride.

Pino chose the bike and went all over the city despite the heat, going through various checkpoints and learning what the Nazis looked for when they stopped him. Long sections of road had been reduced to craters, and he had to walk around them or find another route. Riding on, he passed families living under canvas tarps amid the brick ruins of their homes.

He realized how lucky he was. He sensed for the first time how that could change in the blink of an eye, or the flash of a bomb. And he wondered if Anna had survived.

⇒

In early August, Pino finally understood why the Allies were bombing Milan. A BBC announcer said that the Allies had all but destroyed the Nazi industrial base in the Ruhr Valley, where much of Hitler's munitions had been built. Now they were attempting to blow up the machine tools of northern Italy before the Germans could use them to prolong the war.

The nights of August 7 and 8, British Lancasters dropped thousands of bombs on Milan, targeting factories, industrial facilities, and military installations, but also hitting the neighborhoods around them.

When bombs exploded close enough to make the Lellas' building tremble, Porzia panicked and tried to get her husband to take them all to Rapallo on the west coast.

"No," Michele said. "They won't bomb near the cathedral. It's still safe here."

"All it takes is one," Porzia said. "I'm taking Cicci, then."

Pino's father was sad but determined. "I'll stay and keep the business going, but I think it's time for Pino to go to Casa Alpina."

Pino refused a second time.

"It's for little boys, Papa," Pino said. "I'm not little anymore."

On August 12 and 13, more than five hundred Allied bombers attacked Milan. For the first time explosives struck close to the Duomo. One damaged the church of Santa Maria delle Grazie but miraculously did no harm to Leonardo da Vinci's *The Last Supper*.

La Scala was not as fortunate. A bomb blew through the roof of the opera house and exploded, setting the theater on fire. Another bomb struck the Galleria, which suffered extensive damage. That same detonation rocked the Lellas' building. Pino waited out that horrible night in the basement.

He saw Carletto the next day. The Beltraminis were heading to a train that would take them out into the countryside for the night to sleep and escape the bombardment. The following afternoon, Pino, his father, Aunt Greta and Uncle Albert, and Tullio Galimberti and his latest girlfriend all joined the Beltraminis in overnight exile.

As the train left the central station and headed east, Pino, Carletto, and Tullio stood in the open door of a boxcar crammed with other Milanese fleeing for the night. The train accelerated. Pino looked at the sky, which was so perfectly blue he couldn't imagine it black and filled with warplanes.

＊

They crossed the Adda River, and long before dusk, while the countryside still lay blanketed in summer torpor, the train squealed and sighed to a stop amid gently rolling farmland. Pino carried a blanket over his shoulder and climbed after Carletto to a low grassy hill above an orchard that faced southwest toward the city.

"Pino," Mr. Beltramini said, "watch out, or there will be spiderwebs across your ears by morning."

Mrs. Beltramini, a pretty, frail woman who always seemed to be suffering some malady or another, scolded weakly, "Why did you say that? You know I hate spiders."

The fruit shop owner fought against a grin. "What are you talking about? I was just warning the boy about the dangers of sleeping with his head in the deep grass."

His wife looked like she wanted to argue, but then she just waved him away, as if he were some bothersome fly.

Uncle Albert fished in a canvas bag for bread, wine, cheese, and dried salami. The Beltraminis broke out five ripe cantaloupes. Pino's father sat in the grass next to his violin case, his arms wrapped around his knees and an enchanted look on his face.

"Isn't it magnificent?" Michele said.

"What's magnificent?" Uncle Albert said, looking around, puzzled.

"This place. How clean the air is. And the smells. No burning. No bomb stench. It seems so . . . I don't know. Innocent?"

"Exactly," Mrs. Beltramini said.

"Exactly what?" Mr. Beltramini said. "You walk a little too far here and it's not so innocent. Cow shit and spiders and snakes and—"

Whop! Mrs. Beltramini backhand-slapped her husband's arm. "You show no mercy, do you? Ever?"

"Hey, that hurt," Mr. Beltramini protested through a smile.

"Good," she said. "Now stop it, you. I didn't get a wink of sleep with all that talk of spiders and snakes last night."

Appearing unaccountably angry, Carletto got up and walked down-hill toward the orchard. Pino noticed some girls down by the rock wall that surrounded the fruit grove. Not one of them was as beautiful as Anna. But maybe it was time to move on. He jogged downhill to catch up with Carletto, told him his plan, and they tried to artfully intercept the girls. Another group of boys beat them to it.

Pino looked at the sky and said, "I'm only asking for a little love."

"I think you'd settle for a kiss," Carletto said.

"I'd be happy with a smile." Pino sighed.

The boys climbed over the wall and walked down rows of trees heavy with fruit. The peaches were not quite ripe, but the figs were. Some had already dropped, and they picked them up from the dirt, brushed them off, peeled the skin, and ate them.

Despite the rare treat of fresh fruit right off the tree in a time of rationing, Carletto seemed troubled. Pino said, "You okay?"

His best friend shook his head.

"What is it?" Pino asked.

"Just a feeling."

"What?"

Carletto shrugged. "Like life isn't going to turn out the way we think, that it's going to go badly for us."

"Why would you think that?"

"You never paid much attention in history class, did you? When big armies go to war, everything gets destroyed by the conqueror."

"Not always. Saladin never sacked Jerusalem. See? I did pay attention in history class."

"I don't care," Carletto said, angrier still. "It's just this feeling that I get, and it won't stop. It's everywhere and . . ."

His friend choked up, and tears ran down his face while he fought for control.

"What's going on with you?" Pino said.

Carletto cocked his head, as if peering at a painting he didn't quite understand. His lips trembled as he said, "My mama's really sick. It's not good."

"What's that mean?"

"What do you think it means?" Carletto cried. "She's gonna die."

"Jesus," Pino said. "Are you sure?"

"I heard my parents talking about how she'd like her funeral to be."

Pino thought of Mrs. Beltramini, and then Porzia. He thought about what it would be like to know his mother was going to die. A vast pit opened in his stomach.

"I'm sorry," Pino said. "I really am. Your mama's a great lady. She puts up with your papa, so she's like a saint, and they say saints get their reward in heaven."

Carletto laughed despite his sadness and wiped at his tears. "She is the only one who can put him in his place. But he should stop, you know? She's sick, and he's teasing her like that about snakes and spiders. It's cruel. Like he doesn't love her."

"He loves your mama."

"He doesn't show it. It's like he's afraid to."

They started to walk back. At the rock wall, they heard the strains of a violin.

<hr />

Pino looked up the hill and saw his father tuning his violin and Mr. Beltramini standing there, sheet music in his hand. The golden light of sunset radiated off both men and the crowd around them.

"Oh no," Carletto moaned. "Mother of God, no."

Pino felt equal dismay. At times, Michele Lella could play brilliantly, but more often than not, Pino's father would stutter his rhythm or squall through a section that demanded a smooth touch. And poor Mr. Beltramini had a voice that usually broke or went flat. It was excruciating to listen to either man because you could never relax. You knew some odd note was coming, and it could be so sour at times, it was, well, embarrassing.

Up on the hill, Pino's father adjusted the position of his violin, a beautiful central Italian petite from the eighteenth century that Porzia had given him for Christmas ten years before. The instrument was Michele's most treasured possession, and he held it lovingly as he brought it under his chin and jawbone and raised his bow.

Mr. Beltramini firmed his posture, arms held loosely at his side.

"There's a train wreck about to happen," Carletto said.

"I see it coming," Pino said.

Pino's father played the opening strains of the melody of "*Nessun Dorma,*" or "None Shall Sleep," a soaring aria for tenor in the third act of Giacomo Puccini's opera *Turandot.* Because it was one of his father's favorite pieces, Pino had listened to a recording performed by Toscanini and the full La Scala orchestra behind the powerful tenor Miguel Fleta, who sang the aria the night the opera debuted in the 1920s.

Fleta played Prince Calaf, a wealthy royal traveling anonymously in China, who falls in love with the beautiful but cold and bitchy Princess Turandot. The king has decreed that anyone who wishes to have the princess's hand must first solve three riddles. Get one wrong, and the suitor dies a terrible death.

By the end of act 2, Calaf has answered all the riddles, but the princess still refuses to marry him. Calaf says that if she can figure out his real name before dawn he will leave, but if she can't, she must willingly marry him.

The princess takes the game to a higher level, tells Calaf that if she finds his name before dawn, she'll have his head. He agrees to the deal, and the princess decrees, "*Nessun dorma*, none shall sleep, until the suitor's name is found."

In the opera, Calaf's aria comes with dawn approaching and the princess down on her luck. "*Nessun Dorma*" is a towering piece that builds and builds, demanding that the singer grow stronger, reveling in his love for the princess and surer of victory with every moment that ticks toward dawn.

Pino had thought it would take a full orchestra and a famous tenor like Fleta to create the aria's emotional triumph. But his father and Mr. Beltramini's version, stripped down to its tremulous melody and verse, was more powerful than he could have ever imagined.

When Michele played that night, a thick, honeyed voice called from his violin. And Mr. Beltramini had never been better. The rising notes and phrases all sounded to Pino like two improbable angels singing, one high through his father's fingers, and one low in Mr. Beltramini's throat, both more heavenly inspiration than skill.

"How are they doing this?" Carletto asked in wonder.

Pino had no idea of the source of his father's virtuoso performance, but then he noticed that Mr. Beltramini was singing not to the crowd but to someone *in* the crowd, and he understood the source of the fruitman's beautiful tone and loving key.

"Look at your papa," Pino said.

Carletto strained up on his toes and saw that his father was singing the aria not to the crowd but to his dying wife, as if there were no one else but them in the world.

When the two men finished, the crowd on the hillside stood and clapped and whistled. Pino had tears in his eyes, too, because for the first time, he'd seen his father as heroic. Carletto had tears in his eyes for other, deeper reasons.

"You were fantastic," Pino said to Michele later in the dark. "And 'Nessun Dorma' was the perfect choice."

"For such a magnificent place, it was the only one we could think of," his father said, seeming in awe of what he'd done. "And then we were swept up, just like the La Scala performers say, playing con smania, with passion."

"I heard it, Papa. We all did."

Michele nodded, and sighed happily. "Now, get some sleep."

Pino had kicked out a place for his hips and heels, and then taken off his shirt for a pillow and wrapped himself in the sheet he'd brought from home. Now he snuggled down, smelling the sweet grass, already drowsy.

He closed his eyes, thinking about his father's performance, and Mrs. Beltramini's mysterious illness, and the way her joking husband had sung. He drifted off to sleep, wondering if he'd witnessed a miracle.

Several hours later, deep in his dreams, Pino was chasing Anna down the street when he heard distant thunder. He stopped, and she kept on, disappearing into the crowd. He wasn't upset, but he wondered when the rain would fall, and what it would taste like on his tongue.

Carletto shook him awake. The moon was high overhead, casting a gunmetal-blue light on the hillside, and everyone on their feet looking to the west. Allied bombers were attacking Milan in waves, but there were no sightings of the planes or of the city from that distance, only flares and flashes on the horizon and the distant rumor of war.

※

As the train rolled back into Milan shortly after dawn the next day, black scrolls of smoke unraveled, twisted, and curled above the city. When they left the train and went out into the streets, Pino saw the physical differences between those who had fled the city and those who had endured the onslaught. Explosive terror had bowed the survivors' shoulders, emptied their eyes, and broken the set of their jaws. Men, women, and children shuffled timidly about, as if at any second the very ground they trod might rupture and give way into some unfathomable and fiery sinkhole. There was a smoky haze almost everywhere. Soot, some of it fine white and some a volcanic gray, coated almost everything. Torn and twisted cars. Ripped and crushed buildings. Trees stripped bare by the blasts.

For several weeks, Pino and his father kept on in this pattern, working by day, leaving the city by train in the late afternoon, and returning at dawn to find Milan's newest gaping wounds.

On September 8, 1943, the Italian government, having signed an unconditional armistice on September 3, made public the country's formal surrender to the Allies. The following day, British and American forces landed at Salerno above the instep of the country's boot. The Germans offered mild to fierce resistance. Most Fascist soldiers simply threw up the white flag upon seeing Lieutenant General Mark Clark's US Fifth Army coming ashore. When news of the American invasion reached Milan, Pino, his father, aunt, and uncle all started cheering. They thought the war would be over in days.

The Nazis seized control of Rome less than twenty-four hours later, arrested the king, and surrounded the Vatican with troops and tanks aimed at the golden dome of Saint Peter's Basilica. On September 12, Nazi commandos used gliders to attack the fortress on Gran Sasso Mountain where Mussolini was being held. The commandos fought their way into the prison and rescued Il Duce. He was flown to Vienna and then to Berlin, where he met with Hitler.

Pino heard the two dictators on the shortwave a few nights later, both of them vowing to fight the Allies to the last drop of German and Italian blood. Pino felt like the world had gone mad, and he grew depressed that he hadn't seen Anna in three months.

A week passed. More bombs fell. Pino's school stayed closed. The Germans began a full-scale invasion of Italy from the north, through Austria and Switzerland, and installed Mussolini in a puppet government called the "Italian

Socialist Republic," with its capital the tiny town of Salò on Lake Garda, northeast of Milan.

It was all Pino's father talked about early on the morning of September 24, 1943, as they trudged back to San Babila from the train station after another night spent sleeping in farm fields. Michele was so fixated on the Nazis' seizing control of northern Italy that he did not see one of those black smoke scrolls unraveling above the fashion district and Via Monte Napoleone. Pino did and started to run. As he was weaving through the narrow streets a few moments later, the road curved, and he could see well ahead to the Lellas' building.

Where much of the roof had been, a gaping, smoking hole fed the smoke scroll in the sky. The picture windows of Le Borsette di Lella lay in blackened splinters and blades. The purse shop itself looked like the chipped interior of a coal mine. The blast had incinerated everything else beyond recognition.

"Oh dear God, no!" Michele cried.

Pino's father let go of his violin case and fell to his knees, sobbing. Pino had never seen his father cry, or didn't think he had, and he felt gutted, sorrowful, and humiliated by witnessing Michele's misery.

"C'mon, Papa," he said, trying to get his father to stand.

"It's all gone," Michele wept. "Our life is all gone."

"Nonsense," Uncle Albert said, taking his brother-in-law's other arm. "You've got money in the bank, Michele. If you need a loan, I'll give it to you. An apartment, furniture, purses, you can rebuild."

Pino's father said weakly, "I don't know how I'm going to tell Porzia."

"Michele, you act as if you had something to do with a random bomb hitting your place," Uncle Albert sniffed. "You'll tell her the truth, and you'll start over."

"In the meantime, you'll come stay with us," Aunt Greta said.

Michele started to nod, but then turned angrily to Pino. "Not you."

"Papa?"

"You are going to Casa Alpina. You'll study there."

"No, I want to be in Milan."

Pino's father went berserk. "You are not staying! You have no say in this matter. You are my firstborn. I won't have you die randomly, Pino. I . . . I couldn't take it. And neither could your mother."

Pino was stunned by his father's outburst. Michele was the sort to steam and brood about things, not to rage and yell, and certainly not on the streets of San Babila, where the gossips of the fashion world would take note and never, ever forget.

"Okay, Papa," Pino said quietly. "I'll leave Milan. I'll go to Casa Alpina if you want me to."

PART TWO
THE CATHEDRALS OF GOD

Chapter Five

At the central train station late in the morning of the following week, Michele put a roll of lire in Pino's hand and said, "I'll send your books, and someone will be waiting for you at your stop. Be good, and give my love to Mimo and Father Re."

"But when will I come back?"

"When it's safe to come back."

Pino glanced unhappily at Tullio, who shrugged, and then at Uncle Albert, who studied his shoes.

"This isn't right," he said, furious as he picked up a rucksack filled with clothes and boarded the train. Taking a seat in a near-empty car, he stared out the window, fuming.

He was being treated like a boy. But had he gone to his knees and cried in public? No. Pino Lella had taken the blow and stood there like a man. But what was he supposed to do? Defy his father? Leave the train? Go to the Beltraminis'?

The train lurched and squalled, pulled out of the station and through the train yard where German soldiers guarded hordes of vacant-eyed men, many in shabby gray uniforms, loading flatbed cars with crates of tank parts, rifles, submachine guns, bombs, and ammunition. They had to be prisoners, he thought, and that upset him. Pino stuck his head out the window and studied them as the train left the yard.

Two hours into the trip, the train rolled through the foothills above Lake Como, heading toward the Alps. Ordinarily, Pino would have stared lovingly at the lake, which he thought the most beautiful in the world, and especially the town of Bellagio on the lake's southern peninsula. The grand hotel there looked like some rose castle in a fantasy.

Instead, the boy's focus was down the hill from the train tracks, where he kept catching glimpses of the road that hugged Lake Como's eastern shore and a long line of lorries crowded with filthy men, many in the same sort of dull gray outfits he'd seen back in the train yard. There were hundreds, maybe thousands of them.

Who were they? he wondered. Where were they captured? And why?

He was still thinking about the men forty minutes and a change of trains later, when he got off at the town of Chiavenna.

The German soldiers on duty there ignored him. Pino walked out of the station feeling good for the first time that day. It was a warm, sunny, early autumn afternoon. The air was sweet and clear, and he was heading up into the mountains. Nothing else could go wrong now, he decided. Not today, anyway.

"Hey, you, kid," a voice called.

A wiry guy roughly Pino's age leaned up against an old Fiat two-door coupé. He wore canvas work pants and a grease-stained white T-shirt. A cigarette smoldered between his lips.

"Who you calling kid?" Pino asked.

"You. You the Lella kid?"

"Pino Lella."

"Alberto Ascari," he said, thumbing his chest. "My uncle told me to come pick you up, bring you to Madesimo." Ascari flicked the cigarette and held out his hand, which was almost as big as Pino's and, to his surprise, stronger.

After Ascari had almost broken his hand, Pino said, "Where'd you get the grip?"

Ascari smiled. "In my uncle's shop. Put your stuff in the back there, kid."

The "kid" thing bothered Pino, but otherwise Ascari seemed decent enough. He opened the passenger door. The car was immaculate inside. A towel covered the driver's seat, protecting it from grease.

Ascari started the car. The engine had a sound unlike any other Fiat Pino had ever heard, a deep, throaty growl that seemed to make the entire chassis shake.

"That's no street engine," Pino said.

Ascari grinned, and shifted the car into gear. "Would any race car driver have a street engine or transmission in his own car?"

"You're a race car driver?" Pino said skeptically.

"I will be," Ascari said, and popped the clutch.

They went screeching out of the little train station and swung onto the cobblestone road. The Fiat bounced sideways into a slide before Ascari whipped the wheel the other way. The tires caught traction. Ascari shifted gears and hit the accelerator.

Pino was pinned against the passenger seat but managed to brace his feet and arms before Ascari shot them across the little town square, deftly dodged a lorry filled with chickens, and shifted gears a third time. They were still speeding up when they left the town behind them.

The Splügen Pass road climbed in a steady series of chicanes, S-turns, paralleling a stream at the bottom of a steep-walled valley that cut north into the Alps toward Switzerland. Ascari drove the Splügen like a master, diving the car into every turn and weaving past the few other vehicles on the road like they were standing still.

The whole time, Pino's emotions ran wild from abject fear to joyous exhilaration, envy, and admiration. It wasn't until they were approaching the outskirts of the town of Campodolcino that Ascari finally slowed.

"I believe you," Pino said, his heart still pounding.

"What's that?" Ascari said, puzzled.

"I believe you're going to be a race car driver someday," Pino said. "A famous one. I've never seen anyone drive like that."

Ascari couldn't have smiled more if he tried. "My father, he was better. The European grand prix champion before he died." He raised his right hand off the wheel and pointed his index finger out the windshield and up toward the sky. "God willing, Papa, I will be European champion and more, world champion!"

"I believe it," Pino said again, shaking his head in awe before looking up at a sheer-walled gray cliff that rose more than 450 meters above the east side of the town. He opened the window, stuck his head out, and scanned the top of the cliff.

"What are you looking for?" Ascari asked.

"Sometimes you can see the cross on top of the belfry."

"That's right up ahead here," Ascari said. "There's a notch in the cliff. That's the only reason you can see it." He pointed up through the windshield. "There."

For an instant, Pino caught a glimpse of the white cross and the top of the stone belfry of the chapel at Motta, the highest mountain settlement in this section of the Alps. For the first time that day, he allowed himself to be relieved he was out of Milan.

Ascari took them up the treacherous Madesimo road, a steep, narrow, pot-holed, and switchback route that hugged the steep mountainside. There were no guardrails and no shoulder to speak of in many places, and several times during the climb Pino thought for sure Ascari was going to drive them right off the side of a cliff. But Ascari seemed to know every centimeter of the road, because he'd tweak the wheel or tease the brake and they'd glide through every turn so smoothly Pino swore they were on snow, not rock.

"Can you ski like this?" Pino asked.

"I don't know how to ski," Ascari said.

"What? You live in Madesimo and can't ski?"

"My mother sent me here to be safe. I work in my uncle's shop and drive."

"Ski racing's the same as driving," Pino said. "Same tactics."

"You ski well?"

"I've won some races. Slalom."

The driver looked impressed. "We were meant to be friends, then. You will teach me to ski, and I will teach you to drive."

Pino's grin couldn't have been tamed if he'd tried. "You have a deal."

They reached the tiny village of Madesimo, which featured a stone and slate-roofed inn, a restaurant, and several dozen alpine homes.

"Are there any girls around here?" Pino asked.

"I know a few from below. They like to ride in fast cars."

"We should go for a drive sometime with them."

"A plan that I like!" Ascari said, pulling over. "You know the way from here?"

"I could do it blindfolded in a snowstorm," Pino said. "Maybe I'll come down on the weekends, stay at the inn."

"Come look me up if you do. Our shop's beyond the inn. You can't miss it."

He reached out his hand. Pino winced and said, "Don't break my fingers this time."

"Nah," Ascari said, and pumped his hand firmly. "Nice meeting you, Pino."

"You, too, Alberto," Pino said. He grabbed his rucksack and climbed out. Ascari squealed away, hand out the window waving.

⟜

Pino stood there a moment, feeling like he'd met someone important in his life. Then he put the rucksack up on his back and set out up a two-track path that headed into the woods. The way got consistently steeper until, an hour after he'd started the ascent, he emerged from the forest on a high alpine plateau below a rocky mountain face that climbed nearly twelve hundred vertical meters to a crag of stone called Pizzo Groppera.

The Motta plateau was several hundred meters wide and wrapped around the Groppera to the southeast. The western edge of the wide bench ended where it met a small forest of spruces that clung to the rim of the towering cliff that fell away toward Campodolcino. Late in the day, with the sun like hammered copper shining on the autumn Alps, Pino felt awed by the setting as he always did. Cardinal Schuster was right; being in Motta was like standing on a balcony in one of God's grandest cathedrals.

Motta was scarcely more developed than Madesimo. There were several alpine-style huts at the eastern base of the escarpment, and to the southwest, set back toward those cliffs and spruces, the small Catholic chapel Pino had caught a glimpse of from below and a much larger stone-and-timber structure. Happier than he'd been in months, Pino smelled baked bread and something garlicky and savory the closer he got to the rustic building. His stomach growled.

He ducked under the roof over the entryway, stood before the heavy wooden door, and reached for a cord that hung from a heavy brass bell above a sign that said, "Casa Alpina. All Weary Travelers Welcome." Pino pulled the cord twice.

The clanging of the bell echoed off the flanks of the mountain behind him. He heard the clamor of boys, followed by footsteps. The door swung open.

"Hello, Father Re," Pino said to a burly priest in his fifties. The man, leaning on a cane, was wearing a black cassock, white collar, and leather hob-nailed climbing boots.

Father Re flung open his arms. "Pino Lella! I heard a rumor just this morning you were coming to stay with me again."

"The bombing, Father," Pino said, feeling emotional as he hugged the priest. "It's bad."

"I've heard that, too, my son," Father Re said, sobering. "But come, come inside before we lose the heat."

"How's your hip?"

"It's been better, and it's been worse," Father Re said, limping aside to let Pino in.

"How is Mimo taking it, Father?" Pino asked. "I mean, our house."

"You should be the one to tell him that," Father Re said. "Have you eaten?"

"No."

"Then your timing is perfect. Leave your things there for now. After dinner, I'll show you where you're sleeping."

Pino followed the priest as he caned awkwardly to the dining hall, where forty boys crowded the rough-hewn tables and benches. A fire blazed in the stone hearth at the far end of the room.

"Go eat dinner with your brother," Father Re said. "Then come sit with me for dessert."

Pino saw Mimo regaling his friends with some story of daring. He walked up behind his brother and said in a squeaky voice, "Hey, Mr. Short Stuff, move over."

At fifteen, Mimo was one of the older boys in the room and obviously used to being the center of things. When he turned, his face was hardened, as if he were about to teach the squeaky-voiced kid a thing or two for not knowing his place in the world. But then Mimo recognized his older brother and broke into a puzzled smile.

"Pino?" he said. "What are you doing here? You said you'd never—" Fear robbed Mimo of his enthusiasm. "What's happened?"

Pino told him. His younger brother took it hard, gazed at the dark floorboards of the dining hall for several long moments before raising his head. "Where will we live?"

"Papa and Uncle Albert are going to find a new apartment and a new place for the store," Pino said, sitting down beside him. "But until then, I guess, you and I live here."

"Your supper tonight," a man said in a booming voice. "Fresh bread, fresh-churned butter, and chicken stew à la Bormio."

Pino looked toward the kitchen to see a familiar face. A beast of a man with a shock of wild black hair and absolutely massive hairy hands, Brother Bormio was utterly devoted to Father Re. Brother Bormio served as the priest's assistant in all things. He was also the cook at Casa Alpina, and a fine one.

Brother Bormio oversaw the movement of steaming pots of the stew. When they were in place on the tables, Father Re stood and said, "Young men, we must give thanks for this day and for every day, no matter how flawed. Bow your heads, give your gratitude to God, and have faith in him, and in a better tomorrow."

Pino had heard the priest say these words hundreds of times, and it still moved him, made him feel small and insignificant as he thanked God for getting him away from the bombardment, for meeting Alberto Ascari, and for being back at Casa Alpina.

Then Father Re gave his own thanks for the food on the table, and bid them eat.

After his long day of travel, Pino devoured almost a loaf of Bormio's brown bread and wolfed down three bowls of his heavenly chicken stew.

"Leave some for the rest of us," Mimo complained at one point.

"I'm bigger," Pino said. "I have to eat more."

"Go over to Father Re's table. He hardly eats anything."

"Good idea," Pino said, ruffled his brother's hair, and dodged the sideways punch his brother threw.

⟞⟝

Pino wove through the tables and benches to the one where Father Re sat with Brother Bormio, who was taking a rest and smoking a hand-rolled cigarette.

"You remember Pino, Brother Bormio?" Father Re asked.

Bormio grunted and nodded. The cook took two more spoonfuls of stew, another drag off the cigarette, and said, "I'll get the dessert, Father."

"Strudel?" asked Father Re.

"With fresh apples and pears," Bormio said in a pleased tone.

"However did you get those?"

"A friend," Bormio said. "A very good friend."

"Bless your good friend, and bring us both two servings if there's enough," Father Re said before looking at Pino. "A man can only deprive himself of so much."

"Father?"

"Desserts are my only vice, Pino." The priest laughed and rubbed his belly. "I can't even give them up for Lent."

The pear-and-apple strudel was the equal of any pastry Pino had bought in his favorite bakery in San Babila, and he was grateful Father Re had ordered him two portions. Afterward he was so stuffed, he felt drowsy and content.

"Do you remember the way to Val di Lei, Pino?" Father Re asked.

"Easiest way is southeast to the trail to Passo Angeloga, and then straight north."

"Above the village of Soste." Father Re nodded. "An acquaintance of yours went that way over Passo Angeloga, the Angel's Step, to Val di Lei just last week."

"Who was that?"

"Barbareschi. The seminarian. He said he met you with Cardinal Schuster."

That seemed ages ago. "I remember him. Is he here?"

"He left for Milan this morning. You must have passed each other somewhere in your travels today."

Pino didn't think much of the coincidence, and for a few moments he gazed at the blazing fire, feeling mesmerized and sleepy again.

"Is that the only way you've gone?" Father Re asked. "To Val di Lei?"

Pino thought, then said, "No, I've gone twice on the northern route from Madesimo, and once the hard way, from here up the spine and over the top of the Groppera."

"Good," the priest said. "I couldn't remember."

Then the priest stood, put two fingers in his mouth, and whistled sharply. The room quieted.

Father Re said, "Dish duty: report to Brother Bormio. The rest of you: the tables are to be cleared and wiped down, and then you have to study."

Mimo and the rest of the boys seemed to all know the routine, and they got to their chores with surprisingly few grumbles. Pino retrieved his rucksack and followed Father Re past the entrances to two big dorm rooms to a narrow cubicle with bunk beds built into the wall and a curtain across the front.

"It's not much, especially for someone your size, but it's the best we can do for the moment," Father Re said.

"Who else is with me?"

"Mimo. He's had it to himself until now."

"He's going to be so happy."

"I'll leave you two to figure things out," the priest said. "You are older than the others, so I don't expect you to follow their rules. So here are yours. You must climb every day on a route I prescribe. And you must study at least three hours every day, Monday through Friday. Saturdays and Sundays are your own. Does that work?"

It seemed like a lot of climbing, but Pino loved being in the mountains, so he said, "Yes, Father."

"I'll leave you to unpack, then," Father Re said. "It's good to have you here again, my young friend. I can see now that having you around might prove to be a big help."

Pino smiled. "It's good to be back, Father. I missed you and Motta."

Father Re winked, rapped on the door frame twice with his cane, and left. Pino cleared two shelves and put his brother's clothes on the top bunk. Then he emptied his rucksack and arranged his books, clothes, and the pieces of his beloved shortwave radio, which he'd hidden among his clothes despite the danger he'd have been in if the Nazis had searched his gear. Lying on the bottom bunk, Pino listened to a BBC dispatch on Allied advances, then dropped off into nothingness.

<hr />

"Hey," Mimo said an hour later. "That's where I sleep!"

"Not anymore," Pino said, rousing. "You're top bunk now."

"I was here first," Mimo protested.

"Finders keepers."

"My bunk wasn't lost!" Mimo shouted before lunging at Pino and trying to drag him off the bed.

Pino was much stronger, but Mimo had a warrior's heart and never knew when to admit defeat. Mimo bloodied Pino's nose before Pino could pin him to the floor.

"You lose," he said.

"No," Mimo sputtered as he squirmed, trying to get free. "That's my bed."

"Tell you what. When I'm gone on weekends, you can use it. Four or five days a week it's mine, and two to three it's yours."

That seemed to calm his brother. "Where are you going on weekends?"

"To Madesimo," Pino said. "I have a friend there who will teach me to fix cars and to drive them like a champion."

"You are so full of salami."

"It's true. He gave me a ride up from the train station. Alberto Ascari. The greatest driver I've ever seen. His father was European champion."

"Why would he teach you?"

"It's a trade. I'm teaching him to ski."

"Think he'd teach me to drive, too? I mean, I ski better than you."

"You have vivid dreams, little brother. But how about I teach you what the great Alberto Ascari teaches me?"

Mimo thought about that, and then said, "Deal."

Later, when they'd turned off the light and Pino had buried himself under the covers, he wondered whether Milan was being bombed, how his family was, and whether Carletto was sleeping out in that meadow on the hill or if he was awake and watching more of the city go up in fire and curling smoke. And for a second he thought of Anna leaving the bakery, that moment he first caught her attention.

"Pino?" Mimo said as he'd begun to drift off.

"Yeah?" Pino said, annoyed.

"Do you think I'll grow soon?"

"Any day now."

"I'm glad you're here."

Pino smiled despite the swelling in his nose. "I'm glad I'm here, too."

Chapter Six

Pino was dreaming of car racing when Father Re shook him awake the next morning. It was still dark out. The priest was silhouetted in the light of a hand-held lantern he'd set on the floor outside the brothers' narrow room.

"Father?" Pino whispered, groggily. "What time is it?"

"Four thirty."

"Four thirty?"

"Get up and dress for a hike. You need to get in shape."

Pino knew better than to argue. Though the priest had none of his mother's bravado, he could be as stubborn and demanding as Porzia on her toughest day. With people of this nature, Pino had long ago decided, it was better to get out of their way or go along for the ride.

He grabbed his clothes and went to the washroom to dress. Heavy canvas-and-leather shorts, thick wool socks that came up over his calves, and a pair of brand-new stiff boots his father had bought him the day before. Over his thin loden-green wool shirt, he wore a dark wool vest.

The dining hall was empty except for Father Re and Brother Bormio, who'd cooked him eggs and ham and toast. While Pino ate, the priest gave him two jugs of water that he wanted him to carry in his rucksack. There were also a large lunch and an oilskin anorak in case of rain.

"Where should I go?" Pino said, fighting back a yawn.

Father Re had a map on hand. "Take the easy way to the Passo Angeloga below Pizzo Stella. Nine kilometers there. Nine kilometers back."

Eighteen kilometers? Pino hadn't walked that far in a long time, but he nodded.

"Go straight to the pass and try to stay out of sight of others on the trail unless it's unavoidable."

"Why?"

Father Re hesitated. "Some people from the villages around here think they own the Angel's Step. It's easier if you just stay away from them."

Pino felt confused by that as he set out on a full stomach in the low light before dawn, walking along the trail that led southeast from Casa Alpina. The trail meandered in an easy, long traverse that followed the contour of the mountain, before slanting and losing elevation on the south flank of the Groppera.

By the time he'd neared the bottom, the sun had risen and was shining on the peak of Pizzo Stella ahead and to his right. The air smelled so fragrant there with pine and balsam that it was hard for him to recall the rank scent of bombs.

Pino stopped there, drank water, and ate half of the ham, cheese, and bread Bormio had packed for him. He stretched a bit, looking off and thinking about Father Re's warning to try to stay out of sight of people who thought they owned the pass. What was that about?

Shouldering his pack once more, Pino started up the switchback trail that led to the Passo Angeloga, the Angel's Step, the southern pass toward Val di Lei. Until that point, he had been cutting down a long sidehill. Now he was ascending almost constantly, taking big lungfuls of thin air while his calves and thighs burned.

The trail soon left the forest, and trees dwindled to a few scraggly, wind-gnarled juniper bushes that clung to rocky outcroppings. The sun broke over the ridge, revealing other ground shrubs, mosses, and lichen—all muted oranges, reds, and yellows.

Three-quarters of the way up to the pass, clouds started to scud across the sky, hanging up on the pinnacle of the Groppera far above Pino and to his left. The tundralike terrain gave way to rock and scree fields well below the saddle.

Though there was still a solid trail, loose rocks slid beneath his new boots, the stiff leather of which began to rub at his heels and toes.

His plan had been to reach the stacked-rock cairn at the middle of the Angel's Step, and remove his shoes and socks. But three hours into his hike, the clouds grew large, ominous, and gray. The wind picked up. To the west, he could see the slanting charcoal lines of a storm.

⚊⚊

Putting on the anorak, Pino pressed on toward the cairn at the crossing of several trails at the top of Passo Angeloga, including one that led toward the shoulder of the Groppera, and another toward Pizzo Stella. Fog came swirling in before he reached the stack of rocks.

The rain followed, a few drops at first, but Pino had been in the Alps often enough to sense what was coming. Ditching any idea of checking his feet or having something to eat, he touched the cairn and pivoted into the wind and the building storm. The rain quickly turned to marble-sized hail that battered at his hood and caused him to throw up his forearm to protect his eyes as he dropped back down the mountain.

Hail burst against the rocks and loose stone on the trail, glazing them and forcing Pino to move slower. The hail died with the wind, but the rain kept on in a steady downpour. The trail became an icy sluice box. It took Pino more than an hour to reach the first trees. He was soaked. He was chilled. His feet had blistered.

When he reached where the trail split and climbed back toward Motta and Casa Alpina, he heard shouting from ahead and down toward Soste. Even at a distance, even through the rain, he could tell that the voice was a man's and that he was angry.

Pino remembered Father Re's warning about being seen and felt his heart race as he turned and ran.

Hearing the man's cries turn to outrage behind and below him, Pino sped on the uphill trail into the trees and didn't slow for almost fifteen minutes. His lungs felt like they'd burst. He stood hunched over, gulping for air and feeling nauseated from the exertion and the altitude. But he no longer heard shouting, just the rain dripping from the trees and somewhere far below, a faint train whistle. As he pressed on, he felt good and laughed at having eluded the man.

The rain was starting to let up when Pino reached Casa Alpina. He'd been gone five hours and fifteen minutes.

"What took you so long?" Father Re asked, appearing in the front hallway. "I had faith, but Brother Bormio was starting to get worried."

"Hail," Pino said, shivering.

"Strip to your underwear and go by the fire," Father Re said. "I'll send Mimo to fetch you some dry clothes."

Pino took off his boots and socks, grimaced at the nasty blisters, all of which had popped and were a livid red.

"We'll put iodine and salt on those," Father Re said.

Pino cringed. When he was down to his undershorts, he chattered, hugged his chest, and hobbled into the dining hall where all forty boys were quietly studying under the watchful eye of Brother Bormio. The second they saw mostly naked Pino doing his awkward, exaggerated walk toward the fireplace, they broke into howls of laughter, with Mimo laughing hardest of all. Even Brother Bormio seemed to find it funny.

Pino waved them off, didn't care, just wanted to be as close as he could get to that fire. He stood on the warm hearth for several long minutes, shifting his body one way and then another until Mimo arrived with dry clothes. When Pino had dressed, Father Re came over with a mug of hot tea and a bowl filled with warm salt water for his feet. Pino drank the tea thankfully and had to grit his teeth when he plunged his feet into the salt water.

The priest asked Pino for a complete rundown of the morning's exercise. He told Father Re all about it, including his encounter with the angry man from Soste.

"You didn't get a look at his face?"

"He was kind of far, and it was raining," Pino said.

Father Re thought about that. "After lunch, you can take a nap, and then you owe me three hours of studying."

Pino yawned and nodded. He ate like the proverbial horse, limped down to his bunk, and passed out cold the moment his head hit the pillow.

The following morning, Father Re shook him awake an hour later than he had the previous day.

"Get up," he said. "You have another climb ahead of you. Breakfast in five minutes."

Pino moved, felt sore everywhere, but his blisters were better for the salt bath.

Still, he dressed as if he were in a fog as thick as the one he'd encountered the day before. He was a growing teenage boy. He liked to sleep a lot and couldn't stop yawning as he gingerly made his way in stocking feet back to the dining hall. Father Re was waiting with food and a topographical map.

"I want you to flank to the north today," Father Re said, tapping the wide lines that defined the bench at Motta, including the cart track that dropped down the mountain to Madesimo, and then a series of tight lines indicating increasing steepness beyond it. "Stay high crossing the face here and here. You'll find game trails that will help you cross this ravine. And eventually you'll end up over here in this meadow up the slope from Madesimo. Would you recognize it?"

Pino stared at the map. "I think so, but why don't I avoid that face, drop down to Madesimo on the two-track, and then climb straight up to that spot? It would be faster."

"It would be," Father Re said. "But I'm not interested in your speed, just that you can find your way and not be seen."

"Why?"

"I have my reasons, which I'll keep to myself for now, Pino. It's safer that way."

That only deepened Pino's confusion, but he said, "Okay. And then back?"

"No," the priest said. "I want you to climb into the bowl of the north cirque. Look for the game trail that goes up and over into Val di Lei. Don't climb it unless you feel you're ready. You can come back and try another day."

Pino sighed, knowing he was in for another rough hike.

Weather wasn't a factor. It was a beautiful late September morning in the southern Alps. But Pino's muscles and taped blisters nagged at him as he maneuvered across rocky catwalks on the western face of the Groppera and through a ravine choked with old logs and avalanche debris. It took him more than two hours to reach the meadow Father Re had shown him on the map. He started uphill through deep alpine grasses, already turned paler than brown.

Like Anna's hair, Pino thought, examining the hairs that surrounded the seed pods, mature, and ready to spread on the wind. He remembered Anna on the sidewalk beyond the bakery, and how he'd rushed to keep up with her. Her hair was just like this, he decided, only riper, lusher. As he climbed on, the soft stalks of grass sliding across his bare legs made him smile.

Ninety minutes later he reached the north cirque. It looked like the interior of a volcano, with three-hundred-meter sheer walls to his left and right and ragged, sharp stone teeth along the top. Pino found the goat trail and thought about climbing it, but decided he wouldn't be worth a damn up there with his feet feeling like ground meat. Instead, he dropped straight downhill to Madesimo.

He reached the village at one o'clock that Friday afternoon, went to the inn, ate, and reserved a room. The innkeepers were kind people with three children, including seven-year-old Nicco.

"I'm a skier," Nicco boasted to Pino while he wolfed down his food.

"I am, too," Pino said.

"Not as good as me."

Pino grinned. "Probably not."

"I'll take you skiing when it snows," the boy said. "Show you."

"I look forward to that," Pino said, and tousled Nicco's hair.

Stiff, but no longer ravenous, Pino went in search of Alberto Ascari, but the engine repair shop wasn't open. He left a note telling Ascari of his plan to return in the evening, and hiked back to Casa Alpina.

Father Re listened closely to Pino's description of crossing the cliffy face of the Groppera, and his decision not to climb the north cirque.

The priest nodded. "You don't want to be in the rocks if you're not ready for them. You will be soon enough."

"Father, after I'm done studying, I'm going to go down to Madesimo to spend the night and see my friend Alberto Ascari," Pino said.

When Father Re squinted, Pino reminded him that weekends were his own.

"I did say that," the priest said. "Go, have fun, and rest up, but be ready to start again Monday morning."

Pino took a nap and then studied ancient history and math, before reading the play *The Giants on the Mountain* by Luigi Pirandello. It was past five when he started back down the trail to Madesimo in his street shoes. His feet were killing him, but he hobbled all the way to the inn, checked in, spent time regaling little Nicco with his ski-racing stories, and then went to Ascari's uncle's house.

Alberto opened the door, welcomed him, and insisted he come in for dinner. His aunt was a better cook than Brother Bormio, which was saying something. Ascari's uncle loved to talk about cars, so they got on famously. Pino gorged himself to the point where he almost fell asleep during dessert.

Ascari and his uncle helped him back to the hotel, where Pino kicked off his shoes, flopped on the bed, and slept in his clothes.

⊸

His friend knocked on his door right after dawn.

"Why are you up so early?" Pino asked, yawning. "I was going to—"

"You want to learn to drive or not? The next two days are supposed to be clear, no rain, no snow, so I'm willing to teach you. You pay for petrol, though."

Pino scrambled for his shoes. They ate a quick breakfast in the hotel dining room and then went out to Ascari's Fiat. For the next four hours, they drove above Campodolcino on the road to the Splügen Pass and Switzerland.

On that winding route, Alberto taught Pino how to read the gauges and use them, and how to adapt to terrain, elevation, and direction changes. He showed Pino how to drift through some turns and to knife through others, and how to use the engine and the gears rather than the brakes to keep the car under control.

They drove north until they could see German checkpoints and the Swiss border beyond and turned around. On the way back to Campodolcino, two Nazi patrols stopped them, demanding to know what they were doing on the road.

"I'm teaching him to drive," Ascari said after they'd turned over their papers.

The Germans didn't seem happy about it, but waved them on.

When they returned to the hotel, Pino was as excited as he'd been in a long time. What a thrill it was to drive a car like that! What an amazing gift he'd been given to learn from Alberto Ascari, the future European champion!

Pino again ate dinner at the Ascaris' and enjoyed listening to Alberto and his uncle talk about auto mechanics. They went to the shop after dinner and tinkered with Alberto's Fiat until almost midnight.

The next morning, after early Mass, they set out again for the road between Campodolcino and the Swiss border. Ascari showed Pino how to use crests in the route to his advantage, and to look far ahead whenever he could so his brain was already plotting how best to run the car for optimum speed.

On his last run down the pass, Pino took them around a blind corner going too fast and almost crashed into a German jeep-style vehicle called a Kübelwagen. Both cars swerved and narrowly avoided collision. Ascari looked back.

"They're turning around!" Alberto said. "Go!"

"Shouldn't we stop?"

"You wanted a race, didn't you?"

Pino floored it. Ascari's car had a better engine and was far more nimble than the army vehicle, and the Nazis were out of sight before they left the town of Isola.

"God, that was great!" Pino said, his heart still slamming in his chest.

"Wasn't it?" Ascari said, and laughed. "You didn't do too bad."

To Pino it was high praise, and he felt wonderful leaving for Casa Alpina, having promised to return the following Friday to continue the lessons. The hike back to Motta was far less painful than it had been coming down two days before.

"Good," Father Re said when he showed him the calluses building on his feet.

The priest was also interested in his tales of learning to drive.

"How many patrols did you see on the Splügen Pass road?"

"Three," Pino said.

"But you were only stopped by two?"

"The third tried to stop us, but couldn't catch me in Alberto's car."

"Don't provoke them, Pino. The Germans, I mean."

"Father?"

"I want you to practice being unnoticed," Father Re said. "Driving a car like that gets you noticed, brings you to the Germans' attention. Understand?"

Pino didn't understand, not completely, anyway, but he could see the concern in the priest's eyes and promised not to do it again.

The following morning, Father Re shook Pino awake long before dawn. "Another clear day," he said. "Good for a climb."

Pino groaned, but he got dressed and found the priest and breakfast waiting in the dining hall. On the topographical map, Father Re pointed to a razorback ridge that started a few hundred vertical meters directly above Casa Alpina and made a long, steep, and serpentine climb all the way to the peak of the Groppera.

"Can you do it alone, or do you need someone to guide you?"

"I've been up it once," Pino said. "The really hard parts are here, here, and then that chimney, and the thin spot up top."

"If you get to the chimney and don't think you're up to it yet, don't go farther," Father Re said. "Just turn around and climb back down. And take a walking staff. There are several in the shed. Have faith in God, Pino, and stay alert."

Chapter Seven

Pino set out at dawn, hiking straight up the Groppera. Glad for the staff, he used it crossing a narrow stream before he flanked to the southeast toward that razorback ridge. Busted sheets of rock sheared off the mountain over thousands of years made the bowl chaotic terrain, and the going was slow until he reached the tail of the mountain spine.

There would be no defined trail from here on up, just rock and the occasional grass tuft or tenacious bush. Given the cliffs that fell away on both sides of the spine, Pino knew he couldn't afford a mistake. The one time he'd been on the ridge—two years ago—he'd been with four other boys and a guide friend of Father Re's from Madesimo.

Pino tried to remember how they'd gone up a series of broken staircases and treacherous catwalks that climbed to the base of the spire high above him. He felt a few moments of doubt and fear at the idea he might take the wrong route, but then forced himself to calm down and trust his instincts, handle each section as it came, and then reevaluate his route as he ascended.

Getting up onto the actual spine was his first challenge. A wind-smoothed and rounded column of stone about two meters high defined the very base of the ridge and seemed unclimbable. But on the south side, the rocks were cracked and fragmented. Pino tossed up his staff, heard it clatter to a stop. He jammed his fingers and the toes of his boots into cracks and onto narrow bits of ledge and went up after the staff. A few moments later, he knelt on the razorback, his lungs heaving. He waited until they'd calmed, took the staff, and got to his feet.

Pino began to pick his way higher, finding a rhythm to each footfall, reading the jigsaw terrain before him, and looking for the path of least resistance. An hour later, he faced another major challenge. Slabs of stone had broken away eons before, leaving the way up blocked except for a jagged gouge in the rock face. It was less than a meter wide and again as deep, and it climbed like a crooked chimney from the base up nearly eight meters to a ledge.

Pino stood there for several minutes feeling the fear in him build again. But before it could freeze him, he heard Father Re's voice telling him to have faith and to stay alert. At last, he pivoted 180 degrees and fit himself into the crack in the cliff. He pressed out his hands and levered his boots against the walls of the chimney. He was able to maneuver now and climbed with three points of contact supporting the moving fourth point—a hand, a foot—as it groped and probed for higher ground.

Six meters up, he heard a hawk calling, looked out from the crack and down the ridge toward Motta. He was dizzyingly high up the mountain now, felt a rush of vertigo and almost lost his grip on the rock. That scared him half to death. He couldn't fall. He couldn't live through a fall.

Have faith.

That thought was enough to drive Pino up the chimney and onto the ledge, where he gasped with relief and thanked God for helping him. When his strength returned, he made his way to the southwestern ridge with little pause. The ridge was sheer and razorback, barely a meter wide in places. Avalanche chutes plunged to either side of the jagged way forward to the base of the Groppera's craggy spire, which was more than forty meters tall and shaped like a crooked spearhead.

Pino didn't give the daggerlike crag a second glance. He was straining to spot where the various shoulders and clavicles of the mountain came together below the base of the spire. He found what he was looking for, and his heart began to slam in his chest again. He closed his eyes, told himself to calm down, and to believe. Making the sign of the cross, he went on, feeling like a tightrope artist as he passed between the two main avalanche chutes, not daring to look left or right down them, fixed on creeping straight ahead to where the catwalk widened.

When he reached the end of the catwalk, Pino hugged the stone blocks jutting from the wall like they were long-lost friends. When he was sure he could go on, he climbed up the blocks, which were irregular—almost like a stack of bricks that had tipped over—but stable, unmoving, and he was able to climb higher with relative ease.

Four and a half hours after he left Casa Alpina, Pino reached the base of the crag. He peered to his right and saw a steel cable anchored into the rock and stretched horizontally around the spire at chest height above a ledge perhaps eighteen centimeters wide.

Feeling queasy at what he had to do now, Pino took several deep breaths to shake off his growing jitters before reaching out and grabbing the slack cable. The toe of his right boot probed for and then found the narrow outcropping. It was almost like being on the ledge outside his bedroom window at home. Once he thought about it that way, he was able to hold tight to the cable and scuttle around the base of the crag.

Five minutes later, Pino reached the top of the broadest ridge on the mountain, south-southeast facing, wide, and covered with amber hummocks of lichen, ground moss, edelweiss, and alpine aster. He lay on his back, gasping with the noontime sun beating down on him. The ascent had felt completely different from the time he'd been guided up by a man who'd done the route thirty times, showing him each hand- and foothold. This climb had been the greatest physical challenge of his life. He'd had to think constantly, evaluate constantly, and rely on faith, which he realized was tiring—not easy to sustain at all.

Pino guzzled water, thinking, *But I did it. I made it up the hard way on my own.*

Happy, more confident, he gave thanks for his day and for his food, and then wolfed down the sandwich Brother Bormio had packed for him. Delighted to find more strudel, he ate slowly, savoring each bite. Had there ever been anything that tasted that good?

Pino felt drowsy and lay back, closing his eyes and feeling like everything in that timeless place of mountain and sky was as it should be.

<hr/>

Mist woke him.

Pino checked his watch, surprised to see it was nearly two in the afternoon. Clouds had rolled in. He could see no more than ninety meters down the slope now. With the anorak on, Pino used game and shepherd trails to skirt to his east and north. An hour later, he came to the rim on the back side of the Groppera's north cirque.

It took him a few tries before he found a path that traversed down the steep interior of the bowl and then zigzagged to the point where he'd turned around three days before. He stopped and looked back up what he'd just come down. After the challenges he'd faced earlier in the day, it hadn't seemed that bad at all.

But by the time Pino had trudged down the mountain to Madesimo and then back up to Motta, he was exhausted. Light was dwindling when he reached Casa Alpina. Father Re was waiting in the hall off the dining area where the boys were studying, and the air was filled with the sumptuous odor of Brother Bormio's newest creation.

"You're late," Father Re said. "I didn't want you out there at night."

"I didn't want to be coming off the mountain in the dark, either, but it's a long way, Father," he said. "And the climb. It was more difficult than I remembered."

"But you have faith you could do it again?" the priest asked.

Pino thought about the chimney, the catwalk between the avalanche chutes, and the cable traverse. He didn't exactly want to do any of them again, but he said, "Yes."

"Good," Father Re said. "Very good."

"Father, why am I doing this?"

The priest studied him, and then said, "I'm trying to make you strong. You may need to be in the months ahead."

Pino wanted to ask him why, but Father Re had already turned away.

Two days later, the priest sent Pino on the Angel's Step route to Val de Lei. The day after that, Pino worked the traverse route to the north cirque and climbed the goat trail almost to the rim. On the third day, he took the hard way up, but he had so much more confidence he cut an hour off the time it took him to reach the avalanche chutes.

The weather held through the following weekend and through two more days of driving lessons. Remembering Father Re's warning, he and Ascari stayed off the Splügen Pass road and practiced on the switchbacks around Madesimo.

On Sunday afternoon, they picked up two girls whom Ascari knew in Campodolcino. One was Ascari's friend, Titiana, and the other was Titiana's friend, Frederica. She was dreadfully shy and would hardly look at Pino, who wanted to like her, but he kept thinking of Anna. He knew it was crazy to think about her at all. He'd talked to her all of three minutes and hadn't seen her in almost four months, and she'd stood him up. And yet he had faith he'd see Anna again. She'd become this fantasy he clung to, a story he told himself whenever he was lonely or uncertain about his future.

When Pino reached Casa Alpina after another three days of hard climbing in the second week of October 1943, he was exhausted and ravenous. He ate two bowls of "Spaghetti Bormio" and drank several liters of water before he could lift his head and look around the dining room.

The usual boys were all there. Mimo was commanding an entire table of them on the other side of the room. And Father Re was entertaining guests, two men and a woman. The younger man had sandy hair. His arm was around the shoulder of the woman, who had pale skin and dark, preoccupied eyes. The older man wore a suit, no tie, had a mustache, and smoked. He coughed a lot, and his fingers softly drummed on the tabletop whenever the priest talked.

Pino sleepily wondered who they were. It wasn't that unusual for visitors to come to Casa Alpina. Parents often visited. And many hikers sought refuge there during storms. But these three were no hikers. They were dressed in street clothes.

Pino desperately wanted to go to bed, but he knew that wouldn't go over well with Father Re. He was trying to get up the energy to study when the priest came over and said, "You've earned a day's rest tomorrow. And you can put off studying until then. Okay?"

Pino smiled and nodded. He couldn't remember how he managed to find and get into his bunk.

When he finally awoke, it was broad daylight, and the sun shone in the window at the end of the hall. Mimo was gone. So were all the other boys. When he entered the dining room, it was empty except for those three visitors, who were having a heated whispered discussion at the other end of the room.

"We can't wait any longer," the younger man was saying. "It's all disintegrating. Fifty in Meina! They're raiding in Rome even as we speak."

"But you said we were safe," the woman fretted.

"We are safe here," he said. "Father Re is a good man."

"But for how long?" the older man said, lighting another cigarette.

The woman noticed Pino looking their way, and silenced the men. Brother Bormio brought Pino coffee and bread and salami. The visitors left the room, and he didn't think much about them the rest of the day, which he spent by the fire with his books.

By the time Mimo and the boys trooped in from a long hike it was almost dinnertime, and Pino was feeling not only rested but as fit as he'd been in his entire life. As much as he was exercising, with the massive amounts of food Brother Bormio was feeding him, Pino felt like he was gaining weight and muscle every day.

"Pino?" Father Re said as Mimo and two other boys laid out plates and silverware on the long table.

Pino set his books aside and got up out of his chair. "Father?"

"Find me after dessert, in the chapel."

That puzzled Pino. The chapel was rarely used for anything besides a small Sunday service, usually at dawn. But he left his curiosity aside and sat and joked with Mimo and the other boys, and then entranced them with his description of the perils of the hard way up the Groppera.

"One wrong step up there and it's over," he said.

"I could do it," Mimo boasted.

"Start doing pull-ups, push-ups, and squats. I'll bet you can."

The challenge ignited Mimo as all challenges did, and Pino knew his brother was about to become a pull-ups, push-ups, and squats fanatic.

After dishes had been cleared, Mimo asked Pino if he wanted to play cards. Pino begged off, saying he was going to the chapel to talk to Father Re.

"About what?" Mimo said.

"I'll find out," Pino said, grabbing a wool hat from the rack near the front door. He put it on and went out into the night.

The temperature had fallen below freezing. Above him, a quarter moon shone, and the stars looked as brilliant as firecrackers. A north wind bit his cheeks with the first hint of winter as he walked toward the chapel, beyond which a grove of towering fir trees grew along the rim of the plateau.

Four candles burned when he thumbed the latch to the chapel door and went inside. Father Re was on his knees in a pew, praying, head down. Pino shut the chapel door quietly and sat. After several moments, the priest made the sign of the cross, used his cane to drive himself to his feet, and then limped over and sat closer.

"Do you think you can travel most of the northern route to Val di Lei in the dark?" Father Re asked. "No light other than the moon?"

Pino thought, then said, "Not the face of the cirque, but everything up to that, I think."

"How much more time would it add?"

"Maybe an hour. Why?"

Father Re took a deep breath and said, "I have been praying for an answer to that question, Pino. Part of me wants to keep you in the dark, to keep things simple, focused on your task, and nothing more. But God doesn't make life simple, does he? We cannot say nothing. We cannot do nothing."

Pino was confused. "Father?"

"The three people at dinner tonight. Did you speak with them?"

"No," he said, "but I overheard them say something about Meina."

Father Re turned somber, pained. "In the last month, there were more than fifty Jews hiding in Meina and the surrounding villages. Nazi SS troops found the Jews, executed them, and threw them into Lake Maggiore."

Pino felt his stomach roll hard. "What? Why?"

"Because they were Jews."

Pino understood that Hitler hated the Jews. He'd even known Italians who didn't like Jews and who said disparaging things about them. But to kill them in cold blood? Simply for their religion? It was beyond barbaric.

"I just don't understand."

"Neither do I, Pino. But it's clear now that the Jews of Italy are in grave danger. I spoke with Cardinal Schuster about it by phone this morning."

Father Re said the cardinal told him that after the Meina massacre, the Nazis extorted the Jews still remaining in Rome's ghetto, demanding a payment of fifty kilos of gold in thirty-six hours in return for their safety. The Jews got the gold from their own stocks and from many Catholics. But after the treasure was delivered, the Germans raided the temple and found a list of every Jew in Rome.

The priest stopped, his face tortured, and then said, "Cardinal Schuster says the Nazis have brought in a special SS team to hunt the Jews on that list."

"And do what?" Pino said.

"Kill them. All of them."

Before that moment, Pino could not have imagined such a thing in the remotest and most troubled parts of his young mind. "This is . . . evil."

"It is evil," Father Re said.

"How does Cardinal Schuster know all these things?"

"The pope," Father Re said. "His Holiness told Cardinal Schuster that the German ambassador to the Vatican told him."

"Can't the pope stop it? Tell the world?"

Father Re looked down, kneading his knuckles white. "The Holy Father and the Vatican are surrounded by tanks and the SS, Pino. For the pope to speak out now would be suicide and mean the invasion and destruction of Vatican City. But he has spoken in secret to his cardinals. Through them he has given all Catholics in Italy a verbal order to open their doors to anyone in need of refuge from the Nazis. We are to hide the Jews, and if we can, we are to help them escape."

Pino felt his heart quicken. "Escape to where?"

Father Re looked up. "Have you ever been to the far end of Val di Lei, on the other side of the Groppera, beyond the lake?"

"No."

"There is a triangle of thick woods there," the priest said. "For the first two hundred meters inside that triangle, the trees and ground are Italian. But then Italy narrows to a point, and the land all around becomes Switzerland, neutral ground, safety."

Pino saw the trials of the past few weeks in a different light, and he felt excited and filled with new purpose. "You want me to guide them, Father?" Pino asked. "The three Jews?"

"Three of God's children whom he loves," Father Re said. "Will you help them?"

"Of course. Yes."

The priest put his hand on Pino's shoulder. "I want you to understand that you will be risking your life. Under the new German rules, helping a Jew is an act of treason, and punishable by death. If you are caught, they will likely execute you."

Pino swallowed hard at that, felt shaken inside, but then looked at Father Re and said, "Aren't you risking your life just having them here at Casa Alpina?"

"And the boys' lives," the priest said, his face sober. "But we must help all refugees fleeing the Germans. The pope thinks so. Cardinal Schuster thinks so. And so do I."

"I do, too, Father," Pino said, emotional in a way he never had been before, as if he were about to go out and right a great wrong.

"Good," Father Re said, his eyes glistening. "I had faith you would want to help."

"I do," Pino said, and felt stronger for it. "I'd better go to sleep."

"I'll get you up at two fifteen. Brother Bormio will feed you all at two thirty. You'll leave at three."

Pino left the chapel believing that he'd entered it as a boy and now exited it having made the decision to become a man. He was frightened by the penalty for helping the Jews, but he was going to help them anyway.

He stood out in front of Casa Alpina before going in, staring to the northeast, across the flank of the Groppera, and understanding that three lives were now his responsibility. That young couple. The smoker. They depended on him for this last stage of their escape.

Pino looked up past the massive crag of the Groppera silhouetted in the moonlight to the stars and the black void beyond.

"Dear God," he whispered. "Help me."

Chapter Eight

Pino was up and dressed ten minutes before Father Re came to wake him. Brother Bormio made oatmeal with pine nuts and sugar, and laid out dried meats and cheeses. The smoker and the young couple were already eating when Father Re came over and put his hands on Pino's shoulders.

"This is your guide, Pino," the priest said. "He knows the way."

"So young," the smoker said. "Is there no one older?"

"Pino is very experienced and very strong in the mountains, especially this mountain," Father Re said. "I have great faith he'll get you where you want to go. Or you can find another guide. But fair warning: there are some out there who will take your money and then turn you over to the Nazis anyway. Here we wish only that you find safe haven."

"We're going with Pino," the younger man said, and the woman nodded.

The older one, the smoker, remained unconvinced.

"What are your names?" Pino asked, shaking the younger man's hand.

"Use the names you've been given," Father Re said. "The ones on your papers."

The woman said, "Maria."

"Ricardo," her husband said.

"Luigi," the smoker said.

Pino sat down and ate with them. "Maria" was soft-spoken, but funny. "Ricardo" had been a teacher in Genoa. "Luigi" traded cigars in Rome. At one point, Pino glanced under the table and saw that though none wore boots, their shoes looked sturdy enough.

"Is the way dangerous?" Maria asked.

"Just do what I tell you to do, and you'll be fine," Pino said. "Five minutes?"

They nodded. He got up to clear plates. He took them over to Father Re and said in a soft voice, "Father, wouldn't it be easier for them if I took them up over the Angel's Step into Val di Lei?"

"It would be easier," Father Re said. "But we used that way just a few weeks ago, and I don't want to attract attention."

"I don't understand," Pino said. "Who used it?"

"Giovanni Barbareschi, the seminarian," Father Re said. "Just before you came up from Milan, there was another couple here with their daughter trying to escape. Barbareschi and I came up with a plan. He led the family and twenty boys, including Mimo, on an all-day hike over the Angel's Step to Val di Lei. They had a picnic between the far end of the lake and the woods. Twenty-four people hiked in, twenty-one left."

"No one would ever know the difference," Pino said appreciatively. "Especially if they were seeing the group from a long way off."

Father Re nodded. "Those were our thoughts exactly, but it's not practical to send big groups like that, especially with winter coming."

"Small is better," Pino said, and then glanced over his shoulder. "Father, I can do my best to keep them hidden, but there are a lot of places where we'll have no cover."

"Including the entire length of Val di Lei, which is what makes this especially dangerous to you because you'll be coming part of the way back in the wide open. But as long as the Germans keep patrolling the pass roads, and don't use planes up high to survey the border, you should be fine."

Father Re surprised Pino by giving him a hug. "Go with God on your side, my son, every step of the way."

Brother Bormio helped hoist the rucksack up onto Pino's back. Four liters of water. Four liters of sweet tea. Food. Rope. Topographical map. The anorak. A wool sweater and cap. Matches and lint to make a fire in a little steel canister. A small miner's lamp loaded with dry carbide. A knife. A small hatchet.

Together the load was twenty, maybe twenty-five kilograms, but Pino had been climbing with weight on his back since the day after he arrived at Casa Alpina. It felt normal, and he supposed Father Re had wanted it that way. Of course he had wanted it that way; the priest had to have been planning this for weeks.

"Let's go," Pino said.

⎯⎯◆⎯⎯

The foursome stepped out into a chilly autumn night. The sky was crystal clear, the moon still high and to the south, casting a thin light across the western flank of the Groppera. Pino led them down the cart track at first, just to get them away from the gas lamp outside the school. Then he had them stop so their eyes could fully adjust.

"We speak in whispers from here on out," Pino said in a hushed voice, and pointed up at the mountain. "There are places where noises echo a long way up there, so we want to be timid, quiet as a mouse, you know?"

He saw them nod. Luigi lit a match for a cigarette.

Pino got upset, then realized he had to take control. He took a big step toward the smoker and hissed, "Put that out. Any flame can be seen for hundreds of meters, more through binoculars."

"I need to smoke," Luigi said. "It calms me."

"Not until I tell you to. Or you go back and find another guide, and I take them alone."

Luigi took one last puff, dropped the butt, and crushed it. "Lead on," he said in disgust.

Pino told them to rely on their peripheral vision as he led them in the low light across the plateau to the north, hugging the base of the slope until it petered out to a path about fifty centimeters wide that cut laterally across several steep faces. He uncoiled the rope and tied four waist loops in it with gaps of three meters between each loop.

"Even with the rope, I want you to keep your right hand on the wall, or on any bush that grows out of it," Pino said. "If you feel something to grip, like a little sapling, test it before you commit to its holding your weight. Better yet, put your hands and feet where I do. I know it's dark, but you'll get the idea of what I'm doing by my silhouette."

"I'll follow you," Ricardo said. "Maria, you're right behind me."

"Are you sure?" Maria said. "Pino?"

77

"Ricardo, you can do more for your wife from the back, with Maria walking third, and Luigi right behind me."

That annoyed Ricardo. He raised his voice, "But I—"

"It's safer for her and for all of us if the strongest are at either end of the rope," Pino insisted. "Or do you know more about these mountains and climbing than I do?"

"Do what he says," Maria said. "Strongest at the back and front."

Pino could tell Ricardo was in a quandary, irritated at being ordered around by a seventeen-year-old, and yet flattered at being called the strongest.

"Okay," he said. "I'll be the anchor."

"Perfetto," Pino said after they'd climbed into the waist loops.

He put his gloved right hand on the rock wall and set off. Though the way was wide enough in most places for a normal gait, he imagined the path fifteen centimeters narrower to his left and moved tight to the wall. The worst thing that could happen was for one of them to pitch off the low side of the trail. They might get lucky, and the weight of the other three might be enough to hold them all on the mountainside. Or they might get unlucky, and a second person would go, and then a third. The slope below them was nearly forty degrees. Sharp rock and alpine brush would chew them up if they all started to tumble.

He led them at a cat's pace, slinking along, careful, easy, and sure. They moved with little incident for almost an hour, until they were roughly above the village of Madesimo, when Luigi started to hack and to spit. Pino was forced to stop.

"Signore," he whispered. "I know you can't help it, but cough into the inside of your elbow if you have to. The village is right there below us, and we can't take the chance of being heard by the wrong ears."

The cigar trader whispered, "How much farther?"

"The distance doesn't matter. Just think about your next step."

Five hundred meters farther on, the slopes they crossed became less sheer and the trail more moderate.

"Is that the worst of it?" Luigi asked.

"That was the best of it," Pino said.

"What?" Maria cried in soft alarm.

"I'm joking," Pino said. "That was the worst of it."

By dawn, they were climbing up through the alpine meadows high above Madesimo. The mountain grass that had reminded Pino of Anna's hair was seedless now, and dying. Pino looked around behind him and across the valley at the rugged massif rising on the other side. He wondered if there could be German soldiers over there up this high, watching the Groppera through binoculars. Pino thought it unlikely, but he led the three of them off to the side of the meadows where they could climb in the shadows of trees until those gave way to rock and sparse juniper that offered little concealment.

"We'll need to move faster now," he said. "With the sun behind the peak, there are shadows up in the bowl that will help us. But the sun will be on us soon enough."

Heading into the bowl at the bottom of the north cirque, Ricardo and Maria kept pace with Pino. Luigi, the smoker, lagged behind, sweat pouring off his face, his chest heaving for thin air. Pino had to go back for him twice as they negotiated fields of glacially cast boulders and stuck to the ancient path to the back wall of the bowl.

Pino and the young couple rested and waited for the cigar trader, who was coughing, spitting, and moving at a snail's pace. He reeked of fresh tobacco smoke when he lay down on a flat-topped rock by Pino and moaned.

Pino got out sweet tea, dried meat, and bread from his pack. Luigi devoured his meal. So did the young couple. Pino waited until they were done, then ate and drank smaller portions. He'd save some to eat on the way back.

"Where now?" Luigi asked, as if he'd only just become aware of his surroundings.

Pino gestured at the goat trail that cut a sharp series of steep zigzags up the wall.

The man's chin retreated. "I can't climb that."

"Sure you can," Pino said. "Just do what I do."

Luigi threw up his hands. "No. I can't. I won't. You just leave me here. Death is coming for me sooner than later, no matter what I do to stop it."

For a moment, Pino didn't know what to do. Then he said, "Who says you're going to die?"

"The Nazis," the smoker said, hacking, and then gesturing up at the path. "And this way says that God wants me to die sooner than later. But I will not go up there and fall and bounce over rocks in my last moments. I will sit and smoke and wait for death to come for me here. This spot will do."

"No, you're going with us," Pino said.

"I'm staying," Luigi said forcefully.

Pino swallowed, said, "Father Re told me to get you to Val di Lei. He's not going to like my leaving you, so you're coming. With me."

"You can't make me go, boy," Luigi said.

"Yes, I can," Pino said, angry and moving fast toward the man, "and I will." He loomed over the smoker, whose eyes widened. Even at seventeen, Pino was much bigger than Luigi. He could see those facts playing on the cigar trader's face, which contorted in fear when he glanced again at the steep walls of the cirque.

"Don't you understand?" he said in a defeated tone. "I really can't. I have no faith I can make it—"

"But I do," Pino said, trying to put a growl in his voice.

"Please?"

"No," Pino said. "I promise you you're getting to the top and over into Val di Lei if I have to carry you myself."

Luigi appeared convinced by the resolve in Pino's face. With a quivering lip he said, "Promise?"

"Promise," Pino said, and shook his hand.

He had them rope up again with Luigi right behind him, followed by Maria and her husband.

"You sure I won't fall?" the cigar trader asked, clearly terrified. "I've never done anything remotely like this. I've . . . always lived in Rome."

Pino thought, said, "Okay, so you've climbed around in the Roman ruins?"

"Yes, but—"

"How about those steep, narrow steps in the Colosseum?"

Luigi nodded. "Many times."

"This is no worse than that."

"It is."

"It isn't," Pino said. "Just imagine that you're in the Colosseum and you're cutting back and forth across the seats and steps. You'll be fine."

Luigi seemed skeptical, but he did not fight the rope when Pino started up the first leg. Pino kept up a running banter with the smoker, telling him how he was going to let him have two cigarettes when he reached the top, and advising him to keep the fingers of his inside hand trailing along the slope as they climbed.

"Take your time," he said. "Look ahead, not down."

When the going got rough and the wall turned nearly sheer, Pino distracted Luigi with the story of how he and his brother had survived the first night of bombing in Milan and come home to find music playing.

"Your father is a wise man," the cigar trader said. "Music. Wine. A cigar. The small luxuries of life are how we survive what the mind can't fathom."

"You sound like you do a lot of thinking in your shop," Pino said, wiping the sweat from his eyes.

Luigi laughed. "A lot of thinking. A lot of talking. A lot of reading. It is . . ." The joy left his voice. "It was my home."

<hr />

They were well up the wall of the cirque now, and the trickiest part of the climb was just ahead, where the way cut hard right for two meters and then hard left for three in a cleft in the face of the slope that dropped away sharply. The challenge was a psychological one because the trail through the cleft was plenty wide. But the thirty meters of air right there off the trail could rattle even a veteran climber's confidence if looked at too long.

Pino decided not to warn them and said, "Tell me about your shop."

"Oh, it was a beautiful place," Luigi said. "Just off the Piazza di Spagna at the bottom of the Spanish Steps. Do you know the area?"

"I have been to the Spanish Steps," Pino said, pleased that Luigi had not hesitated to follow him. "That's a fine neighborhood, many elegant stores."

"A wonderful place for business," Luigi said.

Pino walked through the back of the V. He and the cigar smoker were on opposite sides of the cleft now. If Luigi was ever going to look down, it was now. When Pino saw Luigi turn his head to do just that, he said, "Describe your store to me."

Luigi's eyes found Pino's. "Oil-rubbed wood floors and counters," he said, chuckling and taking the turn with ease. "Tufted leather chairs. And an octagonal humidor that my late wife and I designed ourselves."

"I bet the store smelled good."

"The best. I had cigars and tobaccos from all over the world in there. And dried lavender, mints, and Sen-Sen. And fine brandy for my favored customers. I had so many good and loyal customers. They were my friends, really. The shop was like a club until quite recently. Even the filthy Germans came in to buy."

They were all through the cleft and climbing diagonally toward the rim again.

"Tell me about your wife," Pino said.

There was a brief silence behind him, and he felt resistance on the rope before Luigi said, "My Ruth was the most beautiful woman I've ever known. We met at temple when we were twelve. Why she chose me, I'll never know, but she did. It turned out we couldn't have kids, but we spent twenty wonderful years together before she just got sick one day, and sicker the next, and the next. The doctors said her digestive system had reversed, and they couldn't stop it from poisoning her to death."

Pino flashed with a pang on Mrs. Beltramini and wondered how she was, how Carletto was, and his father.

"I'm sorry," Pino said, climbing up over the rim.

"It's been six years," Luigi said as Pino helped him up and then the couple. "And not an hour goes by when I don't think of her."

Pino clapped the cigar trader on the back and grinned. "You did it. We're at the top."

"What?" Luigi said, gazing around in wonder. "That's it?"

"That's it," Pino said.

"That wasn't so bad," Luigi said, and looked to the sky with relief.

"Told you. We can rest ahead. There's something I want you to see first."

He led them to where they could look over the back side of the Groppera.

"Welcome to Val di Lei," he said.

The slope of the alpine valley there was gentle compared to the front side of the mountain and was covered with low, wind-stunted mountain shrubs with leaves turning rust, orange, and yellow. Far down the valley, they could see its namesake. Fewer than two hundred meters wide and perhaps eight hundred long, the alpine lake ran north-south toward that triangle of woods Father Re had described.

The lake surface was silver blue normally, but that day it reflected and radiated the flaming colors of fall. Beyond the lake, a bulwark of stone rose and ran off to the south a long way toward Passo Angeloga, and the stone cairn where Pino had turned around his first day of training. They began to hike down along a game path that ran along a creek fed by glaciated snow still clinging to the highest peaks.

I did it, Pino thought, feeling happy and satisfied. *They listened to me, and I got them over the Groppera.*

"I've never been anywhere more beautiful than this," Maria said when they reached the lake. "It's incredible. It feels like . . ."

"Freedom," Ricardo said.

"A moment to cherish," Luigi said.

"Are we in Switzerland, already?" Maria asked.

"Almost," Pino said. "We go into the woods there a ways to reach the border."

Pino had never been beyond the lake, so he walked to the woods with some apprehension. But he remembered Father Re's description of where he'd find the path, and he soon located it.

The dense grove of fir and spruce was almost like a maze. The air was cooler, and the ground softer. They'd been climbing for close to six and a half hours, but no one looked tired.

Pino's heart beat a little faster at the thought that he'd led these people to Switzerland. He'd helped them escape the—

A big bearded man stepped out from behind a tree three meters ahead. He pointed a double-barreled shotgun at Pino's face.

Chapter Nine

Petrified, Pino threw up his hands. So did his three charges.

"Please—," Pino began.

Over the barrel of the gun, the man snarled, "Who sent you?"

"Father," Pino stuttered. "Father Re."

A long moment passed as the man's eyes flitted from Pino to the others. Then he lowered the gun. "We must be careful these days, yes?"

Pino dropped his hands, feeling sick and weak on his feet. Icy sweat dripped down his spine. He'd never had a gun pointed at him before.

Luigi said, "You will help us now, *signore . . .*?"

"My name is Bergstrom," the man said. "I'll take you from here."

"Where?" Maria asked fretfully.

"Down through the Emet Pass to the Swiss village of Innerferrera," Bergstrom said. "You'll be safe, and we can figure out your next journey from there." Bergstrom nodded to Pino. "Give my best to Father Re."

"I will," Pino promised, and then turned to his three companions. "Good luck."

Maria hugged him. Ricardo shook his hand. From his pocket, Luigi pulled a small metal tube with a screw cap. He handed it to Pino. "It's Cuban," he said.

"I can't take it."

Luigi looked insulted. "You don't think I know how you got me up that last bit? A fine cigar like this is hard to come by, and I don't give it away lightly."

"Thank you, *signore*," Pino said, smiling and taking the cigar.

Bergstrom said to Pino, "Your safety depends on staying unseen. Be careful before you leave the forest. Study the hillsides and the valley before you move on."

"I will."

"We go, then," Bergstrom said, turning away.

Luigi patted Pino on the back and followed. Ricardo smiled at him. Maria said, "Have a good life, Pino."

"And you."

"I hope we have no climbing to do," he heard Luigi say to Bergstrom as they disappeared into the trees.

"A climb down is not a climb up," Bergstrom replied.

After that, all Pino could make out was the snap of a branch, a rock tumbling, and then nothing but the wind through the firs. Though happy, he felt oddly and acutely alone when he turned around and walked back into Italy.

Pino did as Bergstrom had instructed. He stopped and stood inside the tree line to study the valley and the heights above it. When he was sure as he could be that no one was watching, he set out once again. By his watch it was nearly noon. He'd been on the move for nearly nine hours, and he was tired.

Father Re had foreseen his fatigue and told him not to try to make the trip back that day. Instead, his orders were to climb southwest to an old shepherd's hut, one of several on the mountain, and spend the night. Pino would return to Casa Alpina via Madesimo in the morning.

As Pino hiked south through Val di Lei, he felt good and satisfied. They'd done it. Father Re and everyone else who'd helped get the refugees to Casa Alpina. As a team, they'd all saved three people from death. They'd fought back against the Nazis in secret, and they'd won!

To his surprise, the emotions that flooded through him made him feel stronger, refreshed. He decided not to spend the night in the hut but to push on to Madesimo, to sleep at the inn and see Alberto Ascari. When he was almost to the ridge, Pino stopped to rest his legs and eat again.

When he was finished, he looked back at Val di Lei and noticed four tiny figures moving south along the stone outcropping above the lake. Pino shaded his eyes, trying to see them better. He couldn't tell anything about them at first, but then made out that they were all carrying rifles.

Pino got a sickening feeling in his stomach. Had they seen him go into the forest with three people and come out alone? Were they Germans? Why were they out in the middle of nowhere?

Pino had no answers to the questions, which continued to trouble him after the four men disappeared from view. He made his way down the goat trails and through the alpine meadows to Madesimo. It was nearly four in the afternoon when he walked into the village. A group of boys, including his little friend Nicco, the innkeeper's son, was at play not far from the inn. Pino was about to enter and inquire about a room, when he noticed Alberto Ascari hurrying toward him, clearly upset.

"A band of partisans was here last night," Ascari said. "They said they were fighting the Nazis, but they were asking about Jews."

"Jews?" Pino said, and looked away, seeing Nicco squat in the high grass and pick up what at a distance of nearly forty meters looked like a large egg. "What did you say to them?"

"We told them there were no Jews here. Why do you think that they—"

Nicco held the egg out to show his friends. The egg became a flash of fire and light a split second before the force of the explosion hit Pino like a mule's kick.

He almost fell but regained his balance drunkenly, disoriented and unsure what had happened. Even with his ears ringing, he could hear the children's screams. Pino lurched toward them. The boys who had been closest to Nicco were down. One had lost a hand. The other's eyes were bloody sockets. Part of Nicco's face was gone, and most of his right arm. Blood pooled and spattered all around the little boy.

Hysterical, Pino scooped Nicco up, seeing the little boy's eyes roll back in his head, and raced him toward the inn and his mother and father, who'd burst out the front door. The boy started convulsing.

"No!" Nicco's mother screamed. She took her son. He convulsed again, and then sagged dead in her arms. "No! Nicco! Nicco!"

In a daze of disbelief and horror, Pino watched Nicco's sobbing mother go to her knees, lay her son's body on the ground, and cover it with her own—as if she were leaning over his crib when he'd been a baby. For many moments Pino just stood there, numb, watching her grieve. Glancing down, he saw he was smeared in blood. He looked around and noticed villagers rushing to treat the other children, and the innkeeper staring forlornly at his wife and dead son.

"I'm sorry," Pino whimpered. "I couldn't save him."

Mr. Conte said dully, "You didn't do this, Pino. Those partisans last night must have . . . But who would leave a grenade where . . . ?" He shook his head, and choked, "Can you get Father Re? He needs to bless my Nicco's body."

Even though he'd been up since the dead of night, and had covered nearly twenty-three kilometers in steep terrain, Pino was determined to run the entire way, as if his feet and speed alone could separate him from the brutality of what he had just witnessed. Halfway up the trail, though, the smell of the blood on his clothes, and the vivid memories of Nicco boasting about being a better skier than Pino, and the fiery flash that took the little boy were too much for him. Pino stopped, bent over, and vomited his insides out.

Weeping, he staggered the rest of the way to Motta as daylight faded to dusk.

⇌

When he reached Casa Alpina, Pino was ashen, wrung out. Father Re was shocked when Pino came into the empty dining room.

"I told you to stay—," Father Re began, then saw Pino's bloody clothes and struggled to his feet. "What's happened? Are you all right?"

"No, Father," Pino said, starting to cry again, and not caring as he told the priest what had happened. "Why would someone do that? Leave a grenade?"

"I have no idea," Father Re said grimly as he went for his jacket. "What about our friends you guided?"

The memory of Luigi, Ricardo, and Maria disappearing into the woods seemed like ages ago. "I left them with Mr. Bergstrom."

The priest put on his coat and grabbed his cane. "That is a blessing, then, something to be grateful for."

Pino told him about seeing the four men with rifles.

"But they didn't see you?"

"I don't think so," Pino said.

Father Re reached up and put his hand on Pino's shoulder. "You did well, then. You did the right thing."

The priest left. Pino sat on a bench at an empty table in the dining room. He closed his eyes and hung his head, seeing Nicco's missing face and arm, and the boy who'd been blinded, and then the dead girl with the missing arm from the night of the first bombardment. He couldn't get rid of those images no matter how hard he tried. They just kept repeating until he felt as if he were going crazy.

"Pino?" Mimo said sometime later. "You okay?"

Pino opened his eyes to find his brother crouched at his side.

Mimo said, "Someone said the innkeeper's little boy died, and two other boys might."

"I saw it," Pino said, and started to cry again. "I held him."

His brother seemed frozen by the sight of his tears, but then said, "C'mon, Pino. Let's get you cleaned up and to bed. The younger boys shouldn't see you like this. They look up to you."

Mimo helped him to his feet and down the hall to the shower room. He stripped his clothes and then sat a long time in the lukewarm water, mindlessly scrubbing Nicco's blood off his hands and face. It didn't seem real. Except it was.

Father Re gently shook him awake around ten the next morning. For a few moments, Pino had no idea where he was. Then it all came back with such force that it took his breath away all over again.

"How are the Contes?"

The priest turned grim. "It's a terrible blow for any parent to lose a child under any circumstances. But like that . . ."

"He was such a funny little kid," Pino said bitterly. "It's not fair."

"It's a tragedy," Father Re said. "The other two boys will live, but they'll never be the same."

They shared a long silence.

"What do we do, Father?"

"We have faith, Pino. We have faith and continue to do what is right. I got word in Madesimo that we will have two new travelers for dinner tonight. I want you to rest today. I'll need you to guide them in the morning."

It became a pattern over the course of the following weeks. Every few days, two, three, or sometimes four travelers would ring the bell at Casa Alpina. Pino would lead them out in the wee hours of the morning, climbing by what light the moon offered, and using the carbide miner's lamp only during cloud cover and the dark of the moon. On these trips, after handing over his charges to Bergstrom, he went to the shepherd's hut.

It was a crude affair with a stacked-stone foundation dug into the side of the slope, a sod roof supported by logs, and a door that swung on leather hinges. There was a straw mattress and a woodstove with split wood and a hatchet. Those nights in the hut as he stoked the fire, Pino felt lonely. He tried to summon up memories of Anna to comfort him more than once, but all he could recall was the squall of the trolley as it blocked her from his view.

His thoughts would then turn abstract: to girls and to love. He hoped he'd have both in his life. He wondered what his girl would be like and whether she would adore the mountains as he did, and whether she skied, and a hundred other questions with maddeningly unknowable answers.

In early November, Pino led the escape of a British Royal Air Force pilot, shot down during a bombing raid on Genoa. A week later, he helped a second downed pilot to reach Mr. Bergstrom. And almost every day more Jews came to Casa Alpina.

In the dark days of December 1943, Father Re grew worried because of the increased number of Nazi patrols going up and down the Splügen Pass road.

"They're becoming suspicious," he told Pino. "The Germans haven't found many of the Jews. The Nazis know they're being helped."

"Alberto Ascari says there have been atrocities, Father," Pino said. "The Nazis have killed priests helping Jews. They've pulled them right off the altar while they were saying Mass."

"We have heard that, too," the priest said. "But we can't stop loving our fellow man, Pino, because we're frightened. If we lose love, all is lost. We just have to get smarter."

The next day, Father Re and a priest in Campodolcino came up with an ingenious plan. They decided to use watchers to track the Nazi patrols on the Splügen Pass road, and they improvised a communications system.

In the chapel behind Casa Alpina there was a catwalk around the interior of the steeple. From it, through shutters that opened on the flank of the tower, the boys could see the upper floor of the rectory fifteen hundred meters below in Campodolcino, and one window in particular. The shade was drawn in that window when the Germans were patrolling the Splügen. If the shade was up during the day or a lantern shone there at night, refugees could be safely taken up the mountain to Motta in oxcarts, buried under piles of hay to avoid detection.

When it became clear that Pino could not lead every Jew, downed pilot, or political refugee who came to Casa Alpina seeking a way to freedom, he began to teach the routes to several of the other older boys, including Mimo.

Heavy snowfall held off until mid-December of 1943. But then it turned cold, and the skies began to dump, hard and often. Feathery powder snow built up in the chutes and bowls of the upper Groppera, making them avalanche-prone, which soon shut down the preferred northern route to Val di Lei and the Emet Pass into Switzerland.

Because many of the refugees had never faced cold, snowy conditions before, nor had the faintest idea about mountain climbing, Father Re risked sending Pino, Mimo, and the other guides along the easy southern route over the Angel's Step. They started carrying skis with climbing skins to speed the return trip.

The brothers left Casa Alpina the third week of December and joined their family in Rapallo to celebrate Christmas and to wonder whether the war would ever be over. The Lellas had all hoped the Allies would have freed Italy by now. But the Germans' so-called Gustav Line of pillboxes, tank traps, and other fortifications was holding from the town of Monte Cassino east to the Adriatic Sea.

Allied progress had ground to a halt.

⊰⊱

On Pino and Mimo's way back to the Alps, the train passed through Milan. Parts of the city they barely recognized. When Pino reached Casa Alpina this time, he was more than happy to be spending his winter in the Alps.

He and Mimo loved to ski, and they were experts at it by then. They used skins to climb the slopes above the school and schussed in the fresh deep powder that had fallen during their brief time away. Both boys adored the speed and thrill of skiing, but it meant more to Pino than adventure. Swooping down the mountain was the closest he'd ever come to flying. He was a bird on skis. It warmed his soul. It set him free in a way nothing else did. Pino would fall asleep tired, achy, and happy, and wanting to do it all again tomorrow.

Alberto Ascari and his friend, Titiana, decided to host a New Year's Eve party at the Contes' inn in Madesimo. There had been a lull in the number of refugees during the holiday week, and Father Re granted Pino's request to attend the bash.

Excited, Pino oiled his climbing boots, put on his best clothes, and walked down to Madesimo in lightly falling snow that made everything look magical and new. Ascari and Titiana were putting the finishing touches on the decorations when Pino arrived. He spent time with the Contes, who, though still grieving for their son, were glad for the business and distraction the party afforded.

And what a party it was. There were twice as many young ladies present as men, and Pino had a full dance card for much of the evening. The food was wonderful: speck ham, and gnocchi, and polenta with fresh Montasio cheese, and roe deer venison with dried tomatoes and pumpkin seeds. The wine and beer flowed.

Later in the evening, Pino was slow-dancing with Frederica and realized he hadn't once thought of Anna. He was wondering if the night would end perfectly, with a kiss from Frederica, when the door to the inn flew open. Four men with old rifles and shotguns walked in. They were shabbily dressed with filthy red scarves around their necks. Their gaunt cheeks were red from the cold, and their sunken eyes put Pino in mind of feral dogs he'd seen after the bombardments began, scavenging for any scraps they could find.

"We are partisans fighting to free Italy from the Germans," one of them announced, and then licked the left inside corner of his lips. "We need donations to continue the fight." Taller than the others, he wore a knit wool cap that he pulled off and waved at the partygoers.

No one moved.

"You bastards!" Mr. Conte roared. "You killed my son!"

He charged at the leader, who clubbed the innkeeper with the butt of his rifle and knocked him to the floor.

"We did no such thing," he said.

"You did, Tito," Conte said lying on the ground, bleeding from his head. "You or one of your men left a grenade. My son picked it up, thought it was a toy. He's dead. Another boy has been blinded. Another lost his hand."

"Like I said," Tito said, "we don't know a thing about it. Donations, *per favore.*"

He raised his rifle and fired a bullet through the ceiling, which provoked the men at the party to turn out their pockets and the young ladies to open their purses.

Pino fingered a ten-lira note from his pocket and held it out.

Tito snatched it and then stopped to look him up and down. "Nice clothes," he said. "Turn out your pockets."

Pino didn't move a muscle.

Tito said, "Do it or we'll strip you naked."

Pino wanted to punch him, but he pulled out a leather-and-magnet money clip his uncle Albert designed and removed a wad of lira, which he held out to Tito.

Tito whistled and snatched the money. Then he stepped closer and studied Pino, exuding a threat that was as strong as his foul body odor and breath. "I know you," he said.

"No, you don't."

"Yes, I do," Tito said again, his face close to Pino's. "I've seen you in my binoculars. I've seen you climbing over Passo Angeloga and across the Emet with many strangers."

Pino said nothing.

Tito smiled, and then licked the corner of his lips. "What the Nazis would give to know about you."

"I thought you were fighting the Germans," Pino said. "Or was that just an excuse to rob a party?"

Tito hit Pino in the gut with the butt of his rifle, knocking him to the ground.

"Stay off those passes, kid," Tito said. "You tell the priest the same thing. Angel's Step? The Emet. They're ours. You understand?"

Pino lay there gasping for air and refusing to reply.

Tito kicked him. "Understand?"

Pino nodded, which pleased Tito, who studied him.

"Nice boots," he said at last. "What size?"

Pino grunted an answer.

"Couple pairs of warm socks, they'll work just fine. Take them off."

"They're the only boots I have."

"You can take them off alive, or I can take them off you dead. Your choice."

Humiliated and hating the man, but not wanting to die, Pino unlaced the boots and pulled them off. When he glanced at Frederica, she reddened and looked away, making Pino feel like he was doing something cowardly when he handed Tito the boots.

"That money clip, too," Tito said, snapping his fingers twice.

"My uncle made that for me," Pino complained.

"Tell him to make you another. Tell him it's for a good cause."

Sullen, Pino dug in his pocket and got out the money clip. He flipped it at Tito.

Tito snagged it out of the air. "Smart boy."

He nodded to his men. They grabbed food from the buffet, stuffing it into their pockets and packs before leaving.

"Stay off the Emet," Tito said again, and they were gone.

When the door shut behind them, Pino wanted to put his fist through a wall. Mrs. Conte had rushed to her husband's side and was pressing a cloth to his wound.

"Are you all right?" Pino asked.

"I'll live," the innkeeper said. "I should have gotten my gun. Shot them all."

"Who was he, the partisan? You said, 'Tito'?"

"Yes, Tito, from over Soste way. But he's no partisan. He's just a crook and smuggler from a long line of crooks and smugglers. And now a murderer."

"I'm getting my boots and my money clip back."

Mrs. Conte shook her head and said, "Tito's cunning and dangerous. You'll stay away from him if you know what's good for you, Pino."

Pino felt disgusted with himself for not standing up to Tito. He couldn't stay at the party any longer. It was over for him. He tried to borrow some boots or shoes, but no one had his large size. In the end, he took wool socks and low rubber overshoes from the innkeeper, and flailed through the storm back to Casa Alpina.

When he'd finished telling Father Re what Tito had done and that he or one of his men had killed Nicco and maimed the children, the priest said, "You chose the greater good, Pino."

"How come I don't feel good about it?" Pino said, still angry. "And he said to tell you to stay off Angel's Step and the Emet."

"Did he now?" Father Re said, turning stony. "Well, I'm sorry, but that we will not do."

Chapter Ten

A meter of snow blanketed the mountains above Casa Alpina on New Year's Day, followed by a day's break, and then another meter fell. There was so much snow it took until the second week of January before the escapes could resume.

After locating replacement boots, Pino and his brother began leading Jews, downed pilots, and other refugees in groups as large as eight. Despite Tito's warnings about using Passo Angeloga they stuck to the more gradual southern way to Val di Lei by constantly changing the days and times they'd go, and then skiing back along the northern route to Madesimo.

This system worked well into early February 1944. When the lantern was shining in the upper window of the Campodolcino rectory, a steady stream of refugees hiding under hay in oxcarts moved up through Madesimo to Casa Alpina, and then followed Pino or one of the other boys over the Groppera into Switzerland.

Reaching the shepherd's hut in a daze early in the month, Pino found a note nailed to the wall of the hut. It read: *Last warning*.

Pino threw the note in the stove and used it to light the wood stacked inside. He adjusted the damper and went outside to chop more wood. He hoped Tito was out there somewhere in the vast alpine terrain around him, looking through his binoculars and seeing Pino refuse to—

A thunderous explosion blew open the hut door. Pino dove into the snow. He lay there shaking with fear for several minutes before he could build up the courage to look inside. The stove was barely recognizable. The force of the bomb, or grenade, or whatever had been put in the stove had blown the firebox apart, throwing shards of heated metal that chipped the stone foundation and stuck like tiny knives in the beams and woodwork. Glowing wood embers burned holes in his pack and lit the straw bed afire. He dragged them both into the snow and got them snuffed out, feeling completely exposed. If Tito was willing to put a bomb in the hut's stove, he was willing to shoot him.

Pino fought off the sense that someone was aiming at him as he put his skis back on, hoisted his pack onto his shoulders, and picked up his ski poles. The hut was no longer a refuge, and the southern route was no longer a viable option.

"There's only one way left," Pino told Father Re that evening by the fire as the boys and several new visitors ate another of Brother Bormio's masterpieces.

"With the snow piling up, it was inevitable that you would have to use it at some point," the priest replied. "The spine of the ridge will be blown free of snow, and the footing will be the best on the mountain. You'll go again with Mimo the day after tomorrow, teach him the way."

Pino flashed on the chimney, the catwalk, and the cable traverse below the Groppera's crag, and was instantly full of doubt. Any misstep up there in these conditions meant death.

Father Re gestured at the visitors and said, "You'll take that young family, and the woman with the violin case. She used to play at La Scala."

⟨⟩

Pino twisted around, puzzled before recognizing the violinist he'd seen at his parents' party the night of the first bombardment. He knew she was in her late thirties or early forties, but she looked like she'd aged and was ill. What was her name?

He put thoughts of the Groppera out of his mind, got Mimo, and they walked over to her.

"Remember us?" Pino said.

The violinist seemed not to recognize them.

"Our parents are Porzia and Michele Lella," Pino said. "You went to a party at our old apartment on Via Monte Napoleone."

Mimo said, "And you yelled at me in front of La Scala for being a little boy who couldn't see what was happening all around me. You were right."

A slow smile built on her face. "That seems so long ago."

"Are you okay?" Pino asked.

"Just a little queasy in the stomach," she said. "The altitude. I don't think I've ever been this high up. Father Re says I will get used to it in a day or so."

"What shall we call you?" Mimo asked. "What do your papers say?"

"Elena . . . Elena Napolitano."

Pino noticed the wedding ring she wore. "Is your husband here, Mrs. Napolitano?"

She looked ready to cry, hugged her belly, and choked, "He made the Germans chase him while we escaped our apartment. They . . . they took him to Binario Twenty-One."

"What's that?" Mimo asked.

"It's where they take every Jew they catch in Milan. Platform Twenty-One in the central station. They put them into cattle cars, and they disappear, bound for . . . no one knows. They don't come back." Tears rolled down her cheek, and her lips quivered with raw emotion.

Pino thought about the massacre in Meina, when the Nazis machine-gunned the Jews in the lake. He felt sick and helpless. "Your husband. He must have been a brave man."

Mrs. Napolitano wept and nodded. "Beyond brave."

After she'd regained her composure, she dabbed a handkerchief to her eyes and in a hoarse voice said, "Father Re said you two will take me to Switzerland."

"Yes, but with this snow, it won't be easy."

"Nothing in life worth doing is easy," the violinist said.

Pino looked down at her shoes, low black pumps. "Did you climb up here in those?"

"I wrapped them in pieces of a baby blanket. I still have them."

"They won't work," Pino said. "Not where we're going."

"It's all I have," she said.

"We'll find you boots among the boys. What size are you?"

Mrs. Napolitano told him. By afternoon, Mimo had found a pair and rubbed the leather with a mixture of pine tar and oil to make the boots water-proof. He'd also gotten her wool pants to wear beneath her dress, and an over-coat, and a wool hat and mittens.

"Here," Father Re said, handing out white pillow sacks with holes cut out for shoulders and heads. "Wear these."

"Why?" Mrs. Napolitano asked.

"The way you are going is exposed in several places. Someone from far down on the valley floor might see your dark clothes. But with these, you'll blend into the snow."

Accompanying Mrs. Napolitano was the D'Angelo family—Peter and Liza, the parents, and seven-year-old Anthony and his nine-year-old sister, Judith. From Abruzzi, they were physically fit from a lifetime of farming and climbing in the mountains south of Rome.

Mrs. Napolitano, however, had spent much of her life indoors and sitting down playing the violin. She said she walked everywhere in Milan, rarely taking the trolley, but Pino could tell from her breathing at Casa Alpina that the climb was going to be an ordeal for her and for him.

⤙⤚

Rather than dwell on what could go wrong, Pino tried to think of everything he might need. He got an extra nine meters of rope from Brother Bormio and had Mimo carry it bandolier-style in addition to his pack, ice ax, poles, and skis. Pino added several carabiners to his already heavy pack, another ice ax, crampons, skis, climbing skins, poles, and a handful of pitons.

They set out at 2:00 a.m. The moon was half-full, reflecting just enough light off the snow that they did not need the lantern. The early going could have been hellish, with all of them having to post-hole up the first rise to get to the spine, but the afternoon before, Father Re had sent out every boy at Casa Alpina to make the 122-meter vertical climb and descent, in effect boot-packing the hill. Despite the chronic pain in his hip, the priest had broken trail most of the way.

The result was a beaten-down path that climbed straight up the west flank of the Groppera. It probably saved Mrs. Napolitano's life. Though she carried only her beloved violin in its case, she labored long and hard up that initial slope, stopping often, fighting for air, and shaking her head before hugging the violin with both hands and going on.

During the climb, which took her the better part of an hour, Pino said little other than to encourage her with phrases like, "That's it. You're doing fine. Just a little higher and we can rest for a bit."

He sensed that more than that would do no good. This wasn't like the psychological barriers he'd managed to break with the cigar store owner by deflecting his attention. Mrs. Napolitano was simply not in the physical shape necessary to make a climb this demanding. As he followed her up the mountain, he prayed she had enough spirit and will to compensate.

Deepening snow and crevasses had made the boulder field in the bowl all the more treacherous, but with Pino's help, the violinist crossed it without incident. When they reached the tail of the razorback spine, however, Mrs. Napolitano began to shake.

"I don't know if I can do this," she said. "I should go back down with your brother. I'm holding the others up."

"You can't stay at Casa Alpina," Pino said. "It's too dangerous for anyone to stay there for long."

The violinist said nothing, but then turned, held tight to her stomach, and vomited.

"Mrs. Napolitano?" Pino said.

"It's okay," she said. "It passes."

"Are you expecting?" Mrs. D'Angelo said in the darkness.

"A woman can always tell," Mrs. Napolitano gasped.

She's pregnant? A leaden weight came down on Pino's shoulders. *Oh my God! A baby? What if . . . ?*

"You should climb for your baby," Mrs. D'Angelo said to Mrs. Napolitano. "You don't want to go back down. You know what that might mean."

"Pino?" his brother whispered after a long silence that followed. "I can take her back, let her get more used to the altitude."

Pino was about to agree, but then Mrs. Napolitano said, "I'll climb."

But what happens if the altitude gets to her, and her baby . . . ?

Pino forced himself to stop. He could not let fear take control of his brain. Fear had no business here. He had to think, and he had to think clearly.

Telling himself that over and over, Pino took the second rope from Mimo and made a loop under Mrs. Napolitano's armpits. Then he clambered up onto the tail of the ridge. With Mimo behind her, Pino pulled, dragging the violinist up onto the spine. It was a tough chore made tougher by the fact that she held her violin case and would not yield it to Mimo.

"You're going to have to leave the violin," Pino said as he threw the loop back down.

"Never," she said. "My violin stays with me always."

"Let me carry it, then. I'll make room for it in my pack and return it to you when we reach Switzerland."

In the moonlight he could see Mrs. Napolitano struggling with the idea.

"I'm going to need you to have free hands and feet where we're going," he said. "If you keep the violin, you'll put your baby's life in danger."

After a pause, she handed it to him, saying, "It's a Stradivarius. It's all I have now."

"I'll take care of it like my father would," he said, strapping the violin case under the flap of his pack.

⇌

In short order, Pino pulled up the D'Angelo children—who were treating the whole thing as a grand adventure—and then their parents, who were encouraging the idea. As he had with almost every group of refugees, Pino linked them together with rope, with Mrs. Napolitano right behind him followed by Mrs. D'Angelo, the children, Mr. D'Angelo, and Mimo bringing up the rear.

Before they could start up the ridge, the young boy made a whining noise and began bickering at his sister.

"Stop," Pino whispered harshly.

"No one can hear us up here," Anthony said.

"The mountain can hear us," Pino said firmly. "And if you're too loud, it will wake up and shift under its blanket and send avalanches that will bury us all."

"Is the mountain a monster?" Anthony asked.

"Like a dragon," Pino said. "So we have to be careful and quiet, because we're climbing up his scaly back."

"Where's his head?" Judith asked.

"Above us," Mimo said. "In the clouds."

That seemed to satisfy the children, and the group set out once more. What had taken him less than an hour the last time he'd climbed the hard route took them almost two. It was four thirty in the morning when they reached the chimney. Pino could make out the gouge in the nearly vertical mountain face, but he needed more light than the moon's if they were to climb it.

He poured water into the carbide lamp and screwed the lid tight to seal the vapors that were rapidly filling the reservoir. After waiting a minute, he loosened the gas valve and hit the striker. On the second try, a thin blue flame burned against a reflecting pan, throwing enough light up the chimney that they could all see the challenge ahead.

"Oh my God," Mrs. Napolitano groaned. "Oh my God."

He put his hand on her shoulder. "It's not as bad as it looks."

"It's worse than it looks."

"No, it's not. Back in September, when the rock was bare, it was worse, but see the ice on both sides? The ice has narrowed the chimney, made it more climbable."

Pino looked to his brother. "This may take a little time, but I'm going to cut steps. Keep them moving and warm until you hear me whistle that I'm sending down the axes. Then rope up and send Mr. D'Angelo. I'm going to need his strength up there. You'll come up last."

For once, Mimo didn't argue about being last. Pino freed himself from the group rope, dropped his pack, and put on crampons. With Mimo's rope coil slung like a bandolier, he picked up his ice ax and Mimo's and said a prayer before he began to climb. His back to the mountain, Pino reminded himself not to look down before he kicked in the blades of his crampons for support, reached overhead, and jabbed the pick points of the axes into the ice.

With every half meter gained, Pino stopped and carefully chopped out flat spots for the others. It was maddeningly slow work, and the higher he got, the more he was aware of lights coming on, one by one, down in Campodolcino. He knew that with binoculars someone might see the miner's lamp lighting up the inside of the ice chimney, but he felt he had no choice.

Forty minutes later, drenched with sweat, Pino reached the balcony. He kept the lamp on long enough to attach a carabiner to a piton he'd driven into the rock the last time he'd climbed this way, and to pass one end of the rope through the carabiner before testing it with his weight. The anchor held.

Pino tied the ice axes and his crampons to the rope, whistled, and then lowered them down the chimney. Several minutes later, he heard his brother whistle, and he took the slack out of the rope. Mr. D'Angelo came up onto the balcony fifteen minutes later. Together they pulled his son, daughter, and wife up quickly.

———

Pino could hear Mrs. Napolitano moaning with fear even before she entered the icy slot. He lowered the mining lamp down for her to use. The additional light only seemed to deepen the pregnant violinist's terror. Shaking head to toe, she took the ice axes and in crampons clomped into the chimney.

"Right hand first," Mimo said. "Just give it a good whack in there where Pino's leveled things off."

Mrs. Napolitano did so, but halfheartedly, and the ax came free before she could get her full weight on it.

"I can't," she said. "I can't."

Mimo said, "Just climb the stairs Pino made, stabbing the axes and the crampons' blades in tight, back and forth all the way up."

"But I could slip."

Pino called down the chute, "Not with us holding the rope, and definitely not if you kick those crampons and swing those axes like you mean it . . . like your violin bow when you play *con smania.*"

That last bit, referring to playing with passion, seemed to get through to her, because Mrs. Napolitano slashed up and out with her right ax. From above, Pino heard the pick end drive solidly into the ice. He backed up to join Mr. D'Angelo on the rope, and he had his wife lie on her belly, looking over the edge and down the chute to tell them each time the pregnant violinist was going to shift her weight and climb higher. Whereas the others had come up half meter by half meter, her ascent was measured in centimeters.

Almost four meters off the ground, Mrs. Napolitano somehow lost her footing, shrieked, and fell. They caught her, and she dangled there, moaning and blubbering until they could coax her into trying again. Thirty-five nail-biting minutes later, they hauled her up and over onto the balcony. In the wavering light of the miner's lamp, frost coated her clothes and icy snot clung to her face, making her look like she'd been through a frozen hell and back.

"I hated that," she said, collapsing. "Every second of it I hated."

"But you're here," Pino said, grinning. "Not many people could have done that, and you did. For your baby."

The violinist placed her mittens over her overcoat and belly, and closed her eyes. It took another twenty minutes until they could hoist up the packs, tasks made difficult by the poles and skis strapped to the sides, and another fifteen minutes for Mimo to come up the chimney.

"That wasn't too bad," Mimo said.

"You must have been tortured as a child," Mrs. Napolitano said.

By Pino's watch it was almost six o'clock. Dawn would come soon. He wanted them off the face of the Groppera before that. He tied them all back into the rope line, and they started higher.

At six thirty, when they should have been seeing the first paling in the eastern sky, it was suddenly darker than it had been during the entire ordeal. The moon had vanished. Pino felt the wind shift, too, out of the north now, and stronger.

"We have to move faster," he said. "We have a storm coming."

"What?" Mrs. Napolitano cried. "Up here?"

"This is where storms happen," Mimo said. "But don't worry. My brother knows the way."

Pino did know the way, and for the next hour as daylight came amid flurrying snow, they made steady progress. The snowfall was good, Pino decided. It would help hide them from all prying eyes.

Around seven thirty the storm intensified, and Pino dug out a pair of glacier glasses his father had given him for Christmas, with leather side blinders to keep out the snow. Dark clouds enveloped the Groppera. Supercooled by the frozen crag above them, the clouds began to pour snow down on them. Pino fought the urge to panic as he used his ski poles to probe his way forward, intensely aware that the higher they got, the greater the likelihood of a false step. The wind began to swirl, causing whiteouts. The visibility was so low he was almost climbing blind, and it rattled him. Pino was trying to keep faith, but he felt doubt and growing alarm creep into his mind. What if he took the wrong angle on the route? Or made a misstep at a crucial time and fell? With his weight, they'd all be going for a neck-breaking ride. He felt the rope tug him to a halt.

"I can't see," Judith cried.

"Neither can I," her mother said.

"We'll wait, then," Pino said, trying to keep his voice calm. "Turn your backs to the wind."

The snow kept falling. Had the wind stayed a steady gale, they never would have made the catwalk. Instead, it gusted and died to almost nothing every few minutes. During those gaps where Pino could make out the route, they fought their way upward until he felt the ridgeline level out and narrow. Ahead fifteen meters, he could make out the catwalk and the snowy, concave mouths of the avalanche chutes on either side.

———

"We go one by one here," he said. "See the white little bowls of snow next to the spine? Don't step there. Just put your feet exactly where I do, and you'll be fine."

"What's under that snow?" Mrs. Napolitano asked.

Pino didn't want to tell her. Mimo said, "Air. Lots of it."

"Oh," she said. "Ohhh."

Pino wanted to smack his brother.

"C'mon now, Mrs. N," Pino said, trying to sound encouraging. "You've come this far, and done worse. And I'll have the other end of the rope."

The violinist made a puffing noise, hesitated, and then nodded weakly. Pino untied the group line and knotted it to Mimo's to create one long line. While he worked, he whispered to his brother. "From now on, keep your mouth shut."

"What?" Mimo said. "Why?"

"Sometimes the less you know, the better."

"Where I come from, the more you know, the better."

Seeing it was fruitless to argue, Pino tied the rope around his waist. He imagined himself a tightrope walker and held the ski poles horizontally to help him balance.

Each step was dreadful. He'd test first with the toe of his crampon, kicking gently until he heard rock or ice, and then press his heel directly onto that spot. Twice he felt his balance teeter, but managed both times to right himself before reaching the narrow ledge beyond. He paused, his forehead resting against the rock until he felt composed enough to drive a piton into the face.

He got the rope rigged through it. Mimo pulled back the slack, and the rope was taut, like a banister. The wind gusted. The whiteout returned. They were visually separated for more than a minute. When it calmed and he was able to make out the others back on the other side of the catwalk, they looked ghostly.

Pino swallowed hard. "Send Anthony first."

Anthony held on to the taut rope with his right hand and put his boots exactly in Pino's prints. He was across in a minute. Judith followed her brother, holding on to the rope and putting her boots in Pino's prints. They accomplished the task with relative ease.

Mrs. D'Angelo came next. She froze between the avalanche chutes, looking hypnotized.

Then her young son called out, "C'mon, Mama. You can do it."

She pushed on, and when she reached the ledge she wrapped her arms around her children and cried. Mr. D'Angelo came next and accomplished the feat in seconds. He explained that he'd done gymnastics as a boy.

The wind gusted before Mrs. Napolitano could begin the journey. Pino cursed to himself. He knew that the mental trick to crossing something like the catwalk was not to think about it until you were actually in motion. But she couldn't help thinking about it now.

Her ascent of the chimney, however, seemed to have emboldened Mrs. Napolitano, because when the wind ebbed and the visibility returned, she started across without Pino's prompting. When she was three-quarters of the way across the catwalk, the wind picked up again, and she vanished in swirling white.

"Don't move a muscle," Pino shouted into the void. "Wait it out!"

Mrs. Napolitano did not reply. He kept testing the line gently, feeling the weight of her out there until, at last, the wind dropped, and she was standing there coated in snow, as still as a statue.

When she reached the ledge, she held on to Pino tightly for several moments and said, "I don't think I've ever been that scared in my life. I know I haven't prayed that hard in my life."

"Your prayers were answered," he said, patting her on the back, and then whistling for his brother.

With one end of the long rope tightly knotted around his brother's waist, and Pino ready to take in slack, he said, "Ready?"

"I was born ready," Mimo replied, and set off quick and sure.

"Slow down," Pino said, trying to pull the slack rope through the piton and carabiner as fast as possible.

Mimo was already almost between the two avalanche chutes. "Why?" he said. "Father Re says I'm part mountain goat."

Those words had no sooner left Mimo's mouth than he stumbled slightly. His right foot shot out too far, and broke through. There was a sound like someone plumping a pillow. Then the snow in the chute swirled and slid like water cycling down a drain, and to Pino's horror, his little brother went with it, vanishing into a whirlpool of white.

Chapter Eleven

"Mimo!" Pino yelled, and heaved back on the rope. His brother's weight jerked in the void and almost pulled Pino off his feet.

"Help!" Pino cried to Mr. D'Angelo.

Mrs. Napolitano got there first, grabbed hold of the line behind Pino with her mittens, and threw her weight backward. The rope held. The load held.

"Mimo!" Pino shouted. "Mimo!"

No answer. The wind gusted, and with it the world above the avalanche chute whited out once more.

"Mimo!" he screamed.

Silence for a moment, and then came a weak, shaken voice. "I'm here. Jesus, get me up. There's nothing but a lot of air below me. I think I'm going to be sick."

Pino hauled against the rope, but it gave no ground.

"My pack's caught on something," Mimo said. "Lower me a little."

Mr. D'Angelo had taken Mrs. Napolitano's place by then, and though he hated to give up any ground in a situation like this, Pino reluctantly let the rope slide through his leather gloves.

"Got it," Mimo said.

They heaved and pulled and brought Mimo to the lip. Pino tied off the rope and had Mr. D'Angelo pin his legs down so he could reach over to grab his brother's rucksack. Seeing Mimo's hat was gone, seeing him bleeding from a nasty head cut, and seeing how the chute fell away below him, Pino surged with adrenaline and hoisted his brother onto the ledge.

The two brothers sat against the rock face, chests heaving.

"Don't ever do that again," Pino said at last. "Mama and Papa would never forgive me. I'd never forgive me."

Mimo gasped, "I think that's the nicest thing you've ever said to me."

Pino threw his arm around his brother's neck and hugged him once and hard.

"Okay, okay," Mimo protested. "Thanks for saving my life."

"You'd do the same."

"Of course, Pino. We're brothers. Always."

Pino nodded, feeling like he'd never loved his brother as much as he did right then.

Mrs. D'Angelo knew some first aid. She used snow to clean out the scalp wound and stanch the blood flow. They tore pieces of a scarf for bandages, and then wrapped the rest around Mimo's head for an improvised hat that the children said made him look like a fortune-teller.

The gusts slowed, but the snow fell harder as Pino led them up to that ledge along the low neck of the crag.

"We can't climb that," Mr. D'Angelo said, craning his head up at the peak, which was like an icy spearhead above them.

"We're going around it," Pino said. He pressed his stomach to the wall and started to step sideways.

Just before he rounded the corner where the ledge dropped nineteen or twenty centimeters in width, he looked back at Mrs. Napolitano and the others.

"There's a cable here. It's iced up, but you'll be able to grip it. I want you to hold it, right-hand knuckles up, left-hand knuckles down, above and below, right? Do not under any circumstances release your grip until you reach the other side."

"Other side of what?" Mrs. Napolitano asked.

Pino glanced toward the wall and down, saw that snow blocked any real view of what was a very, very long fall—an unlivable fall.

"The rock wall will be right in front of your nose," Pino said. "Look in front of you and sideways, but not behind you or down."

"I'm not going to like this, am I?" the violinist asked.

"I'll bet you didn't like the first night you played at La Scala, but you did it, and you can do this."

Despite the frost on her face, she licked her lips, shuddered, and then nodded.

After everything they'd been through, crossing the face via the cable and ledge proved easier than Pino expected. But that side of the peak was southeast facing and leeward to the storm. All five refugees and Mimo came across without further incident.

Pino collapsed in the snow, thanking God for watching over them, and praying that they'd seen the worst. But the winds picked up again, not in gusts but with steady force that drove the snowflakes into their faces like icy needles. The farther northeast they trudged, the worse the storm got, until Pino wasn't exactly sure where he was. Of all the obstacles they'd faced since leaving Casa Alpina that morning, moving blind in a snowstorm across an open ridge was the most dangerous, at least where Pino was concerned. Pizzo Groppera was pocked with crevasses at that time of year. They could fall six meters or more into one of them and not be found until spring. Even if he could avoid the mountain's physical dangers, with the cold and wet came the threat of hypothermia and death.

"I can't see!" Mrs. Napolitano said.

The D'Angelo children began to cry. Judith couldn't feel her feet or hands. Pino was on the verge of panic when ahead, out of the storm, a cairn appeared. The stack of rocks immediately oriented Pino. Ahead of them lay Val di Lei, but the forest was still a solid four, maybe five kilometers away. Then he remembered that along the trail that climbed north from the cairn there was another shepherd's hut with a stove.

"We can't go on until the storm lets up!" Pino shouted to them. "But I know a place we can take shelter, get warm, and ride it out!"

The refugees all nodded with relief. Thirty minutes later, Pino and Mimo were on their hands and knees, burrowing into the snow to open the door to the hut. Pino ducked inside first and turned on the miner's lamp. Mimo made sure the stove was not booby-trapped, and built a fire. Before they lit it, Pino went out into the snow once more and invited them inside before climbing onto the roof to make sure the chimney was clear.

He pressed the door shut and told his brother to light the stove. The matches caught the dry tinder, and soon the kindling and logs were ablaze. The firelight revealed the exhaustion in all their faces.

Pino knew he'd made the right decision coming here and letting the storm sputter out before they pushed on. But would Mr. Bergstrom be there in the woods beyond Val di Lei? The Swiss man would suspect the storm had delayed their progress. He'd come back when it was over, wouldn't he?

In a few moments, those questions were pushed aside. The little stove was almost red-hot and throwing delicious heat into the dirt-floored, low-ceilinged hut. Mrs. D'Angelo pulled off Judith's boots and began to knead her daughter's frozen feet.

"It stings," Judith said.

"It's the blood returning," Pino said. "Sit closer to the fire and take your socks off."

Soon they were all stripping down. Pino checked Mimo's head wound, which had stopped bleeding, and then got out food and drink. He heated tea on the stove, and they ate cheese and bread and salami. Mrs. Napolitano said it was the best meal of her life.

Anthony fell asleep in his father's lap. Pino turned off the miner's lamp and nodded into a deep, dreamless sleep of his own. He woke long enough to see everyone else dozing around him, then checked the fire, which was down to fading embers.

Hours later, a sound like a locomotive engine woke Pino. The train rumbled right at them, shook the ground, passed, and then there was nothing but a deep silence for many long seconds, broken only by the groaning and popping of the logs supporting the roof. From deep in Pino's gut, he knew they were in trouble once more.

"What was that, Pino?" Mrs. Napolitano cried.

"Avalanche," Pino said, trying to control the tremor in his voice as he groped for the miner's lamp. "It came right over the top of us."

He lit the lamp. He went to the door, pulled it open, and was shaken to his core. Avalanche-hardened snow and debris completely blocked the hut's only exit.

Mimo came up beside him, saw the dense wall of ice and snow, and in a terrified whisper said, "Mary, Mother of God, Pino, it's buried us alive."

⟨⟩

The hut erupted in cries and worries. Pino barely heard them. He was staring at the wall of snow and feeling like the Mother of God and God himself had betrayed him, and everyone else in that hut. *What good is faith now? These people just wanted safety, refuge from the storm, and instead they got—*

Mimo tugged his arm, said, "What are we going to do?"

Pino stared at his brother, hearing the frightened questions the D'Angelos and Mrs. Napolitano were firing at him, and feeling completely overwhelmed. He was only seventeen, after all. Part of him wanted to sit against the wall, hang his head, and cry.

But then the faces looking at him in the glow of the miner's lamp came back into focus. They needed him. They were his responsibility. If they died, it would be his fault. That clicked something inside him, and he looked at his watch. It was a quarter to ten in the morning.

Air, he thought, and with that one word, his brain cleared and he had purpose.

"Everyone be quiet and still," he said, crossing to the cool stove and turning the damper. To his relief it moved. The snow had not come that far down the chimney.

"Mimo, Mr. D'Angelo, help me," Pino said as he put his gloves on and worked to free the chimney from the stove.

"What are you doing?" Mrs. Napolitano asked.

"Trying not to suffocate."

"Oh dear God," the violinist said. "After everything I've been through, my baby and I are going to choke to death in here."

"Not if I can help it."

Pino disconnected the stove and moved it aside. Then, close to the ceiling, they detached the lower section of the blackened sheet metal chimney and put it aside, too.

Pino tried to shine the miner's lamp into the tube, but he couldn't see much. He held his hand across the hole, feeling for a breeze, some sign that air was getting through. Nothing. Fighting panic, he got one of his bamboo ski poles and used his knife to cut the leather and metal basket off the bottom, leaving him with the exposed steel spike.

Pino pushed the ski pole up the chimney hole. It stopped when half the pole had vanished. He jabbed at the blockage. Snow dropped out and to the floor.

He started jabbing and turning and probing with the ski pole, causing a steady stream of snow to fall from the tube. Five minutes. Ten minutes. He could push the ski pole and his arm up the chimney, and it still felt blocked.

"How long can we last in here without air?" Mimo asked.

"I have no idea," Pino said, and pulled the pole down and out again.

He took a second ski pole and cut the leather pieces from the pole baskets into narrower strips. With the strips and his belt, he managed to attach the two poles end to end, spike to handle. It was a wobbly connection at best, and Pino could no longer stab as hard as he could with the single pole.

How long can we survive without air? Four, five hours? Less?

Mimo, Mr. D'Angelo, and Pino took turns chipping at the snow in the chimney, while Mrs. Napolitano, Mrs. D'Angelo, and the children huddled in the corner, watching. All their exertions and exhalations had turned the interior of the hut warm, almost hot. The sweat poured off Pino's head as he kept teasing the ski poles upward, chopping out snow bit by bit.

Two hours after he started, when the handle of the lower ski pole was almost to the ceiling, he hit something that felt unmovable. He kept chipping at it, but all he was getting was slivers of ice. There had to be a block of it above.

"It's not going," Mimo said, frustrated.

"You keep at it," Pino said, stepping aside.

It was now stifling hot in the hut. Pino stripped off his shirt and felt himself struggling for breath. *Is this it? Will it hurt, not having air?* He flashed on a fish he'd seen dying on the beach at Rapallo once, how its mouth and gills had sought water, each movement smaller than the last until there was none. *Is that how we'll die? Like fish?*

Pino did his best to control the panic swirling in his stomach while his brother and then Mr. D'Angelo kept chipping at the obstruction. *Please God,* he prayed. *Please don't let us all die here like this. Mimo and I were trying to help these people. We don't deserve to die like this. We deserve to get out and keep helping people escape the—*

Something came clanking down the chimney and smashed into Mimo's hands.

"Ahhhh," he yelled in pain. "Damn, that hurt. What was that?"

Pino aimed the miner's lamp on the ground. A chunk of ice the size of two fists lay in the dirt. Then he noticed shadows wavering on the walls and the dirt

114

around the ice chunk. He went to the chimney stub, put his hand to it, and felt a small but steady chill draft.

"We've got air!" he said, hugging his brother.

Mr. D'Angelo said, "And now we dig out?"

"And now we dig out," Pino said.

"You think you can?" Mrs. Napolitano said.

"No other choice," Pino said, looking up the chimney tube, seeing pale light, and remembering how high the chimney stuck out of the roof. Then he looked at the open door and the wall of white debris that clogged the entrance. The top of the door frame was low—one and a half meters? He imagined a tunnel angling upward. But how long?

Mimo must have been thinking along the same lines because he said, "We've got at least three meters of digging."

"More," Pino said. "We can't dig a shaft straight up. We're going to have to go at an angle to the door so we can crawl up it."

⧫

They used the ice axes, the hatchet, and the small metal shovel that came with the woodstove to attack the avalanche rubble. They dug at a seventy-degree angle to the door frame, trying to bore out a passage big enough to crawl through. The first part of a meter was relatively easy. The snow was looser. Small blocks and gravel-sized streams of ice and debris came free with each strike of the ax.

"We'll be out after dark," Mimo said, shoveling the snow back into the deepest part of the hut.

Pino's carbide lamp died, leaving them all in pitch-blackness.

"Shit," Mimo said.

"Mommy," Anthony whined.

Mrs. Napolitano said, "How will we see to dig?"

Pino lit a match, dug in his pack, and came out with two devotional candles. He had three. So did Mimo. He lit them and placed them above and beside the doorway. They no longer had the strong glow of the headlamp to rely on, but their eyes soon adjusted to the flickering light, and they set at the avalanche debris again, chopping and picking at what now felt like a monolithic block of snow and ice. Superheated by the friction created in the avalanche, the debris had become as solid as cement in places.

Progress ground to a crawl. But every chunk removed was a cause for celebration, and slowly the tunnel began to form, wider than Pino's shoulders, first a meter, then almost two meters long. They took turns, the man up front chipping at the ice and snow, and the other two moving the snow out into the hut, where the D'Angelo family and Mrs. Napolitano were crowded into a corner, watching the snow mound grow.

"Will we have enough room for all the snow?" the pregnant violinist asked.

"If we have to, we'll start up the stove and melt some of it," Pino said.

By ten o'clock that evening, they were, by Pino's estimate, four meters out from the door when he had to call it quits. He couldn't swing the axes anymore. He had to eat and to sleep. They all had to eat and to sleep.

He divided the remaining provisions in the packs while Mimo and Mr. D'Angelo reassembled the stove. He apportioned one half of the provisions into six shares, and they ate dried meat, dried fruit, nuts, and cheese. They drank more tea and huddled together before Pino lit the stove and blew out the third-to-last candle.

Twice during the night, he dreamed of being buried alive in a casket, and he awoke with a start, listening to the others breathing and the tic-tic-tic of the stove cooling. Snow had melted into the dirt floor, and he knew he'd soon be lying in chill mud. But he was so tired, and his muscles so sore and cramped, he didn't care, and slept a third time.

Mimo budged him hours later. He had the second-to-last candle lit.

"It's six a.m.," his brother said. "Time to get out of here."

It was cold again. Pino's bones ached. Every joint was sore. But he set about dividing up the last of the food and the water he'd melted on the stove the night before.

Mr. D'Angelo went into the tunnel first. He lasted twenty minutes. Mimo lasted thirty and slid out of the tunnel, soaked from sweat and melting ice.

"I left the ax and the candle up there," he said. "You'll have to relight it."

Pino crawled back up the tunnel, now five meters long by his estimate. When he hit the wall, he rolled over and lit one of his last four matches. The candle was dwindling.

He attacked the snow and ice with a fury. He chopped, stabbed, and broke chunks of the snow. He scooped, pushed, and kicked the frozen debris behind him.

"Slow down!" Mimo called thirty minutes into the ordeal. "We can't keep up."

Pino paused, gasping like he'd run a long race, and glanced at the candle, now barely a stub and sputtering against drips of water falling every so often from the ceiling of the tunnel.

He reached up and moved the candle over, set it on a ledge he cut with the ax. Then he set to chopping again, at a slower rhythm than before and with more strategy. He looked for the cracks in the surface and tried to cut into them. Pieces began to peel off in triangular and odder-shaped slabs ten or twelve centimeters thick.

The snow's different, he thought, running the granules through his hand. It was breakable, and the crystals were almost all faceted like his mother's finest jewelry. He sat there, thinking that this kind of snow could cave in from above. As they were chopping their way through that solid block of snow and ice, he'd never considered that the ceiling could collapse. Now, it was all he could think about, and it froze him.

"What's the problem?" Mimo called as he crawled up the tunnel behind him.

Before Pino could reply, the candle's flame sputtered and died, sending him back into total darkness. He buried his face in his hands, finally overwhelmed by the feeling that he, like the candle, was about to die and go black. Waves of emotion—fear, abandonment, and disbelief—crashed over him.

"Why?" he whispered. "What did we—?"

"Pino!" Mimo shouted. "Pino, look up!"

Pino raised his head and saw that the tunnel had not gone pitch dark. A dull, silvery glow showed through the tunnel ceiling, and his tears of despair turned to joy.

They were almost to the surface, but as Pino had feared, the hoary snow broke apart and caved in on him twice, forcing him to back up and dig out before at last he pushed the ax forward and felt it break the final resistance.

When he pulled the ax back, bright sunshine blazed in.

"I'm through," he shouted. "I'm through!"

<hr/>

Mrs. Napolitano, Mrs. D'Angelo, and the children were cheering when he forced his head and then his shoulders up out of the snow crust. The storm had long passed, leaving cold mountain air that smelled delicious and tasted better. The sky was clear and cobalt blue. The sun had only just come over a ridgeline to the east. Fifteen new centimeters of powder snow lay over the rubble field, which he figured was nearly fifty meters wide and fifteen hundred meters long. High above him on the Groppera's crag, he could see a jagged fracture line in the snow.

In places, the slide had stripped the mountain almost bare. Rock and dirt and small trees were mixed into the new snow. Seeing the destruction and getting a sense of the sheer power of the avalanche, he believed it was a miracle that they'd survived.

Mrs. D'Angelo thought so, too, as did her husband, who followed his children out. Mimo exited behind Mrs. Napolitano. Pino went back in, grabbed the skis and packs, and pushed them up the passage.

When he emerged from the tunnel for the last time, he felt spent and filled with gratitude. *It is a miracle we got out. How else can you explain it?*

"What's that?" Anthony asked, gesturing down the valley.

"That, my friend, is Val di Lei," Pino said. "And those mountains over there? That's Pizzo Emet and Pizzo Palù. Way down below those peaks, in those trees there, Italy becomes Switzerland."

"It looks far," Judith said.

"About five kilometers?" Pino said.

"We can do it," Mr. D'Angelo said. "Everybody helps everybody."

"I can't," Mrs. Napolitano said.

Pino turned to find the pregnant violinist sitting on a snow boulder, one hand on her belly and the other holding her instrument case. Her clothes were coated in frost.

"Sure you can," Pino said.

She shook her head, started to cry. "All this. It's too much. I'm spotting blood."

Pino didn't understand until Mrs. D'Angelo said, "The baby, Pino."

His gut fell. She was going to lose the baby? Out here?

Oh God. No. Please no.

"You can't move?" Mimo asked.

"I shouldn't move at all," Mrs. Napolitano said.

"But you can't stay here," Mimo said. "You'll die."

"And if I move, my child might die."

"You don't know that."

"I can feel my body telling me so."

"But if you stay, you'll both die here," Mimo insisted.

"It's better," the violinist said. "I could not live if my baby were to die. So go!"

"No," Pino said. "We are getting you to Switzerland like we promised Father Re."

"I won't take a step!" Mrs. Napolitano shouted hysterically.

Pino decided to stay with her and send on the others with Mimo, but then he looked around, thought a moment, and said, "Maybe you don't have to take a step."

He dropped his pack and put on his long wooden skis with leather and steel cable bear trap bindings. He played with them until they were tight around his boots.

"Ready?" he said to Mrs. Napolitano.

"Ready for what?"

"Get up on my back," Pino said. "I'm taking you piggyback."

"On skis?" she said, terrified. "I've never been on skis in my entire life."

"You never were buried in an avalanche before, either," Pino said. "And you won't be on skis. I will."

She stared at him doubtfully. "What if we fall?"

"I won't let that happen," he said with all the confidence of a seventeen-year-old who'd been skiing almost as long as he'd been walking.

She didn't move.

"I'm giving you a chance to save your baby and be free," Pino said, pulling the violin case from his pack.

"What are you doing with my Stradivarius?" she asked.

"Staying balanced," Pino said, holding out the case in front of him as if it were the wheel of a car. "Like an orchestra, your violin will lead us."

There was a moment's pause where Mrs. Napolitano looked to the sky and then stood up out of the snow, shaking with fear.

"Hold my shoulders, not my neck," Pino said, turning his back to her again. "And wrap your legs tight around my waist."

Mrs. Napolitano grabbed his shoulders. He squatted, got his arms behind her knees, and helped her up onto the small of his back. She got her legs around him, and he let go of them. She didn't feel that much heavier than his pack.

"Think like a jockey on a horse," Pino said, bringing the violin up in front of him and holding it lengthwise. "And don't let go."

"Letting go? No, never. Absolutely the farthest thing from my mind."

Pino felt a glimmer of doubt, but then shook it off, shuffled his feet, and aimed the skis downhill toward the outer edge of the avalanche field, some thirty meters away. They began to slide. There were bumps and ragged chunks of ice sticking up out of the newer snow. He tried to avoid them as they picked up speed. But then one loomed unavoidably in their way. They went right up over the top of it and launched, sailing through the air.

"Ahhhh!!!!" Mrs. Napolitano screamed.

Pino landed awkwardly, skis askew, and for a second he thought the boards were going to get away from him and that he and the pregnant violinist were going to twist and fall hard into the frozen debris.

But then he saw they were going to collide with a stump. He did an instinctual hop move to his left, avoiding the stump, and then another. The two moves restored his equilibrium, and the skis accelerated. Pino and Mrs. Napolitano shot out of the debris field into fluffy powder snow.

With the violin case thrust out in front of him, Pino grinned and began to churn his legs in unison, driving them deep into the snow, and then relaxing them so his feet rose up under his hips as Father Re had taught him. The movement unweighted him momentarily at the top of each turn, which allowed him to shift his weight and turn the skis almost effortlessly. The skis arced left and then right in long, linked curves, building speed and blowing through snowdrifts that exploded and showered their faces.

Mrs. Napolitano hadn't said a word in many seconds. He figured she'd stopped looking and was simply hanging on for dear life.

"Wheeeeeeeeee!" she cried in his ear. "It's like we're birds, Pino! We're flying!"

Mrs. Napolitano giggled and made "whoop!" noises every time they dropped off a knoll. He felt her chin press down on his right shoulder, and understood she could see where they were going as he powered his skis in long, floating, lazy S-turns downslope toward the frozen lake and the woods and freedom beyond.

Pino realized he would lose vertical drop soon. The way would flatten ahead. Even though his thighs were on fire, he pointed the skis straight down the last steep pitch, straight at that forested triangle of Italy that stuck into Switzerland.

Pino wasn't turning now, no slalom here. He was doing straight-line downhill, violin out front for balance, crouched in a semituck. The skis hissed and rode up on top of the snow. They hurtled down that last pitch, thirty, forty, maybe fifty kilometers an hour, one twitch of a knee away from disaster. He saw the transition where the hill met the flat and brought his legs up under him again to absorb it.

They shot past the lake. Pino stayed low, cutting the wind, and they almost made the tree line. When they came to a halt, they were less than a snowball's throw away.

⊷

They were both quiet for a second.

Then Mrs. Napolitano began to laugh. She unwrapped her legs from Pino's waist and let go of her grip on his shoulders. She got down, and, holding her belly, knelt in the soft snow and began chortling like she'd never enjoyed anything so much in her life. Pino was caught up in her snorts and giggles. It was contagious. He fell beside her and laughed until he was crying.

What a crazy thing we've done. Who would have—?

"Pino!" a man's voice called sharply.

Pino startled and looked up to see Mr. Bergstrom standing just inside the tree line. He was carrying his shotgun and looked concerned.

"We made it, Mr. Bergstrom!" Pino cried.

"You're a day late," Bergstrom said. "And get out of the open. Bring her into the woods where she can't be seen."

Pino sobered and took his skis off. He handed Mrs. Napolitano her violin. She sat up and hugged it, saying, "I think everything's going to be all right now, Pino. I can feel it."

"Can you walk?" Pino asked.

"I can try," she said, and he helped her to her feet.

He held her hand and elbow and supported her through the snow to the path.

"What's wrong with her?" Bergstrom asked when they'd slogged into the trees.

Mrs. Napolitano explained about the baby and the spotting with a radiant glow on her face. "But now, I think I can walk however far you need me to."

"Not that far, several hundred meters," Bergstrom said. "Once you're in Switzerland, I can build you a fire. I'll go down and come back for you with a sled."

"A few hundred meters I think I can do," she said. "And a fire sounds like heaven above. Have you ever skied, Mr. Bergstrom?"

The Swiss man looked at her as if she were slightly addled, but he nodded.

"Isn't it grand?" the violinist said. "Isn't it the greatest thing you've ever done?"

Pino saw Mr. Bergstrom smile for the first time.

They waited in the tree line, telling the Swiss man about the storm and the avalanche, and watching Mimo and the D'Angelos work their way slowly down the slope. Mrs. D'Angelo carried her daughter. Mr. D'Angelo had Pino's pack and poles, and his son trailed behind. It took them almost an hour in the deep snow to reach the flat above the lake.

Pino skied out to meet them, took Judith up on his back, and brought her to the woods. They were soon all safely in the trees.

"Is this Switzerland?" Anthony asked.

"Not far," Bergstrom said.

After a brief rest, they set out toward the border with Pino helping Mrs. Napolitano along the well-used path through the forest. When they reached the grove where Italy became Switzerland, they stopped.

"There," Mr. Bergstrom said. "You're safe from Nazis now."

Tears dribbled down Mrs. D'Angelo's cheeks.

Her husband hugged her and kissed away her tears. "We're safe, my dear," he said. "How lucky we are when so many others have . . ."

He stopped and choked. His wife stroked his cheek.

"How can we ever repay you?" Mrs. Napolitano said to Pino and Mimo.

"For what?" Pino said.

"For what! You led us through that nightmare storm and got us out of that hut. You skied me down the side of that mountain!"

"What else could we do? Lose our faith? Give up?"

"You? Never!" Mr. D'Angelo said, now pumping Pino's hand. "You're like a bull. You never give up."

Then he hugged Mimo. Mrs. D'Angelo did, too, as did her children. Mrs. Napolitano hugged Pino the longest.

"A thousand blessings on your head for showing me how to fly, young man," she said. "I'll never forget that as long as I live."

Pino grinned, and felt his eyes water. "Neither will I."

"Isn't there anything I can do for you?" she asked.

Pino was about to say no, but he noticed her violin case. "Play for us as we go back into Italy. Your music will lift our spirits for the long climb and ski out."

That pleased her, and she looked at Bergstrom. "Is it okay?"

He said, "No one here will stop you."

Standing there in the snowy woods, high in the Swiss Alps, Mrs. Napolitano opened her case and rosined her bow. "What would you like to hear?"

For some reason, Pino thought of that August night when he and his father and Tullio and the Beltraminis had taken the train out into the countryside to escape the bombardment of Milan.

"Nessun Dorma," Pino said. "'None Shall Sleep.'"

"I can play that one in my sleep, but I'll play it for you, *con smania,*" she said, her eyes watering. "Go on now. No good-byes among old friends."

Mrs. Napolitano played the opening strains of the aria so perfectly, Pino wanted to stay to hear the entire piece. But he and his brother had hours of effort ahead of them, and who knew what challenges they'd face?

The boys shouldered their packs and set off through the woods. They lost sight of Mrs. Napolitano and the others almost immediately, but they could hear her playing beautifully, with passion, each note carrying through the thin, crisp, alpine air. They reached the tree line and put on their skis as she took the tempo up again, casting forth the melody of the triumphant aria like some radio wave that hit Pino in his heart and vibrated in his soul.

He stopped at the head of the lake to listen to the distant crescendo and was deeply moved when the violin quieted.

That sounded like love, Pino thought. *When I fall in love, I think it will feel just like that.*

Incredibly happy, and using skins on his skis, Pino started uphill after Mimo, heading toward the north cirque of the Groppera in the brilliant winter sunshine.

Chapter Twelve

Pino woke to a clanking sound. Nearly two and a half months had passed since he'd led Mrs. Napolitano and the D'Angelo family into Switzerland. He sat up, grateful that Father Re had let him sleep in after yet another trip to Val di Lei. He stood, noticing he didn't feel sore in the least. He never felt sore anymore. He felt good, strong—the strongest he'd ever been. And why not? He'd made at least a dozen more trips to Switzerland since Mrs. Napolitano had played for him and Mimo.

Hearing the clanking noise again, he looked out the window. Seven oxen with bells around their necks were pushing and shoving against one another, trying to get at bales of hay that had been put out for them.

When he'd had enough of watching them, Pino dressed. He was entering the empty dining hall when he heard male voices outside, shouting, yelling, and threatening. Alarmed, Brother Bormio came out of the kitchen. Together they went and opened the front door to Casa Alpina. Father Re was standing there, just off the little porch, looking calmly into the barrel of a rifle.

Wearing a newer red neckerchief around his neck, Tito looked over the rifle sight at the priest. The same three curs who'd been with Tito at the New Year's Eve party were standing behind him.

"I told your boys all winter to stop using the Emet unless you're going to pay tribute, help the cause of a free Italy," Tito said. "I'm here to collect my money."

"Extorting a priest," Father Re said. "You're coming up in the world, Tito."

The man glared at him, flipped the safety on his rifle, and said, "It's to help the resistance."

"I support the partisans," the priest said. "The Ninetieth Garibaldi Brigade, and I know you're not with them, Tito. None of you are. I think you just wear the neckerchiefs because they suit your purposes."

"Give me what I want, old man, or so help me, I'll burn your school down and then kill you and all your brats."

Father Re hesitated. "I'll get you money. And food. Put the gun away."

Tito studied the priest a second, his right eye twitching. His tongue flicked to the corner of his mouth. Then he smiled, lowered the gun, and said, "You do that and don't be cheap about it, or I'll just have myself a look around inside, see what you really got."

Father Re said, "Wait here."

The priest turned and saw Bormio, and behind him, Pino.

Father Re walked inside and said, "Get them three days' rations."

"Father?" the cook said.

"Do it, Brother, please," Father Re said as he moved on.

Brother Bormio reluctantly turned and followed the priest, leaving Pino in the doorway. Tito caught sight of him, smiled slyly, and said, "Well, look who we got here. My old pal from the New Year's Eve bash. Why don't you come on out? Say hello to me and the boys?"

"I'd rather not," Pino said, hearing the anger in his voice and not caring.

"Rather not?" Tito said, and aimed the gun at him. "You don't have a choice, now do you?"

⬥

Pino hardened. He really hated the guy. He walked out and off the little porch. He stood there facing Tito and stared stonily at him and his gun. "I see you're still wearing the boots you stole from me," he said. "What do you want this time? My underwear?"

Tito licked at the corner of his lips, glanced down at the boots, and smiled. Then he stepped forward, swinging the butt of his rifle stock up hard. It caught Pino in the testicles, and he went down in agony.

"What do I want, kid?" Tito said. "How about a little respect for someone trying to rid Italy of the Nazi filth?"

Pino curled up in the slush, fighting not to puke.

"Say it," Tito said, standing over him.

"Say what?" Pino managed.

"That you respect Tito. That Tito is the partisan leader who runs things around the Splügen. And that you, boy, you answer to Tito."

As hurt as he was, Pino shook his head. Through gritted teeth he said, "Only one person runs things around here. Father Re. I answer to him and God alone."

Tito raised his rifle, butt plate right above Pino's head. Pino was sure he was going to try to bash his skull in. He let go his testicles to guard his head and cringed for a blow that never came.

"Stop!" Father Re roared. "Stop, or by God, I'll call the Germans up here and tell them where to find you!"

Tito threw the rifle to his shoulder and aimed it at Father Re, who'd come off the porch.

"Give us up? That right?" Tito said.

Pino lashed out his boot, kicked Tito flush on the kneecap. Tito buckled. The rifle discharged. The bullet went past Father Re and smacked the side of Casa Alpina.

Pino leaped on Tito and hit him once, hard, right on the nose, hearing it crunch and seeing it gush blood. Then he snatched up the rifle, stood, and cycled the action before pointing the gun at Tito's head.

"Stop this, damn it!" Father Re said, stepping around in front of Pino, blocking him from Tito's men who were aiming at him. "I said I'd give you money for your cause, and three days' food. Be smart. Take it, and go before something worse happens here."

"Shoot him!" Tito screamed, wiping blood on his sleeve and glaring at Pino and the priest. "Shoot them both!"

For a breath, there was stillness and quiet and wondering. Then, one by one, Tito's men lowered their rifles. Pino exhaled with relief, winced at the dull fire still roaring between his legs, and aimed the gun away from Tito's face. He disengaged the clip and ran the bolt to eject the last bullet.

Pino waited while Tito's men took the food and money. Two of them picked up Tito under his armpits, ignoring the curses and insults he hurled at them. Pino handed Tito's empty rifle to the third man.

"Load it! I'll kill them!" Tito raged as blood seeped over his lips and chin.

"Let it go, Tito," one said. "He's a priest, for Christ's sake."

The two men had Tito's arms across their shoulders and were doing their best to get him away from Casa Alpina. But the gang leader was straining to look back.

"This isn't over," Tito bellowed. "Especially for you, boy. This isn't done!"

⤜⬩⤛

Pino stood next to Father Re, shaken.

"Are you all right?" the priest asked.

Pino was quiet for a long time before saying, "Father, is it a sin if I'm asking myself if I did the right thing in not killing that man?"

The priest said, "No, it is not a sin, and you did the right thing not killing him."

Pino bobbed his head, but his lower lip was trembling, and it was taking everything in his power to swallow the emotion surging in his throat. Everything had happened so fast, so—

Father Re patted Pino on the back. "Have faith. You did the right thing."

He nodded again, but couldn't meet the priest's gaze for fear of crying.

"Where did you learn how to handle a gun like that?" Father Re asked.

Pino wiped at his eyes, cleared his throat, and said in a hoarse voice, "My uncle Albert. He has a hunting rifle, a Mauser, kind of like that one. He taught me."

"I can't decide if you were brave or foolhardy."

"I wasn't going to let Tito kill you, Father."

The priest smiled and said, "Bless you for that. I wasn't ready to die today."

Pino laughed, winced, and said, "Me, neither."

They went back inside the school. Father Re got ice for Pino, and Brother Bormio made him breakfast, which he devoured.

"You keep growing and we won't be able to keep up," Bormio grumbled.

"Where's everyone else?" Pino asked.

"Skiing with Mimo," Father Re said. "They'll be back for lunch."

As he was eating his second helping of eggs, sausage, and black bread, two women and four children came timidly into the room, followed by a man in his thirties and two very young boys. Pino could tell in an instant they were new refugees. He'd come to recognize the expressions of hunted people.

"Will you be ready to go again in the morning?" Father Re asked.

Pino shifted, felt a dull ache in his loins, but said, "Yes."

"Good. And can you do me a favor?"

"Anything, Father," Pino said.

"Go to the chapel tower, and watch for the signal from Campodolcino," he said. "You can take your books with you, get some studying done."

Twenty minutes later, Pino gingerly climbed a ladder into the chapel tower. He had a book bag on his back, and his balls still ached. With the sun beating on the tower, it was surprisingly warm, too warm for the amount of clothing he was wearing.

He stood on the narrow catwalk that went around the interior of the chapel spire, glancing at the void where the bell should have been. Father Re had yet to install one. Pino opened a narrow shutter to look down through a slot in the cliff, which allowed him to see the upper two windows of the rectory in Campodolcino over a kilometer below.

Pino took off the book bag and dug out the binoculars Father Re had given him. He peered through them, surprised again at just how close they made the rectory seem. He studied the two windows. Shades drawn. That meant a German patrol of some kind was in the Splügen drainage. They seemed to make the drive up and down the road to the pass near midday, give or take an hour.

Pino checked his watch. It was a quarter to eleven.

He stood there enjoying the warm spring air and watching birds flit among the spruce trees. He yawned, shook his head to clear the incredible desire to go back to sleep, and stared through the binoculars again.

Thirty minutes later, to his relief, the shades came up. The patrol had passed through, heading down the valley toward Chiavenna. Pino yawned and wondered how many more refugees would come to Motta tonight. If there were too many, they'd have to split up. He'd take one group, and Mimo, the other.

His brother had done a lot of growing up in the last few months. Mimo was less—well, less a brat, and as tough as anyone in the mountains. Pino realized for the first time that he saw his younger brother as his best friend, closer even than Carletto.

But he wondered how Carletto was, and how Carletto's mother was, and Mr. Beltramini. He looked down at the catwalk, eyes drooping. He could lie down there, make sure he wouldn't fall off, and snooze in the nice, warm—

No, he decided. He could fall off and break his back. He'd go down the ladder, sleep in one of the pews. It wasn't as warm, but he had his coat and his hat. Just twenty minutes of shut-eye.

Pino had no idea how long and how far he'd gone into dreamless sleep, just that something made him stir. He opened his eyes groggily, trying to figure out what had woken him. He looked around the chapel and up into the tower and—

He heard a far-off donging noise. What was it? Where was it coming from?

<hr />

Pino got up, yawned, and the donging stopped. Then it started again, like a hammer on metal. Then it stopped. He realized he'd left the book bag, binoculars, and the flashlight on the catwalk. He climbed up the ladder, got the bag, and was reaching to close the shutter when the noise started again. Pino realized it was the bell in the church down in Campodolcino pealing.

He glanced at his watch to see how long he'd slept. Eleven twenty? The bell usually rang on the hour. Now it was ringing over and over and—?

Pino snatched up the binoculars, stared down at the window. The blind on the left was closed. A light was flashing in the right window. Pino stared at it, wondering what it meant, and then realized the light was going on for a split second and then longer. It stopped and started again, and Pino realized it was a signal. Morse code?

He picked up his light and flashed it twice. The light below blinked twice, and then went dark. The bell stopped ringing. Then the light came on again, blinking shorts and longs. When it stopped, he grabbed a pen and some paper from his bag, and waited for the light to start again. When it did, he started writing down the sequence of shorts and longs until the end.

Pino didn't know Morse code, or what the watcher in Campodolcino was trying to say, but he knew it couldn't be good. He flashed his own light twice, stowed it, and clambered down the ladder. He sprinted to the school.

"Pino!" he heard Mimo yell.

His brother was skiing down the slope above the school, waving his poles wildly. Pino ignored him, ran into Casa Alpina, and found Father Re and Brother Bormio talking with the refugees in the hallway.

"Father," Pino panted. "Something's wrong."

He explained about the bell, the shades, and the lights flashing below. He showed the priest the paper. Father Re looked at it, puzzled. "How do they expect me to know Morse code?"

"You don't have to," Brother Bormio said. "I know it."

Father Re handed him the paper, saying, "How?"

"I learned it in the—," the cook said, and then he lost all color.

Mimo dashed into the room, covered in sweat, at the same time Brother Bormio said, "Nazis to Motta."

"I saw them from above!" Mimo cried. "Four or five lorries down in Madesimo, and soldiers going door to door. We skied across as fast as we could."

Father Re looked to the refugees. "We have to hide them."

"They'll search," Brother Bormio said.

One of the refugee mothers got up, shaking. "Should we run, Father?"

"They'll track you," Father Re said.

For some reason, Pino thought of the oxen that had woken him up that morning.

"Father," he said slowly. "I've got an idea."

⟨⟩

An hour later, Pino was in the bell tower, nervous as hell, and looking through Father Re's binoculars, when a German army Kübelwagen appeared from the woods on the cart track from Madesimo, the jeep-style vehicle's tires spinning and throwing up mud and snow. A second, larger German lorry lumbered behind it, but Pino ignored it, trying to see through the mud-spattered windshield of the smaller lead vehicle.

The Kübelwagen slid almost sideways, and Pino got a strong look at the uniform and the face of the officer in the front passenger seat. Even at a distance, Pino recognized him. He'd seen the man up close before.

Terrified now, Pino clambered down the ladder and sped out a door behind the altar. Ignoring the ox bells clanking behind him, he sprinted through the back door of Casa Alpina, then into the kitchen and the dining hall.

"Father, it's Colonel Rauff!" he gasped. "The head of the Gestapo in northern Italy!"

"How can you—?"

"I saw him in my uncle's leather shop once," Pino said. "It's him."

Pino fought the urge to flee. Colonel Rauff had ordered the massacre of Jews across the region. If he would order innocent Jews to death, would he stop at executing a priest and a group of boys saving Jews?

Father Re went out onto the porch. Pino hung back in the hallway, not knowing what to do. Was his idea good enough? Or would the Nazis find the Jews and kill everyone at Casa Alpina?

Rauff's vehicle slid to a stop in the slush, not far from where Tito had threatened them all earlier in the day. The Gestapo colonel was as Pino remembered him: balding, medium build, jowly, with a sharp nose, flat, thin lips, and flat, dark eyes that gave away nothing. He wore calf-high black boots, a long black double-breasted leather jacket speckled with mud, and a brimmed cap with the death-head totem.

Rauff's eyes fixed on the priest, and he almost smiled as he climbed out.

"Is it always this difficult to reach you, Father Re?" the Gestapo colonel asked.

"In the spring it can be trying," the priest said. "You know me, but I—"

"Standartenführer Walter Rauff," Rauff said as two lorries came to a stop behind him. "Chief of Gestapo, Milan."

"You've come a long way, Colonel," Father Re said.

"We hear rumors about you, Father, even in Milan."

"Rumors about me? From who? About what?"

"Do you remember a seminarian? Giovanni Barbareschi? Worked for Cardinal Schuster, and, it seems, you?"

"Barbareschi served here briefly," Father Re said. "What about him?"

"We arrested him last week," Rauff said. "He's in San Vittore Prison."

Pino suppressed a shudder. San Vittore Prison had been a notorious and terrible place in Milan long before the Nazis took it over.

"On what charges?" Father Re asked.

"Forgery," Rauff said. "He makes fake documents. He's good at it."

"I don't know anything about that," Father Re said. "Barbareschi led hikes here and helped in the kitchen."

The Gestapo chief seemed amused again. "We have ears everywhere, you know, Father. The Gestapo is like God. We hear all things."

Father Re stiffened. "Whatever you may think, Colonel, you are not like God, though you were made in his loving image."

Rauff took a step closer, gazed icily into the priest's eyes, and said, "Make no mistake, Father, I can be your savior, or your condemner."

"It still doesn't make you God," Father Re said, showing no fear.

The Gestapo chief held his gaze a long moment, and then turned to one of his officers. "Fan out, search every centimeter of this plateau. I will look here."

Soldiers began jumping out of the lorries.

"What are you looking for, Colonel?" Father Re asked. "Maybe I can help you."

"Do you hide Jews, Father?" Rauff asked curtly. "Do you help them get to Switzerland?"

Pino tasted acid at the back of his throat and felt his knees go wobbly.

Rauff knows, Pino thought in a panic. *We're all going to die!*

Father Re said, "Colonel, I adhere to the Catholic belief that anyone in harm's way should be shown love and offered sanctuary. It's also the way of the Alps. A climber always helps someone in need. Italian. Swiss. German. It doesn't matter to me."

Rauff seemed bemused again. "Are you helping anyone today, Father?"

"Just you, Colonel."

Pino swallowed hard, trying not to tremble. *How do they know?* His mind searched for answers. *Has Barbareschi talked? No.* No, Pino couldn't see it. *But how—?*

"Be of help, then, Father," the Gestapo chief said. "Show me around your school. I want to see every bit of it."

"I'd be glad to," the priest said, and stood aside.

Colonel Rauff came up on the porch, kicked his boots free of mud and snow, and drew a Luger pistol.

"What's that for?" Father Re said.

"Swift punishment for the wicked," Rauff said, and stepped into the hallway.

Pino hadn't expected him to come inside, and he was flustered when the Gestapo chief looked at him hard.

"I know you," Rauff said. "I never forget a face."

Pino stammered, "In my aunt and uncle's leather store in San Babila?"

The colonel cocked his head, still studying him. "What's your name?"

"Giuseppe Lella," he said. "My uncle is Albert Albanese. His wife, my aunt Greta, is Austrian. You spoke to her, I believe. I used to work there sometimes."

"Yes," Rauff said. "That's right. Why are you here?"

"My father sent me to escape the bombs and to study, like all the boys here."

"Ahh," Rauff said, hesitated, and then moved on.

Father Re's face was set hard when he glanced at Pino and fell in behind the Gestapo chief, who stopped at the wide entrance to the empty eating hall.

Rauff looked around. "A clean place, Father. I like that. Where are the other boys? How many are here these days?"

"Forty," Father Re said. "Three are sick in bed with the flu, two are helping in the kitchen, fifteen are out skiing, and the rest are trying to catch oxen that got away from a farmer in Madesimo. If you don't catch them before the snow melts, they go wild up in the mountains."

"Oxen," Colonel Rauff said, taking it all in: the tables, the benches, the silverware already set out for the evening meal. He pushed open the galley doors to the kitchen, where Brother Bormio was peeling potatoes along with two of the younger boys.

"Spotless," Rauff said approvingly, and closed the door.

"We are an approved school through the province of Sondrio," Father Re said. "And many of our students come from the finest families in Milan."

The Gestapo chief glanced again at Pino and said, "I see that."

The colonel looked in the dormitories and in Pino and Mimo's room. Pino almost had a heart attack when Rauff stepped on the loose floorboard that hid his shortwave radio. But after a tense moment, the colonel moved on. He looked in every storage room and where Brother Bormio slept. Finally he came to a shut and locked door.

"What's in here?" he asked.

"My room," Father Re said.

"Open it," Rauff said.

Father Re fished in his pocket, came up with a key, and unlocked the door. Pino had never seen the room where Father Re slept. No one had. It was always shut and locked. When Rauff pushed the door open, Pino could see that the space was small and contained a narrow bed, a tiny closet, a lantern, a rough-hewn desk and chair, a Bible, and a crucifix on the wall beside a picture of the Virgin Mary.

"This is where you live?" Rauff asked. "These are all your things?"

"What more does a man of God need?" Father Re said.

The colonel was lost in contemplation for a moment. When he turned, he said, "Living the austere life, the life of purpose, of denial and true nobility, you are an inspiration, Father Re. Many of my officers could learn from you. Most of the Salò army could learn from you."

"I don't know about that," the priest said.

"No, it is the Spartan way you follow," Rauff said earnestly. "I admire that. Such deprivation has always created the greatest warriors. Are you a warrior at heart, Father?"

"For Christ, Colonel."

"I see that," Rauff said, closing the door. "And yet there are these pesky rumors about you and this school."

"I can't imagine why," Father Re said. "You have looked everywhere. If you wish, you can even examine the storage cellar."

The Gestapo chief said nothing for several moments before saying, "I'll send one of my men in to do that."

"I'll show him where to go in," the priest said. "He won't have to dig far."

"Dig?"

"The hatch door still has at least a meter of snow on it."

"Show me," Rauff said.

They went outside with Pino trailing. Father Re had just rounded the corner when boys' hoots and cries started from the spruces beyond the chapel. Four SS soldiers were already moving that way.

"What is this?" Colonel Rauff demanded a split second before an ox broke from the tree line, bawling and lumbering through the snow.

Mimo and another boy chased the beast with switches, herding it toward and into a fenced-in area across from the school while the four SS soldiers watched.

Gasping, grinning, Mimo yelled, "The other oxen are all in the woods back by the cliff, Father Re. We have them surrounded, but we can't get the others to go like that one."

Before the priest could reply, Colonel Rauff said, "You must form a V and get the first one going where you want. The others will follow."

Father Re looked at the Gestapo chief, who said, "I grew up on a farm."

Mimo looked at Father Re uncertainly.

"I'll show you," Rauff said, and Pino thought he was going to faint.

"That's not necessary," the priest said quickly.

"No, it will be fun," the colonel said. "I haven't done this in years." Rauff looked to his soldiers. "You four come with me." Then he looked at Mimo. "How many boys are in the woods?"

"Twenty?"

"More than enough," the colonel said, and he set off toward the spruces.

"Help him, Pino!" Father Re whispered.

Pino didn't want to, but he ran after the Germans.

"Where do you want the boys, Colonel?" Pino asked, hoping he had no quiver in his voice.

"Where are the oxen now?" Rauff said.

Mimo said, "Uh, cornered back by the cliff."

They were almost to the trees, where unseen oxen moaned and lowed. Pino wanted to turn and run for his life, but he kept going. The situation seemed to energize the Gestapo chief. Rauff's eyes had gone from dull and dark to wide and sparkling, and he was grinning with excitement. Pino glanced around, trying to figure out where he could go if this all went bad.

Colonel Rauff entered the wood lot, which was shaped like a crescent that bulged out from the cliff onto the plateau.

"The oxen are to the right, over there," Mimo said.

Rauff holstered his pistol and followed Mimo through the snow, which was nowhere as deep as it was outside the woods. The oxen had been all through the place, packing down the snow and defecating everywhere.

Mimo and then the Gestapo chief ducked several branches and passed beneath one of the biggest spruces, causing Pino's stomach to lurch. The SS soldiers followed Rauff, with Pino bringing up the rear. As he stooped under the branches of the biggest tree, his eye was drawn to a loose cluster of needles twirling and falling in the air. He glanced up and couldn't see any of the Jews hiding high in the trees, their footprints trampled by the oxen.

Thank God, Pino thought as Rauff kept marching toward the boys of Casa Alpina, who were loosely strung out through the woods. They had cornered the six remaining oxen, which were swaying their heads, sounding off, and looking for a way out other than the cliff behind them.

"When I say so, have the middle six boys back up and split into two groups of three," Rauff said, holding his hands pressed at the palms and fingers flared apart. "We want to make the V like this. Once they get moving, the other boys should run ahead to keep them moving where we want them. Stay in V-formation on both sides. Cows, oxen, they're like Jews—followers. They'll go along."

Pino ignored what he'd said at the end, but shouted the original instructions to the boys in the middle. The six backed up fast and then flared out to the sides. When the first ox broke, the rest of the herd went into a frenzied stampede. The beasts bolted through the woods, bellowing and breaking branches as they went, the boys flanking them, shouting, and pressing close so they began to string out and run in a line.

"Yes! Yes!" Colonel Rauff cried, running behind the last ox to leave the cliff area. "This is exactly how you do it!"

Pino followed the Gestapo chief through the trees, but at a distance. The oxen broke from the grove with the boys to either side, and the Nazis all followed, including Rauff, who didn't give a backward glance. Only then did Pino pause to look up another of the bigger firs. Twelve meters up, and through the branches, he caught the vague outline of someone clinging to the tree trunk.

He strolled slowly out of the woods, seeing the oxen were already back in their fenced-off area, eating from the hay bales.

"Ahh," Colonel Rauff said, breathing hard and beaming at Father Re when Pino walked up. "That was fun. I used to do this so many times as a boy."

"It looked like you enjoyed it," the priest said.

The Gestapo chief coughed, laughed, and nodded. Then he looked at the lieutenant and barked something in German. The lieutenant started yelling and blowing a whistle. The soldiers who'd been searching the outbuildings and the handful of homes in Motta came running back to the lorries.

"I remain suspicious, Father," Colonel Rauff said, holding out his hand.

Pino held his breath.

The priest took his hand and shook it. "You're welcome anytime, Colonel."

Rauff got back into the Kübelwagen. Father Re, Brother Bormio, Pino, Mimo, and the other boys stood there, silently watching the German lorries turn around. They waited until Rauff and his soldiers were five hundred meters off, gone down the muddy two-track to Madesimo, before they all broke into wild cheers.

<hr />

"I thought for sure he knew we had you all hidden in the trees," Pino said several hours later. He and Father Re were eating at the table with the relieved refugees.

The father of the two boys said, "I could see that colonel coming the entire way. He walked right under our tree. Twice!"

They all started to laugh as only people who have just avoided death can laugh, with disbelief, gratitude, and infectious joy.

"An inspired plan," Father Re said, clapping Pino on the shoulder and raising his glass of wine. "To Pino Lella."

The refugees all raised their glasses and did the same. Pino felt embarrassed to be the object of so much attention. He smiled. "Mimo was the one who made it work."

But he felt good about it, elated actually. Fooling the Nazis like that made him feel empowered. In his own way, he *was* fighting back. They were all fighting back, part of the growing resistance. Italy was not German. Italy could never be German.

Alberto Ascari came into Casa Alpina without ringing the bell. He appeared in the dining room doorway, hat in hand, and said, "Excuse me, Father Re, but

I have an urgent message for Pino. His father called my uncle's house, and asked me to find Pino and deliver it."

Pino felt hollow inside. What had happened? Who was dead?

"What is it?" he asked.

"Your papa wants you to come home as soon as possible," Ascari said. "To Milan. He said it's a matter of life and death."

"Whose life and death?" Pino said, getting up.

"It sounded like yours, Pino."

PART THREE
THE CATHEDRALS OF MAN

Chapter Thirteen

Twelve hours later, Pino sat in the passenger seat of Ascari's souped-up Fiat, barely noticing the long drops off the side of the serpentine road from Madesimo down to Campodolcino. He didn't look at the lime-green leaves of spring or smell the blooms in the air. His mind was still at Casa Alpina and on how reluctant he'd been to leave.

"I want to stay and help," he'd told Father Re the night before.

"And I could use your help," the priest said, "but it sounds serious, Pino. You need to obey your father and go home."

Pino gestured at the refugees. "Who will take them to Val di Lei?"

"Mimo," Father Re said. "You've trained him well, and the other boys."

Pino had been so upset, he'd slept fitfully and was dejected when Ascari came to pick him up to take him to the train station at Chiavenna. He'd been at Casa Alpina almost seven months, but it seemed like years.

"You'll come to see me when you can?" Father Re asked.

"Of course, Father," Pino said, and they hugged.

"Have faith in God's plan for you," the priest said. "And stay safe."

Brother Bormio had given him food for his journey and hugged him, too.

Pino barely said ten words until they reached the valley floor.

"One good thing," Ascari said. "You have taught me to ski."

Pino allowed a mild smile. "You catch on fast. I wish I could have finished my driving lessons."

"You are already very, very good, Pino," Ascari said. "You have the touch, the feel for the car that is rare."

Pino basked in the praise. Ascari was an amazing driver. Alberto continued to astound him with the things he could do behind the wheel, and, as if to prove it, he took them on a white-knuckle ride down the valley toward Chiavenna that left Pino breathless.

"Scary to think what you'd do in a real race car, Alberto," Pino said when they pulled into the station.

Ascari grinned. "Give it time, my uncle always says. Come back this summer? Finish your training?"

"I'd like that," Pino said, shaking his hand. "Be good, my friend. And stay out of the ditch."

"Every day," Ascari said, and drove off.

Pino had come down so much in altitude, it was nearly thirty degrees warmer than it had been up at Motta. Chiavenna was painted in flowers. Their scent and pollen hung thick in the air. Spring in the southern Alps wasn't always this fabulous, and it made Pino even more reluctant to buy his ticket, show his documents to a German army soldier, and then board the train heading south to Como and Milan.

The first car he entered was filled with a company of Fascist soldiers. He turned around and went forward, finding a car with only a handful of people. Drowsy from lack of rest, he stowed his bag, used his knapsack for a pillow, and fell asleep.

Three hours later, the train pulled into Milan's central station, which had taken several direct hits but stood much as Pino remembered it. Except Italian soldiers no longer guarded the transit hub. The Nazis were in total control now. As he walked down the platform and passed through the station, keeping his distance from the Fascist soldiers from the train, he saw the German troops glancing with contempt at Mussolini's men.

"Pino!"

His father and Uncle Albert hurried to greet him. Both men looked dramatically older than they had at Christmas, grayer about the temples, and their cheeks more sunken and sallow than he'd remembered.

Michele cried, "Do you see the size of him, Albert?"

His uncle gaped at Pino. "Seven months and you go from a boy to a big, strapping man! What was Father Re feeding you?"

"Brother Bormio is a great cook," Pino said, grinning stupidly and pleased by their scrutiny. He was so happy to see them both that he almost forgot to be angry.

"Why did I have to come home, Papa?" he asked as they left the station. "We were doing good things at Casa Alpina, important things."

His uncle's face clouded. He shook his head, said in a low voice, "We do not talk about things good or bad here. We wait, yes?"

They took a taxi. After ten and a half months of bombardment, Milan looked more like a battlefield than a city. In some neighborhoods, nearly 70 percent of the buildings were rubble, yet the streets were passable. Pino soon saw why. Scores of those vacant, bent-back men in gray uniforms were clearing the streets, brick by brick, stone by stone.

"Who are they?" he asked. "Those gray men?"

Uncle Albert put his hand on Pino's leg, pointed a finger at the driver, and shook his head. Pino noticed that the taxi driver kept looking in the rearview mirror, and he surrendered to not talking until they were home.

The closer they got to the Duomo and San Babila, the more structures were still standing. Many were unscathed. They passed the chancellery. A Nazi staff car sat out front, a general's by the flag on the hood.

Indeed, the streets around the cathedral were packed with high-ranking German officers and their vehicles. They had to leave the taxi to go through a sandbagged and heavily fortified checkpoint into San Babila.

After showing their papers, they walked in silence through one of the least damaged areas of Milan. The shops, restaurants, and bars were open and filled with Nazi officers and their women. Pino's father led him to Corso del Littorio, about four blocks from where they'd lived before, still in the fashion district, but closer to La Scala, the Galleria, and the Piazza Duomo.

"Get out your documents again," his father said, pulling out his own.

They entered a building and were immediately confronted by two armed Waffen-SS guards, which surprised Pino. Were Nazis guarding every apartment building in San Babila?

The sentries knew Michele and Pino's uncle, and gave only a cursory glance at their papers. But they studied Pino's long and hard before allowing them to go on. They used a birdcage elevator. As they rose past the fifth floor, Pino saw two more SS guards standing outside a door.

They exited on the sixth floor, went to the end of a short hall, and entered the Lellas' new apartment. It was nowhere near as large as the place on Via Monte Napoleone, but it was already comfortably furnished. He recognized his mother's touch everywhere.

His father and uncle silently motioned for Pino to put his bags down and to follow them. They went through French doors out onto a rooftop terrace. The cathedral's spires attacked the sky to the east. Uncle Albert said, "It's safe to talk now."

Pino said, "Why are there Nazis in the lobby and below us?"

His father gestured to an antenna about halfway down the terrace wall. "That antenna is attached to a shortwave radio in the apartment downstairs. The Germans threw out the old tenant, a dentist, in February. They had workers come in and completely rebuilt the place. From what we've heard, it's where visiting Nazi dignitaries stay when they're in Milan. If Hitler ever came, it is where he'd stay."

"One floor beneath us?" Pino said, unnerved by the idea.

"It's a new and dangerous world, Pino," Uncle Albert said. "Especially for you."

"This is why we brought you home," his father said before he could reply. "In fewer than twenty days, you turn eighteen, which makes you eligible for the draft."

Pino squinted. "Okay?"

His uncle said, "If you wait to be drafted, they'll put you in the Fascist army."

"And all new Italian soldiers are being sent by the Germans to the Russian front," Michele said, wringing his hands. "You'd be cannon fodder, Pino. You'd die, and we can't let that happen to you, not when the war is so close to being over."

The war was close to being over. Pino knew that was true. He'd heard only the day before on the shortwave receiver he'd left with Father Re that the Allies were once again battling over Monte Cassino, a monastery high on a cliff where the Germans had installed powerful cannons. At long last, the monastery and the Germans had been pulverized by Allied bombers. So had the town below. Allied troops all along the Gustav Line of fortifications south of Rome were close to breaking through.

"So what do you want me to do?" Pino asked. "Hide? I'd have been better off staying at Casa Alpina until the Allies drive the Nazis out."

His father shook his head. "The draft office has already been here looking for you. They knew you were up there. Within days of your birthday, someone would have gone to Casa Alpina and taken you."

"So what do you want me to do?" Pino asked again.

"We want you to enlist," Uncle Albert said. "If you enlist, we can make sure you're put in a position out of harm's way."

"With Salò?"

The two men exchanged glances, before his father said, "No, with the Germans."

Pino felt his stomach sour. "Join the Nazis? Wear the swastika? No. Never."

"Pino," his father began, "this—"

"Do you know what I've been doing the past six months?" Pino said angrily. "I've been leading Jews and refugees over the Groppera into Switzerland to escape the Nazis, people who think nothing of machine-gunning innocent people! I cannot and will not do it."

There was silence for several moments as both men studied him.

Finally, Uncle Albert said, "You've changed, Pino. You not only look like a man, you sound like one. So I'm going to tell you that unless you decide to escape to Switzerland yourself and sit out the war, you are going to be drawn into it one way or another. The first way, you wait to be drafted. You will be given three weeks' training, and then be shipped up north to fight the Soviets, where the death rate among first-year Italian soldiers is nearly fifty percent. That means you'd have a one-in-two chance of seeing your nineteenth birthday."

Pino made to interrupt, but his uncle held his hand up. "I am not finished. Or someone I know can get you assigned to a wing of the German army called the 'Organization Todt,' or the OT. They don't fight. They build things. You'll be safe, and you'll probably learn something."

"I want to fight the Germans, not join them."

"This is a precaution," his father said. "As you said, the war will soon be over. You probably won't even make it out of boot camp."

"What will I tell people?"

"No one will know," Uncle Albert said. "We'll tell anyone who asks that you're still in the Alps with Father Re."

Pino said nothing. He could see the logic of it, but it left a nasty taste in his mouth. This wasn't resistance. It was malingering, dodging, the coward's way out.

"Do I have to answer now?" Pino asked.

"No," his father said. "But in a day or so."

Uncle Albert said, "In the meantime, come with me to the store. There is something you can do for Tullio."

Pino broke into a grin. Tullio Galimberti! He hadn't seen him in, what—seven months? He wondered whether Tullio was still following Colonel Rauff around Milan. He wondered about his latest romantic interest.

"I'll come," Pino said. "Unless you need me for something, Papa?"

"No, go on," Michele said. "I have some bookkeeping to take care of."

Pino and his uncle left the apartment and took the elevator again, seeing the guards outside the fifth-floor apartment. The sentries in the lobby nodded as they left.

They wound through the street toward Albanese Luggage, with Uncle Albert questioning Pino about the Alps. He seemed particularly impressed by the signal system Father Re had devised, and the coolness and ingenuity that had gotten Pino through several of his hair-raising predicaments.

The leather shop was thankfully without customers. Uncle Albert put the "Closed" sign up and drew down the blind. Aunt Greta and Tullio Galimberti came out of the back.

"Look at the size of him!" Aunt Greta said to Tullio.

"A brute," Tullio said. "And look at that face, different now. Some girls might even call him handsome. If he wasn't standing next to me."

Tullio was still his bantering self, but the confidence that once bordered on cocksureness had been tamped down by hardship. He looked like he'd lost a lot of weight, and he kept staring off into the middle distance, chain-smoking cigarettes.

"I saw that Nazi you used to follow around, Colonel Rauff, yesterday."

Tullio lost several shades of color. "You saw Rauff yesterday?"

"I spoke to him," Pino said. "Did you know he was raised on a farm?"

"No idea," Tullio said, his eyes darting to Uncle Albert.

Pino's uncle hesitated before saying, "We believe you can keep a secret, yes?"

Pino nodded.

"Colonel Rauff wants Tullio brought in for questioning. If he's caught, he'll be taken to the Hotel Regina, tortured, and then sent to San Vittore Prison."

"With Barbareschi?" Pino said. "The forger?"

Everyone else in the room looked at him, dumbfounded.

"How do you know him?" Tullio demanded.

Pino explained, and then said, "Rauff said he was in San Vittore."

For the first time, Tullio smiled. "He was until last night. Barbareschi escaped!"

That boggled Pino's mind. He remembered the seminarian as he was on the first day of the bombardment, and tried to imagine him becoming a forger and then escaping prison. San Vittore, for God's sake!

"That's good news," Pino said. "So you're hiding here, Tullio? Is that smart?"

"I move around," Tullio said, lighting another cigarette. "Every night."

"Which makes things difficult for us," Uncle Albert said. "Before Rauff took an interest in him, Tullio could move freely about the city, undertaking various tasks for the resistance. Now, he can't. As I said earlier, there is something you might be able to do for us."

Pino felt excited. "Anything for the resistance."

"We have papers that must be delivered before curfew tonight," Uncle Albert said. "We'll give you an address. You carry the papers there, and turn them over. Can you do that?"

"What are the papers?"

"That's not your concern," his uncle said.

Tullio said bluntly, "But if the Nazis catch you with them, and they understand what's written on those papers, they'll execute you. They've done it for less."

Pino looked at the packet his uncle held out to him. Other than the day before, and the day Nicco had died holding the grenade, he'd felt little actual threat from the Nazis. But the Germans were everywhere in Milan now. Any one of them could stop him, search him.

"These are important papers, though?"

"They are."

"Then I won't get caught," Pino said, and took the packet.

An hour later, he left the leather shop on his uncle's bicycle. He showed his documents at the San Babila checkpoint and at another on the west side of the cathedral, but no one patted him down or seemed much interested in him.

It took him until late afternoon to maneuver through the city toward an address in the southeastern quadrant of Milan. The farther he got from the city center, the more devastation he saw. Pino rode and pushed his bike through blistered, charred streets of desolation and want. He came to a bomb crater, slowed, and stopped at the edge of it. It had rained the night before. Filthy water lingered in the bottom of the crater, giving off a putrid stench. Children laughed. Four or five of them, black with filth, were climbing and playing on the skeleton of a burned-out structure.

Were they here? Did they feel the bombs? See the fires? Do they have parents? Or are they street urchins? Where do they live? Here?

Seeing the children living in the destruction upset him, but he pressed on, following the directions Tullio had given him. Pino crossed out of the burned area into a neighborhood that had lost fewer buildings. It put him in mind of a busted piano, with some keys broken, some gone, and some still standing yellow and red against a blackened background.

He found two apartment buildings side by side. As Tullio had instructed, he entered the right one, which teemed with life. Sooty kids roamed the halls. The doors to many of the apartments were open, the rooms packed with people who looked battered by life. A record was playing in one, an aria from *Madama Butterfly* that he realized was being performed by his cousin Licia.

"Who you looking for?" said one filthy boy.

"Sixteen-B," Pino said.

The boy's chin retreated. He pointed down the hall.

At Pino's knock, the door opened slightly on the chain.

A man said in thickly accented Italian, "What?"

"Tullio sent me, Baka," Pino said.

"He is alive?"

"He was two hours ago."

That seemed to satisfy the man. He undid the chain and opened the door just wide enough to allow Pino inside a studio apartment. Baka was Slavic, short, powerfully built, with thick black hair, heavy brows, a flattened nose, and massive arms and shoulders. Pino towered over him, but he still felt intimidated in his presence.

Baka studied him a moment, then said, "You bring something or no?"

Pino dug the envelope out of his pants, and handed it to him. Baka took it without comment and walked away.

"You want water?" he asked. "It is there. Drink and you go. Make it back before curfew."

Pino was parched by the long ride and took a few gulps before he looked around and understood who and what Baka was. A tan leather suitcase with heavy-duty buckles and straps lay open on the narrow bed. The interior of the suitcase had been custom designed with padded cutouts that held a compact shortwave radio, a hand generator, two antennas, and tools and replacement crystals.

Pino gestured at the radio. "Who do you talk to on it?"

"London," he grunted as he read the papers. "Brand-new. We just got it three days ago. The old one died, and we were silent for the two weeks."

"How long have you been here?"

"Parachuted in sixteen weeks ago outside the city and walked in."

"You've been here in this apartment the whole time?"

The radio operator snorted. "If so, Baka would have been a dead man fifteen weeks ago. The Nazis, they have machines now to hunt radios. They use three of them to try to, how do you say, triangulate our transmission location so they can kill us and destroy the radios. You know what is penalty for having transmitter radio these days?"

Pino shook his head.

"No questions, no nothing," Baka said making a slitting sound, and passed his finger across his throat with a smile.

"So you move around?"

"Every two days, in the middle of the day, Baka takes the chance and goes for a long walk with his suitcase to another empty apartment."

Pino had all sorts of other questions he wanted to ask, but he felt he'd already overstayed his welcome. "I'll see you again?"

Baka raised a thick brow, shrugged. "Who can know these things?"

⚬

Pino left the apartment and the building quickly. He recovered his bike and mounted it in the light of a warm spring afternoon. Riding back through the burned wasteland, he felt good, useful again. As small an assignment as that had been, he knew he'd done the right thing, fighting back, taking a risk, and he felt the better for it. He wasn't going to join the Germans. He was going to join the resistance. That was all there was to it.

Pino headed north toward Piazzale Loreto. He reached the fruit and vegetable stand just as Mr. Beltramini was lowering his awnings. Carletto's father had aged terribly since the last time Pino had seen him. Worry and stress were sewn through his face.

"Hi, Mr. Beltramini," he said. "It's me. Pino."

Mr. Beltramini squinted at him, looked him up and down, and then threw his head back and roared with laughter. "Pino Lella? You look like you ate Pino Lella!"

Pino laughed. "That's funny."

"Awww, well, my young friend, how can you survive what life throws at you if you cannot laugh and love, and are they not the same thing?"

Pino thought about that. "I guess so. Is Carletto here?"

"Upstairs, helping his mother."

"How is she?"

Mr. Beltramini's wall-to-wall grin vanished. He shook his head. "Not good. The doctor says maybe six months, maybe less."

"I'm sorry, sir."

"And I'm grateful for every moment I have with her," the shopkeeper said. "I'll go up and get Carletto for you."

"Thanks," Pino said. "Give her my best."

Mr. Beltramini started toward the door, but then stopped. "My son missed you. He says you're the best friend he's ever had."

"I missed him, too," Pino said. "I should have written him a letter, but it was difficult . . . what we were doing up there."

"He'll understand, but you'll look out for him, won't you?"

"Promised I would," Pino said. "And I never go back on a promise."

Mr. Beltramini touched Pino's biceps and shoulders. "My God, you're built like a race horse!"

Four or five minutes later, Carletto came out the door. "Hey."

"Hey," Pino said, punching him lightly on the arm. "It's great to see you."

"Yeah? You, too."

"You don't sound convinced of it."

"My mama has had a tough day."

Pino felt a pang in his gut. He hadn't seen his own mother since Christmas, and he suddenly missed Porzia, and even Cicci.

"I can't imagine," Pino said.

They talked and joked for fifteen minutes, until they noticed daylight beginning to fade. Pino had never dealt with the curfew before, and he wanted to be inside the new apartment long before night fell. They made plans to meet up in the coming days, shook hands, and parted.

It pained Pino to ride away from Carletto. His old friend seemed lost, a shell of himself. Before the bombs had started falling, Carletto had been quick and funny, just like his father. Now, he looked duller, as if inside he'd turned as gray as those men Pino had seen clearing the streets. At the checkpoint into San Babila, the guard recognized him and waved him through. *I could have had a gun on me,* Pino thought as he started to pedal, and then heard shouting behind him.

He looked over his shoulder. Soldiers from the checkpoint came running after him with their machine guns held at their waists. Terrified, he stopped and threw up his hands.

They ran past Pino and around the corner. His heart was racing so fast he got dizzy, and it took several moments before he could move. What had happened there? Where were they going? Then he heard klaxon horns. An ambulance? A police car?

He walked his bike to the corner, looked around it, and saw the three Nazis searching a man in his late thirties. The man had his hands up against a bank wall, legs spread. He was upset and got more so when one of the Germans pulled a revolver from the man's waistband.

"Per favore!" he cried. "I only use this to protect my store and to go to the bank!"

One of the soldiers barked something in German. The soldiers all took a few steps back. One threw up his rifle and shot the man in the back of the head. The man went rag doll and crumpled down the wall.

Pino jumped back, horrified. One of the soldiers saw him, yelled something. Pino leaped on his bike, pedaled like a maniac, and, taking a roundabout route, got to the apartment building on Corso del Littorio without being caught.

The SS sentries in the lobby were new, and they paid closer attention to him than before. One patted him down and inspected his documents twice before allowing him through to the elevator. As the birdcage rose, the memory of the shot man kept playing over and over in his mind.

Numb and sickened, he only became aware of the delicious odors coming from the new apartment when he raised his hand to knock. His uncle opened it and let him in.

"We were worried," Uncle Albert said, shutting the door. "You've been gone too long."

"I went to see my friend Carletto," Pino said.

"Thank God. But otherwise no problems?"

"I saw the Germans kill a man for having a pistol," Pino said dully. "They just shot him like he was nothing. Nothing."

Before his uncle could reply, Porzia appeared in the hallway, threw her arms wide, and cried, "Pino!"

"Mama?"

Pino was flooded with emotions that propelled him across the room to his mother. He scooped Porzia up off her feet, swung her around, and kissed her, which provoked a squeal of fear and delight. Then he swung her around again.

"Okay, okay, that's enough! Put me down!"

Pino placed her gently on the rug. Porzia smoothed her dress before looking at him and shaking her head. "Your father said you were big, but I . . . My Domenico? Is he big like you now, too?"

"Not any taller, but stronger, Mama," Pino said. "Mimo's a tough guy now."

"Well." Porzia beamed, and her eyes began to water. "I am just so happy to be in my new home with my big boy."

His father came out from the kitchen.

"Did you like your surprise?" Michele asked. "Mama came on the train from Rapallo just to see you."

"I like the surprise. Where's Cicci?"

"Sick," Porzia said. "My friends are taking care of her. She sends you her love."

"Where's Greta?" Michele asked. "Dinner's almost ready."

"She's closing the shop," Uncle Albert said. "She'll be here soon."

There was a knock at the door. Pino's father opened it.

Aunt Greta charged in, looking distraught, but waited until the door was shut and locked before sobbing, "The Gestapo caught Tullio!"

"What?" Uncle Albert cried. "How?"

"He decided to leave the shop early. He was going to stay at his mother's tonight. Somewhere along the way, not far from the shop, I guess they arrested him, and took him to the Hotel Regina. Sonny Mascolo, the fancy button man, saw it all, and told me as I was locking up."

Gloom saturated the room. Tullio in Gestapo headquarters. Pino couldn't imagine what he was suffering at that very moment.

"Did they follow Tullio from the shop?" Uncle Albert asked.

"He went out through the alley, so I don't think so," Aunt Greta said.

Her husband shook his head. "We have to think so, even if it isn't true. We may all be under SS scrutiny now."

Pino felt claustrophobic. He could see similar reactions around.

"That settles it, then," Porzia said as if handing down an edict from on high. "Pino, tomorrow morning, you are going to that enlistment office, and you are joining the Germans and staying out of harm's way until the war is over."

"And what do I do then, Mama?" Pino cried. "Get killed by the Allies because of my swastika uniform?"

"When the Allies get close, you take the uniform off," his mother said, glaring at him. "My mind is made up. You are still a minor. I still make decisions for you."

"Mama," Pino complained, "you can't—"

"I can and do," she said sharply. "End of discussion."

Chapter Fourteen

July 27, 1944
Modena, Italy

More than eleven weeks after his parents ordered him to enlist with the Germans, Pino shouldered a Gewehr 43 semiautomatic rifle and marched toward the Modena train station. He wore the summer uniform of the Organization Todt: calf-high black leather combat boots; olive pants, shirt, and peaked cap; a black leather belt; and a holster with a Walther pistol. A red-and-white band high on his left arm completed the uniform and branded him.

Across the white top it read "ORG.TODT." A large black swastika dominated a red circle below. The patch on his other shoulder revealed his rank: Vorarbeiter, or private first class.

Vorarbeiter Lella had little faith in God's plan for him by that point. Indeed, as he entered the station, he was still fuming mad at his predicament. His mother had railroaded him into this. At Casa Alpina, he'd been doing something that mattered, something good and right, guiding as an act of courage, no matter the personal risk. Since then, his life had been boot camp, an endless parade of marches, calisthenics, lessons in German, and other useless skills. Every time he looked at the swastika he wanted to tear it off and head for the hills to join the partisans.

"Lella," called out Pino's Frontführer, or platoon leader, breaking him from his thoughts. "Take Pritoni and guard Platform Three."

Pino nodded without enthusiasm and went to his post with Pritoni, an overweight kid from Genoa who'd never been away from home. They took up position on the elevated platform between two of the most heavily used tracks in the station, which had a high arched ceiling. German soldiers were loading crates of weapons into open boxcars on one track. The other was empty.

"I hate standing here all night," Pritoni said. He lit a cigarette, puffed it. "My feet and ankles, they swell and hurt."

"Lean up against the roof support posts, move one foot to the other."

"I tried that. My feet still hurt."

Pritoni kept up a litany of complaints until Pino tuned him out. The Alps had taught him not to fret and whine at difficult circumstances. It was a waste of energy.

Instead, he started thinking about the war. During boot camp, he hadn't heard a thing. But in the week since he'd been assigned to guard the train station, he'd learned that Lieutenant General Mark Clark's US Fifth Army had liberated Rome on June 5. Since then, however, the Allies had only managed to advance sixteen kilometers north toward Milan. Pino still figured the war would be over by October, November at the latest. Around midnight, he yawned and wondered what he might do after the war. Go back to school? Head to the Alps? And when would he find a girl to—?

Air raid sirens started to moan and wail. Antiaircraft guns opened up. Bombs fell, angry buzzing hornets that rained down on central Modena. At first, the bombs detonated at a distance. Then one exploded outside the rail yard. The next three all struck the train station in rapid succession.

Pino saw a flash before the blasts hurled him backward off the platform and through the air. Still wearing his pack, he landed hard on the empty train tracks and momentarily blacked out. Another explosion roused him, and he instinctively curled into a ball as glass and debris showered down on him.

When the raid ended, Pino tried to get up, smelling smoke and seeing fire. He was dizzy, and his ears had a roar in them like an angry ocean. Everything was disjointed, a broken kaleidoscope, until he saw Pritoni's body on the tracks behind him. The kid from Genoa had taken the brunt of the blast. A chunk of shrapnel had taken off most of his head.

Pino crawled away and vomited. His head pounded so hard he thought it might burst. He found his gun, struggled to get back up on the train platform, and did so before puking again. His ears roared louder. Seeing dead soldiers and others wounded, he felt dizzy and weak, on the verge of passing out. Pino threw out his hands to grab one of the steel support posts still holding up the train station's roof.

Intense, fiery pain shot through his right arm. It was only then that he realized the index and middle fingers of his right hand had nearly been chopped off. They dangled there by ligament and skin. Bone stuck out of his index finger. Blood spurted from the wound.

He passed out a second time.

<hr>

Pino was taken to a field hospital where German surgeons reattached his fingers and treated him for concussion. He lay in the hospital for nine days.

Upon discharge on August 6, Pino was judged temporarily unfit for duty and told to go home for ten days to recuperate. As he rode in the back of a newspaper lorry that gave him a lift back to Milan on a humid, showery summer day, Pino felt nothing like the happy, purposeful man-child who'd left the Alps. He felt weak and disillusioned.

The Organization Todt uniform had its benefits, though. It got Pino waved through several checkpoints, and he was soon walking the streets of his beloved San Babila. He encountered and greeted several old friends of his parents, people he hadn't seen in years. They stared at his uniform and the swastika on the armband and acted like they didn't know him or want to.

Pino was closer to Albanese Luggage than he was to home, so he went there first. Walking down the sidewalk on Via Monte Napoleone, he noticed a Daimler-Benz G4 Offroader, a six-wheel-drive Nazi staff car, parked right in front of the leather store. The hood was up. The driver was under it, working on the engine in the rain.

A Nazi officer wearing a trench coat over his shoulders stepped out of the showroom and said something sharp in German. The driver jerked up and shook his head. The officer looked disgusted and went back inside the leather shop.

Always interested in cars, Pino paused and said, "What's the problem?"

"What's it to you?" the driver said.

"Nothing," Pino said. "I just know a little about engines."

"And I know next to nothing," the driver admitted. "She won't start today, and when she does, she backfires. The idle is horrible, and it bucks between gears."

Pino thought about that and, mindful of his healing hand, looked around under the hood. The G4 had an eight-cylinder engine. He checked the spark plugs and wire heads, saw them gapped correctly. He checked the air filter, found it filthy, and cleaned it. The fuel filter was also clogged. Then he studied the carburetor and saw the screw heads glinting. Someone had recently made adjustments.

He got a screwdriver from the driver, and with his good hand, fiddled with several of the screws. "Try it."

The driver got in, turned over the ignition. The engine caught, backfired, and blew a black cough of smoke.

"See?"

Pino nodded, thought of what Alberto Ascari might do, and tuned the carburetor a second time. Hearing the front door to his uncle's shop open, he said, "Try again."

This time the engine roared to life. Pino grinned, set the tools down, and shut the hood. When he did, he saw that same German officer standing on the sidewalk beside his uncle Albert and aunt Greta. He'd taken off his trench coat. Pino saw by his insignias that he was a major general.

Aunt Greta said something to the general in German. He spoke back.

"Pino," his aunt said, "General Leyers would like a word with you."

Pino swallowed, came around the front of the car, and saluted him with a half-hearted *"Heil Hitler,"* even as he realized that he and the general wore the same uniform and distinctive armband.

Aunt Greta said, "He wants to see your orders, Pino, and to know where you are positioned in the Organization Todt."

"Modena," Pino said, dug in his pocket, and showed the general his papers. Leyers read them, and then spoke in German.

"He wants to know whether you can drive in your present condition," Aunt Greta said.

Pino raised his chin, wiggled his fingers, and said, "Very well, sir."

His aunt translated. The general spoke back. Aunt Greta responded.

Leyers looked at Pino and said, "Do you speak any German?"

"A little," he said. "I understand more than I can speak."

"Vous parlez français, Vorarbeiter?"

Pino said, *"Oui, mon général. Très bien."* Yes, my general, very well.

"You are now my driver, then," the general said. "This other one is an idiot who knows nothing about cars. You are sure you can drive with your hand like that?"

"Yes," Pino said.

"Then report to Wehrmacht headquarters, the German House, tomorrow morning at oh six forty. You'll find this car in the motor pool there. I will leave an address in the glove compartment. You will go to that address and pick me up. Do you understand?"

Pino bobbed his head. *"Oui, mon général."*

General Leyers nodded stiffly and then climbed in the back of the staff car, saying something sharp. The driver gave Pino a filthy look, and the car rolled away from the curb.

"Come inside, Pino!" Uncle Albert cried. "My God! Get inside!"

"What did he say there to the driver?" Pino asked his aunt as they followed him.

Aunt Greta said, "He called him a jackass good only for latrine duty."

His uncle shut the shop door, flipped the sign to "Closed," and shook his fists in triumph. "Pino, do you realize what you've done?"

"No," Pino said. "Not really."

"That's Major General Hans Leyers!" Uncle Albert said, sounding giddy.

Aunt Greta said, "His formal title is *Generalbevollmächtigter fur Reichsminister für Rüstung und Kriegsproduktion für Italien*. It translates as 'Plenipotentiary to the Reich Minister for Armaments and War Production in Italy.'"

Seeing Pino didn't understand, she said, "'Plenipotentiary' means 'full authority.' It's given to someone so high ranking that they have the full authority of a Reich Minister, free to do whatever is necessary for the sake of the Nazi war machine."

Uncle Albert said, "After Field Marshal Kesselring, General Leyers is the most powerful German in Italy. He works with the full authority of Albert Speer,

Hitler's Reich Minister for Armaments and War Production, which puts him two steps from the führer! Whatever Leyers wants to happen, happens. Anything the Wehrmacht needs in Italy, Leyers gets it, or forces our factories to build it, or steals it from us. He makes all of the Nazis' guns, cannons, ammunition, and bombs here. All the tanks. All the lorries."

Pino's uncle paused, staring off at something dawning, and then said, "My God, Pino, Leyers has to know the location of every tank trap, pillbox, land mine, and fortification between here and Rome. He built them, didn't he? Of course he did. Don't you see, Pino? You are the great general's personal driver now. You'll go where Leyers goes. See what he sees. Hear what he hears. You'll be our spy inside the German High Command!"

Chapter Fifteen

His head still reeling from his sudden and dramatic change of fate, Pino rose early on August 8, 1944. He ironed his uniform and ate breakfast before his father was even out of bed. As he sipped coffee and ate toast, he remembered that Uncle Albert had decided that no one but he and Aunt Greta should know Pino's covert role as driver for Major General Hans Leyers.

"Don't tell anyone," Uncle Albert said. "Not your father, mother, Mimo. Carletto. Anyone. Telling someone could lead to someone else knowing, and then a third someone else, and soon you'll have the Gestapo at your door, taking you away for torture. Do you understand?"

"You've got to be careful," Aunt Greta said. "Being a spy is beyond dangerous."

"Just ask Tullio," Uncle Albert said.

"How is he?" Pino said, trying to get his mind off getting caught and tortured.

"The Nazis let his sister see him last week," his aunt said. "She said he'd been beaten, but never talked. He was thin and sick with some stomach thing, but she said his spirits were high, and he spoke of escaping to fight with the partisans."

Tullio will escape and fight, Pino thought as he hurried through the streets as San Babila began to awaken. *And I am a spy. So I am kind of in the resistance now, aren't I?*

Pino was at the German House near the Porta Romana by 6:25 a.m. He was directed to the motor pool, where he caught a mechanic under the hood of Leyers's Daimler-Benz staff car.

"What are you doing there?" Pino demanded.

The mechanic, an Italian in his forties, scowled. "My work."

"I'm General Leyers's new driver," Pino said, looking at the carburetor settings. Two had been moved. "Stop messing with the carburetor."

The mechanic, taken aback, sputtered, "I did no such thing."

"You did," Pino said, taking a screwdriver from the mechanic's box and making several readjustments. "There, she'll purr like a lioness now."

The mechanic stared at him as Pino opened the driver's door, stepped up on the running board, climbed into the seat, and looked around. Convertible roof. Leather seats. Buckets up front, bench in the back. The G4 was easily the biggest vehicle Pino had ever tried to drive. With six wheels and a high ground clearance, it could go virtually anywhere, which was the point, Pino guessed.

Where does a Plenipotentiary General for War Production go? With this car and total authority, anywhere he wants to.

Remembering his orders, Pino looked in the glove compartment and found an address on Via Dante, easy to find. He didn't want to aggravate his wounds, so he played with the shifter to get his hand position and grip right. Then he tested the clutch and found every gear. He used his ring finger and the thumb of his right hand to turn the key. The raw power of the engine vibrated through the steering wheel.

Pino eased out the clutch. It had a hard release. His hand slipped off the shifter. The Daimler lurched forward and stalled. He glanced at the mechanic, who gave him a sneering grin.

Ignoring him, Pino started the car again and teased the clutch out this time. He rolled through the motor-pool yard in first and then second gear. The roads at Milan's center, laid out in horse-and-carriage times, were narrow at best. At the wheel of the Daimler, Pino felt as if he were driving a minitank down the twisting lanes.

The drivers of the two cars he encountered looked at the red Nazi general's flags fluttering on either front fender of the Daimler and immediately backed out of the way. Pino parked the staff car on the sidewalk just beyond the address on Via Dante Leyers left for him.

Pino got looks from several pedestrians, but no one dared protest with those Nazi general's flags flying. He took the keys, climbed out, and went into the lobby of a small apartment building. Sitting on a stool by a closed door near the staircase, an old woman, a crone with thick-lensed glasses, peered his way as if barely seeing him.

"I'm going to three-B," Pino said.

The crone said nothing, just nodded and blinked at him through her spectacles. She was creepy, he decided as he climbed to the third floor. He checked his watch. It was exactly 6:40 a.m. when he rapped sharply on the door.

He heard footsteps. The door opened inward, and his entire life changed.

Flashing her slate-blue eyes at him and smiling, the maid said, "You are the general's new driver?"

Pino wanted to reply, but he was so stunned that he couldn't. His heart boomed in his chest. He tried to speak, but no sound came out. His face felt hot. He ran a finger in his collar. Finally, he just nodded.

"I hope you don't drive like you talk," she laughed, playing with the braid of her tawny-blond hair with one hand and gesturing him inside with the other.

Pino stepped past her, smelled her, and felt so dizzy he thought he might fall.

"I'm Dolly's maid," she said behind him. "You can call me—"

"Anna," Pino said.

When he turned to look back at her, the door was closed, her smile had fallen, and she was regarding him as if he were some form of threat.

"How did you know my name?" she said. "Who are you?"

"Pino," he stammered. "Pino Lella. My parents own a purse store in San Babila. I asked you to go to the movies with me outside the bakery near La Scala last year, and you asked how old I was."

Anna's eyes unscrewed as if she were retrieving some vague, buried memory. Then she laughed, covered her mouth, and studied him anew. "You don't look like that crazy boy."

"A lot can change in fourteen months."

"I can see that," she said. "Is that how long it's been?"

"A lifetime ago," Pino said. *You Were Never Lovelier.*

Anna's eyebrows shot up, annoyed. "Excuse me?"

"The movie," he said. "Fred Astaire. Rita Hayworth. You stood me up."

Her chin dropped; so did her shoulders. "I did, didn't I?"

There was an uncomfortable moment before Pino said, "It's a good thing you did. That theater was bombed that night. My brother and I were inside, but we both made it out."

Anna looked up at him. "True?"

"One hundred percent."

"What's wrong with your hand?" she said.

He looked at his bandaged hand and said, "Just some stitches."

An unseen woman with a thick accent called, "Anna! Anna, I need you, please!"

"Coming, Dolly," Anna cried. She pointed to a bench in the hallway. "You can sit there until General Leyers is ready for you."

He stood aside. The maid passed him close in the narrow hallway. It took his breath away, and he stared after her swinging hips as she disappeared deeper into the apartment. When he sat and remembered to breathe, Anna's female-and-jasmine scent lingered in the air. He considered getting up and wandering through the apartment, just to see and smell her again. He decided he had to take the risk, and his heart began to pound wildly.

Then Pino heard approaching voices, a man and a woman talking and laughing in German. Pino sprang to attention. A woman in her early forties appeared at the other end of the short hall. She sashayed toward him wearing an ivory lace-and-satin robe and beaded gold slippers. She was leggy and pretty in a showgirl way with pendulous breasts, green eyes, and a riot of auburn hair that fell artfully about her shoulders and face. She wore makeup even at this early hour. She eyed Pino while smoking a cigarette.

"You are tall for a driver, and good-looking, too," she said in Italian with a heavy German accent. "Too bad. Tall men are always the ones who die in war. Easy targets."

"Guess I'll have to keep my head down."

"Mmmm," she said, and took a drag. "I am Dolly, Dolly Stottlemeyer."

"Vorarbeiter Lella, Pino Lella," he said with none of the earlier stammering.

Dolly seemed unimpressed, and called out, "Anna? Do you have the general's coffee ready?"

"Coming, Dolly," Anna yelled back.

The maid and General Leyers converged on the short hallway at the same time. Pino snapped to attention, saluted, his eyes darting to Anna as she came over to him, her smell all around him as she held out a thermos. He looked at her hands and fingers, how perfect they were, how—

"Take the thermos," Anna whispered.

Pino startled, and took it.

"And the general's valise," she muttered.

Pino flushed and awkwardly bowed to Leyers, then picked up the large leather valise, which felt full.

"Where is the car?" the general asked in French.

"Out front, *mon général*," Pino replied.

Dolly said something to the general in German; he nodded and replied.

Then Leyers fixed his eyes on Pino and snarled, "What are you doing there, staring at me like a *Dummkopf*? Take my bag to the car. Backseat. Center. I'll be down soon."

Flustered, Pino said, "Oui, *mon général*. Backseat center."

Before leaving, he dared a last glance at Anna and was discouraged to see that she was looking at him as if he had mental problems. He left the apartment and lugged the general's valise down the stairs, trying to remember the last time he'd thought of Anna. Five, six months ago? The truth was he'd stopped believing he'd ever see her again, and now here she was.

Anna was all he could think about as he passed the blinking old crone in the lobby and went outside. The maid's smell. Her smile. Her laugh.

Anna, Pino thought. *What a beautiful name. Rolls right off the tongue.*

Did General Leyers always spend the nights with Dolly? He desperately hoped so. Or was it an unusual thing? Once a week or something? He desperately hoped not.

Then Pino realized he'd better focus if he wanted to see Anna again. He had to be the perfect driver, he decided, one that Leyers would never dismiss.

He reached the Daimler. It was only then, as he was lifting the valise into the backseat, that he thought about what might be inside. He almost tried to open it right there, but then realized that foot traffic was building and there were German soldiers about.

Pino set the briefcase down, shut the door, and came around to the driver's side of the staff car, so he could see back toward the apartment building. He opened the rear door and moved the valise closer. He looked at the hasp, which had a keyhole. He looked up at the fourth floor, wondering how long it took the general to eat.

Less time with every second, Pino thought, and tried the hasp. Locked.

He looked up at the fourth-floor window and thought he saw the drapes flutter as if someone had let them go. Pino shut the back door. A few moments later, the door to Dolly's building opened. General Leyers exited. Pino sprinted around the car and opened the other side.

The Nazis' Plenipotentiary General for War Production barely gave him a glance before climbing in next to his case. Leyers immediately checked the hasp.

Pino shut the door behind the general, his heart hammering. What if he'd been looking inside the valise when the Nazi came out? That thought made his heart hammer all the more as he slid behind the wheel and looked in the rearview mirror. Leyers had set his peaked hat aside and was digging out a thin silver chain from beneath his collar. There was a key on it.

"Where are we going, *mon général*?" Pino asked.

"Don't talk unless spoken to," Leyers said sharply, using the key to unlock his case. "Are we clear, Vorarbeiter?"

"Oui, mon général," Pino said. "Very clear."

"Can you read a map?"

"Yes."

"Good, then. Drive on toward Como. When you cross out of Milan, stop and drop my flags. Store them in the glove compartment. In the meantime, be quiet. I have to concentrate."

After they were moving, General Leyers put on reading glasses and began intently working on a thick stack of papers in his lap. Yesterday at Albanese Luggage and this morning at Dolly Stottlemeyer's, Pino had been too flustered to look at Leyers in any great detail. Now he drove and kept taking glances at the general, really studying the man.

Pino figured Leyers was in his midfifties. Powerfully built, especially through the shoulders, the general had a bull neck that strained against his crisp white shirt and jacket. His forehead, broader than most, was defined by receding salt-and-pepper hair slicked back and glistening with pomade. His thick, dark brows seemed to throw shadows across his eyes as he scanned reports, scribbled on them, and then set them aside in a separate pile on the backseat.

Leyers's concentration seemed total. In the time it took for Pino to drive the Daimler out of Milan proper, he never once saw him raise his head off the work before him. Even when Pino stopped to take down the general's flags, Leyers stayed on task. He had a blueprint spread out across his lap and was studying it when Pino said, "Como, *mon général.*"

Leyers adjusted his glasses. "The stadium. Around back."

⇒⇒

A few minutes later, Pino drove along the long west side of the football stadium on Viale Giuseppe Sinigaglia. Seeing the staff car, four armed guards at an entrance snapped to attention.

"Park it in the shade," General Leyers said. "Wait with the car."

"Oui, mon général."

Pino parked, shot out of the car, and had the back door open in seconds. Leyers seemed not to notice, got out with his valise, and walked by Pino as if he did not exist. Leyers treated the guards the same way as he disappeared inside the stadium.

It was early in the day, and already the August heat was building. Pino could smell Lake Como on the other side of the stadium, and he longed to go down and look up the western arm toward the Alps and Casa Alpina. He wondered how Father Re was, and Mimo.

He thought about his mother, and what her latest purse designs might look like, and whether she knew what had happened to him. He felt melancholy, realized he missed Porzia, especially the way she charged into everything in her life. Nothing had ever frightened his mother, as far as he knew, until the bombing had started. Since then, she and Cicci had been living in Rapallo, listening to the war on the radio, and praying for it all to be over.

It was passive, hiding out, and for that Pino was glad he wasn't with her. He was not hiding out. He was a spy at the heart of Nazi power in Italy. A thrill went through him, and for the first time, he really thought about being a spy, not espionage as a boy's game but as an act of war.

What was he trying to find or see? And where was he trying to find or see it? There was the valise and its contents, to be sure. And General Leyers had offices here in Como, and in Milan, Pino supposed. But would he ever be allowed inside them?

He couldn't see that happening, and realizing there was little for him to do now but wait for the general, he let his thoughts drift to Anna. He'd thought for sure he'd never see her again, but here she was, the maid of the general's mistress! What were the odds of that? Didn't it all seem like it was—?

German lorries, better than a dozen, rumbled past him blowing black diesel smoke, and ground to a halt at the north end of the street. Armed Organization Todt soldiers leaped out of one vehicle and fanned out, training their weapons on the rears of the other lorries.

"Raus!" they shouted, and dropped the gate. Throwing back the canvas, they revealed forty men looking around in bewilderment. *"Raus!"*

They were all emaciated, filthy, with scraggly beards and long tangled hair. Many of them had vacant, dead eyes and wore ragged gray trousers and tops. There were letters on their chests he couldn't make out. Manacled, they moved at no better than a shuffle until the guards tore into them, hitting a few with the butts of their rifles. As lorry after lorry emptied, there were soon three hundred of the men, maybe more, moving en masse to the stadium's north end.

Pino recalled the similar men in the central rail yard in Milan clearing the streets of bomb debris. Were they Jews? Where had they come from?

The gray men, as he'd taken to calling them, rounded the northwest corner of the stadium and headed east toward the lake and out of view. He thought about General Leyers's order to wait by the Daimler, and then Uncle Albert's wish that he become a spy. Pino started walking at a quick pace past the four guards at the near entrance. One said something in German he didn't understand. He nodded, laughed, and kept moving, figuring that acting confident was as good as being confident.

He rounded the corner. The gray men were gone. How was that possible?

Then Pino saw that an overhead door on the north end of the stadium had been rolled up. Two armed guards appeared outside. He thought of Tullio Galimberti, how he used to say that the trick to doing almost anything difficult was to act like someone else, someone who belonged.

Pino saluted the guards and took a right inside a tunnel that led out toward the pitch. He figured if he was going to be stopped, it would be now, but his gamble paid off, and they didn't say a word. He quickly saw why. The tunnel had side hallways in which many men in OT uniforms like his own were stacking boxes and crates. The guards must have figured Pino was just one more in the bunch.

He walked almost to the mouth of the tunnel, then hung back in the shadows and looked out, seeing the gray men lining up in rows on the near side. Beyond them, at the southern end of the stadium, camouflage netting had been raised and lashed in place. There were howitzer cannons on trailers beneath the netting, six of them by Pino's count, dozens of heavy machine guns, and too many wooden crates to ponder. It was a supply depot. Maybe an ammo dump.

Pino turned his attention to the OT soldiers prodding the last few gray men into position just before General Leyers appeared from another tunnel perhaps fifty meters away and down the length of the stadium. An OT captain and a sergeant trailed him.

Pino pressed himself tight to the tunnel wall, only then truly considering what might happen if he were caught snooping about. He'd be questioned, certainly. Maybe punched up. Maybe worse. He thought about walking confidently right back out the way he'd come in, waiting however long it took for Leyers to return, and going on with his day.

But then, ramrod straight and with the full authority of a Nazi Reich Minister, General Leyers strode to a stop in front of the gray men, who were assembled in thirty rows, ten deep, with close to a meter gap between each man, and a three-meter gap between each row. Leyers studied the first man a moment, and then made some kind of pronouncement that Pino couldn't hear.

The captain scribbled on a notepad. The sergeant pointed with the muzzle of his rifle, and the first gray man broke formation. He trudged across the field, turned, and stood looking back at Leyers, who'd moved on to the next man, and the next. Each time Leyers would study the man before him, and then make his pronouncement. The captain would write it down, and the sergeant would point his gun. Some went with the first man. Others were assigned to one of two other groups.

He's grading them. Sorting them.

Indeed, the biggest and strongest of the prisoners stood in a cluster smaller than the other two. The men in the second and larger group looked more beaten up, but they were still grasping at dignity. The third and largest bunch looked like men at their limits, skeletal, and about to drop dead in the building heat.

Leyers was a model of German efficiency in the sorting process. He gave no man more than a five-second appraisal, rendered his verdict, and moved on. He reached the three-hundredth man in less than fifteen minutes, said something to the captain and the sergeant, who snapped into a *Sieg heil* salute. General Leyers returned the Nazi salute with vigor and then strode toward the exit.

He's heading to the car!

Pino spun around, swallowing at the metal taste on his tongue, wanting to run but forcing himself to model the general in his purposeful, authoritative stride. When he walked out the north gate, one of the guards asked him something in German. Before he could answer, their attention moved to the sound of the gray men shuffling into the tunnel behind Pino, who kept moving as if he were leading the parade at a distance.

He rounded the corner. Midway down the stadium, Leyers exited, heading toward the Daimler. Pino exploded into a full sprint.

They'd been seventy-five meters apart when Leyers came out the door. But twelve steps from the staff car, Pino caught up, went by the general, and came to a skidding halt. He saluted, tried to calm his breath, and opened the door. A dribble of sweat left his hairline and ran down between his eyes onto the bridge of his nose.

General Leyers must have seen it, because he stopped before getting in and looked closely at Pino. More sweat beads appeared and dribbled.

"I told you to wait with the car," Leyers said.

"Oui, mon général," Pino gasped. "But I had to piss."

The general showed slight disgust, and climbed inside. Pino shut the door behind him, feeling like he'd taken a steam bath. He wiped both sleeves across his face and got into the driver's seat.

"Varenna," General Leyers said. "Do you know it?"

"East shore of the east arm of the lake, *mon général,*" Pino said, and threw the staff car in gear.

They were stopped at four checkpoints as they made their way to Varenna, but every time, the sentry saw Leyers in the back of the staff car and quickly waved them through. The general had Pino stop at a small café in Lecco for an espresso and a pastry, which Leyers ate and drank as they drove on.

On the outskirts of Varenna, General Leyers gave directions that led out of town and up into the foothills of the southern Alps. The road quickly became a two-track that led to a gated pasture. Leyers told Pino to go through the gate and across the field.

"Are you sure the car will make it?" Pino asked.

The general looked at him like he was a fool. "It is a six-wheel drive. It will go anywhere I tell it to go."

Pino dropped the transmission into full-low gear, and they went through the gate, cruising like a small tank across the uneven terrain with surprising ease. General Leyers told him to park in the far corner of the field near six empty lorries and a pair of OT soldiers guarding them.

Pino pulled in and shut off the staff car.

Before he could get out, the general said, "Can you take notes, too?"

"Oui, mon général."

Leyers rooted in his valise, came up with a stenographer's notepad and a pen. Then he retrieved the chain and key beneath his shirt and locked the case.

"Follow me," he said. "Write down what I tell you."

Pino snatched up the notepad and pen and climbed out. He opened the rear door, and Leyers exited, walking briskly past the lorries to a path that entered woods.

It was nearly eleven o'clock in the morning. Crickets sawed in the heat. The air in the forest smelled good and green and reminded Pino of that grassy hillside where he and Carletto had slept during the bombardment. The trail began to angle steeply downhill, with lots of exposed tree roots and ledges.

A few minutes later, they emerged from the trees onto a railroad track that curved into a tunnel. General Leyers marched toward it. Only then did Pino hear the din of steel on rock, hundreds of hammers striking stone inside the tunnel. The air reeked of spent explosives.

Sentries outside the tunnel snapped to attention and saluted as Leyers passed. Pino followed, feeling their eyes on him. It was gloomy and got gloomier the deeper they walked into the tunnel. With every step, the hammering got closer and turned more painful to the ear.

The general stopped, dug in his pocket, and came out with cotton balls. He handed one to Pino, motioned to him to tear it in half and stuff the pieces in his ear canals. Pino did, and it helped enough that only if the general shouted right next to him could he hear what he was saying.

They rounded a curve in the tunnel. Bright electric bulbs hung from the ceiling ahead, casting a garish light that revealed the silhouettes of a small army of gray men using picks and sledge hammers to attack the walls on both sides of the tunnel, which stank of detonation. Chunks of rock yielded to the onslaught, broke off, and fell at the men's feet. They kicked the rocks behind them to other men loading the debris into ore cars on the rail tracks.

It was hellish, Pino thought, and he wanted to leave immediately. But General Leyers continued on without pause, stopping by an OT guard who handed him a flashlight. The general shone it into the excavations on either side of the track. The gray men had cut a solid meter into the wall in places, and were hollowing out a space that Pino judged at two and a half meters high and twenty-four meters long.

They walked on past the excavations. Fifteen meters on, the walls on either side of the track had already been dug out four and a half meters deep, two and a half meters high, and another thirty meters long. Large wooden crates filled much of the space on both sides of the track. Several were open, revealing bands of ammunition.

General Leyers inspected samples from each of the crates and then asked the sergeant there something in German. The sergeant handed Leyers a clipboard of documents. Leyers scanned several pages and then looked up at Pino.

"Write, Vorarbeiter," he commanded. "Seven point nine two by fifty-seven millimeter Mauser: six point four million rounds ready for shipment south."

Pino scribbled, looked up.

"Nine by nineteen millimeter Parabellum," Leyers said. "Two hundred twenty-five thousand rounds to Waffen-SS Milan. Four hundred thousand rounds to Modena south. Two hundred and fifty thousand rounds to Genoa SS."

Pino was writing as fast as he could and barely keeping pace. When he looked up, the general said, "Read it back to me."

Pino did, and Leyers nodded curtly. He walked on, looking at the printing on some of the crates and barking out notes and orders.

"*Panzerfaust*," Leyers said. "Six—"

"Sorry, *mon général*," Pino said. "I do not know this word *Panzer*—"

"One hundred millimeter rocket grenade," General Leyers said impatiently. "Seventy-five crates to the Gothic Line, per Field Marshal Kesselring's ask. Eighty-eight millimeter tank-wreckers. Forty launchers and one thousand rockets to the Gothic Line, also per Kesselring's ask."

It went on like this for another twenty minutes, with the general barking out orders and destinations of everything from machine pistols to Karabiner 98ks, the Wehrmacht's standard infantry rifle, to Solothurn long-range rifles and the stout 20 x 138 mm ammunition that fed it.

An officer appeared from farther up the tunnel, saluted, and spoke to Leyers, who turned and started back in the other direction. The officer, a colonel, ran to stay abreast with the general, still speaking crisply. Pino lagged a short distance behind.

At last the colonel stopped talking. General Leyers dropped his head slightly, pivoted with military precision, and began to verbally tear into the junior officer in German. The colonel tried to respond, but Leyers went on with his tirade. The colonel took a step back. That seemed to infuriate Leyers all the more.

He looked around, saw Pino standing there, and scowled.

"You, Vorarbeiter," he said. "Go wait by the rock pile."

Pino dropped his head and hurried past them, hearing the general shouting once more. The hammers and the stone cracking ahead made him want to wait for Leyers there. He'd no sooner had that thought than the clamor died, replaced by the sound of tools falling to the ground. By the time he reached the excavation site, the men with the picks and shovels were sitting with their backs to the walls. Many held their heads in their hands. Others looked blankly at the tunnel's ceiling.

Pino did not think he'd ever seen men like this. It was almost unbearable to look at them: how they panted, how they gushed sweat, and how they rolled their tongues along the inside of their parched lips. He looked around. There was a big milk can of water by the near wall and beside it a bucket with a ladle.

None of the guards watching over the men had moved to offer them any water. Whoever they were, whatever they'd done to be here, they deserved water, Pino thought, growing angry. He went to the milk can, tipped it over, and filled the bucket.

One guard protested, but Pino said, "General Leyers," and the protest died.

He walked over to the closest man, ladled him out some water. He was so drawn down his cheekbones and jaw stood out, making his face look like a skull. But he cocked back his head, opened his mouth, and Pino poured the water straight down his throat. When he was finished, Pino moved to the next man, and the next.

Few of them looked at him at all. As Pino was dipping for water, the seventh man stared at the rocks at his feet and muttered curses in Italian, calling him vile names.

"I'm Italian, jackass," Pino said. "Do you want the water or not?"

The man looked up. Pino saw how young he was. They could have been the same age, though he was twisted and aged beyond what Pino could fathom.

"You speak like a Milanese, but you wear a Nazi uniform," he croaked.

"It's complicated," Pino said. "Drink the water."

He drank a sip, and then gulped it down just as eagerly as the other seven had.

"Who are you?" Pino said when he'd finished. "Who are these others?"

The man looked at Pino as if he were studying a bug. "My name is Antonio," he said. "And we're slaves. Every last one of us."

Chapter Sixteen

Slaves? Pino thought, feeling repulsion and pity at the same time.

"How did you get here?" he asked. "Are you Jewish?"

"There are some Jews here, but not me," Antonio said. "I was with the resistance. Fought in Turin. The Nazis captured me, sentenced me to this instead of the firing squad. The others are Poles, Slavs, Russians, French, Belgians, Norwegians, and Danes. The letters sewn on their chests tell you where they're from. In every country the Nazis invade and conquer, they take all able-bodied men and send them into slavery. They call it 'forced labor,' or some such bullshit, but it's slavery any way you look at it. How do you think the Nazis built so many things so fast? All the coastal fortifications in France? And the big defenses down south? Hitler's got a slave army, that's how, just like the pharaohs did in Egypt, and—Jesus, son of Joseph, it's Pharaoh's slave master himself!"

Antonio whispered this last bit, looking in fear past Pino deeper into the tunnel. Pino turned. General Leyers was coming at them, staring at the water bucket and ladle in his hand. Leyers barked at the guards in German. One jumped to take back the water.

"You are my driver," he said as he stomped past Pino. "You do not serve the laborers."

"I'm sorry, *mon général*," Pino said, hurrying after him. "They just looked thirsty, and no one was giving them water. That's just . . . well, stupid."

Leyers spun around in his tracks, got in Pino's face. "What is stupid?"

"Keeping water from a working man makes him weak," Pino stammered. "You want them to work faster, you give them more water and food."

The general stood there, nose to nose with Pino, peering into his eyes as if trying to see into his soul. It took every bit of Pino's spirit not to look away.

"We have policies about the laborers," Leyers said curtly at last, "and food is hard to come by these days. But I'll see what I can do about the water."

Before Pino could blink, the general had turned and marched on. Pino's knees felt wobbly as he followed Leyers out into the bright, hot summer day. When they reached the Daimler, the general asked for the notepad. He tore out the pages Pino had written on and put them in his briefcase.

"Lake Garda, Gargnano, north of Salò," Leyers said, and started in again on the seemingly inexhaustible number of folders and reports that came out of his valise.

⊷

Pino had been to Salò once, but couldn't remember how to get there, so he consulted a detailed map of northern Italy that the general had in the glove compartment. He found Gargnano about twenty kilometers north of Salò on the west shore of the lake, and plotted his route.

He fired up the staff car, and they went rumbling back across the pasture. The air was shimmering and hot when they reached Bergamo. They stopped at a Wehrmacht encampment for petrol, food, and water shortly after noon.

Leyers ate as he worked in the backseat and somehow managed not to get a scrap of food on him. Pino turned off the highway and headed north along the western shore of Lake Garda. There wasn't even the hint of a breeze. The water had a mirror finish that seemed to reflect and magnify the Alps towering above the lake's north end.

They passed through fields of golden flowers and by a church ten centuries old. He glanced in the mirror at the general and realized he hated Leyers. He was a Nazi slave driver. *He wants Italy destroyed, and then rebuilt in Hitler's image. He works for Hitler's architect, for God's sake.*

Part of Pino wanted to find a secluded spot, get out, pull his gun, and kill the man. He would head for the hills, join one of the Garibaldi partisan units.

The powerful General Leyers dead and gone. That would be something, wouldn't it? That would change the war, wouldn't it? At some level?

But Pino knew almost instantly in his gut that he was no assassin. He did not have the ability to kill a man, even a man like—

"Put up my flags before you reach Salò," Leyers said from the backseat.

Pino pulled over and rehung the flags on the front fenders so they snapped and popped as they drove through Salò, and continued on. It was oppressively hot. The lake water looked so inviting, Pino wanted to pull over and dive in with his uniform and bandages on.

Leyers seemed unaffected by the temperature. He'd taken off his jacket, but did not loosen his tie. When they reached Gargnano, Leyers directed him away from the lake through a series of tight streets to a gated estate on a hill guarded by Fascist Black Shirt commandos carrying machine pistols. Taking one look at the Daimler and the red Nazi flags, they opened the gate.

A driveway curved around to a sprawling villa covered in vines and flowers. There were more Black Shirts there. One gestured for Pino to park. He did, got out, and opened the rear door. General Leyers climbed out, and the Fascist soldiers acted like they'd been stuck with a cattle prod, going ramrod straight and looking anywhere but at him.

"Stay with the car, *mon général?*" Pino said.

"No, you come with me," he said. "I didn't arrange for a translator, and this will be quickly done."

Pino had no idea what Leyers was talking about, but he followed him past the Black Shirts to an archway. Stone steps climbed toward a villa with blooming garden beds on either side. They reached a colonnade along the front of the villa and walked down it toward a stone terrace.

General Leyers walked around the corner onto the terrace, came up short, cracked his heels together, and took off his hat before dropping his head in studied deference.

"Duce."

Pino walked up behind the Nazi, wide-eyed in disbelief.

Not five meters from him stood Benito Mussolini.

The Italian dictator wore tan riding breeches, high-glossed boots that hit him below the knee, and a white tunic opened well down his chest, revealing gray hair and the beginnings of an old man's belly that strained against the lower buttons of the shirt. Il Duce's great bald head and the skin above his famous jawline were flushed. He held a glass of red wine. There was a half-empty carafe of wine on the table behind the dictator.

"General Leyers," Mussolini said, nodding, and then turning his rheumy eyes on Pino. "Who the hell are you?"

Pino stammered, "Today I am the general's interpreter, Duce."

"Ask him how he is," Leyers said to Pino in French. "Ask him how I can be of help today."

Pino did so in Italian. Mussolini threw his head back and roared with laughter, then sneered. "How is Il Duce?"

A brunette with formidable breasts bulging against a sleeveless white blouse came out onto the terrace. She wore sunglasses and also carried a glass of wine. A cigarette smoldered between her ruby lips.

Mussolini said, "Tell them, Clara. How is Mussolini?"

She took a drag, blew smoke, then said, "Benito is feeling pretty shitty these days."

Pino tried not to gape. He knew who she was. Everyone in Italy knew who she was. Claretta Petacci was the dictator's notorious mistress. Her picture was always in the papers. He couldn't believe she was there right in front of him.

Mussolini stopped laughing, turned dead serious, looked at Pino, and said, "Tell the general that. Tell him Il Duce is feeling pretty shitty these days. And ask him if he can fix the things that make Il Duce feel shitty."

Pino translated. Irritated, Leyers said, "Tell him, maybe we can help each other. Tell him, if he sees about ending the strikes in Milan and Turin, I'll do what I can for him."

Pino gave it to Mussolini word for word.

The dictator snorted. "I can end the strikes if you pay my workers in hard currency, and make them safer."

"I'll pay them in Swiss francs, but I can't control the bombers," Leyers said. "We have moved many factory operations underground, but there are not enough tunnels to make them all safe. In any case, as far as Italy is concerned, we are at a turning point in the war. The latest intelligence indicates as many as seven Allied divisions were moved out of Italy to France following the invasion there, which means my Gothic Line will hold through the winter if I can keep it supplied. But I cannot be assured of that happening if I do not have competent machinists to turn out weapons and parts. So can you end the strikes for me, Duce? I'm sure the führer will be pleased at your support."

"Done with a phone call," Mussolini said, snapped his fingers, and poured more wine.

"Excellent," General Leyers said. "What else can I help you with?"

"How about control of my country?" the dictator said bitterly, picking up his glass and draining it.

After Pino translated, the general took a long breath and said, "You have much control, Duce. It's why I came to you to stop the strikes."

"Il Duce has much control?" Mussolini said, thick with sarcasm and glancing at his mistress, who nodded encouragement. "Then why are my soldiers in Germany digging ditches or dying on the eastern front? Why no meetings with Kesselring? Why are decisions being made about Italy without its president at the table? Why won't Hitler pick up the goddamned phone?"

The dictator shouted the last question. Leyers seemed unruffled as Pino translated.

Leyers said, "I can't presume to know why the führer hasn't taken your calls, Duce, but fighting wars on three fronts is a busy business."

"I know why Hitler won't take my goddamned calls!" Mussolini bellowed, and slammed his glass on the table. He glared at the general and then Pino in a way that made Pino wonder if he should retreat a step or two. "Who is the most hated man in all of Italy?" Mussolini said, directing the question at Pino.

Flustered, Pino didn't know what to say, but then started to translate.

Mussolini cut him off, still talking to Pino, slapping his chest and saying, "Il Duce is the most hated man in Italy, just like Hitler is the most hated man in Germany. But, you see, Hitler, he does not care. Il Duce cares about his people's love, but Hitler doesn't give a dog's turd for love. All he cares about is fear."

Pino was doing his best to keep up when the dictator seemed to come to some kind of revelation. "Clara, do you know why the most hated man in Italy is not in control of his own country?"

His mistress stubbed out a cigarette, blew smoke, then said, "Adolf Hitler."

"That's right!" Il Duce cried. "It's because the most hated man in Germany hates the most hated man in Italy! It's because Hitler treats his Nazi shepherd dogs better than he treats the president of Italy! Keeps me locked up in the middle of—"

"I don't have time for this madness," General Leyers snapped at Pino. "Tell him I will see about a meeting with Field Marshal Kesselring in the next few days, and to expect a call from the führer within the week. It's the best I can do for now."

Pino translated, expecting another explosion from Mussolini.

Instead, these concessions seemed to please the dictator, who began to button his tunic, saying, "How soon with Kesselring?"

"I am on my way to meet with him now, Duce," Leyers said. "I'll have his aide call before nightfall. Herr Hitler's attention may take a little longer to attract."

Mussolini nodded in a statesmanlike manner, as if he'd gained back some of his illusory power and now planned to use it on the cosmos.

"Very good, General Leyers," Mussolini said, checking his cuffs. "I shall have the strikes ended before nightfall."

Leyers clicked his heels, dropped his head, and said, "I'm sure the field marshal and the führer will be pleased. Thank you again for your time and influence, Duce."

The general pivoted and strode away. Pino hesitated, not quite sure what to do, and then bowed quickly to Mussolini and to Claretta Petacci before bolting after Leyers, who had disappeared around the corner and onto the colonnade. He caught up to him and walked at the general's right shoulder until they'd almost reached the staff car, when he hurried ahead and opened the rear door.

General Leyers hesitated, studied Pino for several seconds before saying, "Well done, Vorarbeiter."

"Thank you, *mon général*," Pino sputtered.

"Now get me out of this insane asylum," Leyers said, and climbed inside. "Take me to the telephone exchange in Milan. Do you know it?"

"Yes, of course, *mon général*," Pino said.

Leyers unlocked the valise and engrossed himself in his work. Pino drove in silence, glancing at the rearview mirror and arguing with himself. When the general had complimented him, he'd swelled with pride. But now he was wondering why. Leyers was a Nazi, a slave driver, a master builder of war. How could Pino feel pride when the compliment had come from someone like that? He couldn't. He shouldn't. And yet he had, and it bothered him.

By the time they reached the outskirts of Milan, however, Pino had decided to feel proud of how much he'd learned driving General Leyers for little more than half a day. His uncle wouldn't believe it. He'd actually talked to Mussolini and Claretta Petacci! How many spies in Italy could say that?

Pino took the route Hannibal had followed with his war elephants and got them to Piazzale Loreto in record time. He took the roundabout, seeing Mr. Beltramini at his post out in front of the fruit and vegetable stand where he was helping an older woman. Pino wanted to wave as he went by, but when he tried to take a right, a German lorry cut him off. They almost crashed. He was able to swerve the staff car out of the way in the nick of time.

He couldn't believe the driver had done that. Hadn't they seen—?

The flags. He'd forgotten to put up the general's flags upon entering Milan. He'd have to make another loop around the rotary. As he did, he saw Carletto walking on the sidewalk toward one of his favorite cafés.

Pino sped up, made the turn onto Viale Abruzzi without incident, and was soon parked at the telephone exchange, which was heavily guarded. The heavy Nazi presence puzzled him at first, until he thought that he who controlled the telephone exchange controlled communication.

"I have two hours of work to do here," General Leyers said. "You do not have to wait. No one would dare touch the car here. Be back at seventeen hundred hours."

"Oui, mon général," Pino said, and opened the rear door.

<hr/>

He waited until Leyers was inside, and then headed back toward Piazzale Loreto and Beltramini's Fresh Fruits and Vegetables. In less than a block, he'd endured enough vile looks to realize he'd be smart to take off the swastika armband and stick it in his back pocket.

That made things better. People barely gave him a glance. He was in uniform, and he wasn't SS or Wehrmacht. That was all they would care about.

He broke into a trot. He could see Mr. Beltramini, right there up ahead, putting grapes in a sack. But he really wanted to see Carletto. It had been four months, and he had so much to tell his old friend.

Pino cut across the street in front of German lorries traveling in a convoy, and took a right. Scanning the sidewalk ahead, he found Carletto sitting with his back to him.

Pino broke into a grin, walked up, and saw Carletto was reading. He pulled back a chair and sat down, saying, "Hope you're not waiting for an elegant young lady."

Carletto looked up. At first his friend looked wearier and more scarred than Pino remembered even in late April. But then Carletto recognized him and cried out, "Oh my God, Pino! I thought you were dead!"

He jumped up and hugged Pino fiercely. Then he pushed Pino back to look at him with misty eyes. "I really did."

"Who said I was dead?"

"Someone told Papa you were guarding the Modena train station when a bomb hit. They said part of your head was taken off! I was devastated."

"No, no!" Pino said. "That was the guy with me. I almost lost these."

He showed him the bandaged hand and wiggled the reattached fingers.

Carletto clapped him on the shoulder and grinned. "Just knowing you are alive," he said. "I think I'm happier than I've ever been!"

"Good to be back from the dead." Pino smiled. "You ordered?"

"Just espresso," Carletto said, taking his seat again.

"Let's eat," Pino said. "I got paid before I left the hospital, so it's on me."

That made his old friend even happier, and they ordered melon balls wrapped in prosciutto, salami, bread, garlic-infused olive oil, and a cold tomato soup that was perfect in the stifling heat. As they waited for their meal to arrive, Pino caught up on the last four months of Carletto's life.

Because of Mr. Beltramini's contacts outside the city, his fruit and vegetable stand continued to prosper. It was one of the few places in the city that had a reliable flow of produce, and it often sold out before closing. Carletto's mother was another story.

"Some days are better than others, but she's weak all the time," Carletto said. Pino could see the strain on him. "She got real sick last month. Pneumonia. Papa was heartbroken, thinking she was going, but somehow she rallied and beat it."

"That's good," Pino said as the waiter started setting plates on the table. His eyes drifted past Carletto, back toward the fruit stand. Between gaps in the German lorry convoy, he caught glimpses of Mr. Beltramini serving a customer.

"So, is that the new Fascist uniform, Pino?" Carletto asked. "I don't think I've seen it before."

Pino started chewing the inside of his cheek. He'd been so ashamed of enlisting in the German army, he'd never told his friend about the Organization Todt.

Carletto went on. "And why were you in Modena? Everyone I know is headed north."

"It's complicated," Pino said, wanting to change the subject.

"What's that mean?" his friend asked, eating one of the melon balls.

"Can you keep a secret?" Pino said.

"What are best friends for?"

"Right," Pino said, then leaned forward and whispered. "This afternoon, Carletto. Not two hours ago. I talked to Mussolini and Claretta Petacci."

Carletto sat back skeptically. "You're making that up."

"No, I am not. I swear."

A car honked on the rotary.

A bicyclist carrying a messenger bag shot by them, so close to their table Pino swore he was going to hit Carletto, who jerked to one side to avoid him.

"Idiot!" Carletto said, twisting around in his chair. "He's riding on the sidewalk against traffic. He's going to hurt someone!"

Seeing the bicyclist from the rear now, Pino noticed a patch of red sticking up from beneath his dark shirt, right at the neckline. He wove through and around pedestrians crowding the sidewalk as three more lorries in the long German convoy began to make the slow turn onto congested Viale Abruzzi. The bicyclist tugged the messenger bag off his shoulder. With his left hand on the handlebar and his right holding the bag's strap, he curved the bike onto Viale Abruzzi and came right up behind one of the lorries.

Pino realized what was about to happen, jumped up, and yelled, "No!"

The bicyclist lobbed the bag up through the canvas cover and into the back of the lorry before streaking away.

Mr. Beltramini had seen the toss, too. He was standing right there, not six meters away, his hands starting to rise a split second before the vehicle exploded in a pluming ball of fire.

The force of the blast punched Pino and Carletto from a block away. Pino dove to the ground, protecting his head from debris and shrapnel.

"Papa!" Carletto screamed.

Cut up and ignoring the blast material raining down on Piazzale Loreto, Carletto sprinted toward the fire, toward the incinerated skeleton of the troop transport, and toward his father, sprawled across the sidewalk beneath the tatters of the fruit stand's awning.

Carletto got to his father before Wehrmacht soldiers from other lorries fanned out to control the area. Two of them blocked Pino's way until he pulled out the red armband and put it on, showing them the swastika.

"I am General Leyers's aide," he said in halting German. "I must get through."

They let him pass. Pino ran from the heat of the still-burning lorry, aware of people screaming and moaning, but caring only about Carletto, who knelt on the sidewalk with his father's scorched and bloody head in his lap. Mr. Beltramini's smock was blackened from the blast and lathered with more blood, but he was alive. His eyes were open, and he was breathing with great difficulty.

Choking back tears, Carletto looked up, saw Pino, and said, "Get an ambulance."

Pino heard sirens wailing in all directions, closing on Piazzale Loreto.

"They're coming," he said, and squatted down. Mr. Beltramini was taking big ragged breaths and twitching.

"Don't move, Papa," Carletto said.

"Your mother," Mr. Beltramini said, his eyes lazing. "You've got to care for . . ."

"Quiet, Papa," his son said, weeping and stroking his father's singed hair.

Mr. Beltramini coughed and hacked, and had to have been in such hideous pain that Pino tried to distract him with some pleasant memory.

"Mr. Beltramini, do you remember that night on the hill when my father played violin and you sang to your wife?" Pino asked.

"*Nessun Dorma,*" he said in a whisper, went far away in his thoughts, and smiled.

"You sang *con smania* and never sounded better," Pino said.

For a moment or two, the three of them were a universe unto themselves, outside all the pain and horror, back on a rural hillside, sharing a more innocent time. Then Pino heard the clanging of the ambulances much closer. He thought to get up to find a medic. But when he tried to stand, Mr. Beltramini clutched at his sleeve.

Carletto's father was staring in bewilderment at the lurid armband Pino wore. "A Nazi?" he choked.

"No, Mr. Beltramini—"

"Traitor?" the fruitmonger said, overwhelmed. "Pino?"

"No, Mr.—"

Mr. Beltramini coughed again and hacked, and this time brought up dark blood that spilled over his chin as he lolled his head back toward Carletto, gazing at his son and wordlessly moving his lips. And then he just eased away, as if his spirit had accepted death, yet lingered, not struggling, but in no hurry to be gone.

Carletto broke down sobbing. Pino did, too.

His friend rocked his father and began to keen with grief. The agony of his loss built and swelled with every breath until it seemed to contort every muscle and bone in Carletto's body.

"I'm sorry," Pino cried. "Oh, Carletto, I'm so damned sorry. I loved him, too."

Carletto stopped rocking his father, looked up at Pino, blind with hatred. "Don't say that!" he shouted. "Don't ever say that! You Nazi! You traitor!"

Pino's jaw felt like it had been broken in twenty places.

"No," he said. "It's not what it looks—"

"Get away from me!" Carletto screamed. "My father saw it. He knew what you are. He showed it to me!"

"Carletto, it's just an armband."

"Leave me alone! I never want to see you again! Ever!"

Carletto dropped his chin and broke down over his father's dead body, his shoulders trembling and tortured sounds hacking up from his chest. Pino was so overwhelmed that he couldn't say a thing. He stood up finally and stepped back.

"Move on," a German officer said. "Clear the sidewalk for the ambulances."

Pino took one last look at the Beltraminis before walking south toward the telephone exchange, feeling like the blast had cut out part of his heart.

That sense of loss still tortured Pino seven hours later when he parked the Daimler in front of Dolly Stottlemeyer's apartment building. General Leyers got out, handed Pino his briefcase, and said, "You've had quite the first day."

"Oui, mon général."

"You're sure you saw a red scarf around the bomber's neck?"

"He had it tucked beneath his shirt, but yes."

The general hardened and entered the building with Pino lugging the valise, which had only gotten heavier since morning. The old crone was right where they'd left her, sitting on her stool and blinking at them from behind those thick glasses. Leyers never gave her a glance, just charged up the stairs to Dolly's apartment and knocked.

Anna opened the door, and at the sight of her, Pino's heart mended a little.

"Dolly's held dinner for you, General," Anna said as he moved past her.

Despite everything that had happened to Pino that day, seeing Anna again was as dazzling an experience as it had been the first two times. The pain of seeing Mr. Beltramini die and losing his friend endured, but he had faith that if he could tell Anna about it all, somehow she'd make it make sense.

"Are you coming in, Vorarbeiter?" Anna asked impatiently. "Or are you just going to stand there staring at me?"

Pino startled, moved past her, and said, "I wasn't staring."

"Of course you were."

"No, I was somewhere else. In my mind."

She said nothing and closed the door.

Dolly came into view at the other end of the hall. The general's mistress wore black stiletto heels, black silk hosiery, and a tight black skirt below a pearl-colored short-sleeve blouse. Her hair looked freshly coiffed.

"The general says you saw the bombing?" Dolly said, lighting a cigarette.

He nodded and put the valise on the bench, feeling Anna's attention on him, too.

"How many dead?" Dolly asked, and took a puff.

"Many Germans, and . . . and several Milanese," he said.

"Must have been horrid," Dolly said.

General Leyers appeared again. His tie was gone. He said something in German to Dolly, who nodded and looked to Anna. "The general would like to eat."

188

"Of course, Dolly," Anna said, glanced at Pino again, hurried down the hallway, and disappeared.

Leyers walked toward Pino, studying him, before picking up the valise. "Return at oh seven hundred sharp."

"*Oui, mon général,*" he said, and stood there.

"You are dismissed, Vorarbeiter."

Pino wanted to linger, to see if Anna might reappear, but instead he saluted and left.

He drove the Daimler back to the motor pool, trying to replay his day, but his mind kept lurching between images of Mr. Beltramini dying, Carletto's grief-driven rage, and the look Anna had given him before leaving the front hall.

Then he remembered his encounter with Mussolini and his mistress, and as he gave the night sentry the keys to the Daimler and walked on through the streets of San Babila toward home, he wondered if he'd hallucinated them. The August night air was thick and warm. The smells of fine cuisine dueled in the air, and many Nazi officers sat at outdoor cafés, drinking and carousing.

Pino reached Albanese Luggage and went around back to the sewing room entrance. When his uncle answered his knock, he felt waves of emotion.

"Well?" Uncle Albert said after he'd come inside. "How did it go?"

Raw grief burst out of Pino. "I don't even know where to start," he cried.

"What in God's name happened?"

"Can I eat something? I haven't had a thing since morning."

"Of course, of course. Greta has saffron risotto waiting for you, and once you've eaten, you can tell us everything, right from the beginning."

Pino wiped at his tears. He hated that he'd cried in front of his uncle, but the emotions had just come over him, or out of him, like a pipe bursting. Wordlessly, he ate two helpings of his aunt's risotto, and then described everything that had happened to him during the course of his day with General Leyers.

They were shocked by his description of the slaves in the rail tunnel, though Uncle Albert said they'd been getting reports of the Germans taking factories and ammo dumps underground.

"You really went to Mussolini's house?" Aunt Greta said.

"To his villa," Pino said. "He and Claretta Petacci were there."

"No."

"Yes," Pino insisted, and repeated what he'd heard about the factory strikes being resolved in return for Mussolini's getting a seat at Kesselring's table, and the promise of a phone call from Adolf Hitler. Then he recounted the worst of it: how Mr. Beltramini died thinking Pino was a traitor, and how his best friend never wanted to see him again because he was a Nazi, a disgrace.

"Not true," Uncle Albert said, looking up from the pad where he'd taken notes. "You're a quiet hero for getting this information. I'll get it to Baka, and he'll transmit what you've seen to the Allies."

"But I can't tell Carletto," Pino said. "And his father—"

"I hate to be blunt about it, Pino, but I don't care. Your position is too valuable and sensitive to risk telling anyone. You're just going to have to swallow all that for now, and have faith that your friendship will come back when you're able to reveal all. I'm serious, Pino. You're a spy behind enemy lines. Take every insult someone may hurl at you, ignore it, and stay as close to Leyers as you can, for as long as you can."

Pino nodded, but without enthusiasm. "So you think what I found out helps?"

Uncle Albert snorted. "We now know of a large ammo dump inside a tunnel near Como. We know the Nazis are using slaves. And we know Mussolini is a eunuch, powerless and frustrated because Hitler won't take his calls. What more could I expect on day one?"

Pino felt good about that and yawned. "I need to sleep. He expects me early."

He hugged them both, went downstairs and through the small factory. The alley door opened. Baka, the radio operator, came in, looked at Pino, and studied his uniform.

"It's complicated," Pino said, and left.

His father had gone to bed by the time Pino walked home and went through a quick security check in the lobby. He set his alarm, stripped, and collapsed on his bed. Terrible images, thoughts, and emotions created a whirlwind in his mind that had him sure he'd never sleep again.

But when he was finally able to limit his spiraling memories to Anna, he felt soothed, and with the maid firmly in his mind, he slipped off into darkness.

Chapter Seventeen

August 9, 1944
6:45 a.m.

Pino jumped from the Daimler he'd parked on Via Dante. He went into Dolly's building, hurried past the blinking old crone and up the stairs, eager to knock on the general's mistress's door.

He was disappointed when Dolly answered. General Leyers was already in the hallway, drinking coffee from a china cup and looking eager to leave.

Pino went and got the valise, still not seeing the maid, and turned back toward Dolly and the apartment door, feeling even more disappointed.

Dolly called out, "Anna? The general needs his food."

A moment later, and to Pino's nervous delight, the maid appeared with the thermos and a brown paper bag. The general headed toward the apartment door. Pino went to Anna and said, "I'll take them."

Anna actually smiled at him as she handed him the thermos, which he slid under one arm before accepting the lunch bag.

"Have a nice day," she said. "And be safe."

He grinned and said, "I'll do my best."

"Vorarbeiter!" General Leyers barked.

Pino startled, spun around, and grabbed the valise. He hurried after Leyers, past Dolly, who held the apartment door open, and gave him a knowing look as he left.

Leyers had a four-hour meeting with Field Marshal Kesselring at the German House that morning. Pino was not invited to the table. The general appeared irritated and upset when he emerged after noon and told Pino to drive him to the telephone exchange.

Pino sat in the Daimler or lounged near it, mad with boredom. He wanted to go somewhere to eat but did not want to leave the car. He was mere blocks from Piazzale Loreto, and debated whether he should go find Carletto, tell him enough that he didn't think him a traitor anymore. It would make Pino feel better, but should—?

He heard a voice calling over a loudspeaker and coming closer.

An SS vehicle with five speakers on top came rolling down Viale Abruzzi.

"A warning to all citizens of Milan," a man brayed in Italian. "The cowardly bombing of German soldiers yesterday will not stand. Turn the bomber in today, or face punishment tomorrow. Repeat: A warning to all citizens of Milan . . ."

Pino was so hungry he felt hollow and jittery as he watched the vehicle go by and heard the echoes of the loudspeakers as it went up and down the streets that fanned off Piazalle Loreto. German soldiers came past him midafternoon, nailing printed copies of the same warning about the bomber on telephone poles and gluing others to the sides of buildings.

Three hours later, General Leyers stormed from the telephone exchange and looked furious when he climbed into the backseat of the Daimler. Pino had not eaten since six that morning, and he felt lightheaded and nervous getting into the driver's seat.

"Verdammte Idioten," Leyers said in a cutting voice. *"Verdammte Idioten."*

Pino had no idea what it meant, and glanced in the rearview in time to see General Leyers pound the seat with his fist three times. It left him red faced and sweaty, and Pino looked away for fear the general would turn his anger on him.

In the backseat, Leyers was taking deep breaths. When Pino at last looked again in the mirror, he saw the general: eyes closed, hands across his chest, his breathing slow and even. Was he sleeping?

Pino didn't know what to do other than to wait and swallow at the hunger that had him shaking.

Ten minutes later, General Leyers said, "The chancellery. Do you know it?"

Pino looked in the rearview, saw Leyers's unreadable face had returned. *"Oui, mon général."* He wanted to ask when he might stop to get something to eat but held his tongue.

"Take down my flags. This is not an official visit."

━━◆━━

Pino did as he was asked, started the car, and put it in gear, wondering what the general wanted at the chancellery. He kept glancing at Leyers as he wove through the city to Via Pattari. But the general seemed lost in thought and revealed nothing.

By the time they reached the chancellery gate, the sun had set. There were no guards, and Leyers told him to pull through to park. Pino drove on into a cobblestoned courtyard surrounded by two-story colonnades. He shut off the Daimler and climbed out. A fountain bubbled at the center of the courtyard. Dusk fell in a listless heat.

Pino opened the door for General Leyers, who stepped out. "I may need you."

Pino wondered whom they were talking to tonight. Then it seemed obvious, and his heart began to pound. They were going to talk with Schuster. The cardinal of Milan had a legendary memory. He would recall Pino as surely as Colonel Rauff had, but unlike the Gestapo chief, the cardinal would remember his name. Cardinal Schuster would also see the swastika and judge him severely, probably damn him to some eternal misery.

General Leyers took a left at the top of the stairs, went to a heavy wooden door, and knocked. It was opened by an older priest, who seemed to recognize Leyers with distaste, but stood aside to let him in. The priest gave Pino the evil eye as he passed.

They went down a paneled hallway to an ornate and impressive sitting room with Catholic iconography sewn into fifteenth-century tapestries, carved into thirteenth-century crucifixes, and cast at every turn in gold and gilt. The only thing not Italianate in the room was the desk, where a short, bald man in a simple crème-colored cassock and red skullcap was writing with his back to Pino and Leyers. Cardinal Schuster seemed unaware of them until the priest knocked on the door frame. Schuster stopped writing for a moment, but then wrote on another four or five seconds, finishing his thought before he looked up, and turned.

Leyers removed his hat. Pino reluctantly did the same. The general walked toward Schuster, but spoke to Pino over his shoulder. "Tell the cardinal that I appreciate his willingness to see me on such short notice, but it is important."

Pino tried to stay behind the general's shoulder where it would be more difficult for the cardinal to see him clearly, and translated Leyers's words into Italian.

Schuster leaned over, trying to see Pino. "Ask the general how I can help him."

Pino looked at the rug and translated into French, which caused the cardinal to interrupt. "I can summon a priest who speaks German if he wishes to make communication easier."

Pino told Leyers.

The general shook his head. "I don't want to take up his time or mine unnecessarily."

Pino told Schuster that Leyers was happy with the interpreting as it stood.

The cardinal shrugged, and Leyers said, "Your Eminence, I'm sure you have heard that fifteen German soldiers were killed in a partisan bombing in Piazzale Loreto yesterday. And I'm sure you know that Colonel Rauff and the Gestapo want the bomber turned in before dawn, or the city faces harsh repercussions."

"I do," Cardinal Schuster said. "How harsh?"

"Any act of violence upon German soldiers by partisans will be countered by an appropriate act of violence on local males," the general said. "The decision was not mine, I assure you. General Wolff has that dishonor."

Pino was shocked as he translated, and saw that the potential repercussions had the same impact on Schuster's face.

The cardinal said, "If the Nazis follow that path, you will turn the population against you, harden the resistance. They'll show you no mercy in the end."

"I agree, Your Eminence, and have said so," General Leyers said. "But my voice isn't being heard here or in Berlin."

The cardinal asked, "What do you want me to do?"

"I don't know that there's much you can do, Your Eminence, other than to ask the bomber to surrender before punishment is imposed."

Schuster was lost in thought for a moment before saying, "When will that happen?"

"Tomorrow."

"Thank you for informing me personally, General Leyers," the cardinal said.

"Your Eminence," Leyers said, bowed his head, clicked his heels, and pivoted toward the door, exposing Pino to Schuster.

The cardinal gazed at Pino with an inkling of recognition.

"My Lord Cardinal," Pino said in Italian. "Please do not tell General Leyers you know me. I'm not what you think I am. I beg you, have mercy on my soul."

The cleric looked puzzled but nodded. Pino bowed, and walked away, following Leyers back out into the chancellery's courtyard and thinking about what he'd just heard inside.

Repercussions in the morning? That wasn't good. What would the Germans do? Appropriate acts of violence on adult males? That was what he'd said, wasn't it?

When they reached the car, Leyers said, "What were you and the cardinal saying at the end?"

Pino said, "I was wishing him a good evening, *mon général.*"

Leyers studied him a moment before saying, "Dolly's, then. I've done all I can."

Although Pino was upset about the pending repercussions, he thought of Anna and drove as fast as he dared through the winding streets around the cathedral until he reached Dolly Stottlemeyer's apartment building. He parked, opened the rear door, and tried to take the valise.

"I'll bring it up," the general said. "Stay with the car. We may go out again later."

That blew the wind out of Pino's lungs.

If Leyers caught his disappointment, he didn't show it as he disappeared through the front door. Only then did Pino's hunger pangs return with a vengeance. What was he supposed to do? Never eat? Never drink?

Miserable, Pino looked up the face of the building, saw slivers of light showing through the blackout curtains across Dolly's windows. Was Anna disappointed? Well, she had definitely smiled at him that morning, and it had been more than your ordinary, run-of-the-mill smile, too, hadn't it? In Pino's mind,

Anna's smile had spoken of attraction, possibility, and hope. She'd told him to be safe and used his name, hadn't she?

In any case, Pino wasn't going to get to see her. Not tonight. Tonight he had to sleep in a car and starve. His heart felt heavy, and then heavier still when thunder drummed. He got the Daimler's canvas top up and snapped down before the rain came in torrents. He slumped in the driver's seat, deafened by the storm and feeling sorry for himself. Was he supposed to sleep out here all night? No food? No water?

A half hour passed, and then an hour. The rain had slowed, but it still pattered off the roof. Pino's stomach was aching, and he thought of driving to his uncle's to report and get some food. But what if Leyers came down and he was gone? What if—?

The front passenger-side door opened.

Holding a basket of delicious-smelling food, Anna climbed inside.

"Dolly thought you might be hungry," she said, closing the door. "I was sent to feed you and keep you company while you ate."

Pino smiled. "General's orders?"

"Dolly's orders," Anna said, peering around. "It will be easier to eat in the backseat, I think."

"That's the general's territory."

"He's busy in Dolly's bedroom," she said, climbed out, opened the back door, and got in. "He should be in there for a long while, if not the night."

Pino laughed, threw open the door, ducked through the rain, and climbed into the back. Anna set the basket where the general usually put his valise. She lit a small candle and set it on a plate. The light flickered, making the staff car's interior golden as she drew back a towel over the basket to reveal two roasted chicken legs with thighs, fresh bread, real butter, and a glass of red wine.

"I have been delivered," Pino said, which made Anna laugh.

On another night, he might have gazed at her as she laughed, but he was so hungry he just chuckled and ate. As he did, he asked her questions, learning that Anna was from Trieste, she had worked for Dolly for fourteen months, and she had gotten the job through a friend who saw Dolly's ad in the newspaper.

"You don't know how much I needed that," he said, finishing his meal. "I was ravenous. Like a wolf."

Anna laughed. "I thought I heard someone howling outside."

"Is that your whole name?" he asked. "Anna?"

"I also go by Anna-Marta."

"No last name?"

"Not anymore," the maid said, cooling, and repacking the basket. "And I must be going."

"Wait," Pino said. "Can't you stay just a little longer? I don't think I've ever met anyone as lovely and elegant as you."

She made a dismissive flip of her hand but smiled. "Listen to you."

"It's true."

"How old are you now, Pino?"

"Old enough to wear a uniform and carry a gun," he said, annoyed. "Old enough to do things that I can't talk about."

"Like what?" she said, sounding interested.

"I can't talk about it," Pino insisted.

Anna blew out the candle, leaving them in darkness. "Then I must go."

Before Pino could protest, she climbed out of the Daimler and shut the door behind her. Pino struggled out of the backseat in time to see her shadow going up the steps to the front door of the apartment building.

"*Buona notte, signorina Anna-Marta,*" Pino said.

"Good night, Vorarbeiter Lella," Anna said, and went inside.

The rain had stopped, and he stood there a long while, looking at that spot where she'd disappeared and reliving every moment of his time in the backseat of the staff car, with her smell all around. He noticed it after the food was gone, when she'd laughed that he'd been hungry as a wolf. Had there ever been anything that smelled like that? Had there ever been a woman who looked like that? So beautiful. So mysterious.

At last he climbed back into the driver's seat and pulled his cap down over his eyes. His thoughts still on her, he questioned everything he'd said to her and dissected her every word as if they were clues to the puzzle of Anna. The horror of Mr. Beltramini's death, being branded a traitor—all these things had vanished from his consciousness. All he knew until sleep took him was the maid.

A sharp rap came at the window, waking Pino. It was barely cracking light. The back door opened. His first happy thought was that Anna had come down to feed him again. But when he looked over his shoulder, he saw the silhouette of General Leyers.

"Fly my flags," Leyers said. "Get me to San Vittore Prison. We don't have much time."

Going for the glove compartment and the flags, Pino fought off a yawn and said, "What time is it, *mon général?*"

"Five a.m.," he barked. "So move!"

Pino bolted from the staff car, mounted the flags, and then drove fast through the city, relying on the flags to get them quickly through checkpoints until they arrived at notorious San Vittore. Built in the 1870s, the prison had six three-story wings connected to a central hub. When San Vittore opened, it was state-of-the-art, but seventy-four years of neglect on, it was a nasty starfish of cells and halls where men fought for their lives every moment of every day. Now that it was under Gestapo rule, Pino couldn't name a place he feared more besides the Hotel Regina.

On Via Vico, which paralleled the prison's high eastern wall, they confronted two lorries stopped by an open gate. The first lorry was backing up through the gate. The other idled on the street, blocking the way.

Dawn glowed over the city when General Leyers got out and slammed the door. Pino jumped out and followed Leyers as he crossed the street and went through the gate with the guards saluting. They went into a large triangular yard that narrowed where the walls of two opposing arms of the prison joined the central hub.

Four steps beyond the gate, Pino stopped to take it all in. Eight armed Waffen-SS soldiers stood about twenty-five meters to his left at ten o'clock. In front of them was an SS captain. Beside the captain, Gestapo Colonel Walter Rauff held a black riding crop behind his back and watched with great interest. Leyers went to Rauff and the captain.

Pino hung back, not wanting Rauff to notice him.

The flaps at the back of the lorry opened. A squad from the Muti Legion of the Black Brigades climbed out. Fanatically dedicated to Mussolini, the elite Fascist commandos wore black turtlenecks, despite the warm air, and jawless death-head symbols on their hats and chests.

"Are you ready?" the SS captain said in Italian.

A Black Shirt brushed past Pino as he called, "Bring them out."

The guards split into two groups of four and moved to open doors set in the walls of the prison wings. Prisoners began to shuffle out. Pino moved, trying to see the men better. Some of them looked like they couldn't handle another step. Those that looked fitter had beards and such long hair that he didn't know if he'd recognize anyone he knew.

Then, from the left-hand door, a tall, imposing young man appeared in the yard. Pino recognized him as Barbareschi, the seminarian, aide to Cardinal Schuster and forger for the resistance. Barbareschi must have been caught and arrested again. Though other men shuffled into a loose formation, staring fearfully at the Black Shirt commandos, Barbareschi went defiantly to the front row.

"How many?" Colonel Rauff said.

"One forty-eight," one of the guards yelled back.

"Two more," Rauff said.

The last man out the right-hand door tossed his head to get the hair from his eyes. "Tullio!" Pino gasped softly.

Tullio Galimberti didn't hear him. Over the sounds of the last men moving into place, no one did. Tullio trudged out of sight behind the lorry. The Black Shirt commander stepped forward. General Leyers confronted Colonel Rauff and the SS captain. Pino could see and hear them arguing. Rauff finally gestured with the riding crop at the Black Shirt and said something that shut Leyers down.

The Fascist commander pointed to his far left and shouted, "You there, start counting off in tens. Every tenth man step forward."

After a moment's pause, the man farthest left said, "One."

"Two," said the second.

It went on down the line until one of the weaker-looking men said, "Ten," and stepped uncertainly forward.

"One," said the eleventh man.

"Two," said the twelfth.

A moment later, Barbareschi said, "Eight."

The second tenth man stepped forward, and soon the third. They were joined by twelve more, all of them standing shoulder to shoulder in front of the assembled prisoners. The count still ongoing, Pino stood on his tiptoes, remembering some of the conversation General Leyers had had with Cardinal Schuster.

To his horror, he heard Tullio say, "Ten," becoming the fifteenth man.

"You fifteen in the lorry," a Black Shirt said. "The rest of you return to your cells."

Pino didn't know what to do, torn between wanting to go to General Leyers and to Tullio. But if he went to Leyers and admitted Tullio was his close friend, and Tullio was in San Vittore for spying for the resistance, wouldn't he begin to suspect—?

"What are you doing in here, Vorarbeiter?" Leyers demanded.

Pino had been so mesmerized by the unfolding scene that he'd lost track of Leyers, who now stood beside him, glaring.

"I'm sorry, *mon général*," Pino said. "I thought you might need a translator?"

"Go to the car, now," Leyers said. "Bring it up after this lorry exits."

Pino saluted, then ran out through the prison gates to the Daimler and climbed in. The lorry parked outside San Vittore began to roll. Pino started the staff car just as the first sun hit the prison's upper walls and around the arch of the gate. In the shadows below, the lorry bearing Tullio and the other fourteen emerged and followed.

Pino drove up to the gate. The general didn't bother waiting for him to open the door. He climbed into the back, his face twisted in barely controlled fury.

"Mon général?" Pino asked after they'd sat there a moment.

"The hell with it," Leyers said. "Follow them, Vorarbeiter."

<hr />

The Daimler quickly caught up to the lorries as they lumbered through the city. Pino wanted to ask the general what was happening. He wanted to tell him about Tullio, but didn't dare.

As he drove around the piazza in front of the Duomo, he glanced up at the highest spire on the cathedral, saw it embraced by the sun while the gargoyles on the lower flanks of the church remained in the deepest of dark shadows. The sight troubled him deeply.

"Mon général?" Pino said. "I know you said not to speak, but can you tell me what is going to happen to the men in that lorry?"

Leyers didn't answer. Pino glanced in the mirror, feared a tongue-lashing, but found the general looking coldly at him.

Leyers said, "Your ancestors invented what's going to happen."

"Mon général?"

"The ancient Romans called it 'decimation,' Vorarbeiter. They used it throughout their empire. The problem with decimation is that the tactic never works for long."

"I don't understand."

"Decimation functions psychologically," Leyers explained. "It's designed to quell the threat of revolt through abject fear. But historically, using brutality against civilians in reprisal breeds more hatred than obedience."

Brutality? Pino thought. *Reprisals? The violent acts Leyers warned the cardinal about?* What were they going to do to Tullio and the others? Would telling General Leyers that Tullio was his close friend help or—?

In the streets parallel to them, he heard the blaring of loudspeakers. The man spoke in Italian, calling "all concerned citizens" to Piazzale Loreto.

Two companies of Black Shirt Fascists had cordoned off the rotary. But they waved the lorries and General Leyers's car through. The lorries drove toward Beltramini's Fresh Fruits and Vegetables, stopped just shy of it, backed up, and turned so the vehicles' backs faced the blank common wall where several buildings joined.

"Drive on around the rotary," Leyers said.

As Pino drove past the fruit stand, the awning still torn, he flashed on the bomb going off there. He was shocked to see Carletto coming out of the shop, staring at the lorries, and then starting to look his way.

Pino hit the accelerator and got quickly out of sight. Three-quarters of the way around the rotary, Leyers ordered Pino to pull into the Esso station, the one with the big iron girder system above the petrol pumps. An attendant came out nervously.

"Tell him to fill the tank and that we are going to park here," Leyers said.

Pino told the man, who looked at the general's flags and scurried away.

With the loudspeakers still calling, the people of Milan came at a trickle of a curious few at first, but then the flow of new arrivals built to a steady stream of pedestrians, coming into Piazzale Loreto from all directions.

Black Shirts put up wooden barriers from the fruit stand west thirty meters and to either side of the lorries heading north forty-five meters. As a result, there was a large open space around the lorries with a crowd building at the fences.

Pino soon figured there were a thousand people, maybe more. Halfway between the 150 meters that separated the Daimler from Tullio's lorry, a second Nazi staff car appeared, pulled to the edge of the rotary, and stopped. From this distance and angle, Pino could not tell who was in the car. More people streamed into the piazza, so many that they soon blocked the view.

"I can't see," General Leyers said.

"Non, mon général," Pino said.

Leyers paused, looked out the window, and said, "Can you climb?"

A minute later, Pino stepped off the top of the petrol pump and pulled himself up onto one of the low girders. He held tight to an iron post and a second girder at head height.

"Can you see?" General Leyers asked from below, standing by the staff car.

"Oui, mon général." Pino had a clear, unobstructed view over the heads of the fifteen hundred people now in the piazza. The lorries were still there, flaps closed.

"Help me up there," Leyers said.

Pino looked down, saw the general had already climbed onto one of the pumps, his hand outstretched. Pino helped hoist him up. Leyers hung on to the overhead cross girder while Pino hugged the post.

In the distance, the Duomo's bells rang the hour nine times. The Black Shirt commander from the prison yard climbed down from the cab of the nearby lorry. The Fascist disappeared from Pino's view behind the other lorry, the one holding the prisoners.

Soon the fifteen began to stream out, one by one, going to the wall to the right of the fruit stand, shoulder to shoulder, facing toward the crowd, which was growing uneasy. Tullio was the seventh man out. By then, Pino knew in his gut what was about to happen, if not how, and he had to wrap his arms around the steel post to keep from falling.

The empty lorry pulled away. The crowd gave it room, and the transport vehicle was soon gone onto the rotary. Hooded Black Shirt gunmen poured out the back of the other transport, and then it was driven away as well. Armed with machine pistols, the Fascist commandos lined up no more than fifteen meters from the prisoners.

A Black Shirt shouted, "Every time a Communist partisan kills a German soldier or a soldier of the Salò army, there will be swift punishment with no mercy."

The piazza fell quiet but for murmurs of disbelief.

One of the prisoners began shouting at the Fascists and the firing squad.

It was Tullio.

"You cowards!" Tullio roared at them. "You traitors! You do the Nazis' dirty work and hide your faces. You're all a bunch of—"

The machine pistols opened up, cutting Tullio down first. Pino's friend danced backward with the bullet impacts and then sprawled slack on the sidewalk.

Chapter Eighteen

Pino screamed and screamed into the crook of his arm as the shooting went on and more men fell. The crowd went mad, crying in horror and stampeding to get away from the machine gunners who sprayed the walls of Piazzale Loreto with blood and gore that dripped and pooled around the fifteen martyrs long after the gunfire had stopped.

Eyes closed, Pino slid down and straddled the lower girder, hearing the screams in Piazzale Loreto as if they were far away and muffled. *The world doesn't work like this,* he tried to tell himself. *The world is not sick and evil like this.*

He remembered Father Re summoning him to a higher cause, and then found himself reciting the Hail Mary, the prayer for the dead and the dying. He'd gotten to the last line, "Holy Mary, Mother of God, pray for us sinners, now and at the hour of our—"

"Vorarbeiter! God damn it!" General Leyers shouted. "Do you hear me?"

In a daze, Pino looked around and up at the Nazi, who was still standing on the girder, his face stony and cold.

"Get down," Leyers said. "We're leaving."

Pino's first thought was to pull the general's feet out from under him, have him fall on his back on concrete from more than four meters up. Then he'd jump down and strangle him with his bare hands just to make sure. Leyers had let this atrocity happen. He'd stood by when—

"I said *get down*."

Feeling like a part of his mind had been permanently burned, he did so. Leyers climbed down after him and got into the back of the Daimler. Pino shut his door and slid behind the wheel.

"Where to, *mon général?*" Pino asked numbly.

"Did you know one of them?" Leyers asked. "I heard you screaming."

Pino hesitated, his eyes welling with tears. "No," he said finally. "I've just never seen anything like that before."

The general studied him in the rearview mirror a moment before saying, "Go. There's nothing more to be done here."

The other German staff car was already turning around, heading for the checkpoint, when Pino started the Daimler. The rear window of the second staff car was down. He could see Colonel Rauff looking out at them. Pino wanted to floor the accelerator and T-bone the Gestapo chief's car. Rauff's vehicle would be no match for the Daimler. Maybe he'd even kill Rauff, make the world an infinitely better place.

General Leyers said, "Wait until they've gone ahead."

Pino watched Colonel Rauff disappear into the city before he started the Daimler.

"Where to, *mon général?*" he said again, unable to stop seeing Tullio rage against his executioners before dancing on the bullets that killed him.

"Hotel Regina," Leyers said.

Pino started in that direction. "If I may, *mon général*, what will happen to the bodies?"

"They'll lie there until dark, when their relatives can claim them."

"All day?"

"Colonel Rauff wants the rest of Milan, especially the partisans, to see what happens when German soldiers are killed," Leyers said as they left the checkpoint. "The savage idiots. Don't they see this will just increase the number of Italians who want to kill German soldiers? You, Vorarbeiter, do you want to kill Germans? Do you want to kill me?"

Pino was shocked by the question, and he wondered if the man could read his mind. But he shook his head, said, "*Non, mon général*. I want to live in peace and prosperity like anyone."

The Nazi's Plenipotentiary for War Production fell silent and pensive while Pino drove back to Gestapo headquarters. Leyers got out and said, "You have three hours."

———

Pino dreaded the task ahead, but he left the Daimler and tore off his swastika armband. He went to the new purse store, but the girl who worked there said his father had gone over to Albanese Luggage.

When Pino entered the leather goods shop, Michele, Uncle Albert, and Aunt Greta were the only ones inside.

His uncle saw him, rushed out from behind the counter. "Where the hell have you been? We've been worried sick!"

"You didn't come home," his father said. "Oh, thank God you're back."

Aunt Greta took one look at Pino and said, "What's happened?"

For a few moments, Pino couldn't say a word. Then he fought back tears as he said, "The Nazis and the Fascists, they did a decimation at San Vittore in retaliation for the bombing. They counted off every tenth man until they got fifteen. Then they took them to the Piazzale Loreto and machine-gunned them to death. I saw . . ." He broke down. "Tullio was one of them."

Uncle Albert and his father looked gut-shot.

Aunt Greta said, "That's not true! You must have seen someone else."

Pino, crying, said, "It was him. Tullio was so brave. Yelling at the men who were about to shoot him, calling them cowards . . . and . . . oh God, it was . . . horrible."

He went to his father and hugged him while Uncle Albert held Aunt Greta, who had turned hysterical. "I hate them," she said. "My own people and I hate them."

When she'd calmed down, Uncle Albert said, "I have to go tell his mother."

"She can't get Tullio's body until sundown," Pino said. "They're keeping the bodies on display as a warning of what happens when partisans kill Germans."

"The pigs," his uncle said. "This changes nothing. It only makes us stronger."

"That's what General Leyers said would happen."

By noon, Pino was sitting on the steps of La Scala where he could see the front of the Hotel Regina and the Daimler parked nearby. He was numb with grief. Gazing across the street at the statue of the great Leonardo and listening to the chatter of citizens who hurried past, he wanted to cry again. Everyone was talking about the atrocity. More than a few called Piazzale Loreto a cursed place now. He was seeing it all again and again in his mind, and he agreed.

At three o'clock, Leyers finally emerged from Gestapo headquarters. He got into the car, told Pino to drive to the telephone exchange yet again. There, Pino waited and thought about Tullio. Merciful night began to fall. Pino felt a little better knowing that his friend's body could be retrieved and readied for burial.

At seven, the general exited the telephone exchange, got in the back of the staff car, and said, "Dolly's."

Pino parked in front of her place on the Via Dante. Leyers had him carry the locked valise. The crone in the lobby blinked behind her glasses and seemed to sniff after them as they passed and climbed up the stairs to Dolly's apartment. When Anna opened the door, he could see she was upset.

"Are you in for the night, General?" Anna asked.

"No," he said. "I'm thinking of taking Dolly out for dinner."

Dolly came to the hallway in a dressing robe, a highball glass in one hand, and said, "A perfect idea. I go crazy sitting here all day, waiting for you, Hans. Where shall we go?"

"That place around the corner," Leyers said. "We can walk. I feel like I need to." He paused, and then looked at Pino. "You can stay here, Vorarbeiter, and eat. When I return, I'll tell you whether I'll have further need of you tonight."

Pino nodded and sat on the bench. Looking unhappy, Anna bustled through the dining area, ignoring Pino as she passed, and saying, "What shall I lay out for you, Dolly?"

General Leyers followed, and they all vanished into the depths of the apartment. None of it seemed real to Pino. Leyers was going on as if he'd not seen fifteen people murdered in cold blood that morning. There was something reptilian about the general, he decided. Leyers could watch men jerking on bullets and spurting blood in the last moments of their lives, and then he could go out to eat with his mistress.

Anna returned and as if it were a chore, said, "You hungry, Vorarbeiter?"

"*Per favore*, if it's a bother, no, *signorina*," Pino said, not looking at her.

After a few moments' pause, the maid sighed, and said in a different tone, "It's not a bother, Pino. I can heat something up for you."

"Thanks," he said, still not looking at Anna because he'd noticed the general's valise at his feet and was wishing he'd learned to pick a lock.

He heard raised, muffled voices, Leyers and his mistress having an argument of some kind. He raised his head, saw the maid was gone.

A door banged open. Dolly passed the hallway where Pino sat. She called, "Anna?"

Anna hurried into the dining and living area. "Yes, Dolly?"

Dolly said something in German that the maid seemed to understand because she left quickly. The general reappeared, dressed in his uniform pants, shoes, and a sleeveless undershirt.

Pino sprang to his feet. Leyers ignored him, came out into the living area, and said something to Dolly in German. She replied curtly, and he disappeared for several minutes while his mistress poured herself a whiskey and smoked by the window.

Pino felt odd inside, as if something about Leyers just then had caught his eye but had not fully registered. What was it?

When the general returned, he wore a freshly ironed shirt and a tie. His jacket was tossed over one shoulder.

"We will be back in a couple of hours," Leyers told Pino, passing closely by.

He stared after the general and Dolly, feeling that oddness again, and then tried to remember Leyers from just a few minutes before, shirtless and . . .

Oh my God, he thought.

⟶⟵

The door shut. Pino heard a board creak. He pivoted his head and saw Anna standing there.

"I heard a grocer say that fifteen members of the resistance were shot in Piazalle Loreto this morning," she said, wringing her hands. "Is that true?"

Sick all over again, he said, "I saw it. My friend was one of them."

Anna covered her mouth. "Oh, you poor thing . . . Please, come to the kitchen. There's schnitzel, gnocchi, and garlic butter. I'll open one of the general's best wines. He'll never know."

Very soon, a place was set at a small table at the end of a galley kitchen that was spotless. A candle burned there, too. Anna sat opposite him, sipping a glass of wine.

Veal? Pino thought as he sat down and smelled the divine aroma wafting up from his plate. When was the last time he'd had veal? Before the bombardment? He took a bite.

"Ohh," he groaned. "That is so good."

Anna smiled. "My grandmother, God rest her, she taught me that recipe."

He ate. They talked. He told her about the scene at the Piazalle Loreto, and she hung her head and held it for a while with both hands. When she lifted her head to look at Pino, her eyes were bloodshot and filmy.

"How do men think of such wickedness?" Anna asked as wax dripped down the candle and pooled about the holder. "Don't they fear for their souls?"

Pino thought about Rauff and the Black Shirts wearing the hoods.

"I don't think men like that care about their souls," Pino said, finishing the veal. "It's like they've already gone to evil, and going a little deeper won't matter."

Anna gazed past Pino into the middle distance for a moment. Then she looked at him and said, "So how does an Italian boy end up driving for a powerful Nazi general?"

Upset by the question, Pino said, "I'm not a boy. I'm eighteen."

"Eighteen."

"How old are you?"

"Almost twenty-four. Do you want some more food? Wine?"

"May I use the toilet first?" Pino said.

"Down the hall, first door on the right," she said, and reached for the wine bottle.

Pino went through the living area, and into a carpeted hall dimly lit by two low-wattage bulbs. He opened the first door on the right, turned on the light, and entered a bathroom with a shower-tub, tiled floor, a vanity crowded with cosmetics, and another door. He went to the second door, hesitated, and then gently tried the knob. It turned.

The door swung open into a darkened space that smelled of Leyers and his mistress so strongly that it stopped him for a moment. A warning voice in his head told him not to go on, to return to the kitchen, and to Anna.

He flipped on the light.

In a sweeping glance, Pino saw that the general occupied the far left side of the room, which was neat and precisely arranged. Dolly's side, which was closer to Pino, resembled an ill-kept theater costume room. There were two racks of fine dresses, skirts, and blouses. Cashmere sweaters bulged from drawers. A mishmash of colorful silk scarves, several corsets, and garter belts hung from the closet doors. Shoes were lined up in rows by the bed, Dolly's only surrender to order. Beyond them, amid stacks of books and hat boxes, was an occasional table that supported a large, open jewelry box.

Pino went to the neater side of the room first, scanning the top of a set of drawers and seeing cuff links on a tray, a clothes brush, a shoehorn, and a shaving kit. But not what he was looking for. Nothing on the nightstand or in it, either.

Maybe I was wrong, he thought, and then shook his head. *I'm not wrong.*

But where would someone like Leyers hide it? Pino looked under the mattress, and under the bed, and was about to search the general's shaving kit when he noticed something in the mirror, something in the chaos of Dolly's side of the room.

Pino circled the bed, going up on tiptoes to avoid stepping on Dolly's things and at last reached the jewelry box. Strings of pearls, gold chokers, and many, many other necklaces hung in bunches from hooks on the inside of the lid.

He pushed them aside, looking for something plain, and then . . .

There it was! Pino felt a thrill go through him as he plucked the thin chain with the key to the general's valise off a hook. He put it in his pants pocket.

"What are you doing?"

⊷

Pino spun around, his heart slamming against his chest. Anna stood in the doorway to the bathroom, her arms crossed, a glass of wine in one hand, and her face etched hard in suspicion.

"Just looking around," Pino said.

"In Dolly's jewelry box?"

He shrugged. "Just looking."

"Not just looking," Anna said angrily. "I saw you put something in your pocket."

Pino didn't know what to say or do.

"So you're a thief," Anna said, disgusted. "I should have known."

"I'm not a thief," Pino said, walking toward her.

"No?" she said, taking a step back. "Then what are you?"

"I . . . I can't tell you."

"Tell me, or I'll tell Dolly where I found you."

Pino didn't know what to do. He could hit her and flee, or . . .

"I'm a spy . . . for the Allies."

Anna laughed dismissively. "A spy? You?"

That made him angry.

"Who better?" Pino asked. "I go everywhere with him."

Anna fell silent, her expression doubtful. "Tell me how you became a spy."

Pino hesitated, and then told her quickly about Casa Alpina and what he'd done there, and how his parents feared for his life and made him join the Organization Todt, and the serendipitous path that had taken him from a bombed train station in Modena to a German hospital bed to the front seat of General Leyers's staff car outside his uncle's luggage store.

"I don't care if you believe me or not," he said at the end. "But I've put my life in your hands. If Leyers finds out, I'll die."

Anna studied him. "What did you put in your pocket?"

"The key to his valise," Pino said.

As if he'd used the key on her somehow, Anna changed in the next moment, transformed from suspicious by a slow, soft smile. "Let's open it!"

Pino breathed a sigh of relief. She believed him, and she wasn't going to tell Leyers. If she was part of opening his valise and the general found out, Anna would be dead, too.

He said, "I have other plans tonight."

"What plans?"

"I'll show you," he said, and led her back to the kitchen.

The candle still flickered on the table. He picked it up and poured a small puddle of wax on the table.

"Don't do that," Anna said.

"It will come right off," Pino said, fishing in his pocket and coming up with the key and chain.

He freed the key from the chain, waited until the wax had congealed to the consistency of putty, and then softly pressed the key into it. "Now I'll be able to make a duplicate and get into the valise anytime I want," he said. "Do you have a toothpick and a spatula?"

Looking at him in reappraisal and some wonder, Anna got him a toothpick from a cabinet. Pino gently pried the key free of the wax and then washed it in hot water. She set a spatula on the table, and he used it to separate the wax from the tabletop. He wrapped the cooling mold in tissue and put it in his shirt pocket.

"Now what?" Anna asked, her eyes flashing. "This is exciting!"

Pino grinned at her. It *was* exciting. "I'm going to take a look in the valise and then put the key back in Dolly's jewelry box."

He thought she'd like that, but instead the maid pouted her lip.

"What's the matter?" Pino asked.

"Well," she said, shrugging, "like you said, once you have the key made, you can get into the valise anytime, and I was thinking we would put the key back, and then . . ."

"What?"

"You could kiss me," Anna said matter-of-factly. "It's what you want, isn't it?"

Pino was going to deny it, but then said, "More than you can imagine."

He returned the key and shut the door to Dolly's bedroom. Anna was waiting for him in the kitchen with a funny smile on her face. She pointed at the chair. Pino sat down, and she set aside her wineglass and sat in his lap. She put her arms on his shoulders and kissed him.

Holding Anna, feeling her lips so soft against his for the first time, and smelling the perfect fragrance of her, Pino felt as if a single violin were playing the first strains of a marvelous melody. The music vibrated so pleasantly through his body that he shivered.

Anna broke the kiss and leaned her forehead against his.

"I thought it would be like that," she whispered.

"I prayed it would be," he said breathlessly. "The first time I saw you."

"Lucky me," Anna said, and kissed him again.

Pino held her tighter, marveling at how right it all felt, as if cellos had joined the violin, like a missing part of him had been found and made more by her touch, the taste of her lips, and the gentle kindness in her eyes. He wanted nothing more than to hold her as long as God would let him. They kissed a third time. Pino nuzzled her neck, which seemed to please her.

"I want to know all about you," he murmured. "Where you come from and—"

Anna drew back a bit. "I told you. Trieste."

"What were you like as a little girl?"

"Strange."

"No."

"My mother said so."

"What was she like?"

Anna put her finger across Pino's lips, gazed into his eyes, and said, "Someone very wise once told me that by opening our hearts, revealing our scars, we are made human and flawed and whole."

He felt his brows knit. "Okay?"

"I'm not ready to reveal my scars to you. I don't want you to see me human and flawed and whole. I want this . . . us . . . to be a fantasy we can share, a diversion from the war."

Pino reached out to stroke her face. "A beautiful fantasy, a wonderful diversion."

Anna kissed him a fourth time. Pino thought he heard a woodwind join the strings vibrating in his chest, and his mind and body were reduced to one thing, to the music of Anna-Marta and nothing more.

Chapter Nineteen

When General Leyers and Dolly returned from dinner, Pino sat on the front hall bench, beaming.

"Have you been sitting there two hours?" Leyers asked.

Amused and drunk, Dolly eyed Pino. "That would be a tragedy for Anna."

Pino blushed and looked away from Dolly, who chuckled and sashayed past him.

"You can go, Vorarbeiter," Leyers said. "Drop the Daimler at the pool, and be back here at oh six hundred hours."

"*Oui, mon général.*"

Driving the Daimler through the streets as the curfew approached, Pino couldn't help thinking that he had just had the best evening of his life at the tail end of the worst day of his life. He'd experienced every emotion possible in a span of twelve hours, from horror to grief to kissing Anna. She was almost six years older, it was true, but he didn't care in the least. If anything, it made her more magnetic.

As Pino walked back to the Lellas' apartment on Corso del Littorio after leaving the staff car at the motor pool, his mind once again lurched between the emotions of seeing Tullio die and the music he'd felt kissing Anna. Riding the birdcage elevator past the Nazi sentries, he thought, *God giveth, and God taketh away. Sometimes in the same day.*

Unless he was up playing music with a group of friends, Pino's father usually went to bed early, so Pino opened the front door to the apartment, expecting a light to be left on for him and the place quiet. But the lights were blazing behind the blackout curtains, and on the floor were suitcases he recognized.

"Mimo!" he cried softly. "Mimo, are you here?"

His brother came out from the kitchen, grinning as he ran over and grabbed Pino in a bear hug. His little brother might have grown an inch, but he'd certainly filled out in the fifteen weeks since Pino left Casa Alpina. Pino could feel the thick cables of muscle in Mimo's arms and back.

"Great to see you, Pino," Mimo said. "Really great."

"What are you doing here?"

Mimo lowered his voice. "I told Papa that I wanted to come home for a short while, but the truth is, as much good as we were doing at Casa Alpina, I couldn't take it anymore, being up there hiding while the real fighting was going on down here."

"What are you gonna do? Join the partisans?"

"Yes."

"You're too young. Papa won't let you."

"Papa won't know unless you tell him."

Pino studied his brother, marveling at his audacity. Just fifteen years old, he seemed to fear nothing, throwing himself into every situation without a shred of doubt. But joining a guerilla group to fight the Nazis could be tempting fate.

He watched the blood drain from Mimo's face before his brother pointed a shaky finger at the red band and the swastika sticking from his pocket and said, "What is that?"

"Oh," Pino said. "It's part of my uniform, but it's not what you think."

"How isn't it what I think?" Mimo said angrily, backing up to take in the entire uniform. "Are you fighting for the Nazis, Pino?"

"Fighting? No," he said. "I'm a driver. That's it."

"For the Germans."

"Yes."

Mimo looked like he wanted to spit. "Why aren't you fighting for the resistance, for Italy?"

Pino hesitated, and then said, "Because I would have to desert, which would make me a deserter. The Nazis are shooting deserters these days, or hadn't you heard?"

"So you're telling me that you're a Nazi, a traitor to Italy?"

"It's not so black and white."

"Sure it is," Mimo said, shouting at him.

"It was Uncle Albert and Mama's idea," Pino shouted back. "They wanted to save me from the Russian front, so I joined this thing—the OT, the Organization Todt. They build things. I just drive an officer around, waiting for the war to be over."

"Quiet!" their father said, coming into the room. "The sentries downstairs will hear you!"

"Is it true, Papa?" Mimo said in a forced whisper. "Pino wears a Nazi uniform to ride out the war while other people step up and free Italy?"

"I wouldn't put it like that," Michele said. "But, yes, your mother, Uncle Albert, and I thought it best."

That didn't mollify his second son. Mimo sneered at his older brother. "Who would have thought it? Pino Lella, taking the coward's way out."

Pino hit Mimo so hard, and so fast, he broke his brother's nose, and dropped him to the floor. "You have no idea what you're talking about," Pino said. "None at all."

"Stop it!" Michele said, getting between them. "Don't hit him again!"

Mimo looked at the blood in his hand, and then at Pino with contempt. "Go ahead and try to beat me down, my Nazi brother. It's the only thing you Germans know how to do."

Pino wanted to bash his brother's face in while telling him about the things he'd seen and done already in the name of Italy. But he couldn't.

"Believe what you want to believe," Pino said, and walked away.

"Kraut," Mimo called after him. "Adolf's little boy's gonna be safe and sound?"

Shaking, Pino shut his bedroom door and locked it. He stripped, got into bed, and set the alarm on his clock. He turned off the light, felt his bruised knuckles, and lay there, thinking that life had swung hard against him again. Was this what God wanted for him? To lose a hero, find love, and endure his brother's scorn, all in one day?

For the third night in a row, the whirlwind of his mind finally slowed on memories of Anna, and he drifted to sleep.

Fifteen days later, a Waffen-SS soldier lashed a team of six mules dragging two heavy cannons up a steep, arid mountainside. The whip laid open the flanks of the mules, and they brayed in pain and fear, dug in their hooves, and kicked up a dust cloud as they climbed toward the heights of the Apennine Mountains north of the town of Arezzo in central Italy.

"Get around them and be quick about it, Vorarbeiter," General Leyers said, looking up from his work in the backseat. "I've got cement pouring."

"Oui, mon général," Pino said, pulling around the mules and accelerating. He yawned, and yawned again, feeling so tired he could have lain right down in the mud and slept.

The pace at which Leyers worked and traveled was stupefying. In the days after the executions in the Piazalle Loreto, he and Pino were on the road fourteen, fifteen, sometimes sixteen hours a day. Leyers liked to travel at night when possible, with slit canvas blinders over the headlights. Pino had to concentrate for hours on end keeping the Daimler on the road with only slivers of light to navigate by.

When he passed the poor mules, it was past two in the afternoon, and he'd been driving since long before dawn. He was further irritated by the fact that the constant movement had hardly left him a moment to be alone with Anna since they'd kissed in the kitchen. He couldn't stop thinking about her, how it had felt when she was in his arms, her lips against his. He yawned but smiled at that happy thought.

"Up there," General Leyers said, pointing through the windshield into rugged, dry terrain.

Pino drove the Daimler until big rocks and boulders blocked the way.

"We'll walk from here," Leyers said.

Pino got out and opened the back door. The general exited and said, "Bring your notebook and pen."

Pino glanced at the valise in the backseat. He'd had the duplicate key for more than a week now, courtesy of some friend of Uncle Albert's, but he'd had no chance to try it. He got the notebook and pen from under the map in the glove compartment.

They climbed up through rocks and friable stones that slid around their feet before they reached the top. They were afforded a view looking over a valley framed by two long, connected ridges that on the map looked like a crab's open claw. To the south, there was a wide plain divided into farms and vineyards. To the north, and high on the crab's inner claw, an army of men worked in ungodly heat.

Leyers walked resolutely up the ridge toward them. Pino trailed the general, stunned at the sheer number of men up and down the side of the mountain, so many they looked like ants with their hill split open, teeming and crawling all over one another.

The closer they got, the ants turned human, and broken, and gray. Fifteen thousand slaves, maybe more, were mixing, transporting, and pouring cement for machine gun nests and artillery platforms. They were digging and setting tank traps across the valley floor. They were running barbed wire across the flanks of the slopes and using pickaxes and shovels to burrow out places for the German infantry to use as cover.

Every group of slaves had a Waffen-SS soldier who goaded them to work harder. Pino heard screaming and saw slaves beaten and whipped. Those who collapsed in the heat were dragged away by other slaves and left to fend for themselves, lying on rocks, dying in the beating sun.

It seemed to Pino a scene as old as time, an update on the pharaohs who enslaved generations of men to build their tombs. Leyers stopped at an overlook. He gazed down upon the vast companies of conquered men at his disposal and, at least by his facial expression, seemed unmoved by their plight.

Pharaoh's slave master, Pino thought.

That was what Antonio, the partisan fighter from Turin, had called Leyers. *The slave master himself.*

⟞⟝

New hatred for General Leyers boiled up from deep in Pino's gut. It was incomprehensible to him that a man who'd fought against something as barbaric as the decimation at San Vittore Prison could in turn rule an army of slaves without so much as a twitch of inner conflict or a tic of self-loathing. But nothing showed on Leyers's face as he watched bulldozers piling tree trunks and boulders on the steep mountainsides.

The general glanced at Pino, then pointed below them. "As the Allied soldiers attack, these obstacles will turn them straight into our machine guns."

Pino nodded with feigned enthusiasm. *"Oui, mon général."*

They walked through a girdle of interconnected machine gun nests and cannon installations, Pino following Leyers and taking notes. The longer they walked, and the more they saw, the more curt and agitated the general became.

"Write this down," he said. "The cement is inferior in many places. Likely sabotage from Italian suppliers. Upper valley is not fully hardened for battle. Inform Kesselring I need ten thousand more laborers."

Ten thousand slaves, Pino thought in disgust as he wrote. *And they mean nothing to him.*

The general then attended a meeting with high-ranking OT and German army officers, and Pino could hear him shouting and threatening inside a command bunker. When the meeting broke up, he saw the officers shouting at their subordinates, who shouted at the men under their authority. It was like watching a wave build until it reached the Waffen-SS soldiers, who hurled the weight of Leyers's demands on the shoulders of the slaves, lashing them, kicking them, driving them by any means necessary to work harder and faster. The implications were clear to Pino. The Germans expected the Allies here sooner than later.

General Leyers watched until he seemed satisfied with the renewed pace of the work, then said to Pino, "We're done here."

They walked back along the mountainside. The general would pause every now and then to observe some work-in-progress. Otherwise, he kept on marching like some unstoppable machine. Did he have a heart? Pino wondered. A soul?

They were near the path that led back to the Daimler when Pino saw a crew of seven men in gray digging and swinging pickaxes, breaking rock and shale under the watchful eye of the SS. Some of them had a ravaged and mad look about them, like a rabid dog he'd once seen.

The closest slave to Pino was uphill from the others, digging weakly. He stopped, put his hands on the end of the handle like a man who'd had enough. One of the SS soldiers started screaming at him and marching across the hill.

The slave looked away and saw Pino standing there, looking down at him. His skin had turned the color of tobacco juice from the sun, and his beard was wilder than Pino remembered it. He'd also lost too much weight. But Pino swore he was looking at Antonio, the slave he'd given water to back in the tunnel the first day he'd driven for Leyers. Their gazes locked, and Pino felt both pity and shame before the SS soldier clubbed the side of the slave's head with the butt of his rifle. He dropped and rolled down the steep embankment.

"Vorarbeiter!"

Pino startled and looked over his shoulder. General Leyers was standing about fifty meters from him, glaring back at him.

With one last glance at the now unmoving slave, Pino broke into a trot toward the general, thinking that Leyers was responsible. The general hadn't ordered the man struck down, but in his mind, Leyers was responsible nonetheless.

<hr />

It was past dark when Pino came through the door to Uncle Albert's sewing room.

"I saw bad things today," Pino said, emotional again. "I heard them, too."

"Tell me," Uncle Albert said.

Pino did the best he could, describing the scene with Leyers and the way the SS soldier had killed Antonio for taking a break.

"They're all butchers, the SS," Uncle Albert said, looking up from his notes. "Because of the reprisal edict, there are stories of atrocities every day now. At Sant'Anna di Stazzema, SS troops machine-gunned, tortured, and burned five hundred and sixty innocents. At Casaglia, they shot down a priest on his altar and three old people during Mass. They took the other hundred and forty-seven parishioners into the church graveyard and opened fire with machine guns."

"What?" Pino said, stunned.

Aunt Greta said, "It goes on. Just the other day, in Bardine di San Terenzo, more than fifty young Italian men, like you, Pino, were strangled with barbed wire and hung from trees."

Pino loathed them all, every single Nazi. "They have to be stopped."

"There are more joining the fight against them every day," Uncle Albert said. "Which is why your information is so important. Could you show me on a map where you were?"

"I've already done it," Pino said, pulling out the general's map from the glove compartment.

Unfolding it on one of the cutting tables, he showed his uncle the light pencil marks he'd made to indicate the rough placement of the artillery, machine gun nests, armories, and ammo dumps he'd seen during the day. He pointed out where Leyers had piled the debris so the Allies would alter course into machine gun fire.

"In this whole area, Leyers said the concrete is inferior, weak," Pino said, gesturing to the map. "Leyers was very concerned about it. The Allies should bomb here first, take it out before they ever attack on the ground."

"Smart," Uncle Albert said, taking notes on the longitude and latitude of the area. "I'll pass it along. By the way, that tunnel you visited with Leyers, when you first saw the slaves? It was destroyed yesterday. Partisans waited until there were just Germans inside and then dynamited both ends."

That made Pino feel better. He actually was making a difference.

"It would sure help if I could get into that valise," Pino said.

His uncle said, "You're right. In the meantime, we'll see about getting you a small camera."

Pino liked that idea. "Who knows I'm a spy?"

"You, me, and your aunt."

And Anna, he thought, but said, "Not the Allies? The partisans?"

"They only know you by the code name I gave you."

Pino liked that idea even more. "Really? What's my code name?"

"Observer," Uncle Albert replied. "As in 'Observer notes machine gun nests at such and such position.' And 'Observer notes troop supplies heading south.' It's deliberately bland. That way, if the Germans ever intercepted the reports, they'd have no clue to your identity."

"Observer," Pino said. "Plain and to the point."

"Exactly my thought," Uncle Albert said, standing up from the map. "You can fold the map up now, but I'd erase those pencil marks first."

Pino did so and left a short time later. Hungry and tired, he started toward home at first, but he hadn't seen Anna in days, and he walked to Dolly's apartment building instead.

As soon as he got there, he wondered why he'd come. It was almost curfew. And he couldn't just go up, knock on the door, and ask to see her, could he? The general had ordered him to go home and to sleep.

He was about to leave when he remembered Anna saying that there was a back stairway just beyond her room off the kitchen. He went around the building, thankful for the moon overhead, and picked his way to where he figured Anna's room and window were, three stories above him. Would she be in there? Or still cleaning dishes and washing Dolly's clothes?

Picking up a small handful of pebbles, he leaned back and threw them all at once, figuring she was either in there or not. Ten seconds went by, then another ten. He was about to leave when he heard a window sash go up.

"Anna!" he called softly.

"Pino?" she called softly back.

"Let me in the back way."

"The general and Dolly are still here," she said, doubt in her voice.

"We'll be quiet."

There was a long pause, and then she said, "Give me a minute."

After she'd opened the utility door, they crept up the back stairs, Anna in the lead, stopping every few steps to listen. At last they reached her bedroom.

"I'm hungry," Pino whispered.

She opened her door, pushed him inside, and whispered back, "I'll find you something to eat, but you must stay here, and be quiet."

She was back soon with leftovers from a ham hock and a fried noodle dish that was the general's favorite. He ate it all by the light of a single candle Anna had burning. She sat on the bed, drank wine, and watched him eat.

"That makes my tummy happy," he said when he'd finished.

"Good," Anna said. "I'm a student of happiness, you know. It's all I really want—happiness, every day for the rest of my life. Sometimes happiness comes to us. But usually you have to seek it out. I read that somewhere."

"And that's all you want? Happiness?"

"What could be better?"

"How do you find happiness?"

Anna paused, then said, "You start by looking right around you for the blessings you have. When you find them, be grateful."

"Father Re says the same thing," Pino said. "He says to give thanks for every day, no matter how flawed. And to have faith in God and a better tomorrow."

Anna smiled. "The first part's right. I don't know about the second."

"Why?"

"I've been disappointed too many times when it comes to better tomorrows," she said, and then kissed him. He took her in his arms and kissed her back.

Then they heard arguing through the walls—Leyers and Dolly.

"What are they fighting about?" Pino whispered.

"What they always fight about. His wife back in Berlin. And now, Pino, you have to go."

"Really?"

"Go on now," she said. Then she kissed him and smiled.

On September 1, 1944, the British Eighth Army punctured the weaker sections of the Gothic Line on the crab-claw ridges north of Arezzo, and then turned east toward the Adriatic Coast. The fighting turned vicious, some of the most intense of the war in Italy after Monte Cassino and Anzio. The Allies rained more than a million mortar and cannon rounds on all the fortifications that separated them from the coastal city of Rimini.

Nine brutal days later, the US Fifth Army drove the Nazis off the highlands at the Giogo Pass, and the British intensified their assault of the east end of the Gothic Line. The Allies rolled north in a pincer fashion, trying to surround the retreating German Tenth Army before it could re-form.

Pino and Leyers went to high ground near Torraccia, where they watched the town of Coriano and the heavy German defenses around it come under bombardment. More than seven hundred heavy shells were dropped on the town before ground forces attacked it. After two days of gruesome, hand-to-hand combat, Coriano fell.

In all, some fourteen thousand Allied soldiers and sixteen thousand Germans died in the area in a two-week span. Despite the heavy casualties, German Panzer and infantry divisions were able to retreat and re-form along a new battle line to the north and northwest. The rest of Leyers's Gothic Line held. Even with the information Pino was providing, the Allied advance in Italy again slowed to a crawl due to loss of men and supplies to France and the western front.

Later in the month, machine workers in Milan went on strike. Some sabotaged their equipment as they left their factories. Tank production halted.

General Leyers spent days getting a tank assembly line restarted, only to hear in early October that Fiat's Mirafiore factory was about to go on strike. They went straight to Mirafiore, an outlying district of Turin. Pino served as interpreter between the general and Fiat management in a room above the assembly line, which was running, but slowly. The tension in the room was thick.

"I need more lorries," General Leyers said. "More armored cars, and more parts for machines in the field."

Calabrese, the plant manager, was a fat, sweaty man in a business suit. But he was not afraid to stand up to Leyers.

"My people are not slaves, General," Calabrese said. "They work for a living— they should be paid for a living."

"They'll be paid," Leyers said. "You have my word."

Calabrese smiled slowly, unconvincingly. "If it were only that simple."

"Did I not help you with factory seventeen?" the general asked. "I had orders to take every piece of machinery there and ship it back to Germany."

"It doesn't matter now, does it? Factory seventeen was destroyed in an Allied attack."

Leyers shook his head at Calabrese. "You know how this works. We scratch each other's backs, we survive."

"If you say so, General," Calabrese said.

Leyers took a step closer to the Fiat manager, looked to Pino, and said, "Remind him that I have the power to force every man on that assembly line to enlist in the Organization Todt or risk deportation to Germany."

Calabrese hardened and said, "Slavery, you mean?"

Pino hesitated, but translated.

"If necessary," Leyers said. "It is your choice whether to leave this plant in your hands or in mine."

"I need some assurance beyond yours that we'll be paid."

"Do you understand my title? My job? I decide the number of tanks to be built. I decide the number of panties to be sewn. I—"

"You work for Albert Speer," the Fiat manager said. "You have his authority. Get him on the phone. Speer. If your boss can give me assurances, then we'll see."

"Speer? You think that weak ass is my boss?" the general said, looking insulted before asking to use the Fiat manager's telephone. He was on it for several minutes, having several agitated arguments in German, before he bobbed his head, and said, *"Jawohl, mein Führer."*

⟞⟝

Pino's attention shot to the general, as did the attention of every man in the room as Leyers continued to speak into the phone in German. About three minutes into the conversation, he yanked the earpiece away from his head.

The voice of Adolf Hitler in full rant came into the room.

Leyers looked at Pino, smiled coldly, and said, "Tell Signor Calabrese that the führer would like to give him his personal assurances of payment."

Calabrese looked like he'd rather have grabbed an electrical wire than the phone, but he took it and held the earpiece a few centimeters from his head. Hitler kept on in full oratorical rage, sounding like he was being ripped apart from the insides, probably foaming at the mouth as it was happening. Sweat poured off the Fiat manager's brow. His hands began to shake, and with them went his resolve.

He shoved the phone back at Leyers and said to Pino, "Tell him to tell Herr Hitler that we accept his assurances."

"A wise choice," Leyers said, and then returned to the phone, saying in a soothing voice, *"Ja, mein Führer. Ja. Ja. Ja."*

A few moments later he hung up the phone.

Calabrese collapsed in his chair, his suit drenched with sweat. As he set the phone down, General Leyers looked at the manager and said, "Do you understand who I am now?"

The Fiat manager would not look at Leyers or reply. He barely managed a weak, submissive bob of his head.

"Very well, then," the general said. "I expect production reports twice weekly."

Leyers handed the valise to Pino, and they left.

It was nearly dark out, but still a nice warm temperature.

"Dolly's," the general said, climbing into the Daimler. "And no talking. I need to think."

"*Oui, mon général,*" Pino said. "Do you want the top up or down?"

"Leave it down," he said. "I like the fresh air."

Pino retrieved the burlap headlamp shields and mounted them before firing up the Daimler and heading east toward Milan with two slits of light to show him the way. But within the hour, the moon rose huge and full in the eastern sky, throwing a mellow glow down on the landscape and making it easier for Pino to follow the route.

"That's a blue moon," Leyers said. "The first of two full moons in one month. Or is it the second one? I can never remember."

It was the first time the general had spoken since leaving Turin.

"The moon looks yellow to me, *mon général,*" Pino said.

"The term doesn't refer to the color, Vorarbeiter. Normally in a single season, in this case, autumn, there are three months and three full moons. But this year, tonight, right now, there's a fourth moon in the three-month cycle, two in one month. Astronomers call it a 'blue moon' because it is such a rare occurrence."

"*Oui, mon général,*" Pino said, driving a long, straight section of road and looking at the moon rising over the horizon like some omen.

When they came to a section of the road that was flanked on both sides by tall, well-spaced trees and fields beyond them, Pino was no longer thinking about the moon. He was thinking about Adolf Hitler. Had that actually been the führer on the phone? He'd sure sounded crazy enough to be Hitler. And that question Leyers had asked of the Fiat manager: *Do you know who I am now?*

Pino stole a glance at the silhouette of Leyers riding in the backseat and answered in his mind: *I don't know who you are, but I sure know who you work for now.*

He'd no sooner had that thought than behind them, to the west, he thought he caught the buzz of some larger engine. He looked in the rearview and side-view mirrors, but saw no slit lights that would indicate an oncoming vehicle. The sound grew louder.

Pino glanced again, seeing General Leyers twisting around, and then something beyond him, something big back there above the trees. The moonlight caught the wings then and the snout of the fighter, its engine a building roar and coming right at them.

⟺

Pino slammed on the Daimler's six brakes. They skidded. The fighter swooped over them like the shadow of a night bird before the pilot could trigger his machine guns and chew up the road out in front of the skidding staff car.

The shooting stopped. The fighter gained altitude and banked to Pino's left, and then was gone behind the treetops.

"Hold on, *mon général*," Pino cried, and threw the vehicle in reverse. He backed up, swung the wheel right, shifted to low range and then first gear, punched off the headlights, and gunned it.

The Daimler went down through the ditch, up the other side, and between a gap in the trees into what looked like a recently plowed field. Pino pulled forward close to the base of a cluster of trees and stopped, clicked the ignition off.

"How did you—?" Leyers began, sounding terrified. "What are you—?"

"Listen," Pino whispered. "He's coming back."

The fighter bore down over the road the same way it had the first time, coming from the west, as if it meant to catch up with the staff car and destroy it from behind. Through the tree branches, Pino couldn't make it out for several seconds, but then the big silver bird blew by them and up the highway, silhouetted against the rarest of moons.

Pino saw white circles with black centers on the fuselage and said, "He's British."

"It's a Spitfire, then," Leyers said. "With .303 Browning machine guns."

Pino started the Daimler, waited, listening, peering. The fighter was making a tighter turn now, coming back above the near tree line six hundred meters ahead of them.

"He knows we're here somewhere," Pino said, and then realized the moon was probably glinting off the hood and windshield of the staff car.

He threw the Daimler in gear, tried to bury the left front quarter panel in the thorn thicket growing up around the hedgerow, and stopped when the plane was two hundred meters out. Pino ducked his head, felt the fighter go over them, and took off.

The Daimler chewed up ground, gathering speed, mowing down clods and ruts the entire length of the plowed field. Pino kept looking back, wondering if the plane would make a third pass. Near the far corner of the field, he pulled into another gap in the trees, with the nose of the staff car facing down the bank into the road ditch.

He turned off the engine a second time and listened. The plane was a distant, fading buzz. General Leyers started laughing, and then clapped Pino on the shoulder.

"You're a natural at the cat-and-mouse game!" he said. "I would not have thought to do any of that, even without being shot at."

"Merci, mon général!" Pino said, grinning as he started the Daimler and headed east again.

Soon, however, he was conflicted. Part of him was appalled that he had basked once more in the general's praise. Then again, he had been smart and crafty, hadn't he? He'd certainly outwitted the British pilot, and he rather enjoyed that.

Twenty minutes later, they crested the hill with the full moon rising before them. Diving out of the night sky, the Spitfire crossed the face of the moon and flew right at them. Pino locked up the brakes. For a second time, the Daimler went into a six-wheel-drive screeching skid.

"Run, *mon général!*"

Before the staff car had stopped, Pino leaped out the door, took one long off-balance stride, and dove for the ditch even as the Spitfire's machine guns opened up and sent bullets skipping down the macadam.

Pino landed in the ditch, felt the wind blow out of him as bullets struck steel and broke glass. Chunks of debris peppered his back, and he curled up, protecting his head and struggling for air.

The shooting stopped then, and the Spitfire flew on to the west.

Chapter Twenty

When the plane was a distant hum, and he could breathe, Pino whispered in the darkness, *"Mon général?"*

There was no reply. *"Mon général?"*

No answer. Was he dead? Pino thought he'd be happy to think that, but instead he saw the downside. No more Leyers, no more spying. No more information for the—

He heard movement and then a groan.

"Mon général?"

"Yes," Leyers said weakly. "Here." He was behind Pino, struggling to sit up. "I must have blacked out. Last thing I remember was diving into the ditch and . . . what happened?"

Pino told the general as he helped him up the bank. The Daimler was backfiring, hesitating, and shuddering, but somehow still running. Pino shut it off, and the engine mercifully died. He got the flashlight and tool kit from the trunk. He flicked the light on and passed its beam over the vehicle with General Leyers gaping along with him. Bullets had ripped the Daimler from front to back, penetrating the hood, which was throwing steam. The machine gun had also blown out the windshield, perforated the front and back seats, and punched more holes through the trunk. The front-right tire was flat. So was the opposite side's outer-rear tire.

"Can you hold this, *mon général?*" Pino asked, holding out the torch.

Leyers looked at it blankly a moment, and then took it.

Raising the hood, Pino saw that the engine block had been hit five times, but the light .303 rounds had not had enough energy left after piercing the hood to do any real damage. A spark plug cable was severed. Another looked ready to go. And there was a hole high in the radiator. But otherwise the power plant, as Alberto Ascari liked to describe it, looked serviceable.

Pino used a knife to strip and twist together the two pieces of the severed spark plug cable and used first-aid tape to bind it and the weaker cable. He got out the tire kit, found patches and rubber glue that he used to seal both sides of the radiator hole. Then he removed the flat front-right tire, and moved the outer back-right tire forward to replace it. He took off the flat outer back-left tire and dumped it. When he started the Daimler, it still ran rough, but it was no longer bucking and coughing like an old smoker.

"I think it will get us back to Milan, *mon général*, but beyond that, who knows?"

"Beyond Milan doesn't matter," Leyers said, sounding clearer-headed as he climbed into the backseat. "The Daimler is too visible a target. We will change cars."

"Oui, mon général," Pino said, and tried to put the staff car in gear.

It bucked and died. He tried again, gave it more petrol, and got it rolling. But running on four wheels instead of six, the Daimler was no longer balanced, and they went shambling and shivering down the road. Second gear was gone. He had to rev the engine as high as he dared to get to third gear, but once they reached a decent speed, the vibrations calmed a bit.

When they were eight kilometers on, General Leyers asked for his flashlight, fumbled around in his valise, and came up with a bottle. He opened the top, took a gulp, and handed it over the seat. "Here," he said. "Scotch whiskey. You deserve it. You saved my life."

Pino hadn't looked at it that way, and said, "I did what anyone would have done."

"No," Leyers said in a scoff. "Most men would have frozen and driven on into the machine guns, and died. But you—you were not afraid. You kept your wits about you. You are what I used to call 'a young man of action.'"

"I like to think so, *mon général*," Pino said, basking once more in Leyers's praise as he took the bottle and had a swig. The liquid spread hot through his belly.

Leyers took the bottle back. "That's enough for you until Milan."

The general chuckled. Over the vibrations in the Daimler, Pino heard Leyers take several more belts of the scotch straight off the bottle.

Leyers laughed sadly. "In some ways, Vorarbeiter Lella, you remind me of someone. Two people, actually."

"Oui, mon général?" Pino said. "Who are they?"

The Nazi was quiet, took a sip, and then said, "My son and my nephew."

Pino hadn't expected that.

"I did not know you had a son, *mon général*," Pino replied, and glanced in the mirror, seeing nothing but the suggestion of the man in the shadows of the backseat.

"Hans-Jürgen. He's almost seventeen. Smart. Resourceful, like you."

Pino didn't know exactly how to react, so he said, "And your nephew?"

There was a moment of silence before Leyers sighed and then said, "Wilhelm. Willy, we called him. My sister's son. He served under Field Marshal Rommel. Died at El Alamein." He paused. "For some reason, his mother blames me for the loss of her only child."

Pino could hear the pain in Leyers's voice and said, "I'm sorry to learn that, *mon général*. But your nephew served with Rommel, the Desert Fox."

"Willy was a young man of action," the general agreed in a hoarse voice before taking a drink. "He was a leader who sought harm's way. And it cost him his life at twenty-eight, in the middle of a flea-infested Egyptian desert."

"Did Willy drive a tank?"

Leyers cleared his throat and said, "With the Seventh Panzers."

"The Ghost Division."

General Leyers cocked his head. "How do you know of these things?"

The BBC, Pino thought, but figured that would not go over well. So he said, "I read all the papers. And there was a newsreel at the cinema."

"Reading newspapers," Leyers said. "A rare thing for someone so young. But both Hans-Jürgen and Willy read all the time, especially the sports sections. We used to go watch sports together. Willy and I saw Jesse Owens run at the Berlin Olympic Games. Fantastic. How angry the führer was that day when a black man bested our best. But Jesse Owens? Vorarbeiter, that Negro was a physical genius. Willy kept saying that, and he was right."

He fell off into silence, pondering, remembering, mourning.

"Do you have other children?" Pino asked at last.

"A young daughter, Ingrid," he said with renewed brightness.

"Where are they? Hans-Jürgen and Ingrid?"

"In Berlin. With my wife, Hannelise."

Pino nodded and focused on driving while General Leyers continued to drink the scotch at a slow but steady pace.

"Dolly's a dear friend," Major General Leyers announced sometime later. "I've known her a long time, Vorarbeiter. I like her a great deal. I owe her a great deal. I look out for her, and I always will. But a man like me doesn't leave his wife to marry a woman like Dolly. It would be like an old goat trying to cage a tigress in her prime."

He laughed with admiration and some bitterness before drinking again.

Pino was shocked that Leyers was opening up to him this way after eight weeks of maintaining a cold reserve, and with the difference in rank and age. But he wanted the general to keep talking. Who knew what he might let slip next?

Leyers fell into silence, sipping the booze once more.

Mon général? Pino said finally. "May I ask you a question?"

Leyers's tongue sounded thick when he said, "What is it?"

Pino slowed at an intersection, winced at the Daimler backfiring, and then glanced in the rearview before saying, "Do you really work for Adolf Hitler?"

For what seemed like an eternity, Leyers said nothing. Then he replied in a slight slur, "Many, many times, Vorarbeiter, I have sat at the left hand of the führer. People say there is a bond between us because both our fathers worked as customs inspectors. There is that. But I am a man who gets things done, a man to depend on. And Hitler respects that. He does, but . . ."

Pino glanced in the rearview and saw the general taking another draw on the scotch.

"But?" Pino said.

"But it is a good thing I am in Italy. If you stay too close to someone like Hitler, you are going to burn someday. So I keep my distance. I do my work. I earn his respect, and nothing more. Do you see?"

"Oui, mon général."

Four or five minutes passed before General Leyers took another swig and said, "I am an engineer by training, Vorarbeiter. I have my doctorate. From the beginning, as a younger man, I worked for the government in armaments, awarding contracts. Millions upon millions of kronen. I learned how to negotiate with great men, industrialists like Flick and Krupp. And because of that, men like Flick and Krupp owe me favors."

Leyers paused, and then said, "I will give you some advice, Vorarbeiter. Advice that could change your life."

"Oui, mon général?"

"Doing favors," Leyers said. "They help wondrously over the course of a lifetime. When you have done men favors, when you look out for others so they can prosper, they owe you. With each favor, you become stronger, more supported. It is a law of nature."

"Yes?" Pino said.

"Yes," Leyers said. "You can never go wrong in this way, because there will be times when you will need a favor, and it will be right there waiting to come to the rescue. This practice has saved me more than once."

"I will keep that in mind."

"You are a smart boy, just like Hans-Jürgen," the general said, and laughed. "Such a simple, simple thing, the doing of favors, but because of them, I lived well before Hitler, I've lived well under Hitler, and I know I'll live well long after Hitler is gone."

Pino glanced at the mirror and saw Leyers's dark silhouette as he drained the scotch bottle. "One last piece of advice from a man older than his years?"

"Oui, mon général?"

"You never want to be the absolute leader in the game of life, the man out front, the one everyone sees and looks to," Leyers said. "That's where my poor Willy made his mistake. He got out front, right there in the light. You see, Vorarbeiter, in the game of life, it is always preferable to be a man of the shadows, and even the darkness, if necessary. In this way, you run things, but you are never, ever seen. You are like a . . . phantom of the opera. You are like . . ."

The scotch bottle fell to the floor. The general cursed softly. A moment later, with his arms wrapped around his valise, using it like a pillow, he began to snorfle, choke, snore, and fart.

When they reached Dolly's apartment building, it was almost midnight. Pino left the comatose general in the Daimler, and left the staff car running for fear it might never start again. He ran through the lobby, past the crone's empty stool, and up the stairs to Dolly's. Anna did not answer until the third series of knocks.

Dressed for bed in her nightgown and robe, Anna looked weary and lovely.

"I need Dolly," he said.

"What's happened?" Dolly said, coming down the hall in a black-and-gold dressing gown.

"The general," Pino said. "He's had too—"

"Too much to drink?" General Leyers said, coming in through the open door, valise in hand. "Nonsense, Vorarbeiter. I'm having another drink, and so are you. Will you join us, Dolly?"

Pino stared at Leyers as if he were Lazarus arisen. As the general passed Pino, his breath was foul with alcohol, and his eyes looked like they were bleeding, but he wasn't slurring his words or weaving on his feet at all.

"What are we celebrating, Hans?" Dolly said, brightening. Anna had said she was always up for a party.

"The blue moon," the general said, setting down the valise. He kissed her lustily before throwing his arm around her shoulder and looking back at Pino. "And we are celebrating the fact that Vorarbeiter Lella saved my life, and that deserves a drink!"

He spun Dolly around the corner into the living area.

Anna looked at Pino with a puzzled smile on her face. "Did you?"

"I saved myself," Pino whispered. "He kind of came along for the ride."

"Vorarbeiter!" Leyers yelled from the other room. "A drink! And fair Anna, too!"

When they entered the living room, the general was beaming and holding out generous tumblers of whiskey. Dolly was already gulping hers. Pino didn't know how Leyers was still standing, but the general took a draw of the liquor and launched into a blow-by-blow description of what he called "the Once-in-a-Blue-Moon Duel between the Sneaky Pilot in the Spitfire and the Daring Vorarbeiter in the Daimler."

Dolly and Anna were on the edge of their seats as Leyers recounted the Spitfire's final return and Pino's locking up the brakes and shouting at him to run. And the machine guns and the Daimler's near destruction.

General Leyers raised his glass at the end of his story and said, "To Vorarbeiter Lella, who I owe a favor or two."

Dolly and Anna clapped. Pino's face felt flushed from the attention, but he smiled and raised his glass in return. "Thank you, General."

A loud rapping came at the door to the apartment. Anna set her glass down and went to the hallway. Pino went with her.

When the maid opened the door, the old crone, the building concierge, was there in her ragged nightclothes, holding a candle lantern.

"Your neighbors can't sleep for all the hell-raising," she scolded, blinking behind her glasses. "There's a lorry or something backfiring out on the street, and you're carrying on drunk in the middle of the night!"

"I forgot," Pino said. "I'll go right down and turn the car off."

Dolly and Leyers appeared at the head of the hallway.

"What is happening?" Dolly asked.

Anna explained, and Dolly said, "We're all going to bed now, Signora Plastino. Sorry to have kept you up."

The crone made a harrumphing noise and, still indignant, turned away, holding the candle lantern high, dragging the filthy hem of her nightgown behind her, and groping her way down the staircase. Pino followed her at a safe distance.

After he turned off the staff car's engine, and after a very drunk General Leyers and Dolly had retired to their bedroom, he was at last alone again with Anna in the kitchen.

She warmed up a sausage, broccoli, and garlic dish and poured him a glass of wine and one for herself. Then she sat opposite him, chin in her hand, and asked him questions about the fighter plane and what it felt like to be shot at, to have someone trying to kill him.

"It felt scary," he said after thinking about it for a moment between bites of the delicious meal. "But I was more scared afterward, when I'd had a chance to think about it. Everything was happening so fast, you know?"

"No, and I don't want to know, not really. I don't like guns."

"Why?"

"They kill people, and I'm a people."

"Lots of things kill people. Are you frightened of mountain climbing?"

"Yes," she said. "Aren't you?"

"No," Pino said, drinking his wine. "I love mountain climbing, and skiing."

"And dueling with airplanes?"

"When it's called for," he said, and grinned. "This is fantastic, by the way. You really are a great cook."

"Old family recipe, and thank you," Anna said, rolling her shoulders forward and studying his face. "You're full of surprises, you know."

"Am I?" Pino asked, pushing the plate back.

"I think people underestimate you."

"Good."

"I'm serious. I underestimated you."

"Did you?"

"Yes. I'm proud of you, that's all."

That made him flush. "Thanks."

Anna continued to gaze at him for several long moments, and he felt himself falling into her eyes, as if they created a world unto themselves.

"I don't think I've ever met anyone quite like you," she said at last.

"I should hope not. I mean, that's a good thing, yes?"

Anna sat back. "Good and frightening all at the same time, if I'm being honest."

"I scare you?" he said, frowning.

"Well, yes. In a way."

"What way?"

She looked off, shrugged. "You make me wish I were different, better. Younger, anyway."

"I like you just the way you are."

Anna gazed at him doubtfully. Pino reached out to her. Anna looked at his hand a long moment, and then smiled and took it in hers.

"You're special," Pino said. "For a fantasy, I mean."

Anna's smile widened, and she got up and came over to sit in his lap.

"Show me I'm special for real," she said, and kissed him.

When they broke apart, they touched foreheads and entwined their hands. Pino said, "You know secrets that could get me killed, but I know so little about you."

After several moments, Anna seemed to come to some kind of decision and touched her uniform above her heart. "I'll tell you about one of my scars. An old one."

Anna said her early childhood was magical. Her father, a commercial fisherman and native of Trieste, owned his own boat. Her mother was from Sicily, superstitious about everything, but a good mother, a loving mother. They had a nice home near the marina and good food on the table. Due to a series of miscarriages, Anna was an only child and doted on by her parents. She loved being in the kitchen with her mother. She loved being on the boat with her father, especially on her birthday.

"Papa and I would go out on the Adriatic before dawn," Anna said. "We'd go west in the darkness several kilometers. Then he'd turn the boat around east and let me take the wheel. I'd drive the boat straight into the sunrise. I loved that."

"How old were you?"

"Oh, maybe five the first time."

On her ninth birthday, Anna and her father got up early. It was raining and windy, so there would be no voyage into the sunrise, but she wanted to go anyway.

"So we did," she said, fell quiet, and then cleared her throat. "The storm got worse. A lot worse. My father put a life preserver on me. We were getting hit by waves, and we got turned broadside to them. A big one hit us hard enough to capsize the boat and throw us into the sea. I was rescued later in the day by other fishermen from Trieste. My father was never found."

"Oh God," Pino said. "That's horrible."

Anna nodded, tears slipping from her eyes and dripping on his chest. "My mother was worse, but she's a scar for another time. I have to sleep. And you have to go."

"Again?"

"Yes," she said, smiled, and kissed him once more.

Though he desperately wanted to stay, Pino felt happy upon leaving Dolly's apartment around 2:00 a.m. He hated seeing Anna's face disappear as she closed the door, but he loved that she looked forward to seeing him again.

Downstairs, the lobby and the old crone's stool were empty. He went outside and looked at the bullet holes in the Daimler, and wondered how they'd survived. He would go home and sleep, and in the morning he would find his uncle. He had much to tell.

⤙⤚

The next morning, while Aunt Greta cut and toasted bread she'd stood hours in a ration line to buy, Uncle Albert took notes as Pino recounted all that had happened to him since they'd last spoken. He finished with the story of General Leyers getting drunk.

Uncle Albert sat there several moments, and then asked, "How many lorries and armored cars did you say are coming off the Fiat lines every day?"

"Seventy," Pino said. "If it weren't for the sabotage, they'd be making more."

"That's good to know," he said, scribbling.

Aunt Greta put toast, butter, and a small jar of jam on the table.

"Butter and jam!" Uncle Albert said. "Wherever did you get that?"

"Everyone has their secrets," she said, and smiled.

"Even General Leyers, it seems," Uncle Albert said.

"Especially General Leyers," Pino said. "Did you know he reports directly to Hitler? That he's sat at the führer's left hand in meetings?"

His uncle shook his head. "Leyers is far more powerful than we thought, which is why I'd love to see what he's got in that valise."

"But he's always got it with him, or where it would be noticed missing."

"He leaves clues, though. He spent the better part of a week dealing with strikes and sabotages, which says to me strikes and sabotage are working. Which says we need more sabotage in the factories. We'll break the Nazis gear tooth by gear tooth."

"The Germans are also having trouble paying," Pino said. "Fiat is working on Hitler's guarantee of payment, not cash."

Uncle Albert studied Pino, thought about that. "Scarcity," he said at last.

"What?" Aunt Greta said.

"The food lines are getting worse, aren't they?"

She nodded. "Longer every day. For nearly everything."

"It's going to get much worse," her husband said. "If the Nazis have no money to pay, their economy is starting to break down. They will start seizing more and more of our stores soon, and that will lead to more scarcity and more misery for everyone in Milan."

"You think so?" Aunt Greta said, worrying her apron.

"It's not necessarily a bad thing, scarcity, in the long run I mean. More misery, more pain, will mean more of us willing to fight until the last German is dead or driven from Italy."

By the middle of October 1944, events were starting to prove Uncle Albert right.

Pino drove General Leyers's new staff car, a Fiat four-door sedan, southeast from Milan one beautiful autumn morning. It was harvest time on the Po River valley floor. Men were taking scythes to grain and picking gardens, groves, and orchards. Leyers sat in the back of the Fiat, as was his custom, the valise open, reports in his lap.

Since they'd survived the strafing, Leyers had been more cordial to Pino, but he showed little of the empathy and openness he had that night. Then again, Pino hadn't seen him take a drink since. He followed the general's directions, and within an hour they arrived at a large meadow in the countryside. Fifty German lorries were parked there along with Panzer tanks, armored cars, and seven or eight hundred soldiers, a full battalion of them. Most were Organization Todt men, but they had a full company of SS soldiers behind them.

General Leyers exited the car, his face hard. At the sight of the general, the entire battalion came to attention. Leyers was met by a lieutenant colonel who led him to a stack of weapons crates. Leyers climbed up on the crates and began to speak rapidly and forcefully in German.

Pino was only catching the odd phrase or word, something about the Fatherland and the needs of brother Germans, but whatever he was saying certainly revved up the troops. They were upright, shoulders back, mesmerized by the general as he exhorted them.

General Leyers finished his speech, shouting something about Hitler, and then threw his arm up and out in the Nazi salute. *"Sieg heil!"* he roared.

"Sieg heil!" they thundered back at him.

Pino stood there, confused by the fear he felt growing inside him. What had Leyers said to them? What was happening?

The general disappeared with several officers into a tent. The eight hundred soldiers climbed into half the lorries and left the others empty. Their diesel engines rattled to life. The vehicles began to snake their way out of the meadow, one lorry full of men followed by an empty one. Some pairs went north on the rural road, and the rest headed south, lumbering into the distance like so many war elephants on parade.

Leyers emerged from the tent. His face betrayed nothing as he climbed into the backseat of the Fiat and told Pino to drive south through the Po River valley, as fertile a place as there was on earth. Three kilometers into the drive, Pino saw a girl sitting in the driveway of a small farm with a grain tower. She was sobbing. Her mother sat on the front stoop, her face in her hands.

Not far down the road, Pino saw the body of a man facedown in the ditch with his white T-shirt bruised purple from drying blood. Pino glanced in the rearview. If Leyers had seen any of it, he wasn't showing a reaction. His head was down. He was reading.

The road ran down through a creek bottom and came up onto a large flat with harvested fields on both sides. Less than a kilometer ahead, a small settlement of houses was clustered next to a large grain bin made of stone.

German lorries were parked on the road and in the farmyards. Platoons of Waffen-SS soldiers marched people out into their front yards, maybe twenty-five of them, and forced them to their knees with fingers laced behind their heads.

"Mon général?" Pino said.

In the backseat, Leyers looked up, cursed, and told him to stop. The general climbed out and shouted at the SS men. The first Todt soldier appeared with large grain sacks on his shoulders. Others came behind, twenty, maybe more, laden with grain sacks.

The SS reacted to something Leyers said, and the families were urged to their feet and then allowed to sit as a group while they watched their grain, their livelihood, their survival, stolen and thrown into the back of a Nazi transport.

One of the farmers would not sit, and started shouting at Leyers. "You can at least leave us enough to eat. It's the decent thing to do."

Before the general could reply, one of the SS soldiers hit the farmer in the head with the butt of his rifle and dropped him in his tracks.

"What did he say to me?" Leyers asked Pino.

Pino told him. The general listened, thought, and then called to one of his Todt officers, *"Nehmen sie alles!"*

Then he headed toward the car. Pino followed, upset because he knew enough German to understand Leyers's command. *Nehmen sie alles.* Take everything.

Pino wanted to kill the general. But he couldn't. He had to swallow his anger and marshal himself. But did Leyers have to take *everything*?

As he slid into the Fiat, Pino silently repeated a vow he'd made to remember what he'd seen, from the slaving to the pillaging. When the war was over, he would tell the Allies everything.

They drove on into the early afternoon, seeing more and more farms with Germans under Leyers's command stealing grain bound for mills, vegetables bound for market, and livestock bound for slaughter. Cows were shot in the head, gutted, and thrown into the lorries whole, their carcasses throwing steam into the cool air.

Every once in a while, the general would tell Pino to stop, and he'd climb out to have a conversation with a Todt officer or two. Then he'd order Pino to drive on and return to his reports. Pino kept glancing at the mirror, thinking how Leyers seemed to shift and change with every moment. *How can he possibly be unmoved by what we've seen? How can he—?*

"You think I'm a wicked man, Vorarbeiter?" Leyers said from the backseat.

Pino looked in the mirror, saw the general looking back at him.

"Non, mon général," Pino said, trying to put on his happy face.

"Yes, you do," Leyers said. "It would be surprising if you didn't hate me for what I've had to do today. A part of me hates myself. But I have orders. Winter is coming. My country is under siege. Without this food, my people will starve. So here in Italy, and in your eyes, I'm a criminal. Back home, I'll be an unsung hero. Good. Evil. It's all a question of perspective, is it not?"

Pino gazed at the general in the mirror, thinking that Leyers seemed infinite and ruthless, the kind of man who could justify almost any action in pursuit of a goal.

"Oui, mon général," Pino said, and couldn't restrain himself. "But now, my people will starve."

"Some might," Leyers said. "But I answer to a greater authority. Any lack of enthusiasm for this mission on my part could be grounds for . . . Well, that's not going to happen if I can help it. Take me back to Milan, the central train station."

Chapter Twenty-One

Lorries stacked high with Nazi booty from Italian farms, orchards, and vineyards jammed into the streets around the train depot. Pino followed General Leyers into the station and out to the loading platforms where German soldiers were loading grain sacks, wine kegs, and full bushel baskets of fruits and vegetables into boxcar after boxcar.

Leyers seemed to understand the whole system, firing questions at subordinates and calling out notes to Pino as he marched up and down the platforms.

"Nine trains travel north through the Brenner tonight," the general said at one point. "Arrival Innsbruck oh seven hundred hours. Arrive Munich thirteen hundred hours. Arrive Berlin seventeen hundred hours. In total three hundred and sixty cars of food will . . ."

Leyers stopped dictating. Pino looked up.

Seven Waffen-SS soldiers blocked their way. Beyond them, a string of seven rickety old cattle cars sat on the track by the far platform. At some point, the cars must have been a barn-red color, but the paint had blistered and peeled, and the wood was splintered and cracked, making them look barely fit for travel.

Leyers said something threatening to the SS soldiers, and they stood aside. The general walked toward the train of old boxcars. Pino followed. Looking up, he saw the sign marked "Binario 21."

He was puzzled, knowing he'd heard of it before, but not placing it. With all the din inside the station from the loading of loot, it wasn't until Pino was beside the last car that he heard children crying inside.

The sound seemed to freeze the general. Leyers stood there, staring at the cracked and splintering walls of the cattle car and the many desperate eyes staring back through the cracks at him and at Pino, who now remembered Mrs. Napolitano saying that Platform 21 was where Jews disappeared on trains heading north.

"Please," a woman inside the cattle car sobbed in Italian. "Where are you taking us? After the prison, you can't leave us in here like this! There's no room. There's . . ."

Leyers looked at Pino with a stricken expression. "What is she saying?"

Pino told him.

Sweat broke out on the general's forehead. "Tell her she's going to an Organization Todt work camp in Poland. It's—"

The locomotive engine sighed. The train rolled back a foot. That set off wailing inside the boxcars, hundreds of men, women, and children screaming to be let out, demanding to know their destination and begging for any small mercy.

"You're going to a work camp in Poland," Pino told the crying woman.

"Pray for us," she said before the wheels squealed on the tracks and the train began to pull away from Binario 21.

Three little fingers stuck out of a crack on the rear wall of the last cattle car. The fingers seemed to wave at Pino as the train gathered speed. He stared after the train, seeing the fingers in his mind long after he couldn't see them anymore. His urge was to go after the train and set those people free, get them to safety. Instead, he stood there, defeated, helpless, and fighting the urge to cry at the image of those fingers, which would not fade.

"General Leyers!"

Pino turned. So did the general, who was pale. Had he seen those fingers, too?

Beyond them, down the platform, Gestapo Colonel Walter Rauff was chugging toward them, his face flushed with anger.

"Colonel Rauff," Leyers said.

Pino took a step away from the general and studied the platform beneath his feet. He didn't want Rauff to recognize him for fear that he might become suspicious of the Italian boy from Casa Alpina somehow becoming the driver to General Leyers.

The Gestapo colonel started yelling at Leyers, who began yelling right back at him. Pino understood little of it, but he did hear Rauff invoke Joseph Goebbels's name. Leyers responded by invoking Adolf Hitler. And in their body language, Pino got the meaning. Rauff answered to Goebbels, a Reich Minister. But Leyers answered to the führer himself.

After several minutes of intense threats and ice-cold conversation, a furious Rauff stepped back and saluted. *"Heil Hitler!"*

Leyers returned the salute with less enthusiasm. Rauff was about to leave, when he fixed on Pino for several seconds. Pino could feel his attention dancing all over him.

"Vorarbeiter," General Leyers called. "We are leaving. Bring the car around."

"Jawohl, General," Pino said in his best German, and then hurried past the two Nazi officers, never once looking at Rauff, but feeling his flat dark eyes fixed on him.

With every step, Pino expected to be called back. But Rauff never said a word, and Pino left Platform 21, praying he'd never have to return.

—◆—

General Leyers climbed into the staff car with his normal unreadable expression back in place.

"Dolly's," he said.

Pino glanced in the rearview and saw Leyers's eyes screwed toward the horizon. He knew he should keep his mouth shut, but he couldn't. *"Mon général?"*

"What is it, Vorarbeiter?" he asked, still looking out the window.

"Are the people in the boxcars really going to an OT work camp in Poland?"

"Yes," the general said. "It's called Auschwitz."

"Why Poland?"

At that, Leyers's eyes came unscrewed and he almost shouted in irritation, "Why all the questions, Vorarbeiter? Don't you know your place? Don't you know who I am?"

Pino felt like he'd been slapped at the back of the head. *"Oui, mon général."*

"Then you will keep your mouth shut. You will not ask questions of me or anyone else, and you will do as you are told. Do you understand?"

"Oui, mon général," Pino said, shaken. "I am sorry, *mon général."*

When they reached Dolly's apartment building, Leyers said he'd take the valise up himself and ordered Pino to return the Fiat to the motor pool.

Pino wanted to follow the general upstairs or go around the back and get Anna to let him in, but it was still daylight and he feared he'd get caught. After a long look at the windows of Dolly's apartment, he drove away, thinking how much he wanted to tell Anna about all that he'd seen that day. The violence. The violation. The despair.

That night and for many nights afterward, Pino's dreams were haunted by the red train and Platform 21. He kept hearing the woman beg him to pray for her. He kept seeing those poor little fingers wiggling at him and dreamed that they belonged to a child of a thousand faces, a child who could not be saved.

Over the ensuing weeks and days, Pino drove General Leyers all over northern Italy. They rarely slept. At the wheel, Pino often wondered about the faceless child and the woman he'd spoken to on Platform 21. Had they gone to Poland to be worked to death? Or had the Nazis just taken them somewhere and machine-gunned them the way they had in Meina and a dozen other desecrated places throughout Italy?

When he wasn't driving, Pino felt powerless and exhausted watching Leyers loot factories for machine tools and seize a staggering quantity of building supplies, vehicles, and food. Entire towns were stripped of basic commodities, which were either shipped to Germany by train or distributed to soldiers on the Gothic Line. Through it all, Leyers remained stoic, pitiless, and committed to his task.

"I keep telling you the Allies need to be bombing the train tracks over the Brenner Pass," Pino told his uncle one night in late October 1944. "They need to cut it off, or there will be no food left for any of us, and winter's coming."

"I've had Baka send that message twice," Uncle Albert said in frustration. "But the world's focused on France, and forgotten Italy."

On Friday, October 27, 1944, Pino again drove General Leyers to Benito Mussolini's villa at Gargnano. It was a warm fall day. The leaves of hardwood trees had turned fiery far up into the Alps. The sky was a crystalline blue, and the surface of Lake Garda mirrored both, causing Pino to wonder whether there was a more beautiful place in the world than northern Italy.

He followed Leyers up onto the villa's colonnade and to the terrace, which was empty and strewn with leaves. The French doors to Mussolini's office were thrown open, however, and they found Il Duce inside, standing at his desk, the suspenders of his riding pants hanging by his sides and his tunic well undone. The dictator had a phone pressed to his ear, and his face was twisted into something spiteful.

"Claretta, Rachele's gone crazy," Il Duce was saying. "She's coming for you. Don't talk to her. She says she's going to kill you, so close the gate, and . . . Okay, okay, call me back."

Mussolini hung up the phone, shaking his head before noticing General Leyers and Pino standing there. He said, "Ask the general if his wife is insane over Dolly."

Pino did. Leyers looked surprised that Il Duce knew about his mistress, but said, "My wife is insane over most things, but she knows nothing of Dolly. How can I be of service, Duce?"

"Why does Field Marshal Kesselring always send you to see me, General Leyers?"

"He trusts me. You trust me."

"Do I?"

"Have I ever done anything to make you question my honor?"

Mussolini poured himself some wine and then shook his head. "General, why doesn't Kesselring trust my army enough to use it? I have so many loyal, well-trained men, true Fascists willing to fight for Salò, and yet they sit in their barracks."

"It doesn't make sense to me, either, Duce, but the field marshal has a far greater military mind than mine. I am but an engineer."

The phone rang. Mussolini grabbed it, listened, and said, "Rachele?"

The dictator pulled his head off the receiver, wincing while his wife's voice came screaming out into the room with remarkable clarity. "The partisans! They're sending me poems, Benito! One line says over and over again, 'We will take you all to Piazzale Loreto!' They blame me, they blame you, and they blame your bitch of a mistress! For that she's going to die!"

The dictator smashed the phone down in its cradle, looking shaken, and then stared at Pino for an indication of how much he'd heard. Pino swallowed and became fascinated by the stitchwork in the rug.

Leyers said, "Duce, I have a busy schedule."

"Preparing your retreat?" Mussolini sneered. "Your run toward the Brenner Pass?"

"The Gothic Line still holds."

"I hear it has holes in it," Il Duce said, and drained his wine. "Tell me, General, is it true that Hitler is building a last redoubt? Somewhere underground in the German Alps, where he will retreat with his most loyal followers?"

"One hears many such stories. But I have no direct knowledge of that one."

"If there is, will there be a place in that underground fortress for me?"

"I can't speak for the führer, Duce."

"That's not what I hear," Mussolini said. "But at the very least, maybe you can speak for Albert Speer. Surely Hitler's architect would know if there was such a place."

"I'll ask the Reich Minister the next time we speak, Duce."

"I'll need a room for two," the dictator said, and poured himself more wine.

"Duly noted," the general said. "And now I must leave. I have a meeting in Turin."

Mussolini looked ready to argue, but the phone rang. He winced, picked it up. Leyers turned to go. As Pino started to follow, he heard Mussolini say, "Claretta? Did you shut the gate?" There was a pause before Il Duce roared, "Rachele's there? Get your guard to get her off the gate before she hurts herself!"

They heard more shouting as they walked off the terrace and down the stairs.

Back in the Fiat, General Leyers shook his head and said, "Why do I always feel like I have been to a madhouse when I leave this place?"

"Il Duce says many strange things," Pino said.

"How he led a country is beyond me," Leyers said. "But they say the train system ran like German clockwork when he was in full power."

"Is there an underground fortress in the Alps?" Pino asked.

"Only a lunatic would believe in something like that."

Pino wanted to remind the general that Adolf Hitler wasn't exactly stable, but he thought better of it and they drove on.

Shortly after sunset on Tuesday, October 31, 1944, General Leyers told Pino to drive him to the train station in the city of Monza, about fifteen kilometers northeast of Milan. Pino was exhausted. They'd been on the road almost constantly, and he wanted to sleep and to see Anna. They'd barely had ten minutes together since the night of the strafing.

But Pino followed orders and turned the Fiat north. The second full moon of the month—the true blue moon—rose, casting a pale light that made the countryside look like dark turquoise. When they reached the Monza station, and the general climbed out, Organization Todt sentries locked at attention. They were Italians, young men like Pino, trying to survive the war.

"Tell them I'm here to oversee a transfer in the yard," General Leyers said.

Pino did, and they nodded and gestured to the far end of the platform.

A small lorry pulled up. Two OT soldiers and four men in shabby gray clothes got out. They had patches on their chests. Three said "OST"; the fourth said "P."

"Wait here, Vorarbeiter," General Leyers told Pino in a cordial tone. "I won't be long, no more than an hour, and then we can get that well-needed sleep and see our lady friends. Okay?"

Feeling punchy, Pino smiled and nodded. He wanted to lie down on one of the benches and go to sleep right then. But watching Leyers take a flashlight from one of the soldiers and lead the way toward the far end of the platform, he came alert.

The general didn't have the valise with him!

It was in the Fiat out in front of the station. An hour, no more, Leyers had said. But that was plenty enough time to go through the valise, wasn't it? Uncle Albert had never gotten him the camera he said he'd look into. But Pino had the general's camera, loaded with what he knew to be a fresh roll of film. Leyers insisted on keeping the camera in the car so he could take pictures of sites for possible artillery installations. And when the general did take pictures, he always removed the film and replaced it with a new roll, even if it wasn't full.

Pino decided that if he came across something that looked important, he'd photograph the papers, take the film, and replace it with another fresh roll from the glove compartment.

He'd taken two steps toward the Fiat when something beyond fatigue bothered him, something about the way Leyers had walked off just then, leading the four slaves and the two OT soldiers. He couldn't put his finger on it, but he wondered what Leyers might be transferring by the light of the full moon. And why didn't the general want him to see the transfer? That was odd. Where Leyers went, Pino usually went as well.

A train whistled not far away. Torn in two directions, Pino went with his gut and padded off toward the end of the platform where Leyers had disappeared. By the time he'd jumped down into the yard and walked well away from the station without seeing the general or the others with him, a freight train came rumbling into the station and squealed to a stop.

Pino scrambled under one of the train's boxcars and crawled over the tracks. When he reached the other side, he heard voices. Peering out from under the train and to his right, he saw the two OT soldiers silhouetted by the general's flashlight. They were coming Pino's way.

Pino pressed himself tight to the wheels of the boxcar and watched the soldiers go by. He looked out and to his right again and made out Leyers standing with his back to him about sixty meters away. The general was watching the four gray men. They had formed a line and were moving objects from a boxcar that was part of the freight train to a lone boxcar on the adjacent track. The objects weren't very big, but the slaves had to put their entire bodies into holding and moving the heavy loads.

If Pino couldn't tell his uncle what he'd seen in Leyers's valise, he at least wanted to be able to tell him what the general was transferring after dark, and why he was personally overseeing the slaves doing the work.

After scrambling back to the other side of the freight train, Pino tried to be as light on his feet as possible and moved forward with the boxcars between him and Leyers, thankful to hear the clunking of heavy metal objects the closer he got. Thunk. Thunk. Clunk.

He caught the rhythm of the timing and moved with it, one foot to the other, until he felt he'd drawn even with the group, and then one knee and hand to the other as he crawled under the freight train. He peeked out the other side to find himself fewer than ten meters from the general.

Leyers had the flashlight aimed at the cinders between the rails, so the men worked in the glow of a light at their feet. Pino could see one man in the boxcar above Leyers handing out narrow rectangular objects that he couldn't quite make out as they were passed above the waist from one man to another and into the opposite boxcar, which was a rusty-orange color.

What the hell was—?

The third man in line fumbled and almost dropped one. Leyers shifted the flashlight beam, shone it on the object in the man's hands, and Pino had to fight not to gasp.

It was a brick, a brick made of gold.

"Das ist genug," Leyers said, telling them in German, "That's enough."

The four slave laborers looked at the general expectantly. He waved with the flashlight toward the boxcars, indicating they should shut and lock them.

Pino realized the gold transfer was complete, which meant Leyers would soon be heading toward the station and the Fiat. He crabbed backward slowly, and then quicker when he heard the door to the boxcar above him sliding shut.

He was back on his feet on the other side of the train when the second boxcar door shut. Pino danced away on his tiptoes and to the side of the cinders where weeds grew and muffled the sound of his passing.

Within a minute, he was clambering up onto the train platform. The freight train's locomotive grumbled at the far end of the track. The wheels creaked, whined, and gained speed. The couplings between the cars ground. And every rail tie crossed made a solid, steady thump, thump, thump. And still Pino heard the flat crack of gunshots clearly.

The first one he doubted. But not the second, third, or fourth, which were spaced at intervals of two to four seconds and coming from Leyers's direction. It was all over in less than fifteen seconds.

The two OT soldiers whom Leyers had ordered away from the transfer site came out onto the platform as if they, too, had heard the shots.

With horror and growing anger, Pino thought, *Four slaves dead. Four witnesses to a gold diversion dead.* Leyers had pulled the trigger. He'd cold-bloodedly executed them. And he'd planned to do it long before tonight.

The last of the freight train boxcars passed the platform and thumped off into the night, carrying a fortune in what Pino assumed was looted gold. There was a fortune out there in the train yard, too. How much gold had there been?

Enough to kill four innocent men, Pino thought. *Enough to—*

He heard the crunch of General Leyers's boots before he saw him as a shade of darkness out there in the moonlit night. Leyers flipped on the flashlight, played it on the platform, and found Pino, who raised his forearm to block the beam and had the quick, panicked thought that the general may have decided to kill him, too.

"There you are, Vorarbeiter," General Leyers said. "Did you hear those shots?"

Pino decided dumb was his best strategy. "Shots, *mon général*?"

Leyers came to the platform, shaking his head in bemusement. "Four of them. All clean misses. I've never been able to shoot worth a damn."

"*Mon général*? I don't understand."

"I was transferring something important to Italy out there, protecting it," he said. "And when I had my back turned, the four laborers took their chance and ran for it."

Pino frowned. "And you shot them?"

"I shot at them," General Leyers said. "Or rather, over them and behind them. I'm a horrible marksman. I didn't care, really. I don't care. Good luck to them." Leyers clapped his hands. "Take me to Dolly's, Vorarbeiter. It's been a long day."

If General Leyers was lying, if he'd killed the four slaves, he was also a superb actor or someone who had no conscience, Pino thought as he drove back to Milan. Then again, Leyers had been shaken by the Jews of Platform 21. Maybe he had a conscience when it came to certain things and not to others. The general seemed in a happy enough mood during the ride, chuckling to himself or smacking his lips with satisfaction every once in a while. And why not? He'd just stashed away a fortune in gold.

The general said he'd done it for Italy, protecting it, but as Pino pulled the Fiat up in front of Dolly's, he remained skeptical. Why would Leyers protect anything for Italy after he'd stolen so much from the country already? And Pino had heard enough stories in life to know that men acted strangely, irrationally, when gold was involved.

When they reached the apartment on the Via Dante, General Leyers climbed out of the car with the valise in his hand.

"You have the day off tomorrow, Vorarbeiter," Leyers said.

"Thank you, *mon général*," Pino said, bobbing his head.

Pino needed a day off. He also needed to see Anna, but he was obviously not being invited to go upstairs for a glass of whiskey.

The general made a move toward the front door, but then stopped.

"You may use the car tomorrow, Vorarbeiter," he said. "Take the maid anywhere you want to go. Enjoy yourselves."

⬦

The next morning, Anna came down the stairs to the lobby just as Pino was coming through the front door. They both nodded uncertainly to the crone blinking on the stool, and then left, laughing and happy to be in each other's company.

"This is nice," she said, taking the passenger seat next to him.

Pino felt good to be out of his OT uniform. He was someone completely different. So was Anna. She wore a blue dress, black pumps, and a fine wool shawl around her shoulders. She'd put on lipstick, and mascara, and . . .

"What?" she said.

"You're just so beautiful, Anna. You make me want to sing."

"You're so sweet," she said. "And I'd kiss you if I didn't want to smear Dolly's expensive French lipstick."

"Where shall we go?"

"Somewhere pretty. Somewhere we can forget the war."

Pino thought about that, and said, "I know just the place."

"But before I forget," Anna said, reaching in her purse and handing him an envelope. "General Leyers says it's a letter of passage, under his signature."

It was astonishing how attitudes changed when Pino showed the letter to sentries along the route to Cernobbio. Pino drove Anna to his favorite spot on Lake Como, a small park near the southern end of the lake's west arm. It was a clear, unusually warm, breezy autumn day. The sky was a thin blue, and snow dusted the tallest crags, the mountains and their reflection in the lake like two joined watercolor paintings. Pino felt hot, and took off his heavy shirt, revealing a sleeveless white T-shirt.

"It's so beautiful," Anna said. "I see why you love it here."

"I've stood here a thousand times, and it still doesn't look real to me, like it's God's vision, nothing human about it, you know?"

"I do."

"Let me take a picture of you here," Anna said, pulling out General Leyers's camera.

"Where did you get that?"

"In the glove compartment. I'll just keep the film and put the camera back."

Pino hesitated, and then shrugged. "Okay."

"Stand in profile," she said. "Chin up, and get your hair back. I want to see your eyes."

Pino tried, but the breeze kept blowing his curly hair over his eyes.

"Hold on," Anna said, digging in her purse. She came up with a white headband.

"I'm not going to wear that," Pino said.

"But I want to see your eyes in the picture."

Seeing how disappointed she'd be if he didn't go along, Pino took the headband, put it on, and made a funny face to make her laugh. Then he stood in profile, lifted his chin, and smiled.

She clicked the camera twice. "Perfect. I'll always remember you like this."

"Wearing a headband?"

"So I could see your eyes," Anna protested.

"I know," he said, and hugged her.

When they broke, he pointed to the far northern stretch of the lake. "Up there, below the snow line? That's Motta, where Father Re runs Casa Alpina. The place I told you about."

"I remember," Anna said. "Do you think he's still helping them? Father Re?"

"Of course," Pino said. "Nothing gets in the way of his faith."

In the next moment he thought about Platform 21. It must have shown in his face, because Anna said, "What's wrong?"

He told her about what he'd seen on the platform and how terrible he'd felt watching the red cattle cars pull away, and the tiny fingers waving.

Anna sighed, rubbed his back, and said, "You can't be the hero all the time, Pino."

"If you say so."

"I do say so. You can't carry the world's problems on your back. You have to find some happiness in your life, and just do your best with the rest."

"I'm happy when I'm with you."

She seemed conflicted, but then smiled. "You know, I am, too."

"Tell me about your mother," Pino said.

Anna stiffened.

"Sore scar?"

"One of the sorest," she said, and they began to walk along the lakefront.

Anna told Pino her mother went slowly crazy after her husband drowned at sea and her daughter survived. Her mother told Anna that she was responsible for her father's death and for all the miscarriages she'd had after Anna's birth.

"She thought I had the evil eye," Anna said.

"You?" Pino said, and laughed.

"It's not funny," Anna said, dead sober. "My mother did horrible things to me, Pino. She made me think things about myself that just weren't true. She even had priests perform exorcisms on me to cast out the demons."

"No."

"Yes. When I could, I left."

"Trieste?"

"Home, and soon after, Trieste," she said, and looked away toward the lake.

"Where did you go?"

"Innsbruck. I answered an ad, and met Dolly, and here I am. Isn't it strange how life is always taking you to places and to people you're supposed to see and meet?"

"You believe that about me?"

A wind came up, blew strands of her hair across her face. "I guess. Yes."

Pino wondered whether God's plan was for him to meet General Leyers, but when Anna brushed back her hair and smiled, he forgot all about that.

"I don't like lipstick from Paris," he said.

She laughed. "Where else can we go? What other beautiful place?"

"You pick."

"Around Trieste, I could show you many places. But here, I don't know."

Pino thought, looked reluctantly at the lake, and then said, "I know a place."

An hour later, Pino drove the staff car over railroad tracks and up a farm lane to the hill where his father and Mr. Beltramini had performed "*Nessun Dorma*," "None Shall Sleep."

"Why here?" Anna asked skeptically as dark clouds were rolling in.

"Let's climb up there, and I'll show you."

They got out and started up the hill. Pino described the trains that had left Milan every night during the summer of 1943, how they'd all come here for safety in the thickest, sweet-smelling grass, and how he and Carletto had seen Michele and Mr. Beltramini perform a minor miracle of voice and violin.

"How did they do it?"

"Love," Pino said. "They played *con smania*, with passion, but the passion came from love. There's no other explanation. All great things come from love, don't they?"

"I guess they do," Anna said, and looked away. "The worst things, too."

"What does that mean?"

"Another time, Pino. Right now, I'm too happy."

They'd reached the crest of the hill. Fifteen months before, the meadow had been green, lush, and innocent. Now, the vegetation had faded to browns. The long grass was matted, gone to stalks, and the fruit trees in the orchard were barren. The sky darkened. It began to drizzle, and then to rain, and they had to run downhill to get to the car.

When they got inside, Anna said, "I have to say, Pino, if it's my choice, here or Cernobbio? I'll take Cernobbio."

"Me, too," he said as he looked up through the rain-streaked windshield toward the hilltop gathering fog. "It's not as wonderful as I remembered, but then again, my friends and family were there. My father played the best violin piece of his life, and Mr. Beltramini was singing to his wife. And Tullio, and Carletto, he . . ."

Overcome with emotion, Pino laid his head on his hands holding the steering wheel.

"Pino, what's the matter?" Anna asked, alarmed.

"They've all left me," he choked.

"Who left you?"

"Tullio, and my best friend, even my brother. They think I'm a Nazi and a traitor."

"Can't you tell them you're a spy?"

"I shouldn't have even told you."

"Oh, that's a lot to bear," she said, rubbing his shoulder. "But they'll know eventually, Carletto and Mimo, when the war's over. And Tullio? The best thing is to grieve for the people you loved and lost, and then welcome and love the new people life puts in front of you."

Pino picked his head up. They gazed at each other for several long moments before Anna put her hand in his, leaned close, and said, "I don't care about the lipstick anymore."

PART FOUR
THE CRUELEST WINTER

Chapter Twenty-Two

Driven by northeast winds, temperatures in northern Italy dropped steadily through November 1944. British Field Marshal Alexander broadcast a plea to the ragtag Italian resistance forces known as GAPs to form into guerilla armies and to attack the Germans. Instead of bombs, leaflets fluttered from the skies onto the streets of Milan, urging citizens to join the fight. The pace of resistance assaults soared. The Nazis were being harassed at almost every turn.

In December, snow buried the Alps. Storm after storm squalled down out of the mountains, blanketed Milan, and fell south as far as Rome. Leyers and Pino began a frenzied series of tours of the defensive fortifications along the Gothic Line in the Apennine Mountains.

They found German soldiers huddling around fires in smoky cement machine gun nests, at cannon installations, and under makeshift canvas tarps. More blankets, OT officers told Leyers. More food. More heavy wool jackets and socks, too. As the bitterness of winter set in, every Nazi soldier on the heights was enduring extreme hardship.

General Leyers seemed genuinely moved by their plight, and he pushed himself and Pino harder to see to their needs. Leyers commandeered blankets from a mill in Genoa, and wool socks and jackets from factories in Milan and Turin. He emptied markets in all three cities, adding to the misery of the Italians.

By the middle of December, Leyers was determined to have more cattle seized, butchered, and delivered to his troops on Christmas Day, along with cases and cases of wine stolen from wineries all over Tuscany.

Early on the morning of Friday, December 22, 1944, Leyers ordered Pino once again to drive to the Monza train station. The general left the Fiat with his valise and told Pino to wait. It was broad daylight. Pino couldn't follow Leyers for fear of being spotted. When the general returned, the valise looked heavier.

"The Swiss border crossing above Lugano," Leyers said.

Pino drove, believing the valise now carried one if not two bars of gold, maybe more. When they reached the border, the general told Pino to wait. It was snowing hard when Leyers crossed into Switzerland and vanished into the storm. Eight bone-numbing hours later, Leyers returned and ordered Pino to drive back to Milan.

⟞⟝

"You sure he took gold to Switzerland?" Uncle Albert said.

"What else would he have done in the train yard?" Pino asked. "Bury the bodies? After six weeks?"

"You're right. I'm . . ."

"What's the matter?" Pino asked.

"The Nazi radio hunters, they are getting good at their jobs, too good. They triangulate in on our broadcasts much faster. Baka has almost been caught twice in the past month. And you know the penalty."

"What are you going to do?"

Aunt Greta stopped cleaning dishes in the sink, turned to look at her husband, who was studying his nephew. "Albert," she said, "I think it's unfair of you to even ask. The boy's done enough. Let someone else try."

"We've got no one else," his uncle said.

"You haven't even discussed this with Michele."

"I was going to have Pino do it."

"Do what?" Pino said, frustrated.

His uncle hesitated before saying, "The apartment below your parents'?"

"The Nazi VIP place?"

"Yes. Now, you're going to think this is a strange idea."

Aunt Greta said, "I thought it was nuts the first time you suggested it, Albert, and now, the more I think about it, it's downright insane."

"I think I'll let Pino decide that."

Pino yawned, then said, "I'm going home to sleep in two minutes whether you tell me what you want me to do or not."

"There's a Nazi shortwave in the apartment below your father's place," Uncle Albert said. "A cable runs out the window and up to a radio antenna mounted on the outer wall of your parents' terrace."

Pino remembered but remained confused, still not sure where this was going.

"So," his uncle continued, "I think to myself that if the German radio hunters are looking for illegal radios broadcasting from illegal antennas, we might fool them by connecting our illegal radio to the Nazis' legal antenna. You see? We splice into their cable, attach our radio, and send out our signal over a known German antenna. When the radio hunters converge, they'll say, 'It's one of us.' And walk away."

"If they know no one is on the Nazi radio, couldn't they come up to the terrace?"

"We'll wait until they are done broadcasting, and then piggyback our signal right when they sign off."

"What would happen if the radio was found in our apartment?" Pino asked.

"Not good."

"Does Papa know what you're thinking?"

"First I want you to tell Michele what you're really doing in German uniform."

Even though his parents had ordered him to join the Organization Todt, Pino had seen how his father reacted to his swastika armband, how he looked away, his lips curled with shame.

Though the chance to tell his father the truth cheered him, Pino said, "I thought the fewer people who knew, the better."

"I did say that. But if Michele knows the kind of risks you are taking for the resistance, he will accept my plan."

Pino thought about it all. "Let's say Papa agrees. How are you going to get the radio up there? Past the lobby guards, I mean."

Uncle Albert smiled. "That's where you come in, my boy."

That evening in the family apartment, Pino's father stared at him.

"You're really a spy?"

Pino nodded. "We couldn't tell you, but now we have to."

Michele shook his head, and then motioned Pino over and hugged him awkwardly.

"I'm sorry," he said.

Pino swallowed his emotions and said, "I know."

Michele released his embrace and looked up at Pino with shining eyes. "You're a brave man. Braver than I could ever be, and capable in ways I never would have guessed. I'm proud of you, Pino. I wanted you to know that, no matter what may happen to us before this war's over."

It meant the world to Pino, and he choked, "Papa—"

His father put his hand on Pino's cheek when he couldn't go on. "If you can get the radio past the sentries, I'll keep it here. I want to do my part."

"Thank you, Papa," Pino said finally. "I'll wait until after you've gone to see Mama and Cicci for Christmas. That way you can deny knowing anything about it."

Michele's face fell. "Your mother will be upset."

"I can't come, Papa. General Leyers needs me."

"Can I tell Mimo about you if he gets in touch?"

"No."

"But he thinks—"

"I know what he thinks, and I'll just have to live with that until a better time," Pino said. "When did you last hear from him?"

"Three months ago? He said he was going south to Piedmont for training. I tried to stop him, but there was no getting in your brother's bullheaded way. He climbed out your window onto the ledge and got out. Six stories up. Who would do such a thing?"

Pino flashed on his younger self using a similar escape route and tried not to smile as he said, "Domenico Lella. The one and only. I miss him."

Michele wiped his eyes. "God only knows what that boy's gotten himself into."

⟻

Late the next evening, after another long day in General Leyers's car, Pino was sitting in Dolly's kitchen eating Anna's excellent risotto and staring off into space.

Anna gave him a light kick in the shin.

Pino startled. "What?"

"You are someplace else tonight."

He sighed, and then whispered, "Are you sure they're asleep?"

"I'm sure they're in Dolly's room."

Pino still whispered. "I didn't want to get you involved, but the more I think about it, you could be a big help with something important that could also be dangerous to the both of us."

Anna gazed at him with excitement at first, but then her expression sobered, and then showed fear. "If I say no, will you do this thing alone?"

"Yes."

After several moments she said, "What do I need to do?"

"Don't you want to know what I want you to do before you decide?"

"I trust you, Pino," Anna said. "Just tell me what to do."

＊

Even amid war, destruction, and despair, Christmas Eve is a day when hope and kindness flourish. Pino saw it early in the day as General Leyers played Weihnachtsmann, Father Christmas, down on the Gothic Line, overseeing the distribution of stolen bread, beef, wine, and cheese. He saw it again that evening when he and Anna stood at the back of the Duomo behind thousands of other Milanese crammed into the three vast apses of the cathedral for a vigil Mass. The Nazis had refused to lift curfew for the traditional midnight celebration.

Cardinal Schuster celebrated the Mass. Though Anna could barely see the cleric, Pino was tall enough to see Schuster clearly as he gave his homily, which was at once a discussion of the hardship of Jesus's birth and a rallying cry to his flock.

"'Let not your hearts be troubled,'" the cardinal of Milan said. "Those six words of Jesus Christ, our Lord and Savior, are more powerful than any bullet, cannon, or bomb. The people who hold these six words true are unafraid, and they are strong. 'Let not your hearts be troubled.' People who hold these words true will surely defeat tyrants and their armies of fear. It has been this way for nineteen hundred and forty-four years. And I promise you it will be this way for all time to come."

When the choir rose to sing, many in the crowd around Pino looked uplifted by Cardinal Schuster's defiant sermon. As they opened their mouths to sing along with the choir, Pino saw battered, war-weary faces taking hope, rejoicing even at a time of sparse joy in the lives of far too many.

"Did you give thanks in there?" Anna said as they left the cathedral after Mass. She shifted a shopping bag she was carrying from one hand to the other.

"I did," Pino said. "I thanked God for making you a present to me."

"Listen to you. That's so nice."

"It's also true. You make me unafraid, Anna."

"And here I'm as afraid as I've ever been."

"Don't be," Pino said, putting his arm around her shoulder. "Do what I sometimes do when I get scared: imagine you're someone else, someone who's far braver and smarter."

As they walked past the dark, damaged hulk of La Scala, heading toward the leather shop, Anna said, "I think I can do that. Act like someone else, I mean."

"I know you can," Pino said, and he walked all the way to Uncle Albert's feeling invincible with Anna at his side.

They knocked at the rear door off the alley. Uncle Albert opened the door to the factory sewing room, and they went in, the smell of tanned leather everywhere. When the door was locked, his uncle flipped on the light.

"Who is this?" Uncle Albert asked.

"My friend," Pino said. "Anna-Marta. She's going to help me."

"I thought I said it would be done better alone."

"Since it's my head on the block, I'll do it my way."

"Which is how?"

"I'm not saying."

Uncle Albert did not look happy about it, but he also showed Pino some respect. "How can I help? What do you need?"

"Three bottles of wine. One opened and recorked, please."

"I'll get them," his uncle replied, and went up to the apartment.

Pino began changing from his street clothes back into his uniform. Anna set down the shopping bag and walked through the workshop, taking in the cutting tables, the sewing stations, and shelves of fine leather goods in various stages of completion.

"I love this," she said.

"What?"

"This world you live in. The smells. The beautiful craftsmanship. It's like a dream to me."

"I guess I've never seen it that way before, but, yes, it's nice."

Uncle Albert came back downstairs with Aunt Greta and Baka. The radio operator was carrying that tan suitcase with the straps and false bottom Pino had seen back in April.

His uncle watched Anna, who was still admiring the leather goods.

Pino said, "Anna loves what you do."

He softened. "Yes? You like these?"

"It's all so perfectly crafted," Anna said. "How do you even learn to do this?"

"You're taught," Aunt Greta said, eyeing her suspiciously. "You learn from a master. Who are you? How do you know Pino?"

"We work with each other, sort of," Pino said. "You can trust her. I do."

Aunt Greta wasn't convinced, but she said nothing. Baka handed Pino the suitcase. Up close, the radio operator looked haggard and drawn, a man who'd been on the run for too long.

"Take care of her," Baka said, nodding at the radio. "She's got a voice that carries everywhere, but she's a delicate thing."

Pino took the case, remarked on how light it was, and said, "How did you get it into San Babila without being searched?"

"Tunnels," Uncle Albert said, looking at his watch. "You need to hurry now, Pino. No need to try this after curfew."

Pino said, "Anna, can you bring the shopping bag and the two unopened bottles?"

She put down a tooled leather bag she'd been admiring, grabbed what he needed, and went with him to the back of the shop. Pino opened the suitcase. They put the wine and the contents of the shopping bag inside, covering the false bottom that hid the radio components and the generator.

"Okay," Pino said after they'd strapped the case shut. "We're off."

"Not without a hug from me," Aunt Greta said, and embraced him. "Merry Christmas, Pino. Go with God." She looked at Anna. "You as well, young lady."

"Merry Christmas, *signora*," Anna said, and smiled.

Uncle Albert held out the leather bag she'd been admiring, and said, "Merry Christmas to the brave and beautiful Anna-Marta."

Anna's jaw dropped, but she took it as a little girl might a treasured doll. "I've never had so wonderful a present in my whole life. I'll never let it go. Thank you! Thank you!"

"Our pleasure," Aunt Greta said.

"Be safe," Uncle Albert said. "The two of you. And merry Christmas."

⊰⊱

When the door shut, the gravity of what lay before them weighed heavily on Pino. Being caught with an American-made shortwave transmitter would be like signing a death warrant. Standing there in the alley, Pino pulled the cork and took a long draw off the bottle of excellent Chianti Uncle Albert had opened, and then handed it to Anna.

Anna took a few swigs, and another longer one. She grinned madly at him, kissed him, and said, "Sometimes you just have to have faith."

"Father Re always says that," Pino said, smiling. "Especially if it's the right thing to do, no matter the consequences."

They exited the alley. He carried the suitcase. Anna put the wine in the open mouth of her new purse. They held hands and threw a few weaves into their steps, and giggled as if they were the only two people in the world. From down the street at the Nazi checkpoint, they heard raucous laughter.

"Sounds like they've been drinking," Anna said.

"Even better," Pino said, and led the way to his parents' apartment building.

The closer they got, the tighter Anna gripped Pino's hand.

"Relax," he said softly. "We're drunk, not a care in the world."

Anna took a long swig of wine, and said, "A couple minutes from now, it will either be the end of things or the beginning."

"You can still back out."

"No, Pino, I'm with you."

Climbing the stairs to the front door of the apartment building and pushing it open, Pino had a moment of panic and doubt, wondered if it was a mistake to bring Anna, to risk her life needlessly like this. But the second he pushed the

270

door open, she burst into laughter, hanging on him and singing snatches of a Christmas carol.

Be someone else, Pino thought, and joined her as they stumbled into the lobby.

Two armed Waffen-SS sentries Pino did not recognize stood at the base of the elevator and stairway, looking at them intently.

"What is this?" one of them asked in Italian, while the other covered them with a machine pistol. "Who are you?"

"I live here, sixth floor," Pino said with a slur, holding out his papers. "Michele Lella's son, Giuseppe, loyal soldier of the Organization Todt."

The German soldier took the papers, studied them.

Anna hung on Pino's arm with an amused look until the other soldier said, "Who are you?"

"Anna," she said, and hiccupped. "Anna-Marta."

"Papers."

She blinked, went for the purse, but then rolled her head drunkenly. "Oh no, this is a new purse, my Christmas present, and I left the papers in my other one at Dolly's. You know Dolly?"

"No. What is your business here?"

"Business?" Anna snorted. "I'm the maid."

"The maid for the Lellas has already left today."

"No," she said, waving a hand at them. "General Leyers's maid."

That got their attention, especially when Pino said, "And I am the general's personal driver. He gave us Christmas Eve off, and . . ." Pino tilted his head to his right shoulder, exposing his neck, and took a step toward them, smiling sheepishly. In a low, conspiratorial voice, he said, "My parents are away. We've got the night off. The apartment is empty. Anna and I thought we'd go up, and, you know, celebrate?"

The eyebrow of the first sentry rose appreciatively. The other one leered at Anna, who responded with a saucy smile.

"Okay?" Pino said.

"Ja, ja," he said, laughing as he gave Pino his papers. "Go on up. It's Christmas."

Pino took the papers, stuffed them sloppily in his pocket, and said, "I owe you."

"We both do," Anna said shyly, and hiccupped again.

Pino thought they were home free when he went to pick up the leather suitcase. But when he did the bottles inside made a distinct clinking noise.

"What's in the suitcase?" the other sentry said.

Pino looked at Anna, who blushed and laughed. "His Christmas present."

"Show me," he said.

"No," Anna complained. "It's supposed to be a surprise."

"Open it," the second sentry insisted.

Pino looked at Anna, who blushed again and shrugged.

Pino sighed, knelt, and undid the straps.

Lifting the lid revealed two more bottles of Chianti; a red satin bustier with matching panties, garters, and thigh-high red stockings; a black-and-white French maid's outfit with garter belt, panties, and sheer black silk stockings; and a black lace bra and panties.

"Surprise," Anna said softly. "Merry Christmas."

⟺

The first soldier howled with laughter and said something fast in German that Pino did not catch. The other soldier cracked up, and so did Anna, who said something back to them in German that got them laughing even more.

Pino didn't know what was going on, but he took the opportunity to remove one of the wine bottles and shut the suitcase. He held the wine out to the sentries. "And merry Christmas to you."

"*Ja?*" one sentry said, taking it. "Is good?"

"*Magnifico*. From a winery near Siena."

The SS soldier held it up to his partner, who was still grinning, and then looked back to Pino and Anna. "Thank you. Merry Christmas to you, and your cleaning lady."

That sent him, his partner, and Anna into another round of laughing. As they made their way to the birdcage elevator, Pino laughed, too, though he didn't know why.

As the elevator began to rise, the Nazi sentries were babbling happily and opening the wine bottle. When the elevator reached the third floor and they were out of sight from below, Anna whispered, "We did it!"

"What did you tell them?"

"Something naughty."

Pino laughed, leaned over, and kissed her. She stepped over the suitcase and into his arms. They were embracing as they passed the fifth floor and the second set of Waffen-SS sentries. When Pino opened his eyes for a peek at them over Anna's shoulders, he caught a glimpse of two envious men. They got inside the apartment, closed the door, turned on a light, and put the suitcase and the radio in a closet before falling into each other's arms on the couch.

"I've never felt like this," Anna gasped, her eyes wide-eyed and glassy. "We could have died down there."

"It makes you see what matters," Pino said, covering her cheeks and face with soft kisses. "It cuts everything else away. I . . . I think I love you, Anna."

He'd hoped she'd say the same, but she pulled back from him, her face hardening. "No, you shouldn't say that."

"Why not?"

Anna struggled, but then said, "You don't know who I am. Not really."

"What could make me not listen to the music in my heart every time I see you?"

Anna wouldn't look at him. "That I'm a widow?"

"A widow?" Pino said, trying not to sound deflated. "You were married?"

"That's usually how it works," Anna said, studying him now.

"You're too young to be a widow."

"That used to hurt, Pino. Now it's just what everyone says."

"Well," he said, still struggling with the news. "Tell me about him."

⊷⊶

It had been an arranged marriage. Her mother, who continued to blame Anna for her husband's death, was keen on getting rid of her and put up a house she'd inherited as dowry. His name was Christian.

"He was very handsome," Anna said with a bittersweet smile. "An army officer. Ten years older than me the day we were married. We had a wedding night and a two-day honeymoon before he was shipped off to North Africa. He died defending a desert town called Tobruk, three years ago now."

"Did you love him?" Pino asked, his throat closed tight.

Anna cocked her chin and said, "Was I crazy for him as he set out to fight Mussolini's stupid war? No. I barely knew him. There'd been no time for real love to kindle, much less burn. But I admit I liked the idea of falling in love with him when I believed he would return to me."

Pino could see she was telling the truth. "But you . . . made love to him?"

"He *was* my husband," she said, irritated. "We made love for two days, and then he went to war and died and left me to fend for myself."

Pino thought about that. He looked into Anna's searching, wounded eyes and felt the music stir in his chest. "I don't care," he said. "It only makes me adore you more, admire you more."

Anna blinked back tears. "You're not just saying that?"

"No," Pino said. "So can I say I love you?"

She hesitated, but then nodded and came to him shyly.

"You can show me you love me, too," Anna said.

They lit a candle and drank the third bottle of Chianti. Anna undressed for Pino. She helped him from his clothes, and they lay down on a bed they made of pillows, cushions, sheets, and blankets on the living room floor.

Had she been any woman other than Anna, Pino might have fixated on the thrill of her skin and touch. But beyond her lips' beckoning and her eyes' bewitching, Pino was seized by something much more compelling and primal, as if Anna were not human but a spirit, a melody, a perfect instrument of love. They caressed, they joined, and in that first ecstasy, Pino felt himself fuse with Anna's soul as deeply as her body.

Chapter Twenty-Three

There was no sleep and no war for Pino that night, only Anna and the pleasure of their duet.

As dawn came on Christmas Day 1944, they drowsed in each other's arms.

"Best present ever," Pino said. "Even without Dolly's outfits."

Anna laughed. "They're not my size anyway."

"Makes me glad the sentries didn't demand a fashion show."

She laughed again and slapped him softly. "Me, too."

Pino began to drift and was right on the verge of falling off into a deep, satisfied sleep when he heard the sound of boots coming down the hall from the bedrooms. He jumped up, clawing for the Walther in his holster on a chair. He got it and spun around.

Already aiming a rifle at his brother, Mimo said, "Merry Christmas, Nazi boy."

Mimo bore a nasty, livid scar down the left side of his face. The rest of him looked as battle-hardened as the German soldiers down along the Gothic Line. Uncle Albert had reports that Mimo had engaged in ambush and sabotage, that he had seen combat and shown great courage in battle. By the hard patina to Mimo's eyes, Pino knew it was true.

"What happened to your face?" Pino asked.

Mimo sneered. "A Fascist put a knife through it and left me for dead, coward."

"Who's a coward?" Anna said, standing up angrily with the sheets around her.

Mimo took one look at her, shook his head at Pino, and said with disgust, "Not only are you a coward and a traitor, you bring some whore to Mama and Papa's house on Christmas and screw her in the living room!"

Before he even felt rage, Pino flipped the pistol, caught it by the barrel, and whipped it overhand at his brother. The Walther hit the wounded cheek, threw Mimo off balance, and he howled with pain. Pino came over the couch in two huge bounds, tried to punch his brother in the face. Mimo dodged and tried to hammer him with the rifle butt. Pino grabbed the gun, twisted it from his brother's grasp, and hit Mimo in the gut the way Tito had hit him back at Casa Alpina. It was enough to blow the wind out of his brother and send him sprawling backward onto the dining room floor.

Pino tossed the rifle aside, leaped astride Mimo, and grabbed him by the throat, wanting to drive a fist into his younger brother's face, once and hard, wound or not. But as he cocked back, Anna cried out.

"No, Pino! Someone will hear, and then everything will have been for nothing."

Pino desperately wanted to hit him but released his throat and spun off him to his feet.

"Who is he?" Anna asked.

"My little brother," Pino said with loathing.

"Used to be your brother," Mimo said from the floor with equal hatred.

Pino said, "Get out of here before I change my mind and kill you on Christmas."

Mimo looked like he wanted to go at him, then settled back on his elbows. "Someday, very soon, Pino, you're going to hate yourself for turning traitor. The Nazis will fall, and when they do, may God have mercy on you."

Mimo got to his feet and picked up his rifle. He didn't glance back but walked down the hall toward the bedrooms and disappeared.

"You should have told him," Anna said after Mimo was gone.

"He can't know. It's for his own good. And mine."

Pino was suddenly shivering. Anna opened the blankets wrapped around her and said, "You look cold and alone."

Pino smiled and went to her. She wrapped the blankets around them both and held him tight, saying, "I'm sorry that had to happen to you on Christmas morning, after the most wonderful night of my life."

"Was it?"

"You're a natural," she said, and kissed him.

He grinned sheepishly. "Think so?"

"Oh, my, yes."

Anna and Pino lay down again and, snuggled in each other's arms, drifted off into the last good sleep they'd have for weeks.

⟞⟝

Storm after storm struck northern Italy in the following days. New Year's brought bitter Russian winds and snow that further buried the landscape in dull whites and sullen grays. For Milan, it was the cruelest winter on record.

Vast sections of the city looked macabre. Scorched fragments of buildings still stood in the rubble and the bomb debris, looking to Pino like so many jagged black-and-white teeth gnashing at a sky that almost constantly threw snow, as if God were doing everything in his power to blot out the scars of war.

The people of Milan suffered for God's cold effort. With Leyers's looting of supplies, heating oil was scarce and allocated to German installations. People began cutting down the city's magnificent old trees for firewood. Campfire smoke belched from ruins and standing buildings alike. Tree stumps flanked Milan's famous shaded streets. Many of the parks were attacked and denuded. Anything that would burn was burned. The air in some neighborhoods turned as foul as a coal stove.

General Leyers rarely stopped moving in the first half of January, which meant Pino rarely stopped moving. Again and again they made the snowy, dangerous drive to the Gothic Line, making sure the troops suffering in the cold would get their rations.

Leyers, however, seemed indifferent to the average Italian's misery. He stopped all pretense of paying the Italians for what they made or provided for the German war effort. If there was something the general needed, he ordered it commandeered. In Pino's eyes, Leyers returned to that reptilian state in which he'd first met him. Cold, ruthless, efficient, he was an engineer tasked with a job and hell-bent on getting it done.

One frigid afternoon in the middle of January, the general ordered Pino to drive him to the Monza train station, where he made his valise heavier before asking to be taken to the Swiss border above Lugano.

Leyers was gone for five hours this time. When he climbed from the sedan that brought him back to the frontier, he carried the valise as if it weighed twice what it had leaving Italy, and he seemed to stumble in the path he took across the border to the Fiat.

"Mon général?" Pino said after Leyers had climbed into the backseat with the valise. "Where now?"

"It doesn't matter," Leyers said. He smelled of liquor. "The war's over."

Pino sat there, stunned, unsure he'd heard him correctly.

"The war's over?"

"It might as well be," the general said in disgust. "We're in economic collapse, on the run militarily, and the ungodly things done for Hitler are about to be uncovered. Take me to Dolly's."

Pino got the Fiat turned around and running downhill while trying to dope out what the general had just said. He understood what an economic collapse was. He also knew from his uncle that the Nazis were in retreat after the Ardennes Offensive in eastern France during the Battle of the Bulge and that Budapest was about to fall.

The ungodly things done for Hitler. What did that mean? The Jews? The slaves? The atrocities? Pino wanted to ask Leyers what he meant, but feared what might happen if he did.

Sipping steadily from a liquor flask, the general sat in silence the entire ride back to Milan. As they were closing on the center of the city, something piqued his interest, and he told Pino to slow. He seemed fixated on the buildings still standing, peering up at them as if they held secrets.

At Dolly's, Leyers slurred, "I need time to think, to plan, Vorarbeiter. Drop the car at the motor pool. Consider yourself on leave until Monday at oh-eight hundred hours."

"Monday," Pino said. *"Oui, mon général."*

Before he could get out to open the rear door, Leyers lurched out and across the sidewalk to Dolly's apartment building and disappeared inside with nothing in his hand. He'd forgotten . . . Pino twisted around and looked over the seat. The valise was there, right on the floor.

After stopping at home to change clothes, Pino drove straight to Uncle Albert's. He parked, got out the valise, which was lighter than he expected. Looking through the leather shop's window and seeing Aunt Greta waiting on two German officers, he went around the back and knocked on the sewing room door.

A worker opened it, stared at him, and said, "Where is your uniform today?"

"I have the day off," Pino said, feeling unpleasantly scrutinized as he walked past her. "Can you tell my uncle I'll be upstairs in the kitchen?"

She nodded, but not happily.

When Uncle Albert arrived, something seemed to be hanging heavy about him.

"Are you all right?" Pino asked.

"How did you come in?"

Pino told him.

"Did you see anyone watching the store?"

"No, but then again, I wasn't looking. Do you think . . . ?"

His uncle was nodding. "Gestapo. We have to back off, slow down, fade into the shadows if we can."

Gestapo? Had they seen him get out of General Leyers's staff car with the valise?

Suddenly the threat of discovery felt as real as it ever had. Was the Gestapo onto Uncle Albert? Were they onto a spy inside the German High Command? He flashed on Tullio raging at his executioners and wondered if he'd have that kind of courage if he were discovered and put against the wall.

Half-expecting Gestapo agents to come bursting through the door, Pino quickly described General Leyers's trip into Switzerland, how he came back drunk and said the war was over, and how he'd walked away from his valise.

"Open it," Uncle Albert said. "I'll get your aunt to translate."

When his uncle left, Pino dug out the key they'd made from the wax mold, said a silent prayer, and then slipped it into the first lock. He had to jigger with it before it gave. The second lock turned more easily.

Coming into her kitchen, Aunt Greta looked pale and uncertain when she saw the folders Pino had removed from the valise.

"I almost don't want to look," she said, but flipped the top file open and started scanning the pages inside as Uncle Albert returned. "These are fortification plans on the Gothic Line. Whole sections. Get the camera."

Uncle Albert hustled off to retrieve the camera, and they started photographing pages and recording positions on the maps that they deemed valuable to the Allies. One file detailed train timetables going to and from Italy into Austria. Others described munitions and their locations.

At the bottom, they found an incomplete, handwritten note from Leyers addressed to General Karl Wolff, the head of the SS in Italy. The note made the case for the war's being lost, citing the rapidly dwindling industrial base, the Allied advance before the snows came, and Hitler's refusal to listen to his combat generals.

"'We must face the fact that we cannot go on much longer,'" Aunt Greta said, reading. "'If we do, there will be nothing left of us or the Fatherland.' That's it. No signature. He's not done with it yet."

Uncle Albert thought, and said, "A dangerous thing to put down in writing. I'll make note of it, and tell Baka to send it in the morning."

The radio operator, posing as a carpenter at work on cabinets and bookcases in the Lellas' apartment, had been transmitting to the Allies over the piggyback radio connection every day since Christmas. So far it had worked like a charm.

"What do you want me to do now?" Pino said after he'd returned the files to the valise.

"Take the valise back to him," Uncle Albert said. "Tonight. Tell him someone in the motor pool found it and found you."

"Be safe," Pino said, and went out through the now quiet factory and into the alley.

He'd almost reached the Fiat when he heard, *"Halt."*

A flashlight played on Pino as he froze, holding Leyers's valise.

An SS lieutenant walked up to him, followed by Colonel Walter Rauff, the head of the Gestapo in Milan.

"Papers," the lieutenant said in Italian.

Pino set the valise down, struggling to remain calm as he dug out his papers, including the letter from General Leyers.

"Why aren't you in uniform?" the lieutenant demanded.

"General Leyers gave me two days' leave," Pino said.

Up until then, Colonel Rauff, the man who'd ordered Tullio's death, had said nothing. "And what is this?" he asked now, toeing the bag with his boot.

Pino thought sure he was about to die. "General Leyers's valise, Colonel. The stitching was broken, and he asked me to bring it to the leather shop for repair. I'm taking it back to him now. Would you like to come? Ask him about it? I can tell you he was drunk and in a foul mood when I left him."

Rauff studied Pino. "Why did you come *here* to get it fixed?"

"It's the best leather shop in Milan. Everyone knows that."

"Not to mention it's your uncle's shop," Rauff said.

"Yes, that, too," Pino said. "Having family always helps in a pinch. Have you herded any oxen lately, Colonel?"

Rauff stared at him so long Pino thought he'd gone too far and blown it.

"Not since the last time," the Gestapo chief said at last, and laughed. "Give General Leyers my best."

"I'll do that," Pino said, bobbing his head as Rauff and his men walked away.

Sweat exploded off Pino as he put the valise on the floor in the backseat, got up front, and gripped the wheel.

"Oh Jesus," he whispered. "Oh sweet Jesus."

As soon as he could stop shaking he started the Fiat and drove it back to Dolly's. Anna answered the door, looking agitated.

"The general's very drunk and angry," she whispered. "He hit Dolly."

"Hit her?"

"He's calmed down, said he didn't mean it."

"Are you okay?"

"I'm fine. I just don't think this is the best time to talk to him. He keeps going on and on about the idiots and traitors who've lost the war."

"Put his valise there by the coatrack," Pino said, handing it to her. "He's given me two days off. Can you come to my place? My father's gone to see my mother again."

"Not tonight," she said. "Dolly may need me. But tomorrow?"

He leaned forward, kissed her, and said, "I can't wait."

After leaving the Fiat at the motor pool, Pino returned to the family apartment. He thought about Mimo. Uncle Albert wouldn't tell him much about what his little brother was doing, which was as it should be. If Pino were ever questioned about Mimo's partisan activities, he could justly claim ignorance. But he longed to know what daring deeds his brother had undoubtedly performed, especially after Uncle Albert said that Mimo's reputation in combat was "ferocious."

Flashing back on cherished memories of the Alps, and how they'd climbed and worked together for a greater good, Pino felt even more miserable that Mimo thought him a coward and a traitor. Sitting there alone in the apartment, he desperately wished General Leyers's words at the Swiss border were true, that the war really was over, and that life, his life, could become something good again.

He closed his eyes and tried to imagine the moment when the war would end and how he'd find out. Would people dance in the streets? Would there be Americans in Milan? Of course there would be. They'd been in Rome for six months now, hadn't they? Wasn't that grand? Wasn't that elegant?

Those thoughts stirred up old dreams of going to America, of seeing the world beyond. *Maybe that's all it takes for the future to exist,* Pino thought. *You must imagine it first. You must dream it first.*

Several hours later, the apartment telephone rang and kept jangling.

Pino didn't want to leave his warm bed, but the phone kept ringing and ringing until he couldn't stand it anymore. He slid from beneath the covers, stumbled down the cold hallway, and turned on the light.

Four o'clock in the morning? Who would be calling now?

"Lella residence," he said.

"Pino?" Porzia cried in a crackly voice. "Is that you?"

"Yes, Mama. What's wrong?"

"Everything," she said, and started to weep.

Pino came wide-awake in a panic. "Is it Papa?"

"No," she sniffed. "He's sleeping in the other room."

"Then what?"

"Lisa Rocha? You remember? My best friend from childhood?"

"She lives in Lecco. She had a daughter I used to play with at the lake."

"Gabriella, she's dead," Porzia choked.

"What?" Pino said, remembering how he'd pushed the girl on a swing in her parents' yard.

His mother sniffed. "She was safe and sound, working in Codigoro, but she was homesick and wanted to go see her parents for a visit. Her father, Lisa's husband, Vito, has been very sick, and she was worried."

Porzia said Gabriella Rocha and a friend had left Codigoro by bus the afternoon before. The driver evidently tried to make up time and took a route that ran through the town of Legnago.

"The partisans were fighting the Fascists in the area," Porzia said. "West of Legnago, near a cemetery and an orchard, toward the village of Nogara, the bus was caught in the battle. Gabriella tried to flee, but she was caught in a cross fire and killed."

"Oh, that's awful," Pino said. "I'm very sorry to learn that, Mama."

"Gabriella's still there, Pino," Porzia said with great difficulty. "Her friend managed to get her body into the cemetery before escaping and calling Lisa. I just got off the phone with Lisa. Her husband is ill and can't go find their daughter. It feels like everything in this world has gone wrong and evil."

His mother was sobbing.

Pino felt horrible. "You want me to go get her?"

She stopped crying, and sniffled, "Would you? And take her home to her mother? It would mean the world to me."

Pino didn't relish the thought of dealing with a dead girl's body, but he knew it was the right thing to do. "She's in the cemetery between Legnago and Nogara?"

"That's where her friend left her, yes."

"I'll go right now, Mama."

⟞⟝

Three hours later, dressed in heavy winter clothes, Pino turned General Leyers's Fiat onto a country road that ran east from Mantua toward Nogara and Legnago. Snow fell that breezy morning. The Fiat whipped and bucked over the frozen, rutty road.

Pino plowed on into farm country, sliding past snowed-over crop fields separated from the road by wooden fences and stacked-rock walls. He fought the sedan up a rise west of Nogara, and stopped to look down a sloping hill. On his left, leafless olive and fruit groves ran out to a large, walled cemetery. The terrain was steeper on the right but gave way quicker to a plain with more barren fruit groves, fields, and farmhouses.

In the softly falling snow, it would have been a gentle pastoral scene but for the burned-out bus blocking the road near the cemetery gate, and the crack, rattle, and screams of a battle still raging several hundred meters down the hill. Pino felt his resolve fragment and scatter.

I didn't sign up for this, he thought, and almost turned around. But in his ears he could hear Porzia pleading with him to bring Gabriella to her mother. And leaving the girl, his childhood friend, to the birds would just be wrong.

Pino reached in the glove compartment and removed General Leyers's binoculars. He stepped from the car into the bitter cold and trained the glasses on the valley below. Catching movement almost immediately, he soon realized that the Fascist Black Shirts controlled the south side of the road and the partisans in red neckerchiefs were holding the north side all the way east to the cemetery wall, which was roughly five hundred meters away from him. Corpses from both armies littered the road, the ditches, the fields, and the groves.

Pino thought about that for a moment, and then formulated a plan that scared him half to death, but it was the best that presented itself to him. For a long moment, the fear of going down that hill locked him. All sorts of what-if questions poured into his thoughts, each of them more gut-wrenching than the next.

Once he made the decision to go, however, he tried to stop thinking about the danger. After checking the loaded Walther in his coat pocket, Pino put on gloves and retrieved two white sheets from the trunk. He'd brought them as shrouds for the body, but now they served another purpose. One sheet he belted about his waist like a skirt, and the other he hung like a shawl over his wool cap and jacket.

Pino headed due north, away from the road. Wrapped in the sheets, he moved ghostlike through the snowstorm across the flank of the hill, and then angled downward, gradually losing elevation until he reached the cover of the closest olive grove.

Pino continued on another two hundred meters before veering east along a rock wall at the far north end of the grove. Through the binoculars and the falling snow, he could see the shapes of partisan fighters far to his right, splayed in prone positions at the base of old olive trees, firing at Fascists who tried to cross the road.

He stayed low and moved, keeping as much of his body as possible behind the rock wall. He heard machine pistols from the Fascist side and bullets striking trees, ricocheting off the stone wall, and every so often making a wet plumping sound that he took to be a partisan being hit.

In the echoing quiet after gunfire, wounded men on both sides screamed out in agony for their wives and mothers, for Jesus, for the Virgin Mary, and for God Almighty, begging for help or an end to their torture. The suffering voices wormed into Pino's head and made him petrified when the shooting started again. He couldn't move. What if he were hit? What if he died? What would his mother do if she lost him? He lay on his belly in the snow behind the rock wall, shaking uncontrollably and thinking he should just turn back and go home.

Then Mimo appeared in his mind, calling him a coward, a traitor, and he was ashamed to be hiding behind a rock wall. *Let not your heart be troubled,* Cardinal Schuster had said on Christmas Eve. *Let not your heart be troubled. Have faith,* Father Re had told him more times than he could remember.

Pino pushed himself up into a hunched-over position and barreled forward and east a solid hundred meters to where the rock wall petered out. He hesitated, and then ran on through the back side of another olive grove, seeing partisans moving in the trees to his right about seventy meters away. A heavy machine gun opened up from the Fascist side of the road.

Pino dove into the snow and hugged the base of an old tree. Bullets raked the grove east to west and back again, tearing the limbs off trees and off partisans, judging by the anguished screaming that followed. For a few moments, everything to Pino was nightmarish, sluggish, and snow-covered, everything except the animal roar of the machine gun and the cries of the wounded.

The big gun came sweeping back Pino's way. Heaving himself to his feet, he sprinted just ahead of the bullets raking after him. He heard them smack trees close behind, but he was almost to the corner of the cemetery wall and thought he'd make it.

A root beneath the snow snagged his foot, tripped him. Pino fought to stay upright, but the ground beneath his next step gave way, and he sprawled face-first into a snow-filled drainage ditch.

⟞⟠⟝

Machine gun slugs ripped the air above him and tore into the corner of the cemetery wall, blowing out rock chunks and mortar before sweeping back again the other way.

Facedown in the snow, Pino heard the god-awful screaming of men and boys clinging to life and calling for help or pleading to be done with it. Their pain goaded him up out of the snow and to his feet. He stood there in the drainage ditch, looking at where he'd sprawled, and understood that if he'd remained upright and tried to get to the cemetery, he would have certainly been dead, probably cut in half.

He saw movement to the south. Fascist Black Shirt soldiers were coming across the road. Pino pulled the sheet around him, climbed out of the ditch, and took several big steps before disappearing from sight behind the cemetery's two-and-a-half-meter rear wall.

Pino balled the sheets and tossed them over the wall. Then he crouched, jumped, and grabbed hold of the icy top. Kicking and pulling himself up, he got one leg over, straddled the wall, and then dropped over into the graveyard, landing in deep fresh snow. The begging of the wounded and the maimed continued outside.

Then, there was a shot. Light caliber, by the flat crack of it. Then another. And a third.

Pino dug out the Walther pistol from his coat pocket, hung the white shrouds over his shoulders again, and moved fast through the snow-clad gravestones, statues, and mausoleums toward the front of the cemetery. He figured Gabriella's friend could not have dragged her very far, so the body had to be ahead of him somewhere.

Another shot outside the cemetery walls, then a fifth, and a sixth. Pino kept going. His head was swiveling as he looked everywhere, but he was seeing no one else inside the graveyard. Swinging wide so he couldn't be seen through the gate from the road, Pino reached the row of tombs closest to the front entrance.

He used the binoculars to scan the open ground before the cemetery's front wall, but again saw nothing. Backing up, he peered between the first row of gravestones and the second, and he saw Gabriella Rocha, or the suggestion of her really, fifteen centimeters beneath the snow. Pino made a beeline toward the shape. When the seventh and eighth shots rang outside the cemetery wall, he glanced at the front gate and was relieved to see no one there.

The daughter of Porzia's best friend lay on her back, tucked up tight to the base of a large tomb that hid her from the gate and the road. He knelt by the snow-covered form, leaned over, and blew at the powdery snow, seeing it waft and clear from her face, which was lovely and ice blue. Gabriella's eyes were shut. Her lips were curled in an almost contented smile, as if she'd heard a funny comment on her way to heaven. Pino blew more snow from her face and dark hair, noticing that blood had seeped into the ice crystals and formed a pale red halo beneath her head.

Grimacing, he lifted her head, found her neck stiff with rigor, but was able to make out where the bullet had gone through both sides of the back of her skull—hardly any damage, just two holes drained of blood on either side of where her spinal cord met her brain. Pino laid her back down and brushed the rest of the snow off her, remembering how much fun they'd had as kids and thinking that it was good she hadn't suffered. Alive and frightened one moment, then dead and content before she could draw her next breath.

After spreading the sheets, Pino set the Walther on the tomb and rolled Gabriella onto the first sheet. As he tucked the fabric up around her, he started to think about how he was going to get her body over the back wall with no rope.

Pino turned to get the second sheet, but it no longer mattered. Three Fascist soldiers had come into the graveyard through the gate. They were aiming rifles at him forty meters away.

<hr />

"Don't shoot!" Pino yelled, going down on his knees and throwing his arms up. "I am not a partisan. I work for Major General Hans Leyers of the German High Command in Milan. He sent me to bring this girl's body to her mother in Lecco."

Two of the soldiers looked skeptical and bloodthirsty. The third started laughing as he moved toward Pino, gun up, and saying, "That's the best partisan excuse I have ever heard, which is gonna make me blowing your head off a real shame."

"Don't do it," Pino warned. "I have the documents to prove what I'm saying. Here, inside my coat."

"We don't give a shit about your forged documents," the Black Shirt sneered.

He stopped ten meters from Pino, who said, "Do you want to explain to Il Duce why you shot me instead of letting me take care of this girl's body?"

That seemed to give the Fascist pause. Then he sniggered. "Now you're saying you're friends with Mussolini?"

"Not a friend. I work for him as a translator when General Leyers visits. It's all true. Just let me show you the papers, and you'll see."

"Why don't we just check, Raphael?" another Black Shirt said, growing nervous.

Raphael hesitated and then motioned for the documents. Pino handed over his identity card from the Organization Todt, the signed letter from General Leyers, and a document of free passage signed by Benito Mussolini, president of the Salò Republic. It was the only thing Pino had stolen from Leyers's valise.

"Put your guns down," Raphael said at last.

"Thank you," Pino said with relief.

"You're lucky I didn't just shoot you for being here," Raphael said.

As Pino got up, Raphael said, "How come you're not in the Salò army? How come you're driving for a Nazi?"

"It's complicated," Pino said. "*Signore*? All I want is to take this girl's body home to her mother, who is heartbroken, and waiting to bury her daughter."

Raphael looked at him with some disdain, but said, "Go on, take her."

Pino retrieved his pistol, holstered it, and then wrapped Gabriella with the second sheet. He dug in his coat pocket, got out the OT swastika armband, and put it on. Then he bent down and scooped up the corpse.

She wasn't terribly heavy, but it took a couple of adjustments before Pino had her rolled firmly into his chest. With a nod, he walked back down the row of gravestones through the deep and falling snow, acutely aware of the Black Shirts watching him every step of the way.

———

When Pino exited the cemetery gate, a slat of sunlight broke through the clouds, shining on the charred bus to his left and making the snowflakes look as dazzling as jewels spiraling to earth. But as he started up the road heading toward the far rise, Pino wasn't looking at the diamonds floating from the sky. His eyes darted left and right at the Black Shirts, who were using axes, saws, and knives to behead the partisan dead below their red scarves.

Fifteen, maybe twenty heads had already been stuck on fence posts facing the road. Many of their eyes were open and their faces were twisted in death's agony. The weight of the dead girl in his arms felt suddenly unbearable under the dark and silent gaze of the bodiless men. Pino wanted to drop Gabriella, to leave her and run from the savagery that surrounded him. Instead, he set her down and rested on one knee with his head down, eyes closed, praying to God for the strength to go on.

"Romans used to do it," Raphael said behind him.

Pino twisted to look up at the Fascist, aghast. "What?"

Raphael said, "Caesar would have the heads of his enemies lining the roads into Rome as fair warning of what happened if you crossed the emperor. I think it has the same effect now. Il Duce would be proud, I think. You?"

Pino blinked dully at the Black Shirt. "I don't know. I'm just a driver."

He picked Gabriella up again and started trudging up the snowy road, trying not to look at the mounting number of heads on bloodstained fence posts or the jerky, butcherous motions of the Fascists still working on the remaining dead.

Chapter Twenty-Four

Porzia's best friend turned hysterical when Pino came to her door in Lecco with Gabriella's body. He helped to lay her daughter out on a table where women in mourning clothes were waiting to prepare her for burial. Pino slipped out as they grieved her, didn't wait for a word of thanks. He couldn't stay around the dead or listen to the echoing pain of the living a moment longer.

Pino got into the Fiat and started it, but did not put the car in gear. Seeing the decapitations had shaken him to his core. Killing a man in a war was one thing. Desecrating his body was another. What kind of barbarians were they? Who would do such a thing?

He thought back on many of the terrible events he'd witnessed since the war came to northern Italy. Little Nicco holding the grenade. Tullio facing the firing squad. The slaves in the tunnel. The little fingers sticking out of the red boxcar on Platform 21. And now bodiless heads on snowy fence posts.

Why me? Why must I see these things?

Pino felt as if he and Italy had been condemned to suffer cruelties that seemed endless. What new brutality was coming his way? Who would be the next to die? And how horribly?

His head spun with these dark thoughts and others. He grew anxious, frightened, and then panicked. He was sitting still, but he was breathing far too fast, sweating and feverish, and his heart felt like he was sprinting uphill. He realized he couldn't go back to Milan like this. He needed somewhere quiet and remote, somewhere he could scream and no one would care. More than that, he needed someone to help him, to talk to . . .

Pino looked north and realized where he was going and whom he wanted to see.

He drove north along the east shore of Lake Como, ignoring its beauty, fixated with getting to Chiavenna and the Splügen Pass road as fast as possible.

The way was barely passable after Campodolcino. Pino had to put chains on the Fiat to make the long climb to Madesimo. He parked the car near the trail to Motta and started uphill with twenty-five centimeters of fresh snow on the boot-packed path.

The sun finally broke through. A strong breeze was blowing out the last of the clouds when Pino reached the plateau, gasping in the bitter air, focused not on the grandeur of the place but on Casa Alpina. He felt so desperate at the sight of the refuge that he ran the length of the plateau and rang the bell on the porch as if it were a fire alarm.

In his peripheral vision, Pino picked up four armed men coming around the side of the building. They wore red neckerchiefs and pointed rifles at him.

Pino threw up his hands and said, "I'm a friend of Father Re."

"Search him," one said.

Pino went into a panic over the documents he still carried in his pockets, one from General Leyers, and the other from Mussolini. The partisans would shoot him just for that.

But before the men could reach him the door opened, and Father Re was looking at him. "Yes?" he said. "Can I help you?"

Pino pulled off his cap. "It's me, Father Re. Pino Lella."

The priest's eyes went wide, first with disbelief, and then with joy and wonder. He threw his arms around Pino and cried, "We thought you were dead!"

"Dead?" Pino said, fighting back tears. "What made you think that?"

The priest stepped back, stared at him, beaming, and then said, "It doesn't matter. What's important is that you are alive!"

"Yes, Father," he said. "Can I come in? Talk to you?"

Father Re noticed the partisans watching. He said, "I vouch for him, my friends. I have known him for years, and there is not a better man in the mountains."

If that impressed them, Pino didn't notice. He followed Father Re down the familiar hallway, smelling Brother Bormio's bread baking, and then hearing men moaning and talking in low voices.

More than half of the dining hall at Casa Alpina had been converted into a field hospital. A man Pino recognized as a doctor from Campodolcino was with a nurse working on one of the nine wounded men lying in cots arranged by the fireplace.

"Members of the Ninetieth Garibaldi," Father Re said.

"Not Tito's boys?"

"The Ninetieth drove those hoodlums out of the valley months ago. The last we heard, Tito and his crew were scavenging and robbing on the road to the Brenner Pass. The cowards. The men you see here are all brave souls."

"Is there somewhere we can talk, Father? I've come a long way to see you."

"Oh? Of course," Father Re said, and took him to his own room.

The priest gestured to the small bench. Pino sat, wringing his hands.

"I wish to confess, Father," he said.

Father Re looked concerned. "To what?"

"My life since I left you," Pino said, and he told Father Re the worst of it.

⟥

He broke down four times describing General Leyers and the slaves and Carletto Beltramini cursing him while his father lay dying, the decimation ceremony at San Vittore Prison, the machine-gunning of Tullio Galimberti, Mimo's ridicule of him, and leaving the graveyard that morning under the dead eyes of the severed heads.

"I don't know why these things are happening to me." Pino wept. "It's just too much, Father. Too much to see."

Father Re put his hand on Pino's shoulder. "It sounds like too much to me, too, Pino, but I'm afraid it's not too much for God to ask of you."

Bewildered, Pino said, "What's he asking me to do?"

"To bear witness to what you've seen and heard," the priest said. "Tullio's death should not go in vain. The murderers in Piazzale Loreto should be brought to justice. Those Fascists this morning, too."

"Seeing them butcher the dead . . . I don't know, Father . . . It makes me question my faith in mankind, in people being good deep down, not savages, not like that."

"Seeing those things would make any man question his faith in mankind," the priest said. "But most people *are* essentially good. You have to believe that."

"Even the Nazis?"

Father Re hesitated, and then said, "I can't explain the Nazis. I don't think the Nazis can explain the Nazis."

Pino blew his nose. "I guess I want to be one of those men out there in the dining room, Father. Fighting openly. Doing something that matters."

"God wants you to fight in a different way, and for a greater good, or he would not have put you where you are."

"Spying on General Leyers," Pino said with a shrug. "Father, other than meeting Anna, the last time I felt really good about myself was here at Casa Alpina, helping people get over to Val di Lei, saving lives."

"Well," Father Re said, "I'm no expert, but I have to believe you've saved the lives of many Allies with the information you've risked your life to provide."

Pino hadn't thought of it that way before. Wiping away tears, he said, "General Leyers—from what I've told you, do you think he's evil, Father?"

"Working a man to death is the same as shooting a man to death," the priest said. "Just a different choice of weapons."

"That's what I think, too," Pino said. "Sometimes Leyers can seem like anyone else, and the next he's like a monster."

"From what you've seen and told me, I'd say you're going to cage the monster someday, make him pay for his sins on earth before he atones for them before God."

That made Pino feel better. "I'd love for that to happen."

"Then you will. Have you really been inside the chancellery in Milan?"

"Once," Pino said.

"And to Mussolini's villa at Gargnano?"

"Twice," Pino said. "It's a strange place, Father. I don't like going there."

"I don't want to know. But tell me more about your Anna."

"She's funny, and pretty, and smart. She's six years older than me and a widow, but I love her, Father. She doesn't know it yet, but I plan to marry her after the war."

The old priest smiled. "Then refind your faith in mankind in your love of Anna, and build your strength through your love of God. These are dark times, Pino, but I really do sense clouds wanting to lift and the sun wanting to rise on Italy again."

"Even General Leyers says the war is all but over."

"Let's pray your general is right about that," Father Re said. "You're staying for dinner? You can spend the night, talk with the wounded men, and I have two downed American pilots coming tonight who could use a guide to Val di Lei. Are you up to it?"

Americans! Pino thought. That would be exciting. A climb to Val di Lei might be good for his body, and helping two Americans escape might be good for his soul. But then he thought of General Leyers, and what he might do if he found out Pino had been driving all over northern Italy with a dead body in the backseat of his staff car.

"Actually, Father," Pino said, "I should go back. The general might need me."

"Or Anna might."

Pino smiled at the mention of her name. "Or Anna."

"Which is as it should be." Father Re chuckled. "Pino Lella. A young man in love."

"Yes, Father."

"Be safe, my son. Don't break her heart."

"No, Father. Never."

Pino left Casa Alpina feeling as if he'd been cleansed somehow. The late afternoon air was fresh and biting cold. The crag of the Groppera stood out like a bell tower against a cobalt sky, and the alpine plateau at Motta seemed once more to Pino like one of God's grandest cathedrals.

Hurrying from the motor pool shortly after dark, Pino felt like he'd lived three lifetimes in a single day. When he entered the lobby of his apartment building, he found Anna standing there, joking with the sentries.

"There you are!" she said, looking like she'd already had her first glass of wine.

One of the sentries said something, the other laughed, and Anna said, "He wants to know if you know how lucky you are."

Pino grinned at the SS soldier. "Tell him I do. Tell him when I'm with you, I feel like the luckiest guy on earth."

"You're sweet," she said, and then translated.

One of the sentries raised an eyebrow skeptically. But the other nodded, perhaps recalling the woman who made him feel like the luckiest guy on earth.

They never asked for Pino's papers, and he and Anna were soon riding in the birdcage elevator. When they passed the fifth floor, Pino grabbed her and they kissed passionately. They broke when the elevator reached their floor.

"So you did miss me?" Anna asked.

"Ridiculously," he said, and took her hand as they exited.

"What's wrong?" she asked as he worked the key into the lock.

"Nothing," he said. "I just . . . I just need to forget this war again with you."

Anna put her hand gently on his cheek. "That sounds like a wonderful fantasy."

They went in, shut the door, and did not leave for nearly thirty hours.

Pino pulled up in front of Dolly's ten minutes early the following Monday morning. He sat there for a few moments, savoring his memories of the hours spent alone with Anna, when time had seemed to stand still, when there was no war, only pleasure, and the giddy happiness of blooming love as triumphant and joyous as Prince Calaf's aria.

The rear door of the Fiat opened. General Leyers climbed in, valise first, wearing his long gray wool business coat.

"Monza," Leyers said. "The train station."

Light snow began to fall when Pino put the Fiat in gear, feeling angry that Leyers was going after his stolen gold again, bringing more of it into Switzerland.

Pino could already see his day unfolding in front of him. He would spend it parked at the border above Lugano, freezing the hours away while the general did secret business. When Leyers returned from the train yard, however, he told Pino to drive not to the Swiss border but instead to the central train station in Milan.

They got there around noon. Leyers would not let Pino carry his valise, and he shifted the heavy load from hand to hand as they walked to that rattletrap train of faded-red cattle cars, sitting in the bitter cold of Platform 21.

Pino had prayed he'd never see the train again, but there it was, and he walked toward it with dread, pleading with God not to let him see tiny fingers waving through the slats in the boxcars. But he could see naked fingers from thirty meters away, dozens of them, and of all ages, beckoning for mercy while voices inside shouted for aid. Through the slats in the boxcar, Pino could see that most of the people were no better dressed than the people he'd seen in the same cars the September before.

"We're freezing!" a voice shouted. "Please!"

"My daughter!" another called. "She's sick with fever. Please."

If General Leyers heard their pleas, he ignored them, and went straight for Colonel Rauff, who stood there waiting for the train to pull out along with ten members of the Waffen-SS. Pino pulled his hat down over his eyes and hung back. The two SS soldiers closest to Rauff had German shepherd attack dogs on short leashes. Leyers looked unimpressed by them and said something calmly to Rauff.

After a moment, the Gestapo colonel ordered the guards to move away. Pino stood in the shadow of an iron post and watched the general and Rauff have an intense argument, which went on until Leyers gestured at his valise.

Rauff stared at the general quizzically, then at the valise, and back to Leyers before he said something. Leyers nodded. The Gestapo colonel barked an order at the SS guards. Two of them went to the rear cattle car, unlocked it, and slid back the doors. Eighty people, men, women, and children, were crammed into a space meant for twenty cows. They were terrified and shivering.

"Vorarbeiter," General Leyers said.

Pino made no eye contact with Rauff as he crossed to Leyers. *"Oui, mon général."*

"I heard someone say, 'My daughter is sick.'"

"Oui, mon général," Pino said. "I heard that, too."

"Ask the mother to show the sick girl to me."

Pino was confused, but he turned to the people in the open cattle car and translated.

A few moments later, a woman pushed through the crowd, helping a pale, sweating little girl about nine years old.

"Tell her that I am going to save her daughter," General Leyers said.

Pino balked a moment before translating.

The woman began to sob. "Thank you. Thank you."

"Tell her I will get the girl medical help and make sure she never comes to Platform Twenty-One again," the general said. "But the girl must come alone."

"What?" Pino said.

"Tell her," Leyers said. "And there is no argument. Either her daughter is saved, or she is not, and I'll find someone more agreeable."

Pino didn't know what to think, but told her.

The woman swallowed but said nothing.

The women around her said, "Save her. Do it!"

At last, the sick girl's mother nodded, and Leyers said to the SS guards, "Take her to my car, and wait with her there."

The Nazis hesitated until Colonel Rauff shouted at them to comply. The girl, though weak and feverish, went hysterical when they took her from her mother's arms. Her shrieks and cries could be heard throughout the station while Leyers ordered the rest of the people out of the boxcar. He walked in front of them, looking at each in turn before stopping in front of a girl in her late teens.

"Ask her if she wishes to be brought somewhere safe," Leyers said.

Pino did, and the girl nodded without hesitation.

General Leyers ordered two more Waffen-SS guards to take her to his car.

The general moved on, inspecting, and Pino couldn't help remembering how he had graded the slaves at the stadium in Como that first day Pino drove for Leyers. In minutes, General Leyers had picked two more, both boys, both in their teens. One boy refused, but his father and mother overruled him.

"Take him," the man said firmly. "If he's safe, he's yours."

"No, Papa," the boy said. "I want to—"

"I don't care," his mother said, crying as she hugged him. "Go. We'll be fine."

When the SS soldiers had led them away, Leyers nodded to Rauff, who ordered the others back into the cattle car. Pino felt overwhelming dread watching them board the train, especially the mother and the father of the last boy chosen. They kept looking back over their shoulders before climbing into the boxcar, as if for one more glimpse of their lost love and joy.

You did the right thing, Pino thought. *It's tragic, but you did the right thing.*

He could not watch when they shut the cattle car door, barred, and locked it.

"Let's go," Leyers said.

They walked past Colonel Rauff. The general's valise sat at the Gestapo chief's feet.

When they reached the Fiat, the four taken off the train were inside and shivering. Three were in the backseat, and one in the front. Two SS soldiers were guarding them. They didn't look happy about it when Leyers dismissed them.

The general opened the rear door and looked in at them, smiling. "Vorarbeiter, tell them my name is Major General Hans Leyers of the Organization Todt. Ask them to repeat that, please."

"Repeat it, *mon général*?"

"Yes," Leyers shot back, irritated. "My name. My rank. The Organization Todt."

Pino did as he was told, and they each repeated his name, rank, and the Organization Todt, even the little sick girl.

"Excellent," the general said. "Now ask them who saved them from Platform Twenty-One?"

Pino felt strange but did as he was told, and the four dutifully repeated his name.

"Have long and prosperous lives, and praise your God as if today were Passover," Leyers said, and shut the car door.

The general looked at Pino, his breath billowing clouds in the frigid air. "Take them to the chancellery, Vorarbeiter, to Cardinal Schuster. Tell him to hide them or get them to Switzerland. Tell him I'm sorry I couldn't bring him more."

"Oui, mon général," Pino said.

"Pick me up at the telephone exchange at six p.m.," he said. He turned and walked back into the train station. "We have much to do."

Pino watched Leyers go before turning back to the car, trying to decipher what he'd just seen occur. *Why was he—? What was he—?* But then, he decided, none of it mattered. Getting these four to the chancellery was the important thing. He got into the car and turned it on.

The sick girl, Sara, cried and moaned for her mother.

"Where are we going?" the older girl said.

"The safest place in Milan," Pino said.

He parked the Fiat in the courtyard of the chancellery and told them to wait inside. Then he climbed the snowy staircase to the cardinal's apartment and knocked.

A priest he did not recognize answered. Pino told him who he was, whom he worked for, and who was in the car.

"Why were they in the boxcars?" the priest asked.

"I didn't ask, but I think they're Jews."

"Why did this Nazi general think Cardinal Schuster would ever get involved with Jews?"

Pino looked at the priest, who'd gone stony, and felt outraged. He pulled himself up to his full height and loomed over the priest, a slight man.

"I don't know why Leyers thought that," Pino said. "But I do know that Cardinal Schuster has been helping Jews escape to Switzerland for the past year and a half because I helped him do it. Now, shouldn't we ask the cardinal what he wants done?"

He'd said this all in such a threatening tone that the priest shrank and said, "I can't promise you anything. He's working in his library. But I'll go—"

"No, I'll go," Pino said. "I know the way."

He brushed past the priest, went down the hall until he reached the library, and knocked.

"I asked not to be disturbed, Father Bonnano," Schuster called from inside.

Pino tore off his hat, opened the door, and stepped through bobbing his head and saying, "I'm sorry, My Lord Cardinal, but it's an emergency."

Cardinal Schuster stared at him curiously. "I know you."

"Pino Lella, My Lord Cardinal. I drive for General Leyers. He got four Jews off the train at Platform Twenty-One. He told me to bring them to you, and to say that he was sorry there couldn't be more."

The cardinal pursed his lips. "Did he now?"

"They're here. In his car."

Schuster did not say a thing.

"Your Eminence," Father Bonnano said, "I explained that you cannot personally be involved with such—"

"Why not?" Schuster said sharply, and then looked to Pino. "Bring them inside."

"Thank you, My Lord Cardinal," Pino said. "One girl is sick with fever."

"We'll get a doctor. Father Bonnano will see to it. Won't you, Father?"

The priest seemed unsure, and then bowed deeply. "At once, Your Eminence."

When Pino had seen the four to the cardinal's library and watched Father Bonnano fetch them blankets and hot tea, he said, "I should go, My Lord Cardinal."

Schuster studied Pino, and then walked him out of earshot of the refugees. "I don't know what to make of your General Leyers," the cardinal said.

"I don't, either. He changes every day. Full of surprises."

"Yes," Schuster said thoughtfully. "He *is* full of surprises, isn't he?"

Chapter Twenty-Five

Polar air continued to pour down out of the Alps on relentless bitter winds that blasted Milan through the end of January and on into early February of 1945. General Leyers ordered the seizure of staples like flour, sugar, and oil. Riots broke out in the long lines that formed for the remaining food. Diseases like typhus and cholera thrived in the unsanitary conditions caused by the bombardment. They were near epidemic in large parts of the city. To Pino, Milan felt like a cursed place, and he wondered why its people were being punished so heartlessly.

The weather and Leyers's ruthlessness bred hatred throughout northern Italy. Despite the frigid conditions, while wearing the swastika Pino could feel the heat of rage building in every resentful Italian face he passed. Tics of disgust. Twitches of rancor. Spasms of loathing. He saw all those reactions and more. He wanted to shout at them, to tell them what he was really doing, but he stayed true, swallowed the shame, and went on.

General Leyers turned erratic after saving the four Jews. He would work at his job at his normal frenzied, sleepless pace for several days, and then grow despondent and get drunk in Dolly's apartment.

"He's up one minute, down the next," Anna said one afternoon in early February as they left a café down the block from Dolly's. "One night, the war's over, the next, the fight's still on."

Snow coated Via Dante, and the air was frigid, but the sun was shining so brightly for a change that they decided to take a walk.

"What happens after the war?" Pino asked as they neared Parco Sempione. "To Dolly, I mean?"

"He's moving her to Innsbruck when the Brenner Pass road opens," she said. "Dolly wants to go now by train. He says it's not safe. Trains are being bombed up on the Brenner. But I think he just needs her here, just like she'll need me there for a while."

Pino's stomach fell. "You'll go to Innsbruck with Dolly?"

Anna stopped by the long, wide, and deep depression in the snow that marked the ancient moat that surrounded Castello Sforzesco. The fifteenth-century stone fortress had been hit during the bombardment of 1943. The medieval round towers to either end were in ruins. The tower above the drawbridge had damage that showed like black, scabbed wounds against the snow.

"Anna?" Pino said.

"Just until Dolly's settled," Anna said, studying the bombed tower as if it held secrets. "She knows I want to come back to Milan. And to you."

"Good, then," Pino said, and kissed Anna's gloved hand. "There're at least fifteen meters of snow up high. It will take weeks to clear that road."

She turned from the castle and said hopefully, "The general did say it could be a month once the snow stops, maybe more."

"I pray for more," Pino said, took her in his arms, and kissed her until they both heard the flapping of wings and broke their embrace.

Big ebony ravens were flushing from the bomb holes in the fortress's central tower. Three birds flew away croaking and squawking, while the largest one flew in lazy circles above the wounded spire.

"I need to get back," Anna said. "You do, too."

They walked hand in hand down Via Dante. A block from Dolly's building, Pino saw General Leyers coming out the front door and heading toward the parked Fiat.

"Got to go," Pino said, blowing her a kiss before sprinting to meet Leyers. He opened the Fiat's door saying, "A thousand pardons, *mon général*."

The general bristled at him. "Where have you been?"

"Taking a walk," Pino said. "With the maid. Where can I drive you?"

Leyers looked like he wanted to lay into Pino, but he glanced through the window and saw Anna approaching.

He let out a long breath and said, "Cardinal Schuster's quarters."

Twelve minutes later, Pino pulled the Fiat through the arch into the chancellery courtyard, which was crowded with vehicles. Pino managed to park, got out, and opened the general's door.

Leyers said, "I may need you."

"Oui, mon général," Pino said, and followed the Nazi across the snowy courtyard and up the exterior stairs to Cardinal Schuster's apartment.

General Leyers knocked, and Giovanni Barbareschi answered the door.

Had the young seminarian escaped again? Leyers showed no sign of recognizing the forger who'd survived the decimation ritual at San Vittore Prison. But Pino did, and was mortified more than ever to be wearing the armband and the symbol of Nazism.

"General Leyers to see His Eminence."

Barbareschi stood aside. Pino hesitated, and then walked past as the seminarian studied him, as if trying to place him. Pino prayed that it wasn't in the yard at San Vittore Prison. Barbareschi had to have seen Leyers there, though. Had he seen the general try to stop the decimation? They entered Cardinal Schuster's private library. The cardinal of Milan stood behind his desk.

"Kind of you to come, General Leyers," Schuster said. "Do you know Signor Dollmann?"

Pino tried not to gape at the other man in the room. Everyone in Italy knew him. A tall, thin, elegantly built man with unnaturally long fingers and an intense, practiced smile, Eugen Dollmann was often in the newspapers. Dollmann was Hitler's translator whenever the führer came to Italy, or when Mussolini went to Germany, for that matter.

Pino began translating to Leyers in French, but Dollmann stopped him.

"I can translate, whoever you are," Dollmann said with a flip of his hand.

Pino nodded, backed up toward the door, wondering if he should leave. Only Barbareschi seemed to notice he did not. Dollmann rose, extended his hand, and spoke to Leyers in German. The general smiled, bobbed his head, and replied.

In Italian, Dollmann told Cardinal Schuster, "He's comfortable with me translating. Shall I ask his driver to leave?"

The cardinal peered past Leyers and Barbareschi toward Pino.

"Let him stay," Schuster said, and then gazed at Leyers. "General, I am hearing that if there is a retreat, Hitler means to scorch the earth and lay waste to Milan's few remaining treasures."

Dollmann translated. Leyers listened and then spoke rapidly back in return. The interpreter said, "The general hears the same things, and he wishes to tell the cardinal that he disagrees with the policy. He is an engineer, a lover of great architecture and art. He is opposed to any more unnecessary destruction."

"And the new field marshal, Vietinghoff?" the cardinal asked.

"The new field marshal, I think, can be persuaded to do the right thing."

"And you are willing to do the persuading?"

"I am willing to try, Your Eminence," Leyers said.

"Then I bless your efforts," Cardinal Schuster said. "You'll keep me informed?"

"I will, Your Eminence. I must also caution you, Cardinal, about your public pronouncements in the days ahead. There are powerful people who are looking for a reason to have you imprisoned, or worse."

"They wouldn't dare," Dollmann said.

"Don't be naïve. Or haven't you heard yet about Auschwitz?"

At that, the cardinal looked weakened. "It's an abomination before God."

Auschwitz? Pino thought. *The work camp where the red cattle cars went?* He flashed on the little fingers sticking out the side of the boxcar. What had happened to that child? To all the others? Dead, certainly, but . . . *an abomination*?

"Until next time, Your Eminence," Leyers said, clicked his heels, and turned away.

"General?" the cardinal called after him.

"Your Eminence?"

"Take good care of your driver," Schuster said.

Leyers glanced hard at Pino, but then seemed to remember something, softened, and said, "What else could I do? He reminds me of my late nephew."

Auschwitz.

Pino kept thinking about that word, that place, that OT work camp as he drove General Leyers to his next appointment at the Fiat factory in Turin's Mirafiore district. He wanted to ask Leyers what the abomination was, but was too frightened to ask, too scared to see how he might react.

So Pino kept his questions to himself, even when they went into a meeting with Calabrese, the Fiat manager, who looked unhappy to see Leyers again.

"There's nothing I can do," Calabrese said. "There have been too many sabotages. We can't run the line anymore."

Pino was sure Leyers would explode. Instead, Leyers said, "I appreciate your honesty, and I want you to know that I am working to make sure Fiat is protected."

Calabrese looked unsure. "Protected from what?"

"Total destruction," the general said. "The führer has called for scorched earth if there is a retreat, but I am making sure the backbones of your company and your economy survive. Fiat will go on, no matter what happens."

The manager thought, and then said, "I'll tell my superiors. Thank you, General Leyers."

⊰⊱

"He's doing them favors," Pino said later that night in his aunt and uncle's kitchen. "That's how he does things."

"At least he's helping Cardinal Schuster to protect Milan," Uncle Albert said.

"After looting the countryside," Pino said hotly. "After working people to death. I've seen what he's done."

"We know you have," Aunt Greta said, seeming preoccupied. For that matter, his uncle was, too.

"What's wrong?" Pino asked.

"There was disturbing news this morning on the shortwave," Uncle Albert said. "About a concentration camp in Poland called Au-something."

"Auschwitz," Pino said, feeling nauseated. "What happened?"

Uncle Albert said that by the time the Russians got to Auschwitz on January 27, parts of the camp had been blown up and the records burned. The SS men who ran the camp had fled, taking fifty-eight thousand Jewish prisoners with them as slaves.

"They left seven thousand Jews behind," Uncle Albert said, his voice choking.

Aunt Greta shook her head, distraught. "They evidently looked like human skeletons because the Nazis had been trying to work them to death."

"Didn't I tell you?" Pino cried. "I've seen them do it!"

"This is worse than what you described," Uncle Albert said. "The survivors said that the buildings the Nazis blew up before leaving the camp were gas chambers used to poison Jews, and a crematorium to burn their bodies."

"They said the smoke covered the sky around the camp for years, Pino," his aunt said, wiping at tears. "Hundreds of thousands of people died there."

The fingers, the little fingers waved in Pino's mind, and the mother of the sick girl, and the father who'd wanted his son saved. They'd gone to Auschwitz just a few weeks before. *Are they dead? Poisoned and burned? Or are they slaves retreating toward Berlin?*

He hated the Germans then, every last one of them, and especially Leyers.

The general had told him that Auschwitz was an Organization Todt work camp. *They build things*, he had said. *Like what? Like gas chambers? Like crematoriums?*

Shame and revulsion poured through Pino at the thought that he'd worn the OT uniform, the same uniform worn by people who built gas chambers to kill Jews and crematoriums to hide the evidence. In his mind, the builders of those camps were as guilty as whoever ran them. And Leyers had to have known. After all, he had Hitler's ear.

⟆

By the time Pino and General Leyers reached the village of Osteria Ca'Ida on February 20, 1945, they had been driving for hours. The last twenty minutes had been spent spinning in greasy cold mud up a steep road to a high promontory that looked southeast toward the medieval fortress of Monte Castello, some three kilometers away.

Pino had been to the spot several times the prior autumn, so Leyers could study the castle from afar to better understand how to fortify it. Monte Castello loomed eight hundred meters above a road that led north toward Bologna and Milan. Controlling that road was essential to holding the Gothic Line.

In the last month, the castle, along with the battlements Leyers built at Monte Belvedere and Monte della Torraccia, had held off the Allied attack four times. But now, on a pale, frigid morning, Monte Castello lay under siege.

Pino had to cover his ears to the whistle and thunder of the artillery shells falling in and around the castle. The blasts felt like hammer blows in his chest. Each hit threw gouts of debris and flame that gave way to uncoiling clouds of oily smoke, which rose, billowed, and blackened the pewter sky.

Pino shivered and watched as Leyers, bundled in a long wool overcoat, used his field glasses to scan the battlefield, and then looked away to the southwest across a series of ridges and mountains. With his bare eyes, Pino could see an army of men about five kilometers away moving over the dull-white and dun winter hills.

"The US Tenth Mountain Division is fighting for della Torraccia," General Leyers said, handing Pino the binoculars. "Very well trained. Very tough soldiers."

Pino used them and saw fragments of the battle before Leyers said, "Glasses."

Pino handed them quickly back to the general, who peered through them southeast past the base of Monte Castello. Leyers cursed, and then chuckled sardonically.

"Here," he said, handing Pino the glasses. "Watch a few black bastards die."

Pino hesitated, but then looked through the binoculars, seeing troops of the Brazilian Expeditionary Force charge across open ground at the base of the mountain's southwest flank. The first line of attacking soldiers was forty meters out from the base when a man stepped on a land mine and was blown apart in a haze of dirt, smoke, and blood. Another soldier stepped on a mine, and then a third before the battlefield came under withering German machine gun fire from above, pinning them down.

But Allied cannons and mortars continued to pound the fortress. By mid-morning, there were breaches in the walls on both sides of the castle, and the Brazilians kept coming, waves of them that finally crossed the minefield, made the base of Monte Castello, and started a deadly climb that would last for hours.

General Leyers and Pino stood there in the cold the entire time, watching the Tenth Mountain Division conquer della Torraccia and, in hand-to-hand combat, the Brazilians take Monte Castello around five that afternoon. The mountainside was cratered when the Allied cannons stopped. The castle lay in smoking ruins. The Germans were in full retreat.

General Leyers said, "I am beaten here, and Bologna will be lost in a matter of days. Take me back to Milan."

The general sat in silence the entire ride back, head down, scribbling on a pad of paper and rifling through documents in his valise until they pulled to the curb outside Dolly's building.

Pino carried his valise, following Leyers past the old crone in the lobby and up the stairs. General Leyers knocked at the apartment door. Pino was surprised when Dolly answered, dressed in a black wool dress that fit her snugly.

Her eyes were rheumy, as if she'd been drinking. Her cigarette smoldering as she teetered on high heels, she said, "How wonderful of you to come home, General." Then she looked at Pino. "I'm afraid Anna is not feeling well. A stomach bug of some sort. Best to stay away."

"Best for all of us to stay away, then," General Leyers said, backing up. "I can't afford to be sick. Not now. I'll sleep elsewhere tonight."

"No," Dolly said. "I want you here."

"Not tonight," Leyers said coldly, pivoted, and left with Dolly shouting angrily after him.

Pino dropped the general at German headquarters under orders to return at 7:00 a.m.

❦

He left the car at the motor pool and trudged toward home, seeing in his mind's eye the carnage and destruction he'd witnessed that day. How many men had he seen die from his safe vantage point? Hundreds?

The sheer brutality of it ate at him. He hated war. He hated the Germans for starting it. For what? Putting your boot on another man's head and stealing him blind, until someone with a bigger boot comes along to kick you out of the way? As far as Pino was concerned, wars were about murder and thievery. One army killed to steal the hill; then another killed to steal it back.

He knew he should be happy to see the Nazis defeated and retreating, but he just felt hollow and alone. He desperately wanted to see Anna. But he couldn't, and that suddenly made him want to weep. He choked back his emotions, forced his mind to put a wall around his memories of the battle.

That wall held as he showed his documents to the sentries in the lobby of his apartment building, and when he rode the birdcage past the Waffen-SS soldiers on the fifth floor, and as he dug in his pocket for his keys. When he opened the apartment door, he thought he'd step inside an empty apartment, fall to the floor, and let it all go.

But Aunt Greta was there already, collapsed in his father's arms. When she saw Pino, she broke into deeper sobs.

Michele's lower lip quivered when he said, "Colonel Rauff's men came to the shop this afternoon. They ransacked the place and arrested your uncle. He's been taken to the Hotel Regina."

"On what charges?" Pino asked, shutting the door.

"Being part of the resistance," Aunt Greta wept. "Being a spy, and you know what the Gestapo does to spies."

Michele's jaw began to tremble, and tears dripped down his cheeks. "You hear her, Pino? What they'll do to Albert? What they'll do to you if he cracks and tells them about you?"

"Uncle Albert won't say a thing."

"What if he does?" Michele demanded. "They'll come for you, too."

"Papa—"

"I want you to run, Pino. Steal your general's car, go to the Swiss border in uniform with your passport. I'll give you enough money. You can live in Lugano, wait for the war to end."

"No, Papa," Pino said. "I won't do that."

"You'll do as I say!"

"I'm eighteen!" Pino shouted. "I can do what I please."

He said this with such strength and resolve that his father was taken aback, and Pino felt bad for having shouted. It had just burst out of him.

Shaking, trying to calm down, Pino said, "Papa, I'm sorry, but I've sat out too much of the war already. I won't run now. Not while the radio still works and the war goes on. Until then, I'm at General Leyers's side. I'm sorry, but that's the way it has to be."

Ten days later, on the afternoon of March 2, 1945, Pino stood by General Leyers's Fiat, studying the exterior of a villa in the hills east of Lake Garda and wondering what was happening inside.

Seven other cars were parked there as well. Two of the drivers wore the uniforms of the Waffen-SS, and one the Wehrmacht. The rest were in plain clothes. Under Leyers's orders, so was Pino. For the most part, Pino ignored the other drivers and continued to watch the house with intense fascination because he'd recognized two of the German officers who'd followed General Leyers inside nearly twenty minutes before.

They were General Wolff, head of the SS in Italy, and Field Marshal Heinrich Von Vietinghoff, who'd recently replaced Kesselring as commander of all German forces in Italy.

Why is Vietinghoff here? And Wolff? What are they all up to?

These questions went round and round in Pino's head until he couldn't take it anymore. He moved through the lightly falling snow toward a hedgerow of ornamental cedar trees that flanked the parking area. He stopped and took a piss in case any of the other drivers were watching, and then pushed through the cedars and disappeared.

Using the hedge for cover, Pino got to the villa's north wall, where he crouched and slunk along, pausing beneath windows to listen, and then rising up to peek through.

From below the third window he heard shouting. One voice roared out, *"Was du redest ist Verrat! Ich werde an einer solchen Diskussion nicht teilnehmen!"*

Pino didn't quite understand. But he did hear the sound of a room door slamming. Someone was leaving. *General Leyers?*

He bolted back down the side of the villa and to the cedar hedge. He ran down the length of it, peering through breaks, seeing Field Marshal Vietinghoff storm from the villa. His driver leaped from his car, opened the door to the backseat, and they soon drove off.

Pino had a moment of indecision. Should he go back to the window, try to hear more? Or should he go back to the car and wait, not risk his luck?

Leyers came out the front door and made the decision for him. Pino eased out through the hedge and jogged to meet him, trying to remember what Vietinghoff had shouted before leaving.

Was du redest ist Verrat!

He kept repeating the phrase silently as he opened the door for a very unhappy General Leyers, who looked ready to bite off a kitten's head. Pino climbed into the front seat, feeling the rage coming off the German like waves.

"*Mon général?*"

"Gargnano," Leyers said. "The insane asylum."

⟢⟶

Pino drove the car through the gates of Mussolini's villa above Lake Garda, fearing what they might encounter. When General Leyers announced himself at the front door, one of Il Duce's aides told him that it was not a good time.

"Of course it's not a good time," Leyers snapped. "That's why I'm here. Take me to him, or I'll have you shot."

The aide became irate. "Under whose authority?"

"Adolf Hitler's. I am here under the führer's direct orders."

The aide remained furious, but nodded. "Very well, if you'll follow me."

He led them to the library and opened the door slightly. Despite the dwindling day, there were no lights on yet in Mussolini's library. The only light came in through the French doors. The pale beam cut diagonally through the room, revealing books strewn everywhere, and papers, and broken glass, and furniture busted and turned over.

In the aftermath of what had to have been a colossal tantrum, Il Duce sat behind his desk, elbows on top, brick jaw in his hands, staring straight down as if looking through the desktop at the ruins of his life. Claretta Petacci lounged in an easy chair in front of Mussolini, smoke lazing from a cigarette in one hand while the other clamped an empty wineglass to her bosom. To Pino, it looked like they could have been frozen in those positions for hours.

"Duce?" General Leyers said, moving deeper into the shambles of a room.

If Mussolini heard him he didn't show it, just stared dully at the top of his desk while Leyers and Pino walked closer and closer. The dictator's mistress heard them, though, and looked over her shoulder with a wan smile of relief.

"General Leyers," Petacci slurred. "It's been a trying day for poor Beno. I hope you're not going to add to his troubles?"

The general said, "Duce and I need to have a frank talk."

"About what?" Mussolini asked, head still down.

Closer now, Pino could see the puppet dictator was staring at a map of Italy. "Duce?" Leyers began again.

Mussolini raised his head, glowered bizarrely at the general, and said, "We conquered Ethiopia, Leyers. And now the Allied swine have brought Negroes north into the land of Tuscany. Negroes rule the streets of Bologna and Rome, too! It is a thousand times better for me to die now than to live. Don't you think?"

Leyers hesitated after Pino translated, and said, "Duce, I can't begin to advise you on such things."

Mussolini's eyes wandered as if searching for something long lost, and then brightened as if enchanted by some new and shiny object.

"Is it true?" the puppet dictator asked. "Does dear Hitler have a secret super-weapon up his sleeve? A missile, a rocket, a bomb like we've never seen before? I hear the führer is just waiting to use the superweapon when his enemies have drawn close enough to wipe them all out with a series of devastating strikes."

Leyers hesitated again, then said, "There are rumors of a secret weapon, Duce."

"Aha!" Mussolini said, springing to his feet with a finger held high. "I knew it! Didn't I say so, Clara?"

"You did, Beno," his mistress replied. She was pouring herself another drink.

Mussolini was as high now as he'd been low. He strode around the desk, full of excitement, almost gleeful.

"It's like the V-2 rocket, isn't it?" he said. "Only so much more powerful, capable of leveling an entire city, isn't that right? Only you Germans have the scientific and engineering brainpower to do such a thing!"

Leyers said nothing for several moments, then nodded. "Thank you, Duce. I appreciate the compliment, but I was sent to ask what your plans are, should things worsen."

That seemed to confuse Mussolini. "But there's a great rocket bomb. How could things worsen in the long run if we have the great rocket bomb?"

"I believe in planning for contingencies," Leyers said.

"Oh," the dictator said, and his eyes started to drift.

Claretta Petacci said, "Valtellina, Beno."

"That's it," Mussolini said, focused again. "If we are pushed, I have twenty thousand troops who will follow me to the Valtellina Valley north of here, right up against Switzerland. They will defend me and my fellow Fascists until Herr Hitler launches his rocket of maximum destruction!"

Mussolini was grinning, looking off and reveling in anticipation of that wondrous day.

General Leyers said nothing for several moments, and Pino glanced at him sidelong. Did Hitler have a superweapon? Was he going to use it on the Allies if they got close enough to Berlin? If Leyers knew one way or the other, he wasn't showing it.

The general clicked his heels and bowed. "Thank you, Duce. That's all we wished to know."

"You'll alert us, Leyers?" Mussolini said. "When Hitler is going to use his magnificent rocket bomb?"

"I'm sure you'll be among the first to know," General Leyers said, turning.

He stopped in front of the dictator's mistress. "Will you, too, go to Valtellina?"

Claretta Petacci smiled as if she'd long ago accepted her fate. "I loved my Beno when times were good, General. I'll love him even more when they're bad."

Later that day, before describing the visit to Mussolini, Pino repeated the few words he'd heard below the window at the villa in the hills east of Lake Garda.

"Was du redest ist Verrat."

Aunt Greta sat upright on the couch. She'd been living at the apartment since Uncle Albert was taken, and helping Baka with the daily radio transmissions.

She said, "Are you sure it was Vietinghoff who said that?"

"No, I'm not sure, but the voice was angry, and right afterward, I saw the field marshal leave the villa very angry. What does it mean?"

"Was du redest ist Verrat," she said. "'What you suggest is treason.'"

"Treason?" Pino said.

His father sat forward. "You mean like a coup against Hitler?"

"I would have to assume so, if they were talking to Vietinghoff in that way," Aunt Greta said. "And Wolff was there? And Leyers?"

"And others. But I never saw them. They arrived before we did, and left afterward."

"They see the writing on the wall," his father said. "They're scheming to survive."

"The Allies should know that," Pino said. "And about Mussolini and the superweapon he thinks Hitler has."

"What does Leyers think about this superweapon?" Aunt Greta said.

"I can't tell. He has a face like granite most of the time. But he would know. He told me himself he started working for Hitler by building cannons."

"Baka is coming in the morning," his father said. "Write down what you want London to know, Pino. I'll have him send it along with the other transmissions."

Pino took paper and pen and scratched his report out. Aunt Greta wrote down the words of treason he'd overheard.

At last Pino yawned, checked his watch. It was almost nine. "I have to report to the general, get my orders for tomorrow."

"Will you be back home tonight?"

"I don't think so, Papa."

"Be careful," Michele said. "You wouldn't have heard those generals talking treason if the war wasn't close to being over for good."

Pino nodded, went for his overcoat, saying, "I haven't asked about Uncle Albert. You saw him this morning in San Vittore, yes? How is he?"

"He's lost weight, which isn't a bad thing," Aunt Greta said, smiling wanly. "And they haven't broken him, though they've tried. He knows many of the other prisoners, so it helps. They protect one another."

"He won't be in there much longer," Pino said.

Indeed, as he walked through the streets back toward Dolly's apartment building, Pino's sense of the time that remained between now and the end of the war was small, much smaller than time after the end of the war, which felt infinitely long, and filled with Anna.

Thoughts of a limitless future with her buoyed Pino to Dolly's door. To his relief, Anna answered, smiling, no longer sick, and very happy to see him.

"The general and Dolly have gone out," Anna said, letting him in.

She closed the door and fell into his arms.

Later, in Anna's bed, their singing bodies glistened with sweat and love.

"I missed you," Anna said.

"You're all I think about," Pino said. "Is it bad that when I'm supposed to be spying on General Leyers, or trying to memorize where we've been, and what we've seen, I'm instead thinking of you?"

"It's not bad at all," Anna said. "It's sweet."

"I mean it. When we're apart, I feel like all the music stops."

Anna gazed at him. "You're a special person, Pino Lella."

"No, not really."

"You are," she insisted, running her finger on his chest. "You're courageous. You're funny. And you're beautiful to look at."

Pino laughed, embarrassed. "Beautiful? Not handsome?"

"You are handsome," Anna said, caressing his cheek now. "But you are so full of love for me, it beams from you, makes me feel beautiful, which makes you beautiful to me."

"Then beautiful we are," he said, and nuzzled her closer.

Pino told Anna about his sense that everything that would happen from now until the war's end would someday seem very short, while time after the war seemed to stretch out toward an invisible horizon.

"We can do anything we want," Pino said. "Life is limitless."

"We can chase happiness, live passionately?"

"Is that really all you want? To chase happiness, and live passionately?"

"Can you imagine any other way to do it?"

"No," he said, kissing Anna and loving her all the more. "I guess I really can't."

Chapter Twenty-Six

General Leyers and Pino were on the move again almost constantly the following two weeks. Leyers went twice to Switzerland after visits to the train yard in Como, not Monza, which caused Pino to think that the general had had the boxcar with the gold moved. Apart from those trips to Lugano, Leyers spent the majority of his time inspecting the state of roads and train lines running north.

Pino didn't understand why, and it wasn't his place to ask, but when they drove to the Brenner Pass road on March 15, the general's intentions were laid plain. The train tracks up through the pass to Austria had been bombed repeatedly. Service had been interrupted in both directions, and gray men were toiling to repair the line.

The Brenner Pass road went through a snowpack that still ran all the way down to the valley floor. The higher they drove, the higher the snowbanks flanking them became, until it seemed they were in a roofless tunnel of gritty white. They came around a bend that gave them a stunning view of the vast Brenner drainage.

"Stop," Leyers said, and climbed out with his binoculars.

Pino didn't need binoculars. He could see the road ahead and a mob of gray men like a single enslaved organism that dug, chopped, and shoveled the snow that blocked the way to the top of the Brenner Pass, and Austria.

They're a long way from the border, Pino thought, and gazed higher. There had to be ten or twelve meters of snow up there. And those dark smudges way up, back toward Austria, looked like avalanche tracks. Below those smudges, there could be fifteen meters of snowpack and debris across the road.

Leyers must have made a similar assessment. When they drove far enough to get to the Waffen-SS troops overseeing the slaves, the general climbed out and lit into the man in charge, a major by his insignia. They had a shouting match, and for a moment Pino thought they were going to come to blows.

When General Leyers returned to the car, he remained in a fury.

"At the rate they're moving, we'll never get the hell out of Italy," he said. "I need lorries, backhoes, and bulldozers. Real machines. Or it's impossible."

"Mon général?" Pino said.

"Shut up and drive, Vorarbeiter!"

Pino knew better than to press the general, and kept silent, thinking about what Leyers had just said and finally understanding what they'd been doing recently.

General Leyers had been put in charge of the escape route. The Germans had to have one to retreat. The train tracks were busted. So the Brenner Pass road was the only sure way out, and it was blocked. Other passes led to Switzerland, but the Swiss had stopped allowing German trains or convoys through their borders in the past few days.

As of now, Pino thought happily, *the Nazis are trapped.*

◆

That night, Pino wrote out a message for Baka describing the huge snow barrier between Italy and Austria. He said the partisans or Allies needed to start bombing the snowy ridges above the road to cause more avalanches.

Five days later, he and Leyers returned to the Brenner. Pino was secretly pleased when the general turned apoplectic over news that Allied bombs had set off huge slides that blocked the road with walls of snow.

With every hour that passed, Leyers grew more erratic, talkative one moment, silent and sullen the next. The general spent six days in Switzerland toward the end of March, which allowed Pino almost unlimited time with Anna and made him wonder why Leyers hadn't moved Dolly to Lugano or even Geneva.

But he didn't think about any of that for very long. Pino was in love, and as love does, it had warped his sense of time. Each moment with Anna seemed breathless and brief, and filled with endless yearning when they were apart.

March turned to April of 1945, and it was as if some cosmic switch flipped. The cold, snowy weather that had plagued northern Italy and the Allied advance gave way to late spring temperatures and melting snow. Pino drove General Leyers to the Brenner Pass road nearly every day. There were backhoes at work on the road by then, and dump trucks hauling away the snow and avalanche debris. The sun beat down on the gray men digging beside the mechanical shovels, their faces burned by its brilliant reflection off the snow, their muscles twisted by the weight of the slush and ice, and their wills broken by the years in slavery.

Pino wanted to comfort them, to tell them to take heart, that the war was almost over. *Weeks left, not months now. Just hold on. Just stay alive.*

⟐

Long after dark on April 8, 1945, Pino and General Leyers reached the village of Molinella, northeast of Bologna.

Leyers took a cot in a Wehrmacht encampment there, and Pino slept fitfully in the Fiat's front seat. By dawn, they were on higher ground, west of the village of Argenta where they could look down on the flatter, wetter terrain on both sides of the Senio River, which ran into Lake Comacchio, an estuary near the coast. The lake blocked the Allies' ability to flank around fortifications Leyers had built on the river's north side.

Tank traps. Minefields. Trenches. Pillboxes. Even from several kilometers away, Pino could see them all clearly. Beyond them, on the other side of the river in Allied territory, nothing moved beyond the odd lorry heading to or from Rimini and the Adriatic Sea.

For many hours on that hill that day there was little sound save that of spring birds and insects, and a warm breeze carried the scent of fields under plow. It all made Pino realize that the earth did not know war, that nature would go on no matter what horror one man might inflict on another. Nature didn't care a bit about men and their need to kill and conquer.

The morning dragged on. The heat built. Around noon, they heard distant thuds, the echoes of explosions coming from the waters off Rimini, and soon, in the distance, Pino could see smoke rising far out to sea. He wondered what had happened.

It was as if General Leyers heard him.

"They're bombing our ships," he said matter-of-factly. "They're choking us off, but down there is where they'll try to break me."

The afternoon ticked on, and soon it was as hot as a summer's day, but not as dry. Instead of baking heat, all the moisture that had fallen during the winter steamed from the ground, making the air thick and oppressive. Pino sat in the shade of the car while Leyers kept up his vigil.

"What will you do after the war, Vorarbeiter?" Leyers asked at one point.

"Moi, mon général?" Pino said. "I don't know. Maybe go back to school. Maybe work for my parents. And you?"

General Leyers lowered his binoculars. "I can't see that far ahead yet."

"And Dolly?"

Leyers cocked his head, as if wondering whether to reprimand him for his impudence, but then said, "When the Brenner opens, she'll be taken care of."

They both caught a rumbling, droning noise to the south. Leyers threw up his glasses and studied the sky.

"It begins," he said.

Pino jumped to his feet, shaded his eyes, and saw the heavy bombers coming out of the south, ten across and twenty deep. Two hundred warplanes flew right at them until they were so close Pino began to fear they'd release their payloads over his head.

A mile out, and a mile up, however, they banked in formation, showing their bellies as the bomb bays opened. The lead flight of bombers dropped altitude, set their wings, and swooped above the Gothic Line and German territory. They released bombs that whistled and trailed behind them, looking like so many fish diving from the sky.

The first one struck well behind the German defenses and erupted, hurling debris and throwing a rainbow of fluorescence and flame. More bombs started blowing up behind the Gothic fortifications, leaving charred blast-holes and copper-red fires stitched in a carpet of violence and destruction that rolled east toward the estuary and the sea.

The last of the birds in the first wave were followed ten minutes later by a second, and a third, and a fourth—more than eight hundred heavy bombers in all. The lumbering planes let loose their ordnance in that same rhythmic pattern, only off by a degree or two so the new bombs struck in different parts of the German rear guard.

Armories exploded. Petrol supplies erupted. Barracks and roads and lorries and tanks and supply dumps evaporated in the initial assault. Then medium and light bombers flew in low over the river, attacking the defensive line itself. Sections of Leyers's tank traps blew up. Pillboxes disintegrated. Cannon emplacements fell.

In the course of the next four hours, Allied bombers dropped twenty thousand bombs on the area. In the gaps between the aerial assaults, two thousand Allied artillery pieces shelled the Gothic Line in thirty-minute-long barrages. When the late afternoon sun shone into the smoke plumes up and down the river, the spring sky looked hellish and low.

Pino glanced at Leyers. As he scanned the battleground south of his broken defenses through the field glasses, the general's hands trembled and he cursed in German.

"Mon général?" Pino said.

"They're coming," Leyers said. "Tanks. Jeeps. Artillery. Entire armies are advancing on us. Our boys will hold as long as they can, and many will die for that river. But at some point, not long now, every soldier down there will be confronted with the inevitable loser's choice: retreat, surrender, or die."

As the day gave way to gathering dusk, Allied soldiers with flamethrowers invaded the German trenches and the pillboxes. A black and starless night fell. As hand-to-hand combat waged out there in the darkness, all Pino could see were explosive flashes and slow whips of fire.

"They'll be overrun by morning," Leyers said at last. "It's over."

"In Italy, we have a saying that it's not over until the fat lady sings, *mon général*," Pino said.

"I hate opera," the general grunted, and walked toward the car. "Get me out of here, back to Milan, before I'm caught without options."

Pino didn't know what that meant exactly, but he eagerly climbed behind the wheel. *The Nazis can retreat, surrender, or die now,* he thought. *The war itself is dying. Only days now from peace and, well, Americans!*

Pino drove through the night back to Milan, elated at the thought that he might at long last get to meet an American. Or an entire army of them! Maybe after he and Anna were married they'd go to the United States like his cousin Licia Albanese did, bring his mother's purses and Uncle Albert's leather goods to New York, Chicago, and Los Angeles. He would make his own fortune there!

Pino felt a thrill go up his spine at that idea, and he caught a glimpse of a future unimaginable to him just a few moments before. The entire drive back he did not once think of the biblical-scale destruction he'd just witnessed. He thought about doing something good and profitable with his life, something *con smania*, and he couldn't wait to tell Anna all about it.

⌁

The Gothic Line along the Senio River was breached later that night. By the following evening, there were Allied forces from New Zealand and India nearly five kilometers beyond Leyers's broken defenses, with the German army retreating and re-forming to the north. On April 14, after another stunning bombardment, the US Fifth Army broke through the western wall of the Gothic Line and rolled north toward Bologna.

Every day brought news of more Allied advances. Pino listened to the BBC each night on Baka's shortwave radio. He also spent almost every day driving Leyers from battlefront to battlefront, or along the escape routes, where they watched long German columns fleeing at a much slower pace than when they'd invaded Italy.

The Nazi war machine looked crippled to Pino. He could see it in the shimmying tanks losing their treads and the shell-shocked infantrymen walking behind teams of mules pulling cannons. Scores of German wounded lay in open lorries, exposed to the blistering hot sun. Pino hoped they'd die then and there.

Every two or three days, he and Leyers would return to the Brenner Pass. With the heat had come snowmelt, and a torrent of filthy ice water ran down the pass, undermining the culverts and the road. When they reached the end of the open route, slaves were ankle and shin deep in the frigid water, still working beside the steam shovels and the dump trucks. On April 17, the gray men were a mile from the Austrian border. One of them collapsed in the water. SS guards dragged him out and threw him to the side.

General Leyers seemed not to notice.

"Work them around the clock," he told the captain in charge. "The entire Wehrmacht Tenth will be coming up this road inside a week."

Chapter Twenty-Seven

Saturday, April 21, 1945

General Leyers stood off to one side as Organization Todt officers doused five large piles of documents with petrol in the yard outside the OT's office in Turin. Leyers nodded to one officer, who lit and flicked a stick match. There was a loud whoosh, and flames seemed to gather and plume everywhere at once.

The general watched the papers burn with great interest. So did Pino.

What in them was so important that Leyers would leave Dolly's bed at 3:00 a.m. to see them destroyed? And then to stand here, waiting to make sure they were all burned? Was there evidence in those papers that incriminated Leyers somehow? There had to be.

Before Pino could begin to think about that, General Leyers barked orders at the OT officers, and then turned to look at Pino.

"Padua," he said.

Pino drove south and looped around Milan to Padua. On the way, he fought not to doze off with thoughts that the war was almost over. The Allies had broken through Leyers's defenses in the Argenta gap. The Tenth Mountain Division of the US Army was closing on the Po River.

Leyers seemed to sense Pino's fatigue, dug in his pockets, and came up with a vial. He spilled a small white pill in his hand and passed it to Pino. "Take it. Amphetamine. Keep you awake. Go ahead. I use them myself."

Pino took the pill and soon felt wide-awake but irritable, and his head ached when they got to Padua, where the general oversaw another mass burning of OT documents. Afterward, they drove up the Brenner Pass yet again. Fewer than two hundred and fifty meters of snow now separated the Nazis from an open road into Austria, and Leyers was told they would break through within the next forty-eight hours.

On Sunday morning, April 22, Pino watched Leyers destroy OT documents in Verona. In the afternoon, the Brescia files went up in flames. At every stop, before each burning, the general carried his valise inside the OT offices and spent time looking through files before overseeing the burns. Leyers would not let Pino touch the valise, which was getting heavier with each stop. In the early evening, he saw OT documents in Bergamo burn before they returned to Leyers's offices behind the Como stadium.

The following morning, Monday, April 23, General Leyers watched OT officers light a huge bonfire of files and documents on the stadium pitch. Leyers oversaw the feeding of that fire for several hours. Pino was allowed nowhere near the documents. He sat in the stands in the building heat, watching the Nazi records turn to smoke and floating ash.

When they returned to Milan later that afternoon, two SS Panzer units had sealed off the neighborhoods around the Duomo, and even Leyers was scrutinized before being allowed inside. At the Hotel Regina, Gestapo headquarters, Pino found out why. Colonel Walter Rauff was drunk, in a rage, and trying to burn anything with his name on it. But when the Gestapo chief saw Leyers he brightened and invited him into his office.

Leyers looked at Pino and said, "You're done for the day, but I have a nine a.m. meeting. Pick me up at Dolly's at eight forty-five."

"*Oui, mon général,*" Pino said. "The car?"

"Take it with you."

General Leyers followed Rauff inside. Pino hated that so many documents were disappearing. The proof of what the Nazis had done to Italy was vanishing, and there seemed little he could do but report it to the Allies. He parked the Fiat two blocks from his apartment building, left his armband on the seat—swastika up—and got past the lobby sentries once more.

Michele held a finger to his lips, and Aunt Greta shut the apartment door.

"Papa?" Pino said.

"We have a visitor," his father said in a hushed tone. "My cousin's son, Mario."

Pino squinted. "Mario? I thought he was a fighter pilot?"

"I still am," Mario said, stepping from the shadows. He was a short, square-shouldered man with a big smile. "I got shot down the other night, but parachuted out and made it here."

"Mario will hide here until the war's over," Michele said.

"Your father and your aunt have been filling me in on your activities," Mario said, clapping Pino on the back. "Takes a lot of guts."

"Oh, I don't know," Pino said. "I think Mimo's had a tougher time of it."

"Nonsense," Aunt Greta said before Pino put up his hands in surrender.

"I haven't had a shower in three days," he said. "And then I need to move the general's car. Glad you're alive, Mario."

"You, too, Pino," Mario said.

Pino went down the hall to the bathroom near his bedroom. He stripped off his smoky clothes, then showered to get the smell off his body and out of his hair. He put on his best clothes and a little splash of his father's aftershave on his cheeks. It had been four days since he'd seen Anna, and he wanted to impress.

In the dining room, he left a note for Baka describing the document burns; said his good-byes to his father, aunt, and cousin; and left.

Dusk was falling, but heat still radiated from the buildings and the macadam, as penetrating as any sauna. It felt good as he walked. The heat and humidity loosened his joints after days of driving and standing and watching. Climbing into the Fiat, Pino reached to start it when someone moved in the backseat and put the cold muzzle of a pistol to the back of his head.

"Don't move," said a man. "Hands on the wheel. Gun?"

"No," Pino said, hearing the waver in his voice. "What do you want?"

"What do you think?"

Pino recognized the voice now, and he was suddenly terrified his brains were about to be blown out.

"Don't, Mimo," he said. "Mama and Papa—"

Pino felt the steel of the muzzle come off his head.

"Pino, I'm so goddamned sorry about the things I said to you," Mimo began. "I know what you've been doing now, the spying, and I'm . . . I'm in awe of your courage. Your dedication to the cause."

Emotion swelled in Pino's throat, but then he got angry. "Then why'd you put a gun to my head?"

"I didn't know if you were armed. I thought you might try to kill me."

"I'd never shoot my baby brother."

Mimo lurched over the seat and threw his arms around Pino. "Do you forgive me?"

"Of course," Pino said, letting go of the anger. "You couldn't have known, and I wasn't allowed to tell you because Uncle Albert said it would be safer that way."

Mimo nodded, wiped his eyes with his sleeve, and said, "I was sent by partisan commanders who told me what you've been doing. I'm to give you your orders."

"Orders? I take my orders from General Leyers."

"Not anymore," Mimo said, handing him a piece of paper. "You are to arrest Leyers the night of the twenty-fifth and bring him to that address."

Arrest General Leyers? At first the idea unnerved Pino, but then he imagined himself aiming a pistol at Leyers's head, and rather liked the idea.

He *would* arrest the general, and when he did, he'd reveal himself as a spy. He'd drub that fact into the Nazi's face. *I've been right here under your nose the entire time. I've seen everything you've done, slave master.*

"I'll do it," Pino said at last. "It will be an honor."

"Then I'll see you when the war's over," Mimo said.

"Where are you going?"

"Back to the fight."

"How? What will you do?"

"Tank sabotage tonight. And we're waiting for the Nazis to start retreating from Milan. Then we're going to ambush them, teach them to never even think about coming back to Italy."

"And the Fascists?"

"Them, too. We need a clean slate if we're going to start over."

Pino shook his head. Mimo was barely sixteen and yet a battle-hardened veteran.

"Don't get killed before it's over," Pino said.

"You, either," Mimo said, slipping from the car and into the shadows.

Pino twisted around in his seat, trying to spot his brother leaving, but he saw nothing. It was as if Mimo were a ghost.

That made Pino smile, and he started General Leyers's car, feeling good about things for the first time in days, at least since he'd last seen Anna.

———⟡———

Pino's heart soared as he parked in front of Dolly's apartment around eight that evening. Giving the old crone in the lobby a wave, he climbed the stairs to the third floor and knocked eagerly on Dolly's door.

Anna answered, smiling. She pecked him on the cheek, whispered, "Dolly's upset. The general hasn't been here in almost four days."

"He's coming back tonight," Pino said. "I'm sure of it."

"Please tell her that," Anna said, and shooed him down the hall.

Dolly Stottlemeyer was on the couch in the living area, dressed in one of Leyers's white tunics and little else. She had whiskey in a tumbler with ice, and she looked like it wasn't her first or second, or even fifth of the day.

Seeing Pino, Dolly set her jaw for a woman scorned and said, "Where is my Hansie?"

"The general's at Wehrmacht headquarters," Pino said.

"We were supposed to be in Innsbruck by now," Dolly said, slurring.

"The pass opens tomorrow," Pino said. "And he told me just the other day that's where he was moving you."

Tears welled up in Dolly's eyes. "He did?"

"I heard him."

"Thank you," Dolly said, and her hand trembled as she raised her glass. "I didn't know what was to become of me." She sipped the whiskey, smiled, and got up. "You two go on now. I need to make myself pretty."

Dolly lurched by them and held on to the wall before disappearing down the hall.

When they heard her bedroom door slam shut they went to the kitchen. Pino spun Anna around, picked her up, and kissed her. Anna threw her legs up around him and kissed him back with equal ardor. When at last their lips separated, she said, "I have food for you. The sausage and broccoli dish you like, and bread and butter."

Pino realized he was starved, put her down reluctantly, and said quietly, "God, I've missed you. You can't know how good it is to be here with you right now."

Anna beamed at him. "I didn't know it could be like this."

"I didn't, either," Pino said, and kissed her again and again.

They ate hot sausages and broccoli sautéed in garlic and olive oil, along with bread and butter, and drank more of the general's wine before slipping off to Anna's room after hearing the knock at the front door and Dolly's cry of not to worry, that she would get it. In the heat, in her small room in the dark, Anna's scent was everywhere around him, and he was instantly drunk on it. He peered for her shape in the pitch black, heard her bed springs creak, and went to her. When he lay by her side and reached out to find her body, Anna was already naked and wanting him.

⚊

There was a knock, and then another at the maid's door.

Pino startled awake the morning of April 24, 1945, and looked around in confusion as Anna roused on his chest and called, "Yes?"

Dolly said, "It's seven forty. The general needs his driver in twenty minutes, and we are to pack, Anna. The Brenner *is* clear."

"We leave today?" Anna said.

"As soon as possible," Dolly replied.

They lay there waiting for Dolly's heels to clip down the hall to the kitchen.

Pino kissed Anna tenderly and said, "That was the most amazing night of my life."

"Mine, too," she said, staring into his eyes as if they held dreams. "I'll never ever forget how magical it was."

"Never. Ever."

They kissed again, their lips barely touching. She inhaled when he exhaled, and exhaled when he inhaled, and Pino felt once again how like a single creature they were when they were like this, together.

"How will I find you?" Pino said. "In Innsbruck, I mean."

"I'll call your parents' apartment once we get there."

"Why don't you just go to my parents' apartment now? Or at least once you've got Dolly packed?"

"Dolly needs me to get settled," Anna said. "She knows I want to come straight back to Milan as soon as possible."

"Does she?"

"Yes. I told her she was going to have to hire a new maid."

Pino kissed her, and they untangled and dressed. Before he went out the door, he took Anna in his arms and said, "I don't know when I'll see you again."

"You'll hear from me, I promise. I'll call for you as soon as I can."

Pino gazed into Anna's eyes, stroked his powerful hands over her face, and murmured, "The war's all but over. Will you marry me when you come back?"

"Marry?" she said, tears glistening in her eyes. "You're sure?"

"More than sure."

Anna kissed his palm and whispered, "Then, yes."

Pino felt joy surge through him as powerful as a crescendo. "Yes?"

"Of course. With all my heart, Pino. With all my soul."

"I know it's corny," Pino said, "but you've just made me the happiest, luckiest guy in all of Italy."

"I think we've made each other happy and lucky," she said, kissing him again.

Hearing the general's boots in the kitchen already, Pino held her as long as he dared and whispered, "Our love will be eternal."

"Forever and ever," she said.

They parted. Pino took one last look at Anna, winked, and left with her beauty, her scent, and her touch dominating his mind.

⟢⟣

General Leyers went first to Gestapo headquarters, emerging from the Hotel Regina an hour later. Then they drove to the telephone exchange, where Leyers disappeared inside for hours while another day of listless heat baked Milan.

Pino took refuge in the shade and noticed that everyone who walked by seemed on edge, as if they'd sensed a violent storm coming. He thought of Anna. When *would* he see her again? He felt hollow at the thought it might be a week, or a month. But what was time after the war? Infinite. And Anna said yes to his sudden proposal! She would love him for ever and ever. And he would love her for ever and ever. No matter what might happen, something was certain about his future now, and it calmed him.

Let not your heart be troubled, Pino thought, and basked in the sureness of being part of something bigger than himself, eternal. He was already envisioning a fantastic life for them, already falling in love with the miracles of what tomorrow might hold. He needed a ring, didn't he? He could—

Pino realized that he was just a few blocks from the Piazzale Loreto and Beltramini's Fresh Fruits and Vegetables.

Was Carletto there? How was his mother? He hadn't seen his oldest friend in more than eight months, since he'd stumbled away from Carletto as he held his poor father's dead body.

Part of Pino wanted to walk there from the telephone exchange and explain himself, but the fear that Carletto might not believe him kept him put, sweating, hungry, and sick of waiting around on the general's whim. He would have Mimo go tell Carletto when the time was—

"Vorarbeiter!" General Leyers barked.

Pino jumped up, saluting and running toward the general, who was already at the back door of the Fiat, holding his valise, an impatient, annoyed look on his face. Pino apologized, blaming it on the heat.

Leyers looked up at the sky and the sun beating down on the city. "Does it always get like this in late April?"

"Non, mon général," Pino said, relieved as he opened the door. "It's very rare. Everything about the weather this year is very rare. Where do we go?"

"Como," Leyers said. "We'll be spending the night."

"Oui, mon général," Pino said, glancing in the rearview, where Leyers was rifling around his valise. "And when will Dolly and Anna go to Innsbruck?"

The general looked engrossed in something, didn't look up. "They're on their way by now, I should think. No more questions. I have work to do."

Pino drove to Como and the stadium. Three days before, he'd seen the bonfire on the pitch. The ash was gone, and there were several companies of Organization Todt soldiers and officers encamped on the field. They'd put up tarps over sections of the grandstands and lounged under them in the shade, as if they were on holiday.

When Leyers went inside, Pino curled up in the front seat of the Fiat. But by the raucous noise echoing from the stadium, he figured the German soldiers were drinking. Leyers was probably in there with them. They lost, but the war was over, or would be any day now. That was cause enough for any man to get drunk, he supposed, and fell into a deep sleep.

Pino woke the next morning, Wednesday, April 25, 1945, to the sound of knuckles rapping against the Fiat's passenger window. He was surprised the sun had risen. He'd slept soundly, dreamed of Anna, and—

The car door opened. An OT soldier said General Leyers needed him inside.

Pino got up, ran his fingers through his hair, looked at himself in the mirror. Grimy, but okay. He followed the soldier inside Leyers's headquarters and down a series of halls to a room with a glass window that overlooked the pitch.

The general was dressed in civilian clothes and drinking coffee with a short man with jet-black hair and a narrow black mustache. He turned to look at Pino and nodded.

"You prefer English or Italian?" the man said in an American accent.

Pino, who towered over him, said, "English is fine."

"Max Corvo," he said, and stuck out his hand.

Pino hesitated, but then shook it. "Pino Lella. Where are you from?"

"America. Connecticut. Tell the general here that I'm with the OSS, the Office of Strategic Services, and that I represent Allen Dulles."

Pino hesitated, but then translated it into French for the general, who nodded.

Corvo said, "We want your assurance that your men will remain in their barracks, General Leyers, and offer zero resistance if they are asked to lay down their arms."

Pino translated. Leyers nodded. "When there's a deal in place, signed by Field Marshal Vietinghoff, my men will comply. And tell him I continue to work to save Milan from destruction."

"The United States of America appreciates that, General Leyers," Corvo said. "I think there'll be something on paper and signed in less than a week, maybe even sooner."

Leyers nodded. "Until then. Wish Mr. Dulles my best."

Pino translated, and then added, "He has been burning documents across northern Italy for the past three days."

Corvo cocked his head. "That true?"

"Yes," Pino said. "They're all burning documents. All of them."

"Okay," the OSS agent said. "Thanks for telling me."

Corvo shook the general's hand, and Pino's, and then he was gone.

Pino stood there for several awkward moments before Leyers said, "What were you saying there just before he left?"

"I asked him what Connecticut was like, and he said it was nowhere as beautiful as Italy."

The general studied him. "Let's go. I have an appointment with Cardinal Schuster."

———

When they drove back into the city at two that afternoon, Milan felt electric and rebellious. Factory whistles were blowing. Conductors and drivers were walking away from the remaining trolley cars and buses, creating havoc for the German convoys trying to forge through the city on their way north. When Pino was stopped at a crossing, he swore he heard the crackle of rifle fire in the distance.

That caused him to glance at General Leyers in the backseat and think about the satisfaction he'd take in arresting the Nazi and telling him he'd been a spy all along. *Where should I do it? And how? In the car? Or on the road somewhere?*

The closer they got to the Duomo, the more Nazis they saw. Most were Waffen-SS, the killers, the rapists, the plunderers, and the slave guards. They were in the streets all around Gestapo headquarters, taking refuge behind the Panzer tanks in and around the cathedral and the chancellery, where Pino parked outside the gates because there were too many cars in the courtyard already.

Pino followed Leyers toward the stairs. A priest intercepted them. "His Eminence is seeing you in his office today, General."

When they entered Schuster's ornate formal offices, the cardinal of Milan sat behind his desk like a judge wearing white robes, his red miter on the shelf behind him. Pino took in the crowded room. Giovanni Barbareschi, the seminarian, stood off the cardinal's left shoulder. Nearest to them was Eugen Dollmann,

Hitler's Italian translator. Beside Dollmann stood SS General Wolff and several men in business suits Pino did not know.

Seated at the far left side of the cardinal's desk, balancing on a cane, was an angry old man whom Pino would not have recognized had his mistress not been sitting next to him. Benito Mussolini looked twisted inside and out, like a spring that had been overwound and sprung. His skin pale and sweaty, the puppet dictator had lost weight and was hunched forward as if against stomach pain. Claretta Petacci stroked Il Duce's hand idly and leaned against him for comfort.

Behind Mussolini and his mistress there were two men wearing red neckerchiefs. *Partisan leaders,* Pino thought.

"Everyone you asked to be here is here, Your Eminence," Barbareschi said.

Schuster eyed them all. "Nothing said here leaves this room. Are we in accord?"

One by one they all nodded, including Pino, who wondered why he was even in the room with Dollmann there to translate.

"Our goal, then, is to save Milan further suffering and limit the amount of German blood spilled as they retreat. Yes?"

Mussolini nodded. After Dollmann translated, Wolff and Leyers did, too.

"Good," the cardinal said. "General Wolff? What can you report?"

"I've been to Lugano twice in the past few days," the SS general said. "Negotiations are moving slower than expected, but moving. We're three, maybe four days away from having a document to sign."

Mussolini came up out of a stupor. "What document? What negotiations?"

Wolff glanced at the cardinal, then at General Leyers, who said, "Duce, the war is lost. Hitler has gone mad in his bunker. We have all been working to end the conflict with as little death and destruction as possible."

Sitting there hunched over his cane, Mussolini went from ashen to beet red. Little bubbles of spittle showed at the corners of Il Duce's lips, which squirmed before he thrust out his chiseled jaw and began shouting and waving his cane at Wolff and Leyers.

"You Nazi bastards," Mussolini roared. "Once more we can say that Germany has knifed Italy in the back! I'll go on the radio! I'll tell the world of your treachery!"

"You'll do no such thing, Benito," Cardinal Schuster said.

"Benito?" Mussolini cried with indignation. "Cardinal Schuster, you will address me as 'Excellency'!"

The cardinal took a long breath, and then bowed his head. "Excellency, it is important to reach an agreement of surrender before the masses rise up and revolt. If not, we will have anarchy, which I intend to prevent. If you are not committed to that goal, Duce, I'll have to ask you to leave."

Mussolini looked around the room, shook his head in disgust, put his hand out to his mistress. "Like how they treat us, Clara? We're on our own now."

Petacci took the Fascist leader's hand and said, "I'm ready, Duce."

They labored to their feet and started toward the door.

"Excellency," Cardinal Schuster called after him. "Wait."

The prelate went to his shelves, pulled down a book, and handed it to Mussolini. "It's a history of Saint Benedict. Repent your sins, and may you find comfort in this book in the sad days that are now on your horizon."

Mussolini got a sour look about him, but took the book and handed it to his mistress. On the way out he said, "I should have them all shot."

The door slammed shut behind them.

"Shall we proceed?" Cardinal Schuster said. "General Wolff? Has the German High Command agreed to my request?"

"Vietinghoff wrote me this morning. He has given orders for his men to stand down from offensive actions, to remain in barracks until they are contacted."

"Not quite a surrender, but a start," said Cardinal Schuster. "And there's still a core group of SS here in the streets around the Duomo. They're loyal to Colonel Rauff?"

"I would think so," Wolff said.

"But Rauff answers to you," Schuster said.

"At times."

"Issue him an order, then. Forbid him and those monsters in uniform from perpetrating any more atrocities before they leave this country."

"Atrocities?" Wolff said. "I don't know what you're—"

"Don't insult me," the cardinal of Milan snapped. "You will not be able to cover up the things done in Italy and to Italians. But you can prevent further massacres from happening. Are we in agreement?"

Wolff looked highly agitated but nodded. "I'll write the orders now."

Barbareschi said, "I'll deliver them for you."

Cardinal Schuster looked at the seminarian. "Are you sure?"

"I want to look the man who tortured me in the eye as he gets the news."

Wolff scribbled the order on stationery, sealed it with Schuster's wax, and put his ring into the wax before handing it to the seminarian. As Barbareschi was leaving, the priest who'd led them in returned and said, "Cardinal Schuster, the prisoners of San Vittore are rioting."

Chapter Twenty-Eight

They were at the chancellery until dusk. General Wolff left. General Leyers and Cardinal Schuster discussed ways for the Germans and the resistance to trade prisoners.

It was only outside with the setting of the sun that Pino remembered again that he was charged with taking Leyers prisoner before midnight. He wished the partisans had given him specific instructions beyond an address where he was to take the general. Then again, they'd given him responsibility, a task, just like they'd given Mimo the task of sabotaging tanks. The details were his to work out.

But as he reached the staff car, Pino was still trying to decide how best to arrest the general, given that he always sat directly behind him in the backseat.

Opening the rear door to the Fiat, Pino saw Leyers's valise there and cursed to himself. It had been there the entire time they'd been inside. He could have excused himself and spent time looking at the files in that valise, probably the ones Leyers had saved from the fires.

General Leyers climbed in without glancing his way and said, "The Hotel Regina."

Pino thought about pulling his Walther and putting Leyers under arrest right then and there, but, unsure of himself, he shut the door and got behind the wheel. Due to all the German vehicles jamming the narrow streets, he had to take a convoluted route to Gestapo headquarters.

Near Piazza San Babila, he saw a German lorry filled with armed soldiers stopped at the exit to a parking garage a half-block away. Someone was standing in the street aiming a machine pistol at the windshield of the Nazi lorry. Pino was stunned when the gunman turned.

"Mimo," he gasped, slamming on the brakes.

"Vorarbeiter?" General Leyers said.

Pino ignored him and climbed out. He was no more than one hundred meters from his brother, who was waving his gun at the Germans and shouting, "All you Nazi swine lay down your weapons, drop them out of the lorry, and then all of you, facedown on the sidewalk there."

The next second seemed like an eternity.

When no Germans moved, Mimo touched off a burst of fire. Lead bullets pinged off the side of the parking garage. In the ringing silence that followed, the Germans in the back of the lorry began to throw down their guns.

"Vorarbeiter!" Leyers said, and Pino was surprised to find he'd gotten out of the car as well and was watching the scene over his shoulder. "Forget the Hotel Regina. Take me to Dolly's instead. I just realized I left some important papers there, and I want to—"

Emboldened by Mimo and without a thought, Pino drew his pistol, spun around, and stuck it into Leyers's gut. He enjoyed the look of shock in the general's eye.

"What is this, Vorarbeiter?" Leyers said.

"Your arrest, *mon général*," Pino said.

"Vorarbeiter Lella," he said firmly. "You will remove that weapon, and we will forget this happened. You will drive me to Dolly's. I will get my papers and—"

"I won't drive you anywhere, slave master!"

The general took that like a slap to the face. His expression twisted with rage.

"How dare you address me like this! I could have you shot for treason!"

"I'll take treason against you and Hitler any day," Pino said, equally angry. "Turn around, and hands behind your head, *mon général*, or I will shoot you in the knees."

Leyers sputtered but saw Pino was serious and did as he was told. Pino reached around and took the pistol Leyers carried when he was in business clothes. He pocketed it, waved the Walther, and said, "Get in."

Leyers moved toward the rear, but Pino shoved him instead into the driver's seat.

With his gun aimed at General Leyers's head, Pino climbed into the backseat and shut the door. He put his forearm on the valise, as Leyers often did, and smiled, liking this role reversal, feeling like he'd earned it, that now, at last, there would be justice done.

He looked past Leyers through the windshield. His brother had twenty Nazi soldiers on their bellies, hands behind their heads. Mimo was unloading and stacking their weapons on the opposite sidewalk.

"It doesn't have to be like this, Vorarbeiter," Leyers said. "I have money, lots of it."

"German money?" Pino snorted. "It will be worthless, if it isn't already. Turn the car around now, and as you have told me so often, don't talk unless you're spoken to."

The general paused, but then started the car and did a three-point turn. When he did, Pino rolled down the back window, yelling, "I'll see you at home, Mimo!"

His brother looked up in wonder, realized who was yelling at him, and threw his fist over his head.

"Uprising, Pino!" Mimo shouted. "Uprising!"

———

Pino felt chills go through him as Leyers drove them out of San Babila and toward the address Mimo had passed along from the partisan commanders. He had no idea why he was supposed to bring Leyers to that specific address, and he didn't care. He was no longer in the shadows. He was no longer a spy. He was part of the rebellion now, and it made him feel righteous as he barked directions and turns at the general, who drove stoop shouldered.

Ten minutes into the ride, Leyers said, "I have more than German money."

"I don't care," Pino said.

"I have gold. We can go and—"

Pino poked Leyers's head with the pistol barrel. "I know you have gold. Gold you stole from Italy. Gold you murdered four of your slaves over, and I don't want it."

"Murdered?" Leyers said. "No, Vorarbeiter, that's not—"

"I hope you face a firing squad for what you've done."

General Leyers stiffened. "You can't mean that."

"Shut up. I don't want to hear another word."

Leyers seemed resigned to his fate then, and drove sullenly through the city as Pino entertained a voice in his head that said, *Don't miss your chance. Exact some punishment. Have him pull over. Shoot him in the leg, at least. Let him go to his fate wounded and in agony. Isn't that the way you're supposed to enter hell?*

The general rolled down his window at one point and put his head out as if to smell his last moments of freedom. But when they rolled up to the gate at the address on Via Broni, Leyers stared straight ahead.

A gunman wearing a red scarf came out the gate. Pino told him he'd been ordered to arrest the general and was there to turn him over.

"We've been waiting," the guard said, and called for the gate to be opened.

Leyers drove into a compound and parked. He opened the door and tried to get out. Another partisan grabbed him, spun him around, and handcuffed him. The first gunman took the valise.

Leyers looked back at Pino with disgust but said nothing before he was dragged off through a door. It slammed shut behind him, and Pino realized he'd never told the general he was a spy.

"What happens to him?" Pino asked.

"He'll go on trial, probably be hanged," the guard with the valise said.

Pino felt acid in his throat as he said, "I want to testify against him."

"I'm sure you'll get your chance. Car keys?"

Pino handed them over. "What do I do?"

"Go home. Here, take this letter. Show it to any partisan who might stop you."

Pino took the letter, folded it, and put it in his pocket. "Can I get a ride?"

"Sorry," he said. "You'll have to walk. Don't worry, in ten or twenty minutes, it won't be hard to see at all."

"Do you know my brother, Mimo Lella?" Pino asked.

The guard laughed. "We all know that terror, and we're happy he's on our side."

Despite their praise for Mimo, Pino walked to the gate feeling let down and cheated somehow. Why hadn't he told Leyers he was a spy? Why hadn't he asked what he was burning in those files? What was it? Evidence of slavery? And what were those papers he wanted to retrieve from Dolly's apartment?

Did the papers matter? The partisans had the valise and at least some of the files Leyers had saved from the bonfires. And Pino would testify against him, tell the world what he'd seen General Leyers do.

When he exited the gate, Pino was on the southeast side of Milan in one of the most heavily bombed neighborhoods. In the darkness, he kicked things and stumbled and worried about falling into some crater in the wasteland before he could find his way home.

A rifle shot rang out not far away. And then another, followed by a burst of automatic gunfire and a grenade explosion. Pino crouched, feeling like he'd walked into a trap. He was about to turn around, try to find another way home, when in the distance he heard the Duomo's smaller bells start to peal. Then the cathedral's big bells and carillon joined, donging and tolling in the darkness.

Pino felt summoned, pulled toward the basilica. He got up and started toward the bells and the Duomo, not caring about the rifle shots that crackled in the streets around him. Other church bells began to peal, and soon it all sounded like Easter morning.

Then, without warning, and for the first time in nearly two years, streetlamps all around Milan flickered on and brightened, banishing the night and the city's long misery in the shadows of war. Pino blinked at how bright the lamps were, and how they made Milan's ruins and scars stand out scorched and livid.

But the lights were on! And the bells were ringing! Pino felt an enormous sense of relief. Was this it? Was it over? All those German units agreed not to fight. Correct? But the soldiers Mimo arrested had not laid down their guns without threat.

Gunfire and explosions went off to the northeast, toward the central train station and the Piccolo Theater, Fascist headquarters. He realized partisans and Fascists must be fighting for control of Milan. It was a civil war. Or perhaps there were Germans there as well, and it was a three-way battle.

In any case, Pino went west, looping toward the Duomo, away from the fighting. On street after street, the people of Milan were tearing down blackout curtains in the buildings that survived and letting more light flood out into the city. Whole families hung out their windows, cheering and calling for the Nazis to be driven into the sea. Many others were out in the streets, looking up at the lights as if they were a fantasy come true.

The elation was short-lived. Machine gun fire erupted from ten different directions. Pino could hear its rattle-and-pause near and far. He recalled the battle that had raged around the cemetery where Gabriella Rocha lay. *The war isn't over,* he realized. *Neither is the insurrection.* The pacts made in Cardinal Schuster's office were falling apart. By the pace of the fighting, Pino soon believed he was absolutely hearing three-way combat: partisans versus Nazis, and partisans against the Fascists.

When a grenade exploded in one of the adjacent streets, people began to scatter and run back into their homes. Pino bolted into an erratic, zigzagging run. When he reached Piazza Duomo, six German Panzer tanks still squatted around the perimeter of the square, their cannon barrels aiming outward. The cathedral's floodlights were still on, illuminating the entire church, and the bells were still tolling, but otherwise the piazza was deserted. Pino swallowed and moved fast and diagonally across the open ground, praying no snipers were waiting on the upper floors of the buildings that framed the square.

He reached the corner of the cathedral without incident and walked on in the shadow of the great church, looking up and seeing how soot from the years of bombardment and fire had darkened the pale-pink marble facade. Pino wondered if the stains of war would ever leave Milan.

He thought of Anna then, and wondered whether she was settled into Dolly's new place in Innsbruck, and sleeping. It comforted him to think of her like that, safe, warm, so elegant.

Pino smiled and moved quicker. In ten minutes he was outside his parents' apartment building. He checked his pocket for his papers, climbed up the stairs, and pushed through the front door, expecting the SS sentries to be eyeing him. But there was no one on guard, and when the birdcage elevator rose past the fifth floor, the guards there were absent as well.

They're gone! They're all running!

He was genuinely happy as he dug out his keys and fit them into the lock. He pushed the door open to find a small party underway. His father had his violin on its stand, and he'd opened two bottles of fine Chianti, which sat on the living room table by two empty bottles. Michele was drunk and laughing by the fireplace with Mario, his cousin's son, the pilot. And Aunt Greta? She was sitting on her husband's lap smothering him with kisses.

Uncle Albert saw Pino, threw his arms up in victory, and cried, "Hey, you, Pino Lella! You come over here and give your uncle a hug!"

Pino burst out laughing and ran over to hug them all. He drank wine and listened to Uncle Albert's dramatic recounting of the uprising in San Vittore Prison—how they'd overpowered the Fascist guards, opened up the cells, and released everyone.

"The best moment of my life, besides meeting Greta, was marching out the front gates of that prison," Uncle Albert said, beaming. "The shackles were off. We were free. Milan is free!"

"Not quite yet," Pino said. "I walked a long way through the city tonight. The pacts Cardinal Schuster made are being ignored. There's fighting in pockets all over."

Then he told them about Mimo and how he had faced down all those German soldiers single-handedly. His father was stunned. "Alone?"

"Completely," Pino said, full of pride. "I think I have a lot of guts, Papa, but my little brother is something else."

He picked up the wine bottle and poured himself another glass, feeling deliriously good. Had Anna been by his side celebrating the insurrection with his family, he would have felt near perfect. Pino wondered when he'd see her again, when he'd hear from her. He checked the phone and to his surprise found it working. But his father said they'd received no calls before his arrival.

Long after midnight, glowing and woozy with wine, Pino crawled into his bed. Through the open window he heard the growl of the Panzer tanks starting up, and then their treads clanking across the cobblestones, moving away to the northeast. He dozed before hearing explosions and automatic rifles in the direction the tanks had taken.

All through the night, the sounds of battle in Milan rose and fell like one chorus after another, each voice singing of conflict, each song reaching a crescendo, and then ebbing off to echoes and strains. Pino wrapped his head in his pillow and finally slept deeply and full of dreams: of that disgusted look General Leyers had given him walking away, of snipers shooting down on him as he ran through the city, but mostly of Anna and their last night together, how magical and powerful it had been, how perfect and God given.

⊷

Pino awoke on Thursday, April 26, and looked at his clock.

Ten a.m.? When was the last time he'd slept that long? He didn't know, but it felt delicious. Then he smelled bacon cooking. Bacon? Where had that come from?

When he'd dressed and reached the kitchen, he found his father setting crisp bacon on a plate and gesturing to a bowl full of fresh eggs Mario was holding.

"A partisan friend of your uncle Albert just brought these," Michele said. "Albert's out in the hall talking to him. And I'm using the last of the espresso I had hidden in the closet."

Uncle Albert came in. He looked very hungover and a little concerned.

"Pino, you are needed for your English," he said. "They want you to go to the Hotel Diana, and ask for a man named Knebel."

"Who's Knebel?"

"An American. That's all I know."

Another American? The second in two days!

"Okay," he said, looking longingly at the bacon frying, the eggs, and the coffee brewing. "But do I have to go now?"

"After you eat," his father said.

Mario the aviator cooked Pino scrambled eggs, and he wolfed them down along with the bacon and a double espresso. Pino couldn't remember when he'd last had such a feast at breakfast, and then he did—at Casa Alpina. He thought about Father Re, wondered how he and Brother Bormio were getting on. The next chance he had, he'd take Anna up to Motta to meet the priest and to ask him to marry them.

That thought made him happy and confident in a way he'd never felt before. It must have shown, because Uncle Albert came over as Pino was cleaning dishes, and said in a whisper, "You're standing there grinning like a fool and staring off, which means you're in love."

Pino laughed. "Maybe."

"The young lady there, who helped you with the radio?"

"Anna. The one who loves your work."

"Does your father know? Your mother?"

"They've never met. Soon, though."

Uncle Albert patted Pino on the back. "To be young and in love. Isn't it remarkable that something like that can happen in the middle of a war? It says something about the inherent goodness of life, despite all the evil we've seen."

Pino adored his uncle. There was an awful lot going on in that man's head.

"I should go now," Pino said, wiping his hands dry. "Meet Signor Knebel."

⟫━━⟪

Pino left the apartment building and headed toward the Hotel Diana on Viale Piave, not far from the telephone exchange and Piazzale Loreto. Within two blocks he saw a body, a man, facedown in the gutter, a bullet wound to the back of his head. He saw the second and third corpses five blocks from the apartment: a man and a woman in their nightclothes, as if they'd been dragged from their beds. The farther he walked the more dead he saw, almost all head shot, almost all lying facedown in the gutter in the building heat.

Pino was horrified and sickened. By the time he reached the Hotel Diana he'd counted seventy corpses rotting in the sun. Sporadic shooting continued to the north of his route. Someone said the partisans had encircled a large number of Black Shirts trying to escape Milan. The Fascists were fighting to the death.

Pino tugged on the front doors to the Hotel Diana and found them locked. He knocked, waited, and got no response. Going around the back, he tried a door and got it open. He entered an empty kitchen that smelled of recently cooked meat. One set of padded swinging doors on the other side of the kitchen led to a dark, empty restaurant, and the other to a dimly lit ballroom.

Pushing the ballroom door open, Pino called out, "Hello?"

Hearing the metal friction of a rifle action loading, Pino threw his hands up.

"Drop da gun," a man demanded.

"I have no gun," Pino said, hearing the shake in his voice.

"Who are ya?"

"Pino Lella. I was told to come here to see an American named Knebel."

He heard a hoarse laugh before a big lanky man wearing a US Army uniform stepped from the shadows. He had a broad nose, a receding hairline, and a wide smile.

"Lower the gun, Corporal Daloia," he said. "This one's got an invitation."

Corporal Daloia, a short beefy soldier from Boston, lowered the gun.

The bigger American walked over to Pino and stuck out his hand. "Major Frank Knebel, US Fifth Army. I flak for the Fifth, do some writing for *Stars and Stripes*, and dabble in psychological operations."

Pino didn't understand half of what he'd said, but nodded. "You just got here, Major Knebel?"

"Last night," Knebel said. "Came in ahead of the Tenth Mountain Division with this advance scout group to get an early sense of the city for my dispatches. So tell me what's going on out there, Pino. What'd you see coming over?"

"There are dead people lying in the gutters from revenge killings, and the Nazis and Fascists are trying to get out," Pino said. "The partisans are shooting at all of them. But the lights went on last night for the first time in years, and there were no bombers, and for a little while it felt like the war was really over."

"I like that," Knebel said, pulling out a notebook. "Vivid. Say it again."

Pino did, and the major wrote it all down. "I'll call you a partisan fighter, okay?"

"Okay," Pino said, liking the sound of that. "How else can I help?"

"I need an interpreter, heard you spoke English, and here you are."

"Who told you I spoke English?"

"Tweety Bird," Knebel said. "You know the score. The point is, I need help. Are you game to give a hand to an American in need, Pino?"

Pino liked the major's accent. He liked everything about him. "Sure."

"Attaboy," Knebel said, putting his hand on Pino's shoulder and continuing on like they were longtime conspirators. "Now, for today, I really need two things from you. First, get me inside that telephone exchange so I can make some calls and file a few stories."

Pino nodded. "I can do that. What else?"

Knebel smiled toothily. "Can you find us some wine? Whiskey? Maybe girls and music?"

"For?"

"A goddamned party," Knebel said, his grin getting bigger. "I have friends sneaking in here after dark, and this son-of-a-bitch war is almost over, so they'll be wanting to blow off some steam, celebrate. Sound good to you?"

The major had an infectious quality that made Pino grin. "Sounds fun!"

"Can you do it? Get a record player, or a shortwave? Some pretty Italian girls for us to cut a rug with?"

"And wine and whiskey. My uncle, he has both."

"Your uncle is hereby awarded a Silver Star for conduct above and beyond the call of duty," the major said. "Can you get everything here by nine tonight?"

Pino looked at his watch, saw it was noon. He nodded. "I'll take you to the telephone exchange and get started."

Knebel looked at the American soldiers, saluted them, and said, "I think I love this kid."

Corporal Daloia said, "He gets a few pretty broads in here, Major. I'll put him up for the Medal of Honor."

"That's saying something for a guy who's up for a Silver Star for valor at Monte Cassino," Knebel said.

Pino reappraised the corporal.

"Who gives a fig about medals?" Daloia said. "We need women, music, and booze."

"I'll find you all three," Pino said, and the corporal saluted him smartly.

Pino laughed and studied the major's uniform. "Take off the shirt. You'll be noticed."

Knebel did so, following Pino out of the Hotel Diana in his T-shirt, fatigue bottoms, and boots. At the telephone exchange, partisan guards blocked the entrance, but once Pino showed them the letter he'd gotten the night before and explained that Knebel was going to write the glorious history of the Milan uprising for his American audience, they let him enter. Pino set up Knebel in a room with a desk and a phone. Once connected, the major covered the mouthpiece and said, "We're counting on you, Pino."

"Yes, sir," Pino said, and tried to salute with the same finesse as Corporal Daloia.

"Almost," Knebel said, laughing. "Now, go round us up a party to remember."

Feeling energized, Pino left the exchange and started north on Corso Buenos Aires toward Piazzale Loreto, trying to figure out how he was going to find everything Knebel asked for in eight and a half hours. A pretty woman in her twenties, no wedding band, came walking down the street toward him, looking anxious.

On impulse, Pino said, "*Signorina, per favore*, would you like to come to a party tonight?"

"A party? Tonight? With you?" she scoffed. "No."

"There will be music, and wine, and food, and rich American soldiers."

She tossed her hair and said, "There are no Americans in Milan yet."

"Yes, there are, and there'll be more at the Hotel Diana, in the ballroom, tonight at nine. Will you come?"

She hesitated, and then said, "You're not lying?"

"On my mother's soul, I'm not."

"I'll think about it, then. The Hotel Diana?"

"That's right. Wear your dancing dress."

"I'll think about it," she allowed, and walked away.

Pino grinned. She'd be there. He was almost sure of it.

He kept walking and when the next attractive woman came along he said the same thing and got roughly the same answer. The third woman reacted differently. She wanted to come to Pino's party immediately, and when he said there would be rich American soldiers, she told him she'd bring four friends.

Pino was so excited that only then did he realize he'd reached the corner of the Piazzale Loreto and Beltramini's Fresh Fruits and Vegetables. The door was open. He caught the silhouette of someone standing in the shadows. "Carletto? Is that you?"

⚓

Pino's oldest friend tried to slam the door shut. But Pino threw his shoulder against it and overpowered the smaller Carletto, who fell onto his back on the floor.

"Get out of my shop!" Carletto shouted, crabbing backward. "Traitor. Nazi!"

His friend had lost a lot of weight. Pino saw it as soon as he slammed the door shut behind him. "I am no Nazi, and no traitor."

"I saw the swastika! Papa did, too!" Carletto sputtered, pointing at Pino's left arm. "Right there. So what did that make you other than a Nazi?"

"It made me a spy," Pino said, and told Carletto everything.

He could see his old friend didn't believe him at first, but when Carletto heard Leyers's name and realized that was who Pino had been spying on, he had a change of heart.

Carletto said, "If they'd known, Pino, they would have killed you."

"I know."

"And you did it anyway?" his friend said, shaking his head. "That's the difference between you and me. You risk and act, while I . . . I watch and fear."

"There's nothing left to be afraid of," Pino said. "The war's over."

"Is it?"

"How's your mama?"

Carletto hung his head. "She died, Pino. In January. During the cold. I couldn't keep her warm enough because we had no fuel and no produce to sell. She coughed herself to death."

"I'm so sorry," Pino said, feeling emotion ball in his throat. "She was as kind as your father was funny. I should have been here to help you bury both of them."

"You were where you were supposed to be, and so was I," Carletto said, looking so crushed Pino wanted to cheer him up.

"You still play the drums?"

"Not in a long time."

"But you still have the set?"

"In the basement."

"Know any other musicians who live around here?"

"Why?"

"Humor me."

"Sure, I think so. If they're still alive, I mean."

"Good. Let's go."

"What? Where?"

"To my house to get you something to eat," Pino replied. "And then we're going to find wine, food, and more young ladies. And when we've got enough, we are going to throw the end-of-war party to end all end-of-war parties."

Chapter Twenty-Nine

By 9:00 p.m. on the second day of the general insurrection in Milan, Pino and Carletto had moved six cases of wine and twenty liters of homemade beer from Uncle Albert's private stock to the Hotel Diana. Pino's father contributed two full bottles of grappa. And Carletto found three unopened bottles of whiskey someone had given his father years before.

Corporal Daloia, in the meantime, had discovered a dismantled stage in the basement of the hotel and saw it reassembled at the far end of the ballroom. Carletto's drum kit was set up at the rear of the stage. He was thumping the bass drum and adjusting his cymbals while a trumpeter, a clarinetist, a saxophonist, and a trombonist were tuning up.

Pino sat at the upright piano the Americans had lifted onto the stage and was fiddling nervously with the keys. He hadn't played in almost a year. But then he let loose with a few chords from each hand and stopped. It was enough.

The crowd began to hoot and call. Pino put his hand to his brow theatrically, looked out at twenty American GIs, a squad of New Zealanders, eight journalists, and at least thirty Milanese women.

"A toast!" Major Knebel shouted, and jumped up onto the stage, holding a glass of wine, spilling some and not caring. He raised his glass. "To the end of war!"

The crowd roared. Corporal Daloia jumped up beside the major and yelled, "To the end of homicidal dictators with weird black bangs and puny square mustaches!"

The soldiers broke into gales of laughter and cheers.

Pino was laughing, too, but he managed to translate for the women, who shouted their approval and raised their glasses. Carletto gulped his wine in one long belt that finished in a lip smack that left him grinning.

Cracking his drum sticks, Carletto yelled, "Eight to the bar, Pino!"

His arms, elbows, wrists, and hands held high, his fingers dangling over the keys, Pino started with high notes, tinkling before he brought in the bass in a bouncy rhythm that rolled over into one of those tunes he used to practice before the bombing began.

This time it was a variation of "Pinetop's Boogie Woogie," pure dance hall music.

The crowd went wild, and wilder still when Carletto went to the brushes and the cymbals, and the bass joined in on top of him. Soldiers started grabbing the Italian girls and dancing swing style, talking through their hands, knees bopping, hips shaking, and spinning. Other soldiers in the room stood around the dancers, nervously looking at the women, or standing in place, drink in one hand and the index finger of the other hand wagging time, hips swaying and shoulders popping along with Pino's wicked boogie tune. Every once in a while, one of them would scream just for the drunken hell of it.

The clarinetist played a solo. So did the sax man and the trombonist. The music died to clapping and shouts for more. The trumpet player stepped forward and slayed the house, blew the opening of "Boogie Woogie Bugle Boy."

Many of the GIs sang the lyrics by heart, and the dancing got frenzied as the other soldiers drank, cheered, and brayed, and danced and drank more and fell away into the sheer fun of letting go. When Pino brought the song to an end, the sweating crowd of dancers cheered and stomped their feet.

"More!" they shouted. "Encore!"

―――◆―――

Pino was drenched with sweat, but he didn't think he'd ever felt this happy. The only thing missing was Anna. She'd never seen Pino play a note. She would have fainted. He laughed at that image and then thought of Mimo. Where was he? Still fighting the Nazis?

He felt a little guilty about celebrating while his younger brother was out being a warrior, but then looked back at Carletto, who was pouring himself another generous glass of wine and smiling like a fool.

"C'mon, Pino," Carletto said. "Give 'em what they want."

"Okay!" Pino shouted to the crowd. "But the piano player needs a drink! Grappa!"

Someone rushed up a glass of the liquor. Pino downed it and nodded to Carletto, who cracked his sticks. And they were off again, pumping the boogie-woogie with Pino messing around with every example he'd ever heard or practiced.

"1280 Stomp." "Boogie Woogie Stomp." "Big Bad Boogie Woogie."

The crowd loved all of it. He'd never had this much fun in his life and suddenly understood why his parents adored having musicians at their parties.

When they took a break around eleven that night, Major Knebel reeled up to him and said, "Outstanding, soldier. Just outstanding!"

"You had fun?" Pino said, grinning.

"Best damned party ever, and it's just getting started. One of your girls lives close by, and she swears her daddy's got all sorts of booze in his basement."

Pino noticed a few couples leaving the ballroom holding hands and heading upstairs. He smiled and went for some water and wine.

Carletto came over, threw his arm around Pino, and said, "Thank you for knocking me on my ass this afternoon."

"What are friends for?"

"Friends always?"

"To the day we die."

The first woman Pino invited to the party walked up and said, "You're Pino?"

"That's right. What's your name?"

"Sophia."

Pino held out his hand. "Nice to meet you, Sophia. Having a good time?"

"So much fun, but I can't speak English."

"A few of the soldiers, like Corporal Daloia over there, speak Italian. The others? Just dance, and smile, and let your body speak the language of love."

Sophia laughed. "You make it sound easy."

"I'll be watching," Pino said before heading back to the stage.

He had another shot of grappa, and they went at it again, boogie-woogie, holding it, and then messing around, and then boogie-woogie again; and the crowd stomping and dancing. At midnight, he glanced at the dance floor and saw Sophia doing back bends and spins with Corporal Daloia, who was grinning ear to ear.

Things could not have gotten better.

Pino had another grappa and then another, and played on and on, smelling the sweat of the dancers and the perfume of the women, all melding into a musk that made him drunk in yet another way. Around two it all became a blur and then black.

Six hours later, on the morning of Friday, April 27, 1945, Pino woke up on the hotel kitchen floor with a splitting headache and a foul stomach. He made it to the bathroom and vomited, which made his stomach better, and his headache worse.

Pino looked out into the ballroom, seeing people sprawled everywhere: in chairs, on tables, on the floor. Carletto was on his back, arm over his face, on the stage behind his drums. Major Knebel was curled up on a couch. Corporal Daloia was on another couch, spooning with Sophia, which made Pino smile through a yawn.

He thought of his own bed and how good it would be to sleep the hangover off there rather than here on a hard floor. He guzzled some water and left the Hotel Diana, heading more or less due south toward Porta Venezia and the public gardens. It was a spectacular day, clear blue and as warm as June.

Within a block of leaving the hotel Pino saw the first body, facedown in the gutter, gunshot to the back of the head. In the next block, he saw three dead. Eight blocks later, he saw five. Two of them were Black Shirt Fascists, by their uniform. Three were in nightclothes.

Despite all the death he saw that morning, Pino knew something had changed in Milan overnight, some critical point had been reached and passed while he'd been partying and sleeping, because the streets near Porta Venezia were crowded and boisterous. Violins played. Accordions, too. People danced and hugged and laughed and cried. Pino felt as if the spirit of the party at the Hotel Diana had moved outside and seduced everyone celebrating the end of a long and terrible ordeal.

He entered the public gardens, taking a shortcut home. People were lying on the lawns, basking in the sun, having a good time. Pino looked ahead on the crowded path he was taking through the park and saw a familiar face coming his way. Wearing the uniform of the Free Italian Air Force, his cousin Mario was beaming, looking like he was having the time of his life.

"Eh, Pino!" he cried, and hugged him. "I am free! No more sitting in the apartment!"

"That's so great," Pino said. "Where are you going?"

"Anywhere, everywhere," Mario said, glancing at his aviator's watch, which gleamed in the sunlight. "I just want to walk and soak it all up, the joy in the city now that the Nazis and the Fascists are kaput. You know this feeling?"

Pino did know. So, it seemed, did almost everyone else in Milan that day.

"I'm going home to get some sleep," Pino said. "Too much grappa last night."

Mario laughed. "I should have been with you."

"You would have had fun."

"I'll see you later."

"You, too," Pino said, and walked on.

He had gone no more than six meters when an argument broke out behind him.

"*Fascista!*" a man shouted. "*Fascista!*"

Pino turned and saw a small, stocky man standing in the path, aiming a revolver at Mario.

"No!" Mario cried. "I am a pilot for free—"

The pistol fired. The bullet blew out the back of Mario's head. Pino's cousin collapsed like a rag doll.

―――――

"He's a Fascist! Death to all Fascists!" the man yelled, and shook his gun.

People began to scream and run.

Pino was so traumatized he didn't know what to do or say, just stared at Mario's body and the blood draining from his head. He started to dry-heave. But then the killer crouched over Mario and started working at his aviator's wristwatch.

Anger boiled up inside Pino. He was about to attack, when his cousin's murderer saw him standing there. "What are you looking at? Hey, he was talking to you. You a Fascist, too?"

Seeing him trying to aim, Pino spun and took off in a series of cuts and feints. The pistol barked behind him, hit one of the few trees left in the garden. Pino didn't slow until he was far from the park, almost to San Babila. Only then did he allow himself to suffer what he'd just witnessed. All the water he'd guzzled came up, and he retched until his sides ached.

He walked on in a daze, taking a roundabout route toward home.

Mario was alive one second and gone the next. The randomness of his cousin's death had him shaking and shivering as he walked through the hot streets. Was no one safe?

In the fashion district, people were outside celebrating, sitting on their front stoops, laughing and smoking, eating and drinking. He walked past the opera house and saw a crowd. He went to it, trying not to see Mario dying in his mind. Partisans had cordoned off the Hotel Regina, Gestapo headquarters.

"What's going on?" Pino asked.

"They're searching the place," someone said.

Pino knew they weren't going to find much of value in there. He'd seen it all burn. He'd seen General Leyers and Colonel Rauff burn so much paper it still baffled him. His mind sought refuge from the horror of his cousin's death in questions about the things the Nazis had burned. What could have been in those documents? And what papers had they kept, and why?

He thought about Leyers two nights before. The general had asked to go back to Dolly's before Pino arrested him, didn't he? Something about getting papers he'd left there, and something else. He'd mentioned those papers at least twice.

Thinking that Leyers might have left something incriminating at Dolly's apartment, he felt more alert, less devastated by Mario's death.

Dolly's was only a few blocks away on Via Dante. He'd go there before going home to tell his father about Mario. He'd find the papers and give them to Major Knebel. With what he could tell the American about Leyers, there had to be a story there. Pino and Knebel would tell the world about the general and his "forced labor-ers," how he'd driven them to their deaths, Pharaoh's slave master at work.

Twenty minutes later, Pino ran up the steps of Dolly's apartment, into the lobby and past the crone, who blinked at him through her thick glasses. "Who's there?"

"An old friend, Signora Plastino," Pino said, and kept climbing.

When he reached Dolly's door, it was busted in and hanging off its hinges. Suitcases and boxes had been slit open. Their contents were strewn about in the front hall.

Pino began to panic. "Anna? Dolly?"

He went to the kitchen, found the dishes smashed and cabinets emptied. He was shaking and thought he was going to be sick again when he reached Anna's room and pushed the door open. The mattress had been pushed off the bed. Her drawers and closet were open and empty.

Then he noticed something sticking out from beneath the mattress. A leather strap. He crouched, lifted the mattress, and pulled. The tooled leather bag his uncle had given Anna on Christmas Eve came out. In his mind, he heard her say, *I've never had so wonderful a present in my whole life. I'll never let it go.*

Where was she? Pino's head began to pound. She left two, three days ago? What had happened? She never would have left the bag behind.

Then he realized who would know. Running back downstairs, Pino went to the crone, gasping. "What happened to Dolly's apartment? Where is she? Where's Anna, her maid?"

Through the thick lenses, the old woman's blinking eyes looked twice their size when a cold, satisfied smile twisted her lips.

"They took the German whores last night," she cackled. "You should have seen the things people took out of that den of perversion afterward. Unspeakable things."

Pino felt disbelief turn to terror. "Where were they taken? Who took them?"

Signora Plastino squinted and then leaned forward, studying him.

Pino grabbed her roughly by the arm. "Where?"

The crone hissed, "I know you. You're one of them!"

Pino let her go and stepped back.

"A Nazi!" she screamed. "He's a Nazi! A Nazi, right here!"

Pino bolted out the front door as the old woman's shrill voice carried behind him. "Stop him! He's a traitor! A Nazi! A friend of the German whores!"

He ran as fast and as hard as he could go, trying to get out of earshot of the crone's squawking alarm. When at last he stopped, he leaned against a wall, feeling disoriented, numb, and frightened. *Anna and Dolly were taken,* he thought, feeling dread that threatened to freeze him. *But where? And who would have taken them? Partisans?* He was sure of that.

Pino could run and find a partisan, but would they listen to him? They would with that letter they'd given him after he delivered Leyers, right? He dug in his pockets. It wasn't there. He searched again. Nothing. Well, he'd just go find a partisan commander in the area anyway. Or since he was without the letter, would they think he was a collaborator because he knew Dolly and Anna, and thereby endanger himself? He needed help. He needed his uncle Albert. He'd go find him and have him use his contacts to—

Pino heard distant shouting, voices he could not make out. But the shouting was getting louder, more voices, and wilder, and he felt even more disoriented. For reasons he couldn't explain, he started not toward home but toward the shouting, as if the voices were calling to him. He wove through the streets fast, tracking the raucous din until he realized it was coming from Parco Sempione, from inside Castello Sforzesco, where he and Anna had walked that snowy day when they'd seen the ravens circling.

Whether it was the hangover, or the fatigue, or the paralyzing fear of knowing Anna had been taken, or all three reasons combined, he felt suddenly unbalanced, as if he might swoon and fall. Time seemed to slow. Every moment took on the surreal quality of the cemetery where he'd gone to retrieve the corpse of Gabriella Rocha.

Only now Pino's senses seemed to shut off one by one, until, like a deaf man who had lost taste and touch, he only saw as he wove on dizzily past a dry fountain toward the lowered drawbridge that crossed the empty moat to the arched main entrance of the medieval fortress.

A mob of other people was ahead of Pino, pushing onto the drawbridge and squeezing to get through the gate. More people crowded in and around behind him, jostling against him, their faces flushed with excitement. He knew they were all shouting and joking, but he understood not a word as he moved forward with the throng. He was looking up. In a brilliant blue sky, ravens were circling the bombed towers again.

Pino was fixated on the birds until he was almost at the entrance. And then someone pushed him through and into a huge, sunbaked, and bomb-cratered courtyard that stretched out one hundred meters to a second fortress wall— not as tall, three stories high—and slotted with windows made for medieval archers to shoot down on their enemies. In the open space between the two fortress walls, the crush around Pino relaxed, and people hurried past him to join hundreds of others pressing against a line of armed partisan fighters standing three-quarters of the way across the courtyard, their backs to the wall of Castello Sforzesco itself.

<hr/>

As Pino walked toward the crowd his senses returned, one by one.

His nose came back first, and he smelled the sick-sweet rankness of all those humans packing together in the heat. Touch returned to his fingers and the skin at the nape of his neck, which registered the sun beating down on him without pity. And then he could hear the mob and its jeering hoots and catcalls for vengeance.

"Kill them!" they were shouting—men, women, and children alike. "Bring them out! Make them pay!"

People toward the front of the mob saw something and began to roar their approval. They tried to surge closer, but the partisan soldiers held them back. Pino, however, was not to be denied. He used his strength, height, and weight to bully his way forward until no more than three men stood between him and the front line of spectators.

Eight men wearing white shirts, red scarves, and black pants and hoods marched out into the open ground beyond the fighters. They held carbine rifles on their shoulders and tried for discipline as they moved into position some forty meters directly in front of Pino.

"What's happening?" Pino asked one old man.

"Fascists," he replied with a toothless smile, and made a cutting gesture across his neck.

The hooded men stopped in a line three meters apart, set their guns and bodies at ease facing the wall of the inner fortress. The crowd calmed on its own, and grew quiet when a door in the far left corner of that wall opened.

Ten seconds passed. Then twenty. Then a minute.

"C'mon!" someone shouted. "It's hot. Bring them out!"

A ninth hooded man appeared in the doorway. He held a pistol in one hand and gripped the end of a stout rope with the other. He stepped out. Nearly two meters of rope played behind him before the first man appeared: tubby, chicken-legged, in his fifties, and dressed only in his underwear, socks, and shoes.

People began to laugh and clap their approval. The poor man looked like he might collapse at any moment. Behind him came another man in trousers and a cutoff T-shirt. He was keeping his chin up, trying to act brave, but Pino could see he was shaking. A Black Shirt came out next, still in uniform, and the crowd howled its disapproval.

Then a sobbing, middle-aged woman in bra, panties, and sandals stepped from the doorway, and the mob went wild. Her head had been shaved. Something had been written on her skull and face with lipstick.

The rope went on another meter before a second bald woman stepped out, and then a third. When Pino saw the fourth woman emerge, blinking in the hot sun, he started to tremble in his gut and quake in his marrow.

It was Dolly Stottlemeyer. She was in her ivory dressing gown and green slippers. When Leyers's mistress saw the executioners she began to pull against the rope like a horse against its rein, trying to dig in her heels, twisting, fighting, and screaming in Italian, "No! You can't do this! It's not right!"

A partisan stepped up and hit Dolly between the shoulder blades with the butt of his rifle, stunning her into a forward stumble, which yanked Anna out the door.

⟞⟝

Anna had been stripped to her slip and bra, and her hair had been horribly shorn. Tufts of it stuck out from her bare scalp. Her lips were smeared with so much red lipstick she was like some grotesque creature in a cartoon. Her terror elevated now that she'd seen the firing squad and heard the crowd heaping its scorn, calling for her death.

"No!" Pino said, and then screamed it. "No!"

But his voice was drowned out by a song of savageness and bloodlust that built and swept through the courtyard of Castello Sforzesco, echoing around and off the condemned beings lined up against the wall. The crowd squeezed forward again and pinned Pino from all sides. Helpless, sick, and disbelieving, he watched Anna pushed into position beside Dolly.

"No," he said, his throat constricting and tears welling in his eyes. "No."

Anna had gone hysterical, her cries wracking through her body. Pino didn't know what to do. He wanted to go crazy, fight, scream at the partisans to let Anna go. But he kept freezing at the image of the crone, and how she'd recognized him and called him a Nazi and a traitor. And he had no letter. They could just as well throw Pino up there against the wall, too.

The partisan leader drew his pistol and fired it into the air to quiet the crowd. Anna wrenched up with fear and fell back against the wall, shaking and sobbing.

The partisan leader yelled, "The charges against these eight are treason, collaboration, whoring, and profiting from the Nazi and Salò occupation of Milan. Their just punishment is death. Long live the new Republic of Italy!"

The crowd cheered lustily. Pino couldn't take it. His eyes burned with tears, and he began to lash out in frustration, throwing his elbows and kicking with his knees until he'd fought to the very front of the mob.

A partisan saw him coming and stuck his rifle barrel against his chest.

"I had a letter, but I can't find it," Pino said, patting at his pockets. "I am with the resistance. There's been a mistake."

The partisan barely looked at him. "I don't know you. Where's the letter?"

"It was in my pocket last night, but I . . . There was a party and . . . ," Pino said. "Please, just let me talk to your commander."

"Not without something that says he should be talking to you."

"We needed to eat!" cried a woman's voice. Pino looked over the partisan's shoulder and saw the first woman on the rope line pleading, "We needed to eat and to live. Is that too much?"

Down the line, seeming resigned to her fate, Dolly shook back her hair and tried to lift her chin but did not succeed.

"Ready?" the commander said.

Anna started screaming, "No! I'm not a whore! I'm not a collaborator! I'm a maid. That's all I am. Someone, please believe me. I'm just a maid. Dolly, tell them. Dolly? Tell them!"

Dolly didn't seem to hear her. She was staring at the guns rising to the shoulders of the execution squad.

"My God!" Anna wailed. "Someone tell them I'm just a maid!"

"Aim."

Pino's mouth opened. He looked at the fighter, who was studying him, suspicious now. Pino willed his diaphragm to tense and yell out that it was true, that she was innocent, that this was all a mistake and—

"Fire!"

The rifle shots rang out like cymbals and kettledrums.

Anna-Marta took a bullet to her heart.

She bucked up at the impact, looking surprised before seeming to gaze toward Pino, as if her spirit had sensed him there and called out for him in that last moment before she crumpled back against the wall, and died in the dust.

Chapter Thirty

Watching Anna's body twitch while a bloom of blood unfolded across her bosom, Pino felt his heart breach and flush out all love, all joy, all music.

The crowd around him bellowed and jeered its approval while he just stood there, hunch shouldered, whimpering at the agony that possessed him, so powerful it almost made him think it couldn't be real, that his beloved was not lying there in a pool of blood, that he'd not watched her take the bullet, that he'd not watched life flee her in a blink, that he'd not heard her begging him to save her.

The crowd around him started pushing the other way, leaving now that the show was over. Pino stayed where he was, gazing over at Anna's corpse sprawled against the bottom of the wall and seeing her dull stare like an accusation of betrayal.

"Move away now," the partisan said to him. "It's over."

"No," Pino said. "I—"

"Move, if you know what's good for you," the soldier said.

With one long last shuddering look at Anna, Pino turned and trudged off with the last of the crowd. He went through the gate and across the drawbridge, unable to grasp what had just happened. It felt like he had been shot in the chest, and only now was he beginning to sense the true pain to come. But then a realization came battering down upon his shoulders and threatened to destroy him. He hadn't stood up for Anna. He had not died for her love the way great and tragic men did in lasting stories and librettos.

Pino's brain burned with failure. His heart soured with self-loathing.

I'm a coward, he thought in darkest despair, and wondered why he'd been sentenced to such hell. In the roundabout in front of the castle, it all became too much. Pino felt dizzy, and then sick. He stumbled to the dry fountain. He retched and retched again, knowing that he was weeping as well, and that people were watching him.

When Pino finally stood, coughing, spitting, and wiping his eyes, a guy on the other side of the fountain said, "You knew one of them, didn't you?"

Pino saw suspicion and the threat of violence in the man's expression. Part of Pino wanted to admit his love for Anna and have a noble end to it all. But then the man started to walk toward him, quickening his pace, and then jabbing his finger at Pino.

"Someone grab that guy!" he shouted.

<hr>

The primitive instinct to survive took over, and Pino took off, sprinting diagonally away from the fountain toward Via Beltrami. Shouts went up. One man tried to tackle Pino, but Pino threw a fist that drove the man to the pavement. Running pell-mell, knowing people were chasing him, he noticed men trying to cut in at him from the side.

Pino threw an elbow into one man's face, kneed another in the groin, and dodged through cars onto Via Giuseppe Pozzone. He jumped up on and over the hood of one before cutting off onto Via Rovello, where he leaped across a water-filled bomb crater and put distance between him and his pursuers. When he glanced back at the corner of Via San Tomaso, he saw six men still chasing him and still yelling, "He's a traitor! Collaborator! Stop him!"

But those streets were Pino's backyard. He sped into a higher gear, taking a right on Via Broletto and a left on Via Del Bossi. There was a knot of people ahead in Piazza Della Scala. Pino feared getting past them and through the Galleria before the calls of "traitor" caught up to him.

Diagonally across the street, in the wall of the great opera house, a door was open. He ran over and through it into a hallway, moving beyond the shadows into a wedge of blackness. Pino stopped there, sure he couldn't be seen from outside, watching and waiting until the six men sprinted past, heading toward the piazza. Gasping for breath in the darkness, he stayed there, wanting to make sure he'd lost them.

———✦———

Deeper inside La Scala, a tenor began to sing, running scales.

Pino turned and accidentally kicked something metal. It clattered enough that he looked to the doorway and saw the man from the fountain, who was peering in from the sidewalk.

He stepped inside, dusting off his hands. "You're in here, aren't you, traitor?"

Pino said nothing and held his position in the darkest shadow, almost sure the man could not see him pivot toward him and crouch ever so slowly. The man kept coming even as Pino's fingers groped on the floor and found a piece of discarded steel reinforcement rod, probably left over from the repair job on the opera house after the bomb hit it. It was as thick as Pino's thumb, as long as his forearm, and heavy. When the man from the fountain was just a couple of meters from him and squinting to see better, Pino whipped the rod backhand, aiming at his shins. But his aim was high, and he hit the man in the kneecap.

The man screamed. Pino came up fast, took two big steps, and drove a fist into the side of the man's face. He went down. But behind him, two of the others who'd been chasing Pino appeared. He spun and took off, deeper into the darkness, hands out, groping and navigating toward the tenor who'd started to sing. Pino stumbled twice and caught his pants on wire while also trying to listen for pursuers behind him, so he did not recognize the aria the tenor was practicing at first.

But then he did. "*Vesti la Giubba*," "Put on the Costume," from the opera *Pagliacci*, *The Clowns*. The aria reeked of grief and loss, and Pino's thoughts of escape were slashed by images of the bullet's impact and Anna falling. He tripped, hit his head against something, saw stars, and almost went down.

When he roused himself, the aria was into its second verse. Canio, the heart-broken clown, was telling himself to go on, to put on a mask and shield his inner pain. Pino had heard recordings of the aria dozens of times and felt prodded to action by it, and by the sound of footsteps pounding in the passages behind him.

He pushed on, still groping until he felt air on his cheek, then turned and saw a slant of light ahead. Running now, he pushed open a door and found himself backstage in the great opera house. He'd been there several times watching Licia, his cousin, practice. A young tenor stood center of La Scala's stage. Pino caught glimpses of him out there under the low lights as he launched into the third verse.

> *"Ridi, Pagliaccio, sul tuo amore infranto."*
> (*"Laugh, clown, at your broken love."*)

Pino went through a curtain and down stairs that led to the side aisle for loge seating. He started up the aisle toward the exit even as the tenor sang, *"Ridi del duol, che t'avvelena il cor!"* (*"Laugh at the grief that poisons your heart."*)

The words seemed to hit Pino like arrows that weakened him until the tenor stopped and cried out in alarm, "Who are you? What do you want?"

Pino glanced back and saw he was addressing Pino's three pursuers, who'd joined the tenor on the stage.

"We're after a traitor," one of the men said.

⊰⊱

Pino pushed through the door, and it made an ear-splitting squeak. He took off again, across a landing, down the stairs, and into the lobby. The doors were open. He jogged out, tearing off his shirt, which left him in a sleeveless white T-shirt.

He glanced to his left. Home was only five or six blocks away. But he couldn't go there and risk jeopardizing his family. Instead, he went straight across the trolley tracks and into a knot of people celebrating the end of the war around the statue of Leonardo da Vinci. He tried to stay focused, but in his head he kept hearing the clown's devastated aria, kept seeing Anna crying for help, hunching up at the bullet's strike, and then crumpling.

It took everything he had not to lie down and dissolve into sobs. It took everything he had to put on a smiling face, as if he, too, were overjoyed by the Nazis' retreat. He kept it up through the Galleria, smiling and moving, not quite sure where he was going.

Then he stepped free of the shopping mall and knew. A huge crowd was celebrating on Piazza Duomo, eating, drinking, playing music, and dancing.

Pino melted into them, slowing, smiling, and trying to look normal as he moved toward the trickle of people heading into the cathedral to pray.

To Pino, the Duomo meant sanctuary. They could chase him inside the cathedral, but they couldn't bring him out.

He was almost to the front doors when he heard a man shouting behind him. "There he is! Stop him! He's a traitor! A collaborator!"

Pino looked back and saw them coming across the piazza. Following several women old enough to be his mother, he slipped into the basilica.

⸻

With the stained-glass windows boarded over, the only light in the Duomo came from votive candles flickering in the various alcoves and chapels to either side of the cathedral's central aisle, and more burning at the far end around the altar.

Even with the candles, the inner cathedral was a charcoal-shadowed place that day, and Pino acted swiftly to take advantage of it. He moved away from the chapels on the Duomo's left side, heading toward the right aisle and the confessionals: bleak affairs offering no privacy to the penitent, who knelt outside a tall wooden box and whispered their sins to the priest inside.

It was humiliating, and Pino hated going to confession there. But from his times kneeling at the Duomo confessionals as a young boy, he knew there was a space between the booth and the wall, thirty centimeters, fifty at best. He hoped it would be enough as he eased behind the third confessional booth, farthest from the candle stands.

He stood there, shaking, hunched down so he'd be fully hidden, and was glad that no priests seemed to be taking confessions on liberation day. The aria started again in his head, and with it the horror of Anna's death, until he shook it off and forced himself to listen. The clicking and murmurs of women praying the Holy Rosary came to him. A cough. The squeak of the main doors. Men talking. Pino fought the urge to peek out and waited, hearing loud footsteps coming. Men moving fast.

"Where did he go?" one said.

"He's in here somewhere," said another, sounding like he was right in front of the confessional booth.

"I'm coming," a male voice said, amid other footsteps approaching.

"No, Father," one man said. "Not today. We're, uh, going to one of the chapels to pray."

"If you sin on the way there, I'll be waiting," the priest said, and the door to the confessional booth opened.

Pino felt the box settle under the priest's weight. He heard the two men move off deeper into the cathedral. He waited, hardly breathing, giving it time. Once more the clown sang in his head. Once more he tried to will it away, but the aria would not leave his head.

He had to move for fear he'd burst out crying again. Pino tried to step gingerly out from behind the confessional, but his shoe caught the kneeler.

"Ahh," the priest said. "A customer at last."

The screen slid back, but all Pino could see in there was blackness. He did the only thing he could think of and knelt.

"Bless me, Father, for I have sinned," Pino choked.

"Yes?"

"I said nothing," Pino sobbed in lament. "I did nothing."

"What are you talking about?" the priest said.

Feeling like he might collapse if he confessed more, Pino lurched to his feet and charged deeper into the cathedral. He crossed beneath the transept and found a door he remembered. He went through it and was outside again, facing Via dell'Arcivescovado.

There were more happy people walking toward the piazza. He went against the grain and looped around the back of the Duomo. He was considering going home or to Uncle Albert's, when he noticed a priest and a workman come out a door on the far side of the Duomo near Corso Vittorio. There was a staircase behind them that he remembered going up as a boy with a school class.

Another workman exited. Pino caught the door before it closed and started up a steep and narrow staircase that climbed thirty stories to a walkway that ran the long side of the basilica, up there among the gargoyles, spires, and Gothic arches. He kept glancing up at the pristine, polychrome statue of the Madonna atop the Duomo's highest tower, wondering how she'd survived the war, and how much destruction she'd seen.

Drenched with cold sweat, shivering despite the baking heat as he moved between and under the flying buttresses that supported the roof, Pino stopped at last when he reached a balcony high above the cathedral's front doors. He looked out over his bombarded city, his bombarded life, splayed out around him like some tattered and bullet-riddled skirt.

Pino lifted his head to the sky and from an anguish that knew no bottom, whispered, "I said nothing to save her, God. I did nothing."

Those confessions transfixed him right back into the tragedy, and he choked back sobs. "After everything . . . After everything, now I have nothing."

Pino heard laughter, music, and singing float up to him from the piazza. He stepped out onto the balcony and looked over the railing. Ninety meters below, down where he'd seen the workmen erecting the spotlights nearly two years before, violins played, and accordions, and guitars. He could see bottles of wine being passed around, and couples were beginning to kiss and dance and love on the back side of war.

Pain and grief sawed through Pino. This torment was his punishment, he decided. He bowed his head, understanding that this was between God and . . . The aria of the heartbroken clown echoed in his ears and Anna crumpled and fell again, and again, and . . . in a matter of seconds, his faith in God, in life, in love, and in a better tomorrow drained away to empty.

Pino held on to a marble post and climbed up onto the balcony rail, a betrayer, abandoned and alone. He gazed at the puffy clouds scudding across the azure sky and decided that clouds and sky were good enough to look at while dying.

"You saw all that I did, Lord," Pino said, letting go of the post to take the worst step of all. "Have mercy on my soul."

Chapter Thirty-One

"Stop!" a man shouted behind him.

Pino startled, almost lost his full balance, almost pitched off the railing, almost plunged thirty stories to the stone piazza and death. But his mountaineering reflexes were too ingrained. His fingers caught the post. He steadied himself enough to look over his shoulder and felt his heart try to crawl out of his chest.

The cardinal of Milan was standing there, not three meters away.

"What are you doing?" Schuster demanded.

"Dying," Pino said dully.

"You'll do no such thing, not in my church, and not on this day of all days," the cardinal said. "There's been too much bloodshed already. Get down from there, young man. Now."

"Really, My Lord Cardinal, it's better this way."

"My Lord Cardinal?"

The prince of the church squinted, adjusted his glasses, and looked closer. "Only one person I know calls me that. You're General Leyers's driver. You're Pino Lella."

"Which is why jumping is better than living."

Cardinal Schuster shook his head, took a step toward him. "Are you the traitor and collaborator who's supposedly hiding in the Duomo?"

Pino nodded.

"Get down, then," Schuster said, holding out his hand. "You're safe. I'm granting you sanctuary. No one will harm you under my protection."

Pino wanted to cry, but said, "You wouldn't if you knew what I've done."

"I know what Father Re told me about you. It's enough for me to know I should save you. Take my hand now. You're making me ill standing up there like that."

Pino looked down and saw Schuster's hand and his cardinal's ring, but he did not take it.

"What would Father Re have you do?" Cardinal Schuster said.

At that, something gave way inside Pino. He grabbed the cardinal's hand, got down, and stood there, stooped and trying not to break down.

Schuster put his hand on Pino's trembling shoulder. "It can't be all that bad, my son."

"It's worse, My Lord Cardinal," Pino said. "The worst. The go-to-hell kind of act."

"Let me be the judge of that," Schuster said, guiding him away from the balcony.

He got Pino to sit down in the shade of one of the cathedral's flying buttresses. Pino did, vaguely aware of the music still playing below, vaguely aware of the cardinal calling to someone to get food and water. Then Schuster crouched beside Pino.

"Tell me now," the cardinal said. "I will hear your confession."

Pino gave Schuster the spine of his story with Anna, how he'd met her on the street the first day of the bombardment, and then fourteen months later through General Leyers's mistress, how they'd fallen in love, and how they'd planned to marry, and how she'd tragically died in front of a firing squad not an hour before.

"I said nothing to stop them," he wept. "I did nothing to save her."

Cardinal Schuster closed his eyes.

Pino choked, "If I really loved her, I . . . I should have been willing to die with her."

"No," the prelate said, opening his eyes and fixing them on Pino. "It is a tragedy that your Anna died that way, but you had the right to survive. Every human has that basic, God-given right, Pino, and you feared for your life."

Pino threw up his hands and cried, "Do you know how many times I've feared for my life in the last two years?"

"I can't imagine."

"Every time before, I had faith in doing the right thing, no matter the danger. But I just . . . couldn't believe in Anna enough to . . ."

He started to cry again.

"Faith is a strange creature," Schuster said. "Like a falcon that nests year after year in the same place, but then flies away, sometimes for years, only to return again, stronger than ever."

"I don't know if it will ever return for me."

"It will. In time. Why don't you come with me now? We'll get you fed, and I'll find a place for you to spend the night."

Pino thought about that, and then shook his head, saying, "I'll come off the roof with you, My Lord Cardinal, but I think I'll slip out after dark, go home to my family."

Schuster paused, and then said, "As you wish, my son. Bless you, and go with God."

After dark, Pino slipped into the lobby of his parents' apartment building and immediately recalled the prior Christmas Eve and how Anna had played the sentries to get the suitcase with the radio transmitter safely upstairs. Riding up in the birdcage elevator provoked another round of crushing memories, how they'd kissed going past the fifth-floor guards, and how they'd—

The elevator stopped. He shuffled to the door and knocked.

Aunt Greta opened the door with a big grin on her face. "There you are, Pino! We've been holding dinner for you and Mario. Have you seen him?"

Pino swallowed hard and said, "He's dead. They're all dead."

His aunt stood there in shock as he moved past her into the apartment. Uncle Albert and Pino's father had heard him and were getting up from the living room couch.

"What do you mean he's dead?" Michele asked.

"A man who wanted his wristwatch called him a Fascist and shot him in the head in the public gardens near Porta Venezia," Pino said dully.

"No!" his father said. "That's not true!"

"I saw it happen, Papa."

His father broke down, crying, "Oh dear God. How will I tell his mother?"

Pino was staring at the living room rug, remembering how he and Anna had made love there. The best Christmas present of his life. He wasn't hearing the questions Uncle Albert was firing at him. He just wanted to lie down there and mourn and grieve.

Aunt Greta stroked his arm. "It's going to be okay, Pino," she soothed. "Whatever you've seen, whatever you've suffered, you're going to be okay."

Tears welled in Pino's eyes and he shook his head. "No, I won't. Not ever."

"Oh, my poor boy," she cried softly. "Please, come and eat. Tell us all about it."

In a wavering voice, he said, "I can't talk about it. I can't think about it anymore, and I'm not hungry. All I want to do is sleep." He was shivering as if it were the middle of winter again.

Michele came over, put his arm around Pino. "Then we'll get you to bed. You'll feel better in the morning."

Pino barely understood where he was as they led him down the hall to his bedroom. He sat on the edge of the bed, all but catatonic.

"Do you want to listen to the shortwave?" his father asked. "It's safe now."

"Father Re has mine."

"I'll get Baka's."

Pino shrugged listlessly. Michele hesitated, but then left and returned with Baka's radio. He set it on the end table.

"It's there for you if you want it."

"Thanks, Papa."

"I'm right down the hall if you need me."

Pino nodded.

Michele shut the door behind him. Pino could hear him talking to Uncle Albert and Aunt Greta in worried whispers that faded to nothing. Through the open window he heard a single shot to the north and people laughing and carrying on in the streets below.

It felt like they were all taunting him with their joy, kicking him at his lowest moment. He slammed down the window. He pulled off his shoes and pants, lay down on the bed, shaking with rage and regret as he turned off the light. He tried to sleep, but was haunted not by the aria but by the black accusatory look Anna held on to as she died, and the love that fled from him with her soul's passing.

He turned on the shortwave and tuned it until he heard a slow piano solo playing against the whisk of a drum cymbal. Soft, warm jazz. Pino closed his eyes and tried to go with the music, which was as gentle and playful as a summer stream. He tried to imagine the stream, tried to find peace in it, and sleep, and nothingness.

But then the piece ended, and "Boogie Woogie Bugle Boy" came on. Pino sat up with a start, feeling like every twitching beat in the song was there to goad and torture him. He saw himself the night before in the Hotel Diana with Carletto playing and partying. Anna had been alive then, not yet taken by the mob. If he'd just gone by Dolly's rather than . . .

Feeling destroyed all over again, Pino grabbed the radio and almost hurled it against the wall, intending to bust it into a thousand pieces. But all of a sudden he was so overwhelmed, so exhausted, he merely turned the dial until the radio emitted static. Pino rolled up in the fetal position. He closed his eyes, listening to the hiss and crackle of the wireless and praying that the gaping wound in his heart was enough to stop it from beating before he awoke.

———

In Pino's dreams, Anna was alive. In his dreams, she still laughed like Anna and kissed like Anna. She smelled of her own perfume and gave him that sidelong, amused look that always got him wanting to hold her and tickle her and—

Feeling someone shaking his shoulder, he startled awake in his bedroom. Sunlight poured through the window. Uncle Albert and his father were standing by his bed. Pino looked at them as though they were strangers.

"It's ten," Uncle Albert said. "You've been asleep almost fourteen hours."

The nightmare of the day before rushed back in. Pino so longed for sleep and the dreams where Anna still lived that he almost started to cry again.

"I know this is difficult for you," Michele said. "But we need your help."

Uncle Albert nodded. "We have to go look for Mario's body at Cimitero Monumentale."

Pino still wanted to roll over and search for Anna in his dream, but he said, "I left him in the public gardens. I ran from his body there."

Uncle Albert said, "I went to look last night after you'd gone to sleep. They said he was taken to the cemetery and we could look for him there along with all the other bodies that have been found in the streets the past few days."

"So get up," Michele said. "Three of us will find Mario quicker than two. We owe his mother that much."

"I'll be recognized," he said.

"Not with me, you won't," Uncle Albert said.

Pino saw there was no stopping them. "Give me a minute. I'll be right out."

They left him, and he sat up, aware of the pounding in his head and the deep and vast emptiness that fluctuated between his throat and gut. His brain sought memories of Anna, but he stopped the urge. He couldn't think of her. Otherwise, he'd just lie there and mourn.

Pino put on clean clothes and walked back into the living room.

"Do you want anything to eat before we go?" his father asked.

"I'm fine now," Pino said, hearing the flatness in his voice and not caring.

"You should at least drink some water."

"I'm fine!" Pino shouted. "Are you deaf, old man?"

Michele took a step back. "Okay, Pino. I just want to help."

He stared at his father, unable and unwilling to tell them about Anna.

"I know, Papa," he said. "I'm sorry. Let's go find Mario."

Eleven in the morning and already it was stifling hot outside. Barely a breeze blew as they walked through the streets, took one of the few trams running, and then caught a ride from a friend of Uncle Albert's who'd managed to find petrol.

Pino would remember little of the journey. Milan, Italy, the world itself had become unhinged for him, disjointed and savage. He watched the scarred city as if from afar, not at all a part of the teeming life that was beginning to return after the Nazis' retreat.

The car dropped them in front of the cemetery piazza. Pino felt like he was in a dream turning nightmare again as he walked toward the Famidio, the octagonal-shaped memorial chapel of the Cimitero Monumentale, and the long, two-story, arched and open-air colonnades that jutted off the chapel left and right.

Cries of grief echoed from the colonnades before rifle shots sounded at a distance, followed by the deep rumbling exhale of some larger explosive. Pino didn't care about any of it. He welcomed a bomb. He'd hug one and smash the primer with a hammer if he could.

A dump truck honked. Uncle Albert pulled Pino out of its way. In a daze, Pino looked at the vehicle as it passed. It was like any other dump truck he'd seen until it got upwind. The stench of death poured out. Stacked like cordwood, corpses filled the vehicle's bed. Blue and swollen bodies stuck out the top, some clothed, some naked, men, women, and children. Pino doubled over, started to dry-heave and then retch.

Michele rubbed his back. "It's all right, Pino, with the heat, I knew to bring us handkerchiefs and camphor."

The dump truck did a 180-degree turn and backed up to the lower arches of the western colonnade. A lever was thrown. A hundred or more bodies spilled out of the bed and flopped onto the gravel.

Pino stopped and gaped in horror. Was Anna in there? Buried?

He heard one of the drivers say that there were hundreds more bodies coming.

Uncle Albert tugged Pino's arm.

"Come away from there now," he said.

Like an obedient dog, Pino followed them into the memorial chapel.

"Are you looking for a loved one?" asked a man standing inside the door.

"My cousin's son," Michele said. "He was mistaken for a Fascist and—"

"I'm sorry for your loss, but I don't care why or how your cousin's son died," the man said. "I just want the body to be claimed and removed. This is an extraordinary health hazard. Do you have masks?"

"Handkerchiefs and camphor," Pino's father said.

"That will help."

"Is there some order to the bodies?" Uncle Albert said.

"The order they came in, and where we found a place to lay them. You'll just have to search. Do you know what he was wearing?"

"His Italian Air Force uniform," Michele said.

"Then you should find him. Take those stairs. Start on the lower eastern colonnades and work your way out to the rectangular series of hallways off the main galleries."

Before they could thank him, he'd already moved on to tell the next distraught family how to find its dead loved one. Michele handed out white handkerchiefs and fished the mothballs from a paper sack. He put the camphor into the center of the handkerchiefs and tied the ends to make a pouch, showed them how to press it to their lips and nose.

"I learned to do this in the first Great War," he said.

Pino took the pouch and stared at it.

"We'll search the lower galleries," Uncle Albert said. "You start up here, Pino."

—✦—

His mind was barely functioning as he went out an open side door on the east side of the chapel and out onto the upper floor of the colonnade. Parallel open arches hemmed the gallery some ninety meters to an octagon-shaped tower that marked a triple intersection of passages.

On any other day, these halls would have been largely empty save for the statues of long-forgotten Lombardy statesmen and members of the nobility. Now, however, the length of the colonnade and the galleries beyond were part of a colossal morgue taking in nearly five hundred corpses a day in the wake of the Nazi retreat. The dead bodies were lined up on both sides of the open-air halls, feet to the wall, faces close to a meter-wide path that ran between them.

Other Milanese walked the galleries of the dead that morning. Old women dressed for grief held black lace shawls across their lips and noses. Younger men guided the quaking shoulders of wives, daughters, and sons. Greenhead blowflies had begun to gather. They whined and buzzed. Pino had to swat at them to keep them from getting at his eyes and ears.

The flies swarmed the nearest body, a man in a business suit. He'd been shot through the temple. Pino looked at him no more than a second, but the image seared in his brain. The same happened when he looked at the next corpse, a woman in her fifties, dressed in her nightclothes, a lone curler still clinging to her iron-gray hair.

Back and forth he went, scanning the clothes, the sex, the faces, trying to find Mario among them. Pino moved faster now, giving no more than a glance at the naked couples he figured for once prosperous and powerful Fascists and their wives. Portly. Older. Their skin had turned pallid and mottled in death.

He walked the first gallery to the octagonal intersections of the hallways and took a right. This colonnade, longer than the first, overlooked the cemetery piazza.

Pino saw strangled bodies there, hacked bodies, shot bodies. Death became a blur. The sheer numbers were more than he could handle, so he focused on two things. *Find Mario. Get out of this place.*

A short time later, he found his cousin lying among six or seven dead Fascist soldiers. Mario's eyes were shut. Flies danced on his head wound. Pino looked around and saw an empty sheet across the hallway. He got it and laid it over Mario's corpse.

Now all he had to do was find Uncle Albert and his father and leave. He felt claustrophobic as he ran back toward the chapel. He dodged through other searchers and got there out of breath and brimming with anxiety.

He went through the chapel, barreled down the stairs to the lower colonnades. A family was shrouding a body on his right. When he looked left, his uncle was coming toward him from down the gallery, his lips and nose pressed into the camphor and his head shaking to and fro.

Pino ran to him. "I found Mario."

Uncle Albert dropped the camphor pouch and looked up at him with piteous, bloodshot eyes. "Good. Where is he?"

Pino told him. His uncle nodded, and then put his hand on Pino's forearm. "I understand now why you were so upset last night," he said hoarsely. "And I'm . . . I'm so sorry for you. She seemed like such a fine young lady."

Pino's stomach cored out. He'd tried to tell himself Anna wasn't here. But where else? He stared over Uncle Albert's shoulder and down the long gallery behind him.

"Where is she?" he demanded, trying to push by.

"No," Uncle Albert said, blocking the way. "You are not going down there."

"Get out of my way, Uncle, or I'll throw you out of my way."

Albert dropped his eyes, stepped aside, and said, "She's in the far hall, on the right. Do you want me to show you?"

"No," he said.

Chapter Thirty-Two

Pino found Dolly Stottlemeyer first.

General Leyers's mistress was still dressed in her ivory gown. Between Dolly's breasts a chrysanthemum of blood had bloomed, wilted, and dried. Her slippers were gone. Her eyes and mouth were half-open, frozen in rigor. Her fingers had died clutching her thumbs, exposing the red nail polish, and making it all the more lurid against the robin's egg color of her skin.

Pino looked up then and saw Anna down the hall. His eyes clouded with tears, and his breath became short and ragged as he tried to keep down the emotion surging everywhere within him, trying to thrash its way out of his chest and through his windpipe. Mouth open, lips moving to form silent words of sorrow, he went and knelt beside her.

There was a bullet hole below Anna's bra, and a flower of blood on her exposed belly similar to the one on Dolly. *Whore* had been written across her brow in the same red gloss the partisans had used to make her lips look so garish.

Pino stared down, engulfed by misery, swallowing against grief and trembling with loss. He lowered the camphor pouch from his lips and nose. Breathing in the ungodly putrid air in the hallway, he untied the pouch and put the camphor aside. He used the handkerchief to wipe the lipstick from her brow and from about her lips until she was almost the Anna he remembered. He set the handkerchief down, clasped his hands, and gazed at her as he sucked in the smell of her death, drawing it deep into his lungs.

"I was there," Pino said. "I saw you die, and I said nothing, Anna. I did . . ."

The pain threw tears from his eyes and doubled him over.

"What did I do?" he moaned. "What did I do?"

Tears dripped off his cheeks as he rocked back and forth on his haunches and stared down at the wreckage of his love.

"I failed you," Pino choked. "Christmas Eve, you were there to stand by me, come what may. And I wasn't there for you. I . . . I don't know why. I can't even explain it to myself. I wish I'd stood against the wall with you, Anna."

He lost track of time as he knelt there by her, vaguely aware of people moving past him, glancing at Anna's chopped hair and making comments about her under their breath. He didn't care. They couldn't hurt her now. He was there, and they couldn't hurt her any further.

<hr/>

"Pino?"

He felt a hand on his shoulder and looked up to find his father and uncle there.

"We were supposed to have . . . everything, Papa," Pino said in bewilderment. "Our love was supposed to be forever and ever. We didn't deserve this."

Michele was tearing up. "I'm so sorry, Pino. Albert's only just told me."

"We're both so sorry," his uncle said. "But we have to go, and I hate to tell you this, but you have to leave her now."

Pino wanted to rise up and beat his uncle to a pulp. "I'm staying with her."

"You're not," Michele said.

"I've got to bury her, Papa. Make sure she has a funeral."

"You can't," Uncle Albert said. "There are partisans checking who's claiming the bodies. They'll think you were a collaborator, too."

"I don't care," Pino said.

"We do," Michele said firmly. "I know this is hard, son, but—"

"Do you?" Pino screamed. "If this were Mama, would you leave her?"

His father cringed and stepped back. "No, I . . ."

Uncle Albert stopped him. "Pino, it's what Anna would want."

"How do you know what Anna would want?"

"Because I saw in her eyes how much she loved you that Christmas Eve at the shop. She would not want you to die because of her."

Pino looked down at Anna again, choking back emotion. "But she won't get a funeral, a headstone, anything."

Uncle Albert said, "I asked the man in the chapel what happens to the unclaimed bodies, and he said they'll all be blessed by Cardinal Schuster, cremated, and buried."

Pino's head swung slowly back and forth. "But where will I go to . . ."

"See her?" his father said. "You go to where you were both happiest, and she'll always be there. I promise you that."

Pino thought of that small park in Cernobbio at the southwest end of Lake Como, where he and Anna had stood at the rail and she'd taken his picture wearing the headband, and everything had seemed perfect. He looked down at Anna's cold face. Leaving her seemed a second betrayal, one with no possibility of forgiveness.

"Pino," his father said softly.

"I'm coming, Papa." He sniffed and wiped his eyes with the handkerchief, smearing some of her lipstick on his face, and then tucked the tear-stained hankie in her bra.

I loved you, Anna, Pino thought. *I'll love you forever and ever.*

Then he leaned over, kissed her, and said his good-bye.

Pino stood, wobbly. With his uncle and father holding on to each elbow, he left, and did not look back. He couldn't. If he did, he swore he'd never move again.

By the time they returned to the chapel, Pino could walk without their help. He was already trying to get the image of her corpse out of his head by recalling Anna in Dolly's kitchen the night after he'd saved the general's life, and how she told him about her childhood birthday mornings with her father out on the sea.

That memory carried him through the rest of the process of shrouding Mario and moving him out of the upper gallery to the partisans checking the bodies. They recognized Mario's uniform for what it was and waved them through. They found a cart and pushed the corpse through the city to an undertaker who was a friend of the family.

They didn't make it home until after dark. Pino was spinning from exhaustion, from grief, from lack of food and water. He forced himself to eat, and he drank too much wine. He went to bed the way he had the night before, with the shortwave tuned to static. He closed his eyes, praying that he'd see Anna alive again in his dreams.

But she wasn't alive there, not that night. In Pino's dreams, Anna was dead and lying alone in the lower galleries of the Cimitero Monumentale. Behind his eyelids, Pino could see her, as if lit from above in a dark place. Every time his dream self tried to get closer to her, however, she slipped farther and farther away.

The cruelty of it made him cry out in pain. Pino startled alert into the waking nightmare of Anna being gone all over again. He gasped and held his sweating head for fear of its bursting. He tried to clear his thoughts of Anna but could not, and he could not sleep. That was done. He could either lie here while memories and regrets ripped him up, or he could walk and let movement calm his mind as it had since he was a boy.

Pino checked his watch. It was 3:00 a.m. on Sunday, April 29, 1945.

He dressed and slipped out of the apartment, took the stairs, and went out through the empty lobby. The night was dark and the streetlamps infrequent as he wove through San Babila, heading north, retracing much of the route they'd used to bring Mario's body to the funeral home. At ten past four, Pino was back at the Cimitero Monumentale. Partisans stopped him, checked his papers. He told them his fiancée was inside. Someone had seen her body there.

"How are you going to see her?" one of the guards asked.

Another guard lit a cigarette.

Pino said, "Could you give me three of your matches?"

"No."

"C'mon, Luigi," the first guard said. "The kid's trying to find his dead sweetheart, for Christ's sake."

Luigi took a deep drag, sighed, and flipped Pino the box.

"Bless you, *signore*," Pino said, and hurried across the piazza toward the colonnades.

Rather than walk among the corpses, Pino looped around to a door that took him to the long hallway where Anna lay. When he got to where he thought she'd been, he lit a match and shone it around.

She wasn't there. He looked about, tried to get his bearings, and thought he might be short. The match went out. He walked another three meters and lit another match. She wasn't there. No one was there. The gallery floor was empty for at least twelve meters on either side of where she'd been. The unclaimed bodies were gone. Anna was gone.

The finality of it felt smothering. He sank against the wall there and sobbed until he could not cry anymore.

When Pino at last trudged down the steps from the memorial chapel, he felt the burden of her death like a yoke that could never be shed.

"Find her?" the guard asked.

"No," Pino said. "Her father must have gotten here first. A fisherman from Trieste."

They exchanged glances. "Sure," Luigi said. "She's with her papa."

⁂

Pino wandered aimlessly through the city, skirting the central train station, now heavily guarded by partisan forces. He got turned around in an unlit area, had no idea where he was at one point. But then dawn began to glow across rippling low clouds, and he could soon see well enough to realize he was northwest of Piazzale Loreto and Beltramini's Fresh Fruits and Vegetables. He ran and got to the fruit stand in the first good light of day. He pounded on the door, called out toward the upstairs windows. "Carletto? Carletto, are you there? It's Pino!"

He got no answer. He kept pounding and calling, but his friend did not reply.

Despondent, Pino walked south. It wasn't until he'd walked past the telephone exchange that he understood where he was going and why. Five minutes later, he cut through the kitchen of the Hotel Diana and pushed on through the double doors into the ballroom. There were American GIs and Italian women passed out here and there—not as many as two mornings before, but empty bottles were everywhere, and broken glass on the floor crunched under his shoes. He looked into the hallway that led to the lobby.

Major Frank Knebel was there, sitting at a table against the wall. He was drinking coffee and looking very hungover.

"Major?" Pino said, walking toward him.

Knebel looked up and laughed. "Pino Lella, the boogie-woogie kid! Where the hell have you been, buddy? All the girls have been asking for you."

"I . . ." Pino didn't know where to begin. "Can I talk to you?"

The major saw the seriousness in his eyes and said, "Sure, kid, pull up a chair."

But before Pino could, a boy about ten years old burst in the front door and yelled in broken English, "Il Duce, Major K! They bring the Mussolini to Piazzale Loreto!"

"Now?" Major Knebel said, getting up fast. "Are you sure, Victor?"

"My father, he hears this."

"Let's go," Knebel said to Pino. Pino hesitated, wanted to talk to the major, to tell him—

"C'mon, Pino, you'll be a witness to history," the American said. "We'll take the bikes I bought yesterday."

<hr>

Pino felt a break in the fog of Anna's death and nodded. He'd wondered what would become of Il Duce the last time he saw him in Cardinal Schuster's office, when Mussolini was still praying for Hitler's superweapon to be unleashed and still hoping for a bed in the führer's secret Bavarian bunker.

By the time they'd grabbed two bikes Knebel had stashed behind the registration desk and exited the hotel, other people were running toward Piazzale Loreto, crying, "They've got him! They've got Il Duce!"

Pino and the American major jumped on the bikes, pedaled hard. Other bikes soon joined them, racing and waving red scarves and flags, all of them lusting to see the dictator now that he'd been deposed. They rode past Beltramini's Fresh Fruits and Vegetables and into Piazzale Loreto, where a thin crowd was already gathering around the Esso station and the girders Pino had stood on to witness the execution of Tullio Galimberti.

Pino and Major Knebel put the bikes aside, and went forward to see four men clambering up onto the girders. They carried ropes and chains. Pino followed the American as he fought his way to the front of the growing crowd.

Sixteen bodies lay there by the petrol pumps. Benito Mussolini was in the middle, barefoot, his massive head resting on his mistress's chest. The puppet dictator's eyes were vacant and opaque, the madness Pino had seen in them at the villa on Lake Garda just a memory. Il Duce's upper lip was pulled back, baring his teeth and making him look as if he were about to launch into one of his tirades.

Claretta Petacci sprawled beneath Mussolini with her head turned away from her lover, as if being coy. Some of the partisans in the crowd were saying that Mussolini had been having sex with his mistress when the executioners arrived.

<hr/>

Pino looked around. The crowd had quadrupled, and there were more coming, throngs from every direction, like a chorus gathering on a stage at the end of a tragic opera. Shouting, angry, they all seemed to want to wreak personal vengeance on the man who'd brought the Nazis to their doors.

Someone put a toy scepter in Mussolini's hand. Then a woman old enough to have been the crone in Dolly's apartment building waddled out. She squatted over Il Duce's mistress and pissed on her face.

Pino was repulsed, but the crowd went feral, sinister, and depraved. People were laughing hysterically, cheering, and feeding on the anarchy. Others began shouting for more desecrations while ropes and chains were being rigged. A woman darted forward with a pistol and put five rounds in Mussolini's skull, which provoked another round of jeers and catcalls to beat the bodies, to tear the flesh from their bones.

Two partisans fired their guns into the air to get the mob back. Another tried to turn a fire hose on them. Pino and Major Knebel had retreated by then, but others kept pressing toward the bodies, eager to vent their rage.

"Hang them!" a voice in the chorus cried. "Get them up where we can see them!"

"Put the hooks into their hocks!" others sang. "String 'em up like pigs!"

Mussolini went up feet first, head and arms dangling below the girder. Those in the ever-growing mob went insane. Cheering, they stamped their feet, threw their fists high, and brayed their approval. Il Duce had been beaten so badly by then, his skull was caved in. He looked beyond grotesque, a figment in a nightmare and nothing like the man Pino had spoken to repeatedly over the past year.

They hoisted Claretta Petacci up next. Her skirt fell toward her breasts, revealing that she wore no panties. When a partisan chaplain climbed up beside her to tuck the skirt up between her legs, he was pelted with trash.

Four more bodies were strung from the girders, all high-ranking Fascists. The desecrations went on in the building heat until the barbarity finally broke through Pino's grief-dazed state and sickened him. He felt dizzy, nauseated, and thought he might faint.

A man was brought forward. His name was Starace.

They placed Starace beneath the hanging corpses of Mussolini and his mistress. Starace gave the straight-arm Fascist salute, and six partisans shot him dead.

The bloodthirsty chorus in Piazzale Loreto sang deliriously and called for more. But seeing Starace shot caused Pino to reel off into the memory of Anna's dying. He thought he might go mad and join the mob.

"This is how tyrants fall," Major Knebel said, disgusted. "That would be the lead if I were writing this story. 'This is how tyrants fall.'"

"I'm going to leave, Major," Pino said. "I can't take this anymore."

"I'm with you, buddy," Knebel said.

They pushed their way back through a crowd that had grown to twenty thousand or more. It wasn't until they were across from the fruit stand that they could walk easily against the grain of more and more people coming to Piazzale Loreto to pay their disrespects.

"Major?" Pino said. "I need to talk to you—"

"You know, kid, I've been meaning to talk to *you* since you showed up this morning," Knebel said as they crossed the street.

The door to Beltramini's Fresh Fruits and Vegetables was open now. Carletto stood in the doorway, looking green with a hangover. He smiled wanly at Pino and the American.

"Another drag-the-knuckle night, Major," Carletto said.

"That's knuckle-dragger," Knebel said with a laugh. "But even better. I've got the both of you at once."

"I don't understand," Pino said.

"Would you boys be willing to help America?" the major asked. "Do something for us? Something tough? Something dangerous?"

"Like what?" Carletto asked.

"I can't tell you right now," Knebel said. "But it's vital, and if you pulled it off, you'd have a lot of friends in the United States. Ever thought of going stateside?"

"All the time," Pino said.

"There you go," the major said.

"How dangerous?" Carletto asked.

"I won't B.S. it. You could get killed."

Carletto thought about that, then said, "Count me in."

Feeling his heart race with a strange mania, Pino said, "I'm in, too."

"Excellent," Knebel said. "Can you get a car?"

Pino said, "My uncle has one, but it's up on blocks, and the tires won't go far."

"Uncle Sam will take care of the tires," he said. "Get me the keys and an address where the car is, and I'll see it's ready and waiting for you at the Hotel Diana, three a.m., day after tomorrow. May first. Okay?"

Carletto said, "When will we know what we're doing?"

"Three a.m., day after—"

Knebel stopped. They all heard the tanks then. The roar of diesels. The treads clanking. As they poured into Piazzale Loreto, Pino saw war elephants in his mind.

"Here come the Shermans, buddies!" Major Knebel crowed, throwing his fist overhead. "That's the US Fifth Army Cav. As far as this war goes, the fat lady's singing."

PART FIVE
"VENGEANCE IS MINE,"
SAYETH THE LORD

Chapter Thirty-Three

Tuesday, May 1, 1945

As Pino and Carletto neared the Hotel Diana at 2:55 a.m., they were almost as drunk as they'd been before passing out just a few hours before. Only now their stomachs were queasy, and their headaches blazing. On the other hand, Adolf Hitler was dead. The Nazi führer had shot himself in his bunker in Berlin, committing suicide along with his mistress the day after Mussolini and Petacci swung in Piazzale Loreto.

Pino and Carletto had heard the news the afternoon before, and found another bottle of Mr. Beltramini's whiskey. Holed up in the fruit and vegetable stand, they celebrated Hitler's death and told each other their war stories.

"You really loved Anna enough to marry her?" Carletto asked at one point.

"Yes," Pino said, and tried to control the raw emotion that pulsed through him whenever he thought of her.

"You'll find another girl someday," Carletto said.

"Not like her," Pino said, his eyes watering. "She was different, Carletto. She was . . . I don't know, one of a kind."

"Like my mama and papa."

"Special people," Pino said, nodding. "Good people. The best people."

They had more drinks, and retold Mr. Beltramini's best jokes, and laughed. They talked about the night on the hill the first summer of the bombardment when their fathers had performed so flawlessly. They cried at too many things. By eleven, they'd finished the bottle and drunk themselves into forgetfulness, nonsense, and not enough sleep. It took an alarm to wake them three and a half hours later.

Bleary-eyed, they turned the corner, and Pino saw Uncle Albert's old Fiat parked out front of the Hotel Diana, running like a top, with brand-new tires that he kicked and admired before they went inside. The end-of-war party was winding down for the night. A few couples danced slowly to a scratched and popping record on a phonograph. Corporal Daloia climbed the staircase, clinging to Sophia, both of them giggling. Pino watched them until they disappeared.

Major Knebel came out a door behind the registration desk, saw them, and grinned. "There you are. Knew I could count on old Pino and Carletto. Got a few presents to give you both before I explain what we're going to have you do."

The major squatted down behind the registration desk and lifted up two brand-new Thompson submachine guns with rotary magazines.

Knebel cocked his head. "You know how to run a tommy gun?"

Pino felt fully awake for the first time since passing out, and regarded the machine gun with some awe. "No," he said.

"Never," Carletto said.

"It's simple really," Knebel said, setting one gun down and pressing a latch to release the rotary magazine. "You've got fifty .45 ACP rounds already loaded in here." He set the magazine on the counter before clearing the breech and showing them a lever above and behind the rear pistol grip. "Your safety," he said. "You want to fire, you push that lever all the way forward. You want safe, all the way back."

The major repositioned the Thompson, right hand on the rear grip and left hand on the front grip, the side of the weapon mashed tight to his torso. "Three points of contact if you want control over your fire. Otherwise, the recoil will have the muzzle bouncing all over the goddamned place, shots going high and wide, and who needs that?"

"So both hands on the grips, and the stock pressed into your hip—three points of contact. See how I'm turning my hips with the gun?"

"What if we have to shoot from the car?" Carletto asked.

Knebel threw the gun tight to his shoulder. "Three points: shoulder, my cheek to the stock, and both hands. Short bursts. That's all you really need to know."

Pino picked up the other gun. He liked how heavy and compact the Thompson was. He grabbed the grips, held it tight to his body, and fantasized about mowing down Nazis.

"Your backup magazines," the major said, setting two drums on the counter. He reached into his pocket and came out with an envelope. "These are your papers. They'll get you through all Allied-held checkpoints. Beyond that, you'll be on your own."

"You ever going to tell us what we're doing?" Carletto demanded.

Knebel smiled. "You'll be taking a friend of America to the top of the Brenner Pass."

"The Brenner?" Pino said, remembering something Uncle Albert had told him the day before. "The Brenner's still at war. It's anarchy up there. The German army's in full retreat, and the partisans are ambushing them, trying to kill as many as they can before they get across the border into Austria."

Knebel showed no expression and said, "We need our friend at the border."

"It's a suicide mission, then," Carletto said.

"It's a challenge," the major said. "But we've got you a map, and there's a flashlight to read it. Shows all the major Allied checkpoints. You won't leave Allied-held territory until north of the A4 heading toward Bolzano."

After a short silence, Carletto said, "I'm going to need two bottles of wine to do this."

"I'll make it four," Knebel said. "Make it a party. Just don't crash."

Pino said nothing. Carletto looked at him. "I'm going with or without you."

Pino saw an intensity in his old friend that he'd never witnessed before. Carletto looked eager to go into battle and die. Suicide by war. That thought pleased Pino as well.

"Okay, then, who are we taking up there?" Pino said, looking at Knebel.

The major got up and disappeared through the door behind the counter. A few moments later, the door reopened and Knebel exited, followed by a man in a dark business suit, dark trench coat, and a brown fedora pulled down low over his eyes. He struggled to carry a large rectangular leather suitcase handcuffed to his left wrist.

Major Knebel and the man came out from behind the counter.

"I believe the two of you know each other," Knebel said.

⊷

The man raised his head and from under the fedora's brim stared into Pino's eyes.

Pino's shock was complete. He stepped back as rage plumed through his body.

"Him?" he shouted at Knebel. "How is he any friend of America?"

The major's expression hardened. "General Leyers is a hero, Pino."

"A hero?" Pino said, wanting to spit at the ground. "He was Hitler's slave master. He drove people to their deaths, Major. I saw it. I heard it. I witnessed it."

Knebel was rattled by that and glanced at the Nazi general before saying, "I can't know if that's true, Pino. But I'm under orders here, and that's what I've been told, that he's a hero who deserves our protection."

Leyers just stood there, not understanding a bit of the conversation but watching them with that detached amusement that Pino had so grown to despise. He started to say he wouldn't do it, but then another idea, a much more satisfying one, wormed its way into his mind. He thought of Anna and Dolly. He thought of all the slaves and knew it was the right thing to do. God had a plan for Pino Lella after all.

Pino grinned with bonhomie then, and said, "*Mon général,* shall I take your bag?"

Leyers shook his head crisply. "I will carry the bag, thank you."

"Good-bye, Major Knebel," Pino said.

"Look me up when you get back, bud," Knebel said. "I've got other plans for you. Be right here, waiting to tell you all about them."

Pino nodded, certain he would never see the American or Milan again.

⊷

He left the hotel with his machine gun cradled and Leyers following. He opened the rear door to the Fiat and stood aside. Leyers glanced at Pino and then struggled into the seat with the suitcase.

398

Carletto got into the front passenger seat, the Thompson between his legs. Pino got behind the wheel, put his machine gun between Carletto and the stick shift.

"Keep control of my gun, too," Pino said with a glance in the mirror at Leyers, who'd set his hat aside and was using his fingers to comb back his iron-gray hair.

"I think I can shoot this thing," Carletto said, his finger wandering in admiration over the machine gun's oiled surface. "I've seen how they do it in gangster movies."

"All you need to know," Pino said, and put the car in gear.

He drove on with Carletto reading the map by flashlight and navigating. The route led back through Piazzale Loreto, and then east toward the city limits, where they encountered the first US Army checkpoint.

"America is the best," Pino said to the skeptical GI who came to his window with a flashlight. Pino handed him the envelope with their papers.

Taking them out of the envelope, the soldier shone his light on them, and his chin retreated. He quickly folded the papers, stuffed them in the envelope, and said nervously, "Jesus. You can go right on through, then."

Pino put the papers in his breast pocket, pulled through the gate, and headed east toward Treviglio and Caravaggio.

"What do those papers say?" Carletto asked.

"I'll look later," Pino said. "Unless you read English?"

"Can't read it. Speak it a little. What do you suppose is in his suitcase?"

"I have no idea, but it looks heavy," Pino said, glancing in the rearview when they passed beneath a streetlight. General Leyers had moved the suitcase off his lap. It sat beside him, to his right. Leyers's eyes were closed, and he could have been dreaming of Dolly or his wife, or children, or the slaves, or nothing at all.

In that single glance, something sharp and ice-cold forged in Pino's heart. For the first time in his short, complicated life, he knew the feeling of ruthlessness, and the sweet anticipation of setting things right.

"I say he's got some of those gold bars you saw locked in that case," Carletto said, breaking him from his thoughts.

Pino said, "Or maybe he's got files in that suitcase. Hundreds. Maybe more."

"What kind of files?"

"The dangerous kind. The kind that give you a little power in powerless times."

"What the heck does that mean?"

"Leverage. I'll explain later. Where's the next checkpoint?"

Carletto turned on the light, studied the map, and said, "Where we pick up the main road this side of Brescia."

⟞⟝

Pino pressed down on the accelerator, and they hurtled on through the night, reaching the second checkpoint at four in the morning. After a quick review of their papers, they were waved through again and warned to avoid Bolzano, where a battle was raging. The problem was they had to get past Bolzano to reach the Brenner Pass road.

"I'm telling you, he's got gold in his suitcase," Carletto said after they were under way again. He'd uncorked one of the wine bottles and was taking sips. "No way it's just files. I mean, gold's gold, right? Buy your way out of anything with gold."

"When it comes down to it, I don't care what's in his suitcase."

The highway ahead was pocked with bomb craters and diversions where the snowmelt from the previous winter had washed out culverts, so Pino couldn't go as fast as he wanted. It was 4:45 a.m. before he took the turn toward Trento and Bolzano, heading north toward Austria. They drove along the east shore of Lake Garda, on the bank opposite Mussolini's old villa, causing Pino to remember the anarchy in Piazzale Loreto. He glanced back at the general, who was dozing, and wondered how much Leyers knew, how much he cared, or whether he was just a man out for his skin.

Favors, Pino thought. *That's what he trades in. He told me so himself. That suitcase is full of favors.*

He drove aggressively now. There were fewer vehicles on the road and less damage than there'd been on the main highway. Carletto's eyes closed, and his chin slumped to his chest, the bottle and the machine gun between his legs.

Just north of Trento, around five fifteen, Pino saw lights ahead and started to slow. A shot rang out and smacked the side of the Fiat. Carletto startled awake even as Pino hit the accelerator hard and started weaving down the road as shots came at them from both sides, some hitting, others whistling by.

"Get your gun!" Pino shouted at Carletto. "Shoot back!"

Carletto fumbled with the machine gun.

"Who's shooting at us?" General Leyers demanded. He was lying sideways across the suitcase.

"Doesn't matter," Pino said, and gained speed toward those lights. There was a barrier there, sawhorses, and a group of ragtag armed men. There was no order about them, and that made Pino's decision.

"When I say so, shoot at them," Pino said. "Safety off?"

Carletto got up on one knee, head and shoulders stuck out the window, the machine gun stock rammed against his shoulder.

Pino tapped the brakes when they were seventy meters out, as if he meant to stop. But at fifty meters, with the headlights blinding the men at the barrier, Pino hit the accelerator again and shouted, "Shoot!"

Carletto yanked the trigger, and the Thompson began spitting bullets that went high, low, and everywhere in between.

The gunmen scattered. Pino bore down on the barrier. Carletto had no control. He kept holding down on the trigger, and the machine gun kept firing wild. They smashed through the barrier. The Thompson was knocked from Carletto's grip. It bounced off the road and vanished.

"Shit!" Carletto yelled. "Go back!"

"No," Pino said, shutting off the lights and speeding on as guns cracked behind them.

"That's my machine gun! Go back!"

"You shouldn't have held the trigger so long," Pino shouted. "Knebel said short bursts."

"It almost tore my shoulder off," Carletto said angrily. "God damn it! Where's my wine?"

Pino handed him the bottle. Carletto pulled the cork with his teeth, took a drink, and cursed, and cursed again.

"It's okay," Pino said. "We've got my gun and two extra magazines."

His friend looked at him. "You'd take the chance, Pino? Let me shoot again?"

"Just hold on this time. And touch the trigger. On/off. No yanking."

Carletto grinned. "Can you believe that just happened?"

From the backseat, Leyers said, "I have often thought you were an amazing driver, Vorarbeiter. That time last fall when the plane was strafing us? In the

Daimler? Your driving that night was why I requested that you take me to the border. It's why you're here. If anyone can get me to the Brenner, it's you."

Pino heard the words as if they were coming from a man he did not know and did not want to know. He loathed Leyers. He despised the fact that he'd convinced some fool in the US Army that he was a hero. Hans Leyers was not a hero. The man in the backseat was Pharaoh's slave master, a war criminal, and he deserved to suffer for his actions.

"Thank you, *mon général*," Pino said, and left it at that.

"Not at all, Vorarbeiter," General Leyers said. "I have always believed in giving credit where credit is due."

———

The sky started to lighten as they pushed on toward Bolzano. Pino believed it would be his last dawn. It came in rose fingers that fanned across a blue sky framed by snowcapped mountains rising beyond the last forty kilometers of war. Pino didn't give the danger that lay ahead more than a passing thought. He was thinking about General Leyers, feeling the anticipation again, feeling the adrenaline trickle.

Pino reached over and tugged the wine bottle from between Carletto's legs, which provoked a mild grumble of protest, for his friend had fallen asleep again.

He took a gulp of the wine, and then another. *It has to be somewhere high,* he thought. *It has to be done in the grandest of God's cathedrals.*

Pino pulled over on the road's shoulder.

"What're you doing?" Carletto said, eyes still shut.

"Seeing if there's a way around Bolzano," Pino said. "Gimme the map."

Carletto groaned, found the map, and handed it over.

Pino studied it, tried to commit to memory the major routes he might take to get north of Bolzano and onto the actual Brenner Pass road.

Leyers, meanwhile, used a key to unlock the handcuff from the suitcase and climbed out to take a piss.

"Let's take off," Carletto said. "We'll split the gold."

"I've got other plans," Pino said, staring at the map.

The general returned, scooted forward in the backseat, and looked over Pino's shoulder at the map.

"The main route will be the best defended," Leyers said. "You'll want to go up that secondary road near Stazione, take it to the northwest of Bolzano, all the way to Andriano/Andrian on the Switzerland road. The Swiss border is shut to us, so the Wehrmacht doesn't care about that route. You'll get past the Americans, then across the Adige River on their far left flank. Across the river, you go back along the mountains there, right behind the Germans, until you reach the Brenner Pass road. Do you see it?"

Pino hated to admit it, but his plan seemed their best chance. He nodded and looked in the rearview, seeing how animated Leyers was as he locked himself to his suitcase once more. The general was enjoying himself.

It is just a game to him, Pino thought, and got angry all over again. *It's all a game of favors and shadows.* Leyers wanted to have fun? He'd show him fun. He threw the Fiat in gear, popped the clutch, and drove on like a man possessed.

It was full daylight when they rolled up to a US checkpoint blocking the road near the mountain town of Laghetti Laag. A US Army sergeant walked toward them. They could hear the echoes and thuds of combat somewhere not far ahead.

"Road's not open," the sergeant said. "You can turn around here."

Pino handed him the envelope. The sergeant took it, opened it, read the letter, and whistled. "You can go. But are you sure you want to? We've got companies battling with Fascists and Nazis for Bolzano. And sometime in the next couple of hours, the Mustangs are going to strafe the German column, try to wipe out what they can."

"We're going," Pino said, took the envelope, left it in his lap.

"Your lives, gentlemen," the sergeant said, and waved at the gatekeeper.

The barricade was pulled aside. Pino drove through.

"My head hurts," Carletto announced, and rubbed at his temples before taking another swig of wine.

"Knock the wine off for now," Pino ordered. "There's a battle right ahead of us, and we're going to need your help to live through it."

Carletto stared at him, saw he was serious, and corked the bottle. "Get the gun?"

Pino nodded. "Put it on your right side, parallel to the door, the butt up against the side of the seat. You'll get to it quicker."

"How do you know that?"

"Just makes sense."

"You think different than I do."

"I guess that's true," Pino said.

Ten kilometers beyond the checkpoint, he took a secondary road heading northeast, as Leyers had recommended. The way was rough and ran through little alpine settlements, twisting toward Saint Michael and northern Bolzano.

Clouds rolled in. Pino slowed enough to hear the artillery, the tanks and rifles engaged to their right and south, at least a mile, maybe more. They could see the outskirts of Bolzano and plumes of smoke rising as the Fascists tried to hold ground and the Germans tried to defend their rear to give their countrymen more time to make Austria.

"Head north again," General Leyers said.

Pino did as he was told, taking a sixteen-kilometer detour that brought them to a bridge across the Adige that was unguarded, just as Leyers had predicted. They reached Bolzano's northwestern outskirts around eight forty that morning.

The fighting to the immediate southeast was intense now. Machine guns. Mortars. And so close they could hear tank turrets pivoting. But it looked like Leyers was right again. They'd managed to stay nearly four hundred meters behind the battle lines, slipping along a rear seam of the conflict.

At some point, though, we'll see Nazis. They'll be on the Brenner Pass road for—

"Tank!" Leyers cried. "American tank!"

Pino ducked his head, looked fast to his right, trying to see past Carletto.

"There it is!" Carletto cried, pointing across a large open lot on the outskirts of the city. "A Sherman!"

Pino kept them moving, flanking to the tank's left.

"He's turning his cannon on you," General Leyers said.

Pino glanced, saw the tank seventy meters away, the turret and the barrel pivoting toward them. He hit the accelerator.

Carletto leaned out the window, waved both arms at the tank, and yelled in English, "American friends! American friends!"

The tank fired a shell that went right behind them, right off their rear fender, and blew a smoking hole in a two-story factory building on the other side of the street.

"Get us out of here!" Leyers bellowed.

Pino downshifted and took evasive action. But before he could get out of the tank's line of fire, machine guns opened up from the smoking building.

"Duck!" Pino shouted, and crouched down, hearing bullets cracking overhead and pinging downrange off the tank's armor and treads.

They shot into an alley and out of sight.

Leyers pounded Pino on the shoulders. "A genius behind the wheel, this one!"

Pino smiled sourly, weaving them through side streets. US forces seemed bogged down behind the confluence of two streams that joined the Adige River. Leyers found a way around the pinch point, beyond the battle, and then away from the city itself, heading east toward the village of Cardano/Kardaun.

Pino soon turned onto the Brenner Pass road, finding it nearly empty. He accelerated, heading north again. Ahead, the Alps vanished in a gathering storm. Mist began to fall, and chains of fog appeared. Pino remembered the slaves digging at the snow here only a month before, flailing in the slush, collapsing, and being dragged away.

He drove on past Colma and Barbiano. It wasn't until they were on a curve south of the village of Chiusa/Klausen that he was able to see far ahead up the road to the tail end of a long German column clogging both sides of the route, a crippled army creeping north toward Austria through the town of Bressanone/Brixen.

"We can get around them," General Leyers said, studying the map. "But this little road goes off to the east just ahead here. It climbs, goes way up to here, where you can take a road north and then this one back down to the Brenner Pass road. Do you see?"

Pino saw it, and again took the route Leyers chose.

They spun their way across a short, muddy flat before the road began to climb a steep, narrow draw, which broadened into a high alpine valley choked on the north flank by spruces and by sheep meadows facing south. They continued up the north flank through switchbacks that took them beyond the alpine settlement of Funes.

The road ascended another thousand meters almost to the tree line, where the fog and clouds began to break. The road ahead was two-track and slick. It cut through a sea of yellow and pink wildflowers.

The clouds lifted more, revealing the scree fields and the long wall of the Dolomites, the grandest of God's cathedrals in Italy: limestone spire after limestone spire after limestone spire, eighteen of them soaring thousands of meters toward heaven and looking for all the world like an enormous crown of pale gray thorns.

General Leyers said, "Pull over there. I need to piss again, and I want to take a look."

Pino felt it was all fated at that point because he'd been getting ready to use that excuse to stop himself. He pulled over by a narrow meadow in a large gap in the spruces that revealed the Dolomites in all their majesty.

It's a fitting place to make Leyers confess and pay for his sins, Pino thought. *Out in the wide open. No favors to call in. No way to hide in the shadows. Alone in God's church.*

Leyers unlocked the handcuff and got out Carletto's side. He walked off into wet grass and alpine flowers. He stopped at the edge of the cliff there, gazing across the narrow valley and up at the Dolomites.

"Give me the gun," Pino muttered to Carletto.

"Why?"

"Why do you think?"

Carletto got wide-eyed, but then smiled and handed him the Thompson. The machine gun felt oddly familiar in Pino's hands. He'd never fired one, but he'd seen them in gangster movies, too. *Just do what Major Knebel said. How hard can it be?*

"Do it, Pino," Carletto said. "He's a Nazi monster. He deserves to die."

Pino got out, held the Thompson one-handed and behind his legs. He need not have bothered hiding it. General Leyers had his back to Pino, his own legs spread as he pissed over the edge of the cliff and enjoyed the spectacular view.

He thinks he's a man in charge, Pino thought coldly. *He thinks he's a man in control of his fate. Except he's not in control anymore. I am.*

Pino walked around the back of his uncle's Fiat and took two steps into the meadow, slightly short of breath, feeling time slow as it had before he entered Castello Sforzesco. But he was fine now, as sure of what he was about to do as he'd been about the depths of Anna's love. Pharaoh's slave master was going to pay. Leyers was going to go down on his knees and beg for mercy, and Pino was going to show him none.

General Leyers zipped and took another scan of the stunning scenery. He shook his head in wonder, adjusted his jacket, and turned around to find Pino ten meters away, the Thompson glued to the side of his hip. The Nazi came up short and stiff.

"What is this, Vorarbeiter?" he said, fear seeping into his voice.

"Vengeance," Pino said calmly, feeling weirdly out of his body. "Italians believe in it, *mon général*. Italians believe bloodshed is good for the wounded soul."

Leyers's eyes darted about. "You're going to just shoot me down?"

"After what you did? After what I saw? You deserve to be shot down by a hundred guns, a thousand if there was any justice."

The general held out both of his hands, palms to Pino. "Didn't you hear your American major? I'm a hero."

"You're no hero."

"And yet, they let me go. And yet, they sent me with you. The Americans."

"Why?" Pino demanded. "What did you do for them? What favor did you call in? Who did you bribe with gold or information?"

Leyers looked conflicted. "I am not at liberty to tell you what I've done, but I can tell you I was valuable to the Allies. I remain valuable to the Allies."

"You're worthless!" Pino cried, the emotion bulging up the back of his throat again. "You care about no one but yourself, and you deserve to—"

"That's not true!" the general shouted. "I care about you, Vorarbeiter. I care about Dolly. I care about your Anna."

"Anna's dead!" Pino screamed. "Dolly's dead, too!"

General Leyers looked stunned as he took a step back. "No. That's not true. They went to Innsbruck. I'm supposed to meet Dolly . . . tonight."

"Dolly and Anna died in front of a firing squad three days ago. I saw it happen."

Leyers was rocked by the blow. "No. I gave orders they were to be . . ."

"No car ever came for them," Pino said. "They were still there waiting when a mob took them because Dolly was your whore."

Pino calmly moved the Thompson's safety to fire.

"But I gave the orders, Vorarbeiter," Leyers said. "I swear to you I did!"

"But you didn't make sure the orders were followed!" Pino shouted, throwing the machine gun to his shoulder. "You could have gone to Dolly's and made sure they'd been moved. But you didn't. You left them to die. Now I'm going to leave you to die."

Leyers's face screwed up in desperation, and he raised his hands as if to ward off the bullets. "Please, Pino, I wanted to go back to Dolly's apartment. I wanted to check on them, don't you remember?"

"No."

"Yes, you do. I asked you to take me there to get some papers I'd left behind, but you arrested me instead. You turned me over to the resistance when I could have been making sure that Dolly and Anna had gotten out of Milan and reached Innsbruck."

The general looked at him without remorse and added, "If there's anyone directly responsible for Dolly and Anna's death, Pino, it's you."

Chapter Thirty-Four

Pino's finger was on the trigger.

He'd been planning to shoot General Leyers from the hip, to spray bullets across his abdomen so he'd go down but not die. Leyers would have suffered like that, gut-shot, maybe for a good long while. And Pino had wanted to stand there and watch his every twitch of pain, to relish each moan and pleading.

"Shoot him, Pino!" Carletto yelled. "I don't care what he's saying to you. Shoot that Nazi pig!"

He did ask me to take him to Dolly's that night, Pino thought. *But I arrested him instead. I arrested him instead of . . .*

Pino felt dizzy and sick to his stomach again. He heard the clown's aria, and the rifles firing, and saw Anna falling once more.

I did this. I could have helped Anna. But I did everything I could to kill her.

Pino lost all strength then. He let go of the front grip of the machine gun. The Thompson hung at his side. He stared vacantly up at the vastness of God's grand cathedral and altar of atonement, and wanted to go to bone and dust, to blow away on the wind.

"Shoot him, Pino!" Carletto cried. "What the hell are you doing? Shoot him!"

Pino couldn't. He felt weaker than a dying old man.

General Leyers nodded curtly to Pino, said icily, "Finish your job, Vorarbeiter. Take me to the Brenner, and we end our war together."

Pino blinked, unable to think, unable to act.

Leyers gave him a contemptuous look and barked at him, "Now, Pino!"

⸺

Pino dumbly followed the general back to the Fiat. He held the rear door open, closing it after Leyers had climbed in. He locked the safety on the Thompson, handed the weapon to Carletto, and got behind the wheel.

In the back, the general was handcuffing himself again to the suitcase.

"Why didn't you kill him?" Carletto said in disbelief.

"Because I want him to kill me," Pino said, started the Fiat, and put it in gear.

They took off, sliding in greasy mud that soon caked the sides of the car. They drove cross-country to the north before finally meeting up with a two-track road that led downhill through switchbacks and long traverses that put them parallel to the Brenner Pass road above the town of Bressanone/Brixen. The German army column choked the town and the route ahead for more than a mile. Nothing was moving.

Gunshots sounded below. Out the window, bouncing along on the two-track, Pino looked toward the front of the column and saw why it had all but halted. There were six or seven pieces of heavy artillery at the head of the line. Many of the mules that had pulled the cannons through Italy had finally given up; they stood their ground and refused to work any longer.

The Nazis were whipping the mules, trying to get the artillery pieces out of the way so the rest of the column could get by. The mules that wouldn't pull were being shot and dragged to the shoulders of the road. The last cannon was almost out of the way. The Nazi caravan was about to retreat on.

"Go faster," Leyers ordered. "Get in front of that column before it blocks us."

Pino downshifted and said to Carletto, "Hold on."

⸺

The track was drier here, and Pino was able to double and then triple his speed, still parallel to the convoy, almost to the head of the snake. A kilometer farther on, the lane met another crude route that dropped downhill seven hundred meters to the Brenner Pass road where it passed through the village of Varna/Vahrn and no more than one hundred meters from the cannons and the dying mules.

Pino downshifted and slid them neatly into a track that headed steeply downhill. He floored the accelerator. The Fiat bounced and flew down the last flank of the mountain even as the last cannon cleared and the Panzer tanks at the head of the German column fired up and began to roll once more toward Austria.

"Get ahead of them!" Leyers shouted.

It took everything Alberto Ascari had taught Pino to keep the car from flipping or rolling. He chuckled madly as he barreled them down the last stretch to the road even as the first Panzer built speed.

But then, out of nowhere and a mile to the south, a US Mustang P-51 fighter plane dive-bombed and opened fire on the Nazi column, strafing its way up the line.

The general must have understood the physics of all that was involved now because he began to shout, "Faster! Faster, Vorarbeiter!"

⬥

They were neck and neck with the tank, which was some eighty meters from blocking the intersection. The Fiat was one hundred and ten meters from the Brenner Pass road but closing faster as the Mustang flew closer, letting loose machine gun fire every few seconds.

Forty meters shy of the road, Pino finally hit the brakes and downshifted, which hurled the Fiat into a series of wild muddy zigzags and then up on two wheels, with the Panzer right there, before they shot off an embankment and landed in front of the tank. They skidded, went up on two wheels again, and almost flipped before Pino got the Fiat righted and accelerating.

"Soldier coming up out of the tank!" Leyers yelled. "He's at the machine gun!"

Pino had widened the gap, but the distance was still child's play for a heavy-caliber machine gun. The shooter could cut the Fiat apart like cheese. Hunched over the wheel, Pino held the accelerator flat against the floorboard, expecting to take a bullet to the back of the head.

But before the Nazi could open fire, the US fighter came round the bend, strafing up the neck and head of the German column. Bullets rattled off the Panzer armor and ricocheted off the road right behind the Fiat. Suddenly, the shooting stopped, and the plane banked off.

They rounded another bend and were out of the Germans' sight. For a moment there was stunned silence in the car. Then Leyers began to laugh, pounding his fists on his thighs and on the suitcase.

"You did it!" he cried. "You crazy Italian son of a bitch, you did it again!"

Pino hated that he'd done it. He'd fully expected to die in the trying, and now that he was putting distance between them and the retreating Nazis and gaining ground on the Austrian border, he didn't know what to do. He seemed destined to get General Leyers out of Italy, and he finally surrendered to the task.

The twenty-four kilometers of road between Bressanone/Brixen and Vipiteno/Sterzing climbed to the level of the snowpack, which looked granular, wet, and névé, but still deep. When they met fog again, it was hard to tell where the snow ended and the air began. Cut off by the German column behind them, the Brenner Pass road was deserted and wound up into patches of thicker cloud and mist. Their pace slowed to a crawl.

"Not far now," Leyers said after they passed through Vipiteno. He pulled the suitcase back up onto his lap. "No time at all."

"What are you going to do, Pino?" Carletto asked, drinking again. "What's this all been for if he just gets away with the gold?"

"Major Knebel says he's a hero," Pino said, feeling numb. "I guess he goes free."

Before Carletto could respond, Pino downshifted and braked hard, entering a hairpin turn on the last climb toward the border. A low wall of snow blocked the way, and he had to slam on the brakes and come to a full stop.

Six rough-looking men wearing red scarves stood up from behind the snowbank, aiming rifles at them from point-blank range. Out of the forest on

Carletto's side, another man appeared holding a pistol. An eighth man stepped out of the trees to Pino's left. He was smoking a cigarette and carrying a sawed-off shotgun. At first glance, even after a year, Pino knew him.

Father Re had said Tito and his men were robbing people on the Brenner Pass road, and now here he was, strolling Pino's way.

⋙

"What have we here?" Tito said, coming up alongside the open window, the sawed-off shotgun leading. "Where do you think you all are going on this fine May morning?"

Pino had his hat pulled down over his brows. He held out the envelope and said, "We're on a mission for the Americans."

Tito took it, opened it, and looked at the paper in a way that made Pino think he couldn't read. He stuffed the letter back in the envelope and tossed it aside. "What's the mission?"

"We're taking this man to the Austrian border."

"That right? What's in the suitcase he's got handcuffed to his hand?"

"Gold," Carletto said. "I think."

Pino groaned inside.

"Yeah?" Tito said. He used the muzzle of the shotgun to push Pino's cap up higher so he could see his face.

After a second or two, Tito laughed scornfully and said, "Isn't this *perfetto*?"

Then he jabbed Pino's cheek with the shotgun muzzle, opening up a gash below his eye.

Pino grunted with pain and reached up, feeling blood already flowing.

Tito said, "Tell your man back there to unlock that handcuff and give me that suitcase, or I am going to blow your head off and then his."

Carletto was breathing heavy and fast. Pino glanced at him and saw his friend was shaking with alcohol and rage.

"Tell him," Tito said, and jabbed Pino again.

Pino did, in French. Leyers said nothing, didn't move a muscle.

Tito shifted the shotgun barrel toward the general.

"Tell him he's about to die," Tito said. "Tell him you're all about to die, and I'll take the suitcase anyway."

—

Pino thought of Nicco, the innkeeper's dead son, jerked on the door handle, threw his weight against the door, and slammed it against the left side of Tito's body.

Tito stumbled to his right, slipped on the snow, and almost went down.

A pistol fired from the backseat of the Fiat.

The man standing by Carletto's door died of a bullet through the cheek.

Tito got his balance, shouldered the shotgun, and tried to swing it at Pino, screaming, "Kill them all!"

The next second seemed endless.

Carletto pulled the trigger on the Thompson and blew out the Fiat's windshield; at the same moment General Leyers fired a second time, hitting Tito square in the chest. As Tito fell, his shotgun went off, blasting the Fiat's lower-quarter panels with buckshot. Carletto's second machine gun burst killed two of the six remaining men in Tito's gang of smugglers and highwaymen. The other four were trying to get away.

Carletto threw open his door and ran after the fleeing men. One of them was hit already and stumbling. Carletto shot him as he ran by in pursuit of the last three, screaming hysterically, "You partisan bastards killed my father! You killed him and broke my mother's heart!"

He skidded to a halt and opened fire again.

He hit one man in the spine and dropped him. The other two turned to fight. Carletto mowed them both down dead.

"Paid in full!" Carletto screamed wildly. "Paid in . . ."

Shoulders sagging and shaking, Carletto began to weep. Then he went to his knees and sobbed.

Pino came up behind him and put his hand on his friend's shoulder. Carletto jerked around, crazed. He pointed the barrel up at Pino and looked ready to shoot.

"Enough," Pino said softly. "Enough, Carletto."

His friend stared at him, and then broke down all over again. He dropped the gun and stepped up into Pino's arms, bawling. "They killed my papa, and they made my mama want to die, Pino. I had to take revenge. I had to."

"You did what you had to do," Pino said. "We all did."

The sun began to burn through the clouds. It didn't take them long to clear the snow and move the bodies from the road. Pino went through Tito's pockets, thinking about Nicco, until he found the money clip stolen from him two New Year's Eves before. He looked at Tito's boots and left them, but picked up the envelope with their papers. Pausing at the driver's door, he peered into the backseat where General Leyers still sat, still holding a US Colt M1911 pistol, just like the one Major Knebel carried.

Pino said, "We're even. No favors owed."

Leyers said, "Agreed."

In the last eight kilometers toward Austria, Carletto acted like someone head shot. He sat there empty with no spirit in his skin or bones. Pino was not much better. He drove on because it was all he could do. There was no thinking at the wheel for him now, no grief, no shell shock, and no regret, just the road ahead. A little more than three kilometers from the border crossing, he punched on the radio and tuned it to dance music and static.

"Turn that off," Leyers snapped.

"Shoot me if you want," Pino said, "but the music's staying on."

He glanced in the rearview, saw his own defeated eyes and the general staring back at them in victory.

American paratroopers and two Mercedes-Benz sedans waited at the border crossing in a narrow, forested valley. There was a Nazi general in uniform, whom Pino did not recognize, standing there by one Mercedes, smoking a cigar and enjoying the building sunshine.

This isn't right, Pino thought as he pulled the Fiat to a stop. Two paratroopers came toward him. Pino opened the envelope and scanned the paper inside before handing it to them. It was a letter of free passage signed by Lieutenant General

Mark Clark, commander of the US Fifth Army, at the behest of General Dwight D. Eisenhower, Supreme Allied Commander.

A redheaded paratrooper nodded to Pino and said, "Showed a lot of moxie and grit to get him up here, safe and sound. The US Army thanks you for your help."

"Why are you helping him?" Pino said. "He's a Nazi. A war criminal. He worked people to death."

"Just following orders," the GI said, glancing at the general.

The second soldier opened the backseat and helped General Leyers out, the suitcase still handcuffed to his wrist.

Pino climbed out. The general stood there waiting for him. He held out his free hand. Pino stared at it a long beat, and then reached out his own.

Leyers shook his hand hard, and then pulled Pino close, and whispered in his ear.

"Now you understand, Observer."

━━━

Pino stared at him in disbelief. *Observer? He knows my code name?*

General Leyers winked, released his grip, and whirled in his tracks. Striding away, Leyers never looked back. The paratrooper opened the backseat of one of the waiting cars. The general disappeared inside with the suitcase while Pino gaped after him.

Behind Pino, in the Fiat, the radio turned to a news bulletin that Pino couldn't make out for all the static. He just stood there, Leyers's last words to him spinning in his mind and adding confusion to his despair and defeat when not an hour ago he'd had such homicidal clarity, sure that vengeance was his and not the Lord's.

Now you understand, Observer.

How could he have known? How long had he known?

"Pino!" Carletto yelled. "Do you hear what they're saying?"

The car bearing the general drove away and was quickly gone, heading down the road toward Stubaital and Innsbruck.

"Pino," Carletto shouted, "Germany has surrendered! The Nazis have been told to lay down their weapons by eleven o'clock tomorrow morning!"

Pino said nothing, just watched the point in the road where Major General Hans Leyers vanished from his life.

Carletto came over and put his hand gently on Pino's shoulder. "Don't you understand?" he said. "The war's over."

Pino shook his head and felt tears stream down his face as he said, "I don't understand, Carletto. And the war's not over. I don't think it ever will be over for me. Not really."

AFTERMATH

By the end of World War II, a third of Milan lay in ruins. The bombardment and the fighting had left twenty-two hundred Milanese dead and four hundred thousand homeless.

The city and its people began to rebuild, burying the past and the rubble under new roads, parks, and high-rise structures. They cleaned the soot of war off the Duomo. They put up a monument to Tullio Galimberti and the martyrs of Piazzale Loreto around the corner from a bank that used to be Beltramini's Fresh Fruits and Vegetables. The Hotel Diana still stands, as do the chancellery, San Vittore Prison, and the haunted colonnades of the Cimitero Monumentale.

The towers of Castello Sforezsco were repaired, but bullet marks remain on the inner walls. In an effort to forget the savagery that occurred in the Piazzale Loreto, the Esso station was torn down. So was the building that once housed the Hotel Regina and the Gestapo. A plaque on Via Silvio Pellico is all that memorializes the people murdered and tortured inside SS headquarters. Milan's Holocaust Memorial is inside the central train station, beneath Platform 21.

Of the roughly forty-nine thousand Jews in Italy at the time of the Nazi invasion, some forty-one thousand evaded arrest or survived the concentration camps. Many were put on the Catholic underground railroad that ran north along several different routes into Switzerland, including Motta. Others were helped by courageous Italians, Catholics, and clergy who hid Jewish refugees in the basements of monasteries, convents, churches, homes, and even a handful in the Vatican.

Alfredo Ildefonso Schuster, who fought to save Jews and his city from further destruction, remained the cardinal of Milan until his death in August 1954. A future pope said Cardinal Schuster's funeral Mass. One of his pallbearers took up his cause for sainthood. That pallbearer became Pope John Paul II, who beatified Cardinal Schuster in 1996. His blessed body lies in a sealed glass case beneath the Duomo.

Father Luigi Re continued to offer Casa Alpina as sanctuary to people in danger. In the days following the end of World War II, he infamously protected Eugen Dollmann, Hitler's Italian translator, and refused demands from the US Army to hand him over.

Father Re was honored by the Israeli Community of Milan for selflessly risking his own life to save Jews. Father Re died in 1965 and is entombed on the ski slopes above Motta, beneath a golden-plated statue of the Madonna said to have been paid for by all the people he'd helped before, during, and after the war. His boys' school has since been rebuilt as a hotel named Casa Alpina. His chapel is gone.

Giovanni Barbareschi became a priest shortly after Tullio Galimberti's execution. He was also the cofounder of OSCAR, an underground resistance group that opposed the Nazi occupation and its aims. Affiliated with the Aquile Randagie, a banned group similar to the Boy Scouts of America, Barbareschi and others in OSCAR forged more than three thousand fake identities for refugees to use in their escape to Switzerland. With the help of OSCAR, more than two thousand Jews escaped Italy through the Splügen Pass, Motta, Val Codera, and other northern routes. After the war, Barbareschi was honored by the Israeli Community of Milan and, more recently, a tree was planted in his honor in a memorial park in Milan for the Righteous of Italy, who risked their lives selflessly to save Jews.

Alberto Ascari, who taught Pino Lella to drive, went on to live his childhood dreams and became an Italian national hero. At the wheel of a Ferrari, Ascari won the Formula 1 World Drivers' Championships in 1952 and 1953. In May 1955, while he was taking training laps on the Monza circuit, his car somersaulted and crashed, hurling Ascari onto the racetrack. He died in Mimo Lella's arms. Thousands of people crowded the Duomo and the piazza the day of Ascari's funeral. Buried next to his father in the Cimitero Monumentale, Ascari is widely considered one of the greatest race car drivers of all time.

Colonel Walter Rauff, the head of the Gestapo in northern Italy, was believed to be directly responsible for the deaths of more than one hundred thousand people, and indirectly responsible for the hundreds of thousands who died in the portable gas chamber he designed and deployed in eastern Europe before his transfer to Milan. Rauff was captured, but broke out of a prisoner of war camp and ended up in Chile as a shadowy spy-for-hire who became close to the country's dictators.

Simon Wiesenthal, the famous Nazi hunter, tracked Rauff down in 1962. The German government tried to have Rauff extradited. He fought it, and the case went to the Chilean Supreme Court. Rauff was freed five months later. He died in Santiago in 1984 of a heart attack. Attended by many former Nazi officers, his funeral was described as a raucous celebration of Rauff, Adolf Hitler, and the Third Reich in general.

Major J. Frank Knebel returned to the United States, left the army, and picked up his life in newspaper journalism. He was the publisher of the *Garden Grove News* in California and later the *Ojai Valley News*. In 1963, he bought the *Los Banos Enterprise*. Knebel and Pino corresponded on and off until the newspaperman's death in 1973. Knebel left behind little about the war except for a cryptic note in one of his files that alluded to his plans to write a "never-before-told true story of great intrigue in the last days of the war in Milan." He never did.

Corporal Peter Daloia returned to Boston. When he died decades after the war ended, his son was shocked to find a Silver Star for valor for his father's heroics at the battle of Monte Cassino. It was buried in a box in the attic. Typical of so many, Daloia told no one about his war in Italy.

Albert and Greta Albanese continued to flourish in business. They made a fortune when Uncle Albert decided to wrap meerschaum pipes in leather and sell them around the world. They died in the 1980s. Their shop at #7 Via Pietro Verri is now Pisa Orologeria, or Pisa Luxury Watches.

Michele and Porzia Lella ran a series of successful purse and sportswear companies after the war and were active in the fashion district their entire lives. Before their deaths in the 1970s, #3 Via Monte Napoleone, the site of the original purse store, was rebuilt and now houses a Salvatore Ferragamo boutique. The street known as Corso del Littorio was changed to Corso Matteotti after the war. The apartment building where the Lellas lived still stands, though the birdcage elevator has been removed.

Pino's sister, Cicci, became as dynamic a businesswoman as her mother. She promoted Milan as a global fashion center and worked in the family business, focusing on the boutiques in San Babila. She died in 1985.

Domenico "Mimo" Lella was cited for courage fighting for the resistance, most notably for his actions on the first day of the general insurrection. Mimo worked in the family business before founding his own manufacturing company, Lella Sport, which catered to the weekend athlete and outdoor enthusiast. A short, pugnacious, and successful businessman, Mimo married a beautiful fashion model, Valeria, who stood a foot taller than him. They had three children. He built a cabin at Motta beside Casa Alpina that was said to be his favorite place on earth. In 1974, at age forty-seven, Mimo died of skin cancer.

Carletto Beltramini and Pino Lella were lifelong friends. Carletto became a successful salesman for Alfa Romeo and lived all over Europe. He never married and did not talk about the war for fifty-three years. But in 1998, as he lay ill in the hospital, Pino and an American named Robert Dehlendorf paid him a visit. Carletto recounted the last days of the war almost as a confession. He remembered the wild party at the Hotel Diana and the vengeful look on Pino's face when he learned they were taking General Leyers to Austria. Carletto remained convinced that Leyers carried gold in his suitcase. He also admitted shooting the highwaymen as they tried to get away, broke down sobbing, and asked God's forgiveness for the insanity of his acts.

Carletto died a few days later with Pino at his side.

⎯⎯◆⎯⎯

After watching General Leyers drive away into Austria, Pino made it back to Milan and became Major Knebel's guide in Italy for two weeks. The major refused to discuss Leyers, saying that those matters were top secret and the war was over.

But it wasn't over for Pino. He was ravaged by grief and memory, his faith in constant peril, and dogged by questions no one could answer. Had General

Leyers known Pino was a spy all along? Had everything he'd seen and heard while in Leyers's company been deliberately shown to him so he could report to Uncle Albert and to the Allies through Baka's radio?

Uncle Albert claimed to have been as surprised as Pino that Leyers had known his code name. His uncle and his parents were more concerned that Pino was still a target for reprisal. Their fears were justified. By the end of May 1945, thousands of Fascists and Nazi collaborators lost their lives in executions and vendetta killings across northern Italy.

At his family's urging, Pino left Milan for Rapallo. He worked at odd jobs in the coastal town until late in the fall of that year. Then he returned to Madesimo, where he taught skiing and tried to come to terms with his tragedy in long discussions with Father Re. They talked of love. They talked of faith. They spoke of the crushing weight of their loss.

Pino prayed for help in the mountains, for relief from the constant grief and confusion and sadness. But Anna would not leave him. She was the memory of the best moments of his life—her smile, her smell, and the music of her laughter that kept playing in his ears. She was a damning force that swirled around him in the dark of night, accusatory, bitter, and demanding.

Someone tell them I'm just a maid.

Pino lived for more than two years in the dull haze of guilt and grief, blind to any kind of future, deaf to any words of hope. He walked for kilometers along the beaches in the summers, and he climbed in the Alps in the autumns before the snow fell in the cathedrals of God, and begged daily for forgiveness that never came. With every day that passed, though, Pino still believed that someone would come and ask him about General Leyers.

But no one did. Returning to Rapallo for a third summer in 1947, Pino was still trying to come to grips with his war experience, and still trying to deal with Anna's ghost. He grieved the fact that she never told him her surname, or her married name, for that matter. He couldn't even try to find her mother to tell her that her daughter had died.

It was as if Anna had never existed for anyone but him. She'd loved him, but he'd failed her. He'd been put in an impossible situation, and through his silence, he had denied knowing her, denied loving her. He'd had faith and been selfless in the Alps guiding the Jewish refugees and in his life as a spy, but he had been faithless and self-serving when faced with the firing squad.

The mental torture went on and on until, on one of those long beach walks where Anna still lived in his mind, Pino remembered her telling him that she didn't believe much in the future, that she tried to live moment by moment, looking for reasons to be grateful, trying to create her own happiness and grace, and to use them as a means to a good life in the present and not a goal to be achieved some other day.

Anna's words rang in Pino's head, and for some reason, after all that time, they clicked and unlocked him somehow, made him admit he wanted more than to pine for her and to feel gutted for not trying to save her.

On that deserted beach, he ached for Anna one last time. But in his mind, his memories were not of her death, nor of her lifeless body on the colonnade floor, nor of the clown's aria that taunted him in his faithless hours.

Instead, he heard Prince Calaf's aria, "*Nessun Dorma*," "None Shall Sleep," playing in his head, and recalled snapshots of their strange falling in love: Anna outside the bakery the first day of the bombardment; Anna disappearing behind the trolley; Anna opening Dolly's front door a year and a half later; Anna catching him in Dolly's room with the general's key; Anna taking his picture in the park by Lake Como; Anna acting drunk in front of the sentries on Christmas Eve; Anna naked and wanting him.

Hearing "None Shall Sleep" swell toward its crescendo, Pino looked out at the Ligurian Sea, and he thanked God for having had Anna in his life, even for so short and tragic a time.

"I still love her," he told the wind and the sea where she'd been happiest. "I'm grateful for her. She was a gift that I'll always treasure in my heart."

Over the course of several hours, Pino felt the iron grip her spirit had on him ease, slip, and float away. When he left the beach, Pino vowed to put the war behind him, to never think again about Anna, General Leyers, Dolly, or the things he'd seen.

He would pursue happiness above all, and he would do so *con smania*.

⟐

Pino returned to Milan and for a time tried to find that happiness and passion by working for his parents. His gregarious personality returned, and he was a fine salesman. But Pino was restless in the city and happiest in the cathedrals of

God, on foot and on skis. His alpine talents brought him in a roundabout way to become a coach and interpreter with the Italian National Ski Team that went to Aspen, Colorado, in 1950 for the first postwar world championships.

Pino went to New York first, and listened to jazz in a smoky nightclub and saw Licia Albanese, his cousin, sing soprano in *Madama Butterfly* under Toscanini's direction at the New York Metropolitan Opera.

His first night in Aspen found him striking up a conversation and drinking with two men he met by chance in a bar. Gary was from Montana, and an avid skier. Hem had skied in Italy at Val Gardena, one of Pino's favorite mountains.

Gary turned out to be the actor Gary Cooper, who tried to convince Pino to go to Hollywood for a screen test. Hem turned out to be Ernest Hemingway, who drank a lot and said little. Cooper ended up being a longtime friend of Pino's. Hemingway did not.

When the ski team returned to Italy, Pino wasn't with them. He went to Los Angeles but never took the screen test. The idea of millions of people scrutinizing his every move was unappealing, and he doubted he could remember lines.

Instead, through his friendship with Alberto Ascari, he got a job at International Motors in Beverly Hills, selling Ferraris and other luxury sports cars. Pino's fluent English, his understanding of high-performance cars, and his love of fun made him a natural.

His favorite sales tactic was to take one of his Ferraris and park it at a lunch stand across the street from Warner Bros. He met James Dean that way, and claimed to have warned the young actor away from the Porsche he wanted to buy, telling Dean he wasn't ready for the power of it. He was crushed when Dean didn't listen.

At International Motors, Pino worked with mechanics Dan Gurney, Richie Ginther, and Phil Hill, local Santa Monica boys who became Formula 1 drivers. In 1952, Hill started racing for Ferrari after Pino introduced him to Alberto Ascari at Le Mans. Like Ascari, Hill would go on to become world champion.

In the winters, Pino traveled to Mammoth Mountain in the central Sierra Nevada and joined the ski school there. On the slopes, teaching, he found his greatest happiness and passion in life. He taught skiing as a form of joyful fun and creative adventure. Dave McCoy, Mammoth's founder, said seeing Pino on skis in deep powder snow was "like watching a dream."

Pino was soon so popular that the only way to hire him was privately, which led to his friendship with Lance Reventlow, the son of Barbara Hutton—the Poor Little Rich Girl—and to a blind date with Patricia McDowell, the heiress to a newspaper fortune her family made with the *Los Angeles Daily Journal*, the *San Diego Times*, and the *San Bernardino Sun*.

After a whirlwind courtship, Pino and Patricia married, bought a home in Beverly Hills, and led a jet-set life, splitting time between California and Italy. Pino no longer sold Ferraris. He owned them and raced them on sports car circuits. He skied. He mountain climbed. He lived a vigorous life and was genuinely happy, day after day, for years.

Pino and Patricia had three children, Michael, Bruce, and Jamie. He doted on the children and taught them to ski and love the mountains. And he was always the life of the party that seemed to trail Pino no matter where they were in the world.

But every once in a while, late at night, often outside, he'd have memories of Anna and General Leyers, and they would all fill him once again with melancholy, confusion, and loss.

In the 1960s, when Pino was in his midthirties, he and Patricia began to fight. He thought she drank too much. She thought he paid too much attention to other women, and chided him for never making much of himself beyond being a world-class ski instructor.

In that toxic environment, Pino thought more and more of Anna, and grew ever more restless at the thought that he might never know a love as deep and as true again in his lifetime. He felt caged and with it the overwhelming need to walk, to move, to roam, to search.

A year of travel ended in Pino's asking his wife for a divorce. He'd met an exotic, stunningly beautiful young woman named Yvonne Winsser, who was related to the Sukarno family in Indonesia. Pino was smitten the moment they met. The divorce and remarriage hit Pino's first family hard. Patricia descended into alcoholism. Pino sent the boys off to a Swiss boarding school. They were angry with him for years.

When Pino's parents died, he inherited a third of the family business, which caused a rift between him and his sister. Cicci resented the fact that while he'd been off living a life in pursuit of happiness, she'd been working to build the Lella brand, and that he was now taking a third of the profits for doing next to nothing.

The money gave Pino even more freedom, but for many years that desire to roam wasn't there. He and Yvonne had two children, Jogi and Elena. And he tried to be a better father to his older kids, with whom he reconciled.

After Mimo's death, however, the old restlessness returned. And he started having dreams and nightmares of Anna. Pino took off on a trip that was supposed to begin in Frankfurt, on a Pan Am jet bound for Detroit via London and New York. But an old friend talked Pino into delaying his departure by a day so they could catch up. Pino did, only to learn that his original flight, Pan Am Flight 103, went down over Lockerbie, Scotland, killing everyone aboard.

Pino was gone for months that time, traveling, looking, and not really understanding what he was searching for. When he returned, after thirteen years of marriage, Yvonne decided that while she loved him, she couldn't live with him anymore. Oddly, though divorced, they stayed the best of friends.

Pino aged. He watched his children grow and his bank account dwindle, but he remained in remarkably good spirits through his sixties. He skied. He wrote about motor sports for several Italian publications. He had interesting friends and girlfriends. He never once spoke of Anna, or General Leyers, or Father Re, or Casa Alpina, or what he'd done in the war.

—◆—

A researcher from the Altruistic Personality and Prosocial Behavior Institute at California's Humboldt State University approached Pino in the 1980s. She was doing a study on people who had risked their lives to save others. She said she'd gotten his name through Yad Vashem, which was a surprise to Pino. He'd never been contacted by anyone regarding his activities with Father Re.

Pino spoke with the young woman briefly, but her study's focus upset him, brought up memories of Anna that led him to end the interview with a promise to fill out her detailed questionnaire and return it to her. He never did.

Pino maintained his silence until the late 1990s, when he had a chance meeting in northern Italy with Robert Dehlendorf, a successful American who'd owned, among other things, a small ski area in California. Dehlendorf was retired and staying on Lake Maggiore.

The two men, roughly the same age, bonded. They ate. They talked. They laughed. Late the third night, Dehlendorf asked, "What was the war like for you, Pino?"

Pino got a faraway look in his eye, and after a long hesitation, said, "I've never told anyone about my war, Bob. But someone very wise once told me that by opening our hearts, revealing our scars, we are made human and flawed and whole. I guess I'm ready to be whole."

Long into the night, fragments of the tale spilled out. Dehlendorf was stunned. How was it possible that so little of the story had ever been told?

⟫⟫

That chance meeting between Dehlendorf and Pino led serendipitously and eventually to a dinner party in Bozeman, Montana—the evening of the lowest day of my life—and to my decision to fly to Italy to hear the story firsthand and in full. Pino was in his late seventies when I landed in Milan the first time. He had the cheer and vigor of someone twenty years younger. He drove like a maniac. He played beautiful piano.

When I left three weeks later, Pino looked much older than his age. Opening up a story he'd kept locked away for six decades had been traumatizing, and he remained haunted by a lifetime of unanswered questions, especially concerning General Hans Leyers. What had become of him? Why hadn't he been charged with war crimes? Why had no one ever come to hear Pino's side of the story?

It took nearly a decade of research on my part to give Pino Lella answers to some of his questions, largely because General Leyers had been so devastatingly good at burning his way out of history. So were other officers of the Organization

Todt. Even though the Nazis were compulsive record keepers, and even though the OT had literally millions of prisoners and slaves under its command, the organization's surviving documents would fill only three file cabinets.

General Leyers, who by his own admission had sat at the left hand of Adolf Hitler and who was arguably the second-most powerful man in Italy during the last two years of World War II, left behind fewer than one hundred pages from his time there. In most of those documents, his name is merely noted as a participant in one meeting or another. It is rare to see a paper where Leyers appears as a signatory.

However, from the documents that did survive, it is clear that after Pino delivered Leyers to paratroopers on the Brenner Pass, the general's assets in Germany and Switzerland were frozen. Leyers was taken from the pass to an Allied prisoner of war camp outside Innsbruck. Strangely, no records of Leyers's interrogation statements remain or have been made public, nor is he mentioned in the open proceedings of the Nuremberg war crimes trials.

The general did, however, write a report for the US Army on the Organization Todt's activities in Italy. The report is on file in the US National Archives, and is, in short, a total whitewash of Leyers's own actions.

In April 1947, twenty-three months after the end of the war, Hans Leyers was released from prison. Thirty-four years later, he died in Eschweiler, Germany. Those two dates were the only things about Leyers I was certain of for nearly nine years.

⊷

Then, in June 2015, while working with an excellent German researcher and translator named Sylvia Fritzsching, I tracked down General Leyers's daughter, Ingrid Bruck, who was still living in Eschweiler. Though on her deathbed, Mrs. Bruck agreed to talk to me about her father and what had happened to him after the war.

"He was taken to the prisoner of war camp, awaiting his prosecution at Nuremberg," she said, wan and sick in her bedroom in the sprawling German manor she had inherited from her parents. "He was charged with war crimes, but . . ."

Mrs. Bruck started coughing and got too sick to go on beyond that. But it turned out that General Leyers's spiritual adviser of twenty-five years and his friend and aide of three decades were both available to explain the rest to me, or at least what Leyers had told them about his time in Italy and his miraculous release from the prisoner of war camp.

⸻◆⸻

According to Georg Kaschell and retired Reverend Valentin Schmidt of Eschweiler, General Leyers was indeed indicted for war crimes. They weren't familiar with the specific charges, and they claimed to know nothing about Leyers's taking slaves or participating in genocide through his implementation of "*Vernichtung durch Arbeit*," the Nazi policy of "Extermination by Labor" that was part of Hitler's final solution.

The reverend and the estate manager did agree, however, that Leyers was to be tried at Nuremberg along with other Nazis and Fascists who committed war crimes in Italy. A year and then two went by after the war's end. During that time, most of Hitler's surviving henchmen were tried and hanged, many of them after being testified against by the führer's Reich Minister for Armaments and War Production and the leader of the Organization Todt, Albert Speer.

At Nuremberg, Speer claimed he knew nothing about the concentration camps even though the Organization Todt built them, and even though many of the camps featured signs that identified them as OT work camps. Whether the Allied prosecutors actually believed Speer, or just valued the damning testimony he offered, the tribunal saved Hitler's architect from the hangman's noose.

After being told that Speer had turned on Hitler's inner circle and sent them to the gallows, General Leyers cut his own deal with prosecutors. On his own behalf, Leyers provided evidence that, among other things, he had helped Jews escape Italy, he had protected high-ranking Catholics, including Cardinal Schuster, and he had saved the Fiat company from total destruction. The general also agreed to testify in closed court against his titular boss, Albert Speer. Based in part on evidence provided by Leyers, Hitler's architect was ultimately convicted of taking slaves and sent to Spandau Prison for twenty years.

At least that's how the minister and Leyers's longtime aide told the story of why the general came to be released from a POW camp in April 1947.

Though the account was thoroughly plausible, the Leyers' family legend was no doubt somewhat more complex. Less than two years after the war's end, the world was sick of its aftermath and growing apathetic about the ongoing Nuremberg trials. There was also increasing political concern about the expanding power of Communism in Italy. The thinking went that a series of sensational trials against Fascists and Nazis would only play into pinko hands.

The "Missing Italian Nuremberg," as historian Michele Battiti has called it, never happened. Nazis and Fascists who had committed unspeakable atrocities, including General Leyers, were simply allowed to walk in the spring and summer of 1947.

There was no trial for Leyers's crimes. No assignment of blame for the slaves who died under his watch. All the evil and savagery done in northern Italy in the last two years of the war was kicked into a legal hole, buried, and forgotten.

⤛⤜

Leyers returned to Düsseldorf with his wife, Hannelise; son, Hans-Jürgen; and daughter, Ingrid. During the war, the general's wife had inherited Haus Palant, a medieval manor and estate in Eschweiler. It took six years of legal wrangling after the war for Leyers to regain full control of the sprawling property, but he did, and spent the rest of his life restoring and running it.

He started by rebuilding the large manor house and the barns, which ironically had been burned to the ground shortly before the war ended by Polish men taken slave by Organization Todt. Leyers's minister and aide said he never spoke about the nearly twelve million people abducted by the Germans and forced into labor all over Europe.

Nor did they know where the general got the enormous sums of money required to rebuild his estate, other than to say that for years after the war he provided consulting work to various German supercompanies, including steelmaker Krupp and munitions manufacturer Flick.

Leyers, they said, had an incredible network of connections, and someone always seemed to owe him a favor. He would want something—a tractor, say—and, poof, someone would give him a tractor. It happened all the time. Fiat was said to be so grateful to Leyers that the company used to send him a new free car every other year.

Postwar life was good for Hans Leyers. As he had prophesied, things had gone his way before Adolf Hitler, during Adolf Hitler, and after Adolf Hitler.

Leyers was also a devout churchgoer after his release from the Allied prison camp. He paid for the construction of Eschweiler's Church of the Resurrection, which is just a stroll down the lane from the estate on Hans-Leyers-Weg, a road named in the general's memory.

Leyers was said to be the kind of man who "got things done," and people, including his minister and aide, urged him to enter politics. The general refused, telling them he preferred to be "the man in the shadows, in the darkness, pulling the levers." He never wanted to be the man out front.

As he turned elderly, Leyers watched his son grow up and earn a doctorate in engineering. His daughter married and had a family. He rarely spoke of the war other than to boast at times that he never worked for Albert Speer, having always reported directly to Hitler.

Soon after the führer's architect was released from Spandau Prison in 1966, Speer paid Leyers a visit. Speer was reportedly congenial at first, and then drunken and antagonistic, hinting that he knew the general had testified against him. Leyers threw Speer out of his house. When Leyers read *Inside the Third Reich*, Speer's bestselling account of Hitler's rise and fall, he became irate and called the entire account "one lie after another."

After a period of declining health, General Leyers died in 1981. He is buried beneath a huge boulder in a cemetery between the church he built and the house where he lived, long after leaving young Pino Lella on the Brenner Pass.

"The man I knew was a good person, a man who stood against violence," Reverend Schmidt said. "Leyers was an engineer who joined the army because it was a job. He wasn't a member of the Nazi party. If he was involved in war crimes, I can only believe he was forced to be part of them. He must have had a gun to his head, no choice in the matter at all."

A week after I learned all this, I paid Pino Lella one more visit on Lake Maggiore. He was eighty-nine by then, with a white beard, wire-rim glasses, and a stylish black beret. As always, he was affable, funny, and spry, living *con smania,* which was extraordinary, given that he'd had a recent motorcycle accident.

We went to a café he liked on the lakeshore in the town of Lesa where he lived. Over glasses of Chianti, I told Pino what had become of General Leyers. After I finished, he sat for a long time looking out at the water, his face rippling with emotions. Seventy years had passed. Seven decades of not knowing had ended.

Maybe it was the wine, or maybe I'd thought about his story for too long, but Pino at that moment seemed to me like a portal into a long-ago world where the ghosts of war and courage, the demons of hatred and inhumanity, and the arias of faith and love still played out within the good and decent soul who'd survived to tell the tale. Sitting there with Pino, recalling his story, I got the chills and thought again of how privileged I'd been, and how honored I was to have been vested with his tale.

"You're sure about all this, my friend?" Pino asked finally.

"I've been to Leyers's grave. I spoke to his daughter, and the minister he confessed to."

Pino shook his head in disbelief finally, shrugged, and threw up his hands. "*Mon général*, he stayed in the shadows, he remained a phantom of my opera right to the end."

Then he tossed his head back and laughed at the absurdity and unjustness of it.

After several moments of quiet, Pino said, "You know, my young friend, I will be ninety years old next year, and life is still a constant surprise to me. We never know what will happen next, what we will see, and what important person will come into our life, or what important person we will lose. Life is change, constant change, and unless we are lucky enough to find comedy in it, change is nearly always a drama, if not a tragedy. But after everything, and even when the skies turn scarlet and threatening, I still believe that if we are lucky enough to be alive, we must give thanks for the miracle of every moment of every day, no matter how flawed. And we must have faith in God, and in the Universe, and in a better tomorrow, even if that faith is not always deserved."

"Pino Lella's prescription for a long, happy life?" I said.

He laughed at that, and wagged his finger in the air. "The happy part of a long life, anyway. The song to be sung."

Pino gazed north then, across the lake to his beloved Alps, rising like impossible cathedrals in the summer air. He drank from his Chianti. His eyes misted and unscrewed, and for a long time we sat in silence, and the old man was far, far away.

The lake water lapped against the retaining wall. A white pelican flapped by. A bicycle's bell rang behind us, and the girl riding it laughed.

When at last he took off his glasses, the sun was setting, casting the lake in coppers and golds. He wiped away tears and put his glasses back on. Then he looked over, gave me a sad, sweet smile, and put his palm across his heart.

"Forgive an old man his memories," Pino said. "Some loves never die."

(Firma del titolare)

ACKNOWLEDGMENTS

I am grateful to and humbled by Giuseppe "Pino" Lella for entrusting me with his remarkable story, and for opening up his scarred heart so I could tell the tale. Pino taught me too many lessons about life to count, and changed me for the better. Bless you, old man.

My thanks go out to Bill and Deb Robinson for inviting me to their home on the worst day of my life, and to Larry Minkoff for sharing the first snippets of the story over dinner. I am deeply grateful to Robert Dehlendorf, who tried to write about Pino first, and then gave the project to me when he hit a dead end. Other than my wife and sons, it is the greatest gift I have ever received.

I am blessed to be married to Elizabeth Mascolo Sullivan. When I came home from the dinner party to tell her, out of the blue and almost out of money, that I was thinking of going to Italy without her to chase an untold sixty-year-old war story, she did not hesitate or try to dissuade me. Betsy's unwavering belief in me and in this project has made all the difference.

Michael Lella, Pino's son, read every draft, helped me find other witnesses, and was critical to getting everything Italian right. Thanks, Mike. I could not have done it without you.

I am also indebted to Fulbright Scholar Nicholas Sullivan, who helped me immensely during the weeks we spent in the Bundesarchiven in Berlin and Friedrichsberg, Germany. I am likewise thankful for Silvia Fritzsching, my German translator and research assistant, who helped me piece together General Leyers's life after the war and put Pino's questions to rest.

My heartfelt thanks to all the people in Italy, Germany, Great Britain, and the United States who helped me research Pino's tale. It seemed as if every time

I hit a wall, some generous person would come along and help point me in the right direction.

These individuals include but are not limited to Lilliana Picciotto of the Fondazione Memoria della Deportazione and Fiola della Shoa in Milan, the retired Rev. Giovanni Barbareschi, and Giulio Cernitori, another of Father Re's boys at Casa Alpina. Mimo's friend and former partisan fighter Edouardo Panzinni was a great help, as was Michaela Monica Finali, my guide in Milan, and Ricardo Surrette, who took me on the Brenner Pass escape route.

Others include Steven F. Sage of the Mandel Center for Advanced Holocaust Studies at the United States Holocaust Memorial Museum, Paul Oliner of the Altruistic Personality and Prosocial Behavior Institute at Humboldt State University, US National Archives researchers Dr. Steven B. Rogers and Sim Smiley, Italian and Vatican historian and researcher Fabian Lemmes, and Monseigneur Bosatra at the archives of the chancellery of Milan. In Madesimo, I was helped by Pierre Luigi Scaramellini, and Pierino Perincelli, who lost an eye and a hand in the grenade explosion that took the innkeeper's son. Thanks as well to Victor Daloia for describing the discovery of his father's buried war medal; and to Anthony Knebel for sharing his father's correspondence; and to Horst Schmitz, Frank Hirtz, Georg Kaschell, Valentin Schmidt, and Ingrid Bruck for bringing General Leyers's saga to a close.

Various organizations, historians, authors, researchers, and organizations were also of great help to me as I tried to understand the context in which Pino's tale unfolded. Among them were the staff of Yad Vashem, the members of the Axis History Forum, and writers and researchers Judith Vespera, Alessandra Chiappano, Renatta Broginni, Manuela Artom, Anthony Shugaar, Patrick K. O'Donnell, Paul Nowacek, Richard Breitman, Ray Moseley, Paul Schultz, Margherita Marchione, Alexander Stille, Joshua D. Zimmerman, Elizabeth Bettina, Susan Zuccotti, Thomas R. Brooks, Max Corvo, Maria de Blasio Wilhelm, Nicola Caracciolo, R. J. B. Bosworth, and Eric Morris.

I am also grateful to the patient readers of the early drafts, including Rebecca Scherer of the Jane Rotrosen Agency, NPR Pentagon Correspondent Tom Bowman, David Hale Smith, Terri Ostrow Pitts, Damian F. Slattery, Kerry Catrell, Sean Lawlor, Betsy Sullivan, Connor Sullivan, and Lawrence T. Sullivan.

Meg Ruley, my amazing agent, recognized the sweep and emotional clout of Pino's story the first time she heard it, and supported me and my pursuit of this project when few did. I'm a lucky guy to have her in my corner.

As we set out to find a home for the book, I wrote down that I wanted an editor who was as passionate about the story as I was. I got my wish in Danielle Marshall, my editor at Lake Union, and the novel's champion at Amazon Publishing. She and fellow editor David Downing believed in the story and pushed me to hone the narrative to its final state. I can't thank either of you enough.

READING GROUP GUIDE

By Mark Sullivan, www.readinggroupguides.com

1. *Beneath a Scarlet Sky* is a work of historical fiction. As you were reading did you feel that the story was authentic? Given that the truth about what actually happened to each character is included at the end, talk about how Mark Sullivan crafted an interesting story while also sticking to the facts.

2. Throughout the book, Sullivan describes horrific scenes filled with human sacrifice, violence, bombings, and ruthless executions. How well do you think he captures the fear in the air? Does he strike the right balance between page-turner and paying homage to the brutal truth?

3. At the beginning of *Beneath a Scarlet Sky*, bombs are dropped on Milan, destroying sections of the city. At this point, Mr. Beltramini's grocery is saved. In talking to Pino Lella, Beltramini says, "If a bomb's coming at you, it's coming at you. You can't go around worrying about it. Just go on doing what you love, and go on enjoying your life." What are your thoughts about his advice? Given what's going on in the world today, do you live in fear of terrorism or war? How do you balance "enjoying your life" in spite of your fear?

4. If you or members of your book discussion group lived through World War II, here or abroad, how do your recollections match the emotions that you are reading here?

5. Father Re enlists Pino's help to usher Italian Jews through the mountains to Switzerland and to safety. Catholics and Jews clearly have different belief systems. In today's world, what do you think it would take for a Christian to help, say, a Muslim in a similar manner in a place of war? Do you think it's possible for such an underground network to exist today?

6. Mrs. Napolitano is a pregnant Italian Jew who successfully escapes over the mountain pass in the dead of winter, in one of the most dramatic passages of the book. She almost dies along the way. If you were in her shoes, do you think you'd be brave enough to attempt the trek? What does it mean to be brave in the face of death?

7. There is a moment when Colonel Rauff, the head of the Gestapo in Milan, helps Father Re's boys corral oxen into a pen. He enjoys himself and almost seems . . . human. What do you think the author intended by choosing to portray such an evil man in this light? Was it effective?

8. Just a few months shy of Pino's eighteenth birthday, his father calls him back to Milan and demands that he enlist instead of waiting to be drafted. The catch? Enlisting with the Germans is safer. He is given a choice and chooses to enlist. Knowing you'd have to work for the enemy, what would you have done if you were in Pino's shoes?

9. Almost by chance, Pino becomes the driver for one of the highest-ranking German officers in Italy. It's a chance for Pino to become a spy, once again risking his life. If you were Pino, would you take advantage of the opportunity, knowing it could put your family in significant danger?

10. Pino's best friend from childhood finds out that he's a Nazi and accuses him of being a traitor. Pino can't, of course, tell him the truth because it would put the mission in danger. What would it take for you to make a similar sacrifice? Is there a cause for a "greater good" that you'd risk anything for?

11. Anna catches Pino in the act of rifling through the Major General Hans Leyers's things. When he tells her the truth, she softens and they kiss. What was your initial reaction during that scene? Did you trust Anna? Why or why not? How did your gut feeling change as the novel progressed? Do you think she deserved her fate?

12. After Pino and Major General Leyers are nearly killed by a British fighter plane, Leyers opens up to Pino and shares a bit about his life. Did this scene change the way you thought about him? Are people 100 percent evil, or is it possible to find humanity or goodness in everyone?

13. Major General Leyers gives Pino advice: "Doing favors. They help wondrously over the course of a lifetime. When you have done men favors, when you look out for others so they can prosper, they owe you. With each favor, you become stronger, more supported. It is a law of nature." How does this statement inform Leyers's character? Do you agree with this statement? Is doing and receiving favors about "owing," or is it about something else?

14. Major General Leyers saves four children from Platform 21 . . . and from death. Why do you think he does this? Out of the goodness of his heart, or is it one of his favors?

15. When the Germans surrender, the Italians turn on each other, and many butcher each other to death, either for doing nothing or for being friendly with the Germans. Are their actions justified? Or is this violence just as condemnable?

16. Toward the end, Pino is given the chance to execute Major General Leyers. He doesn't take it. Why do you think that is? What would you have done?

17. The ending is quite a shocker. Did you see it coming? Why or why not?

18. In certain sections, particularly in conversations between characters, Sullivan writes in a modern style. What effect, if any, does this have on the story or your perception of events? Does he capture the mood of the 1940s?

19. Sullivan provides information about what actually happened to the characters in the novel. After completing the book and finding out their destinies, did you feel each character got what they deserved?

20. In the preface, author Mark Sullivan admits to being suicidal the night he came up with the idea for Beneath a Scarlet Sky. Did that information have any impact on how you perceived the book?

STORY OF A LIFETIME: MARK SULLIVAN ON HIS ODYSSEY TO *BENEATH A SCARLET SKY*

By Alynda Wheat

Triumph and tragedy live side by side in Pino Lella's memories. During World War II, the seventeen-year-old Lella went from normal teenage pursuits in his native Milan to risking his life guiding Jewish refugees to safety over the Italian Alps into Switzerland. After landing a job as driver for a Nazi official with close ties to Adolf Hitler, Lella then became a spy—and fell in love. It's an astonishing story, brought to life in the bestselling *Beneath a Scarlet Sky* by author Mark Sullivan, no stranger to triumph and tragedy himself.

Sullivan, who previously had written mostly thrillers, spent the better part of a decade traveling around Europe to research the story and get to know Lella, age ninety-one, who still lives in Italy. The book, published in May 2017, hit #1 on Amazon Charts' Most Sold list in August and recently was optioned for a movie starring *Spider-Man*'s Tom Holland.

You write in the preface of *Beneath a Scarlet Sky* that you had a road-to-Damascus moment before you wrote the book. What was going on in your life at that point?

My little brother—and best friend—had drunk himself to death, and I'd written a book that tanked in the United States. I was involved in a lingering business dispute that would've taken me and my family to the brink of bankruptcy. And I realized, on a snowy Montana highway driving to Costco, that I was worth more dead than alive. I considered driving into a bridge abutment. I pulled into the Costco parking lot, put my head on the steering wheel, and asked the universe for a story. Three hours later, my wife forces me to go to a dinner party, and this guy starts telling me the snippets of Pino Lella's story.

How did you know this story was for you?

First of all, it was the proximity to the asking, right? I asked, and then there was an answer. But the idea of this Catholic school high in the Alps, where Jews staged up before attempting to cross the Alps in the winter into Switzerland—and the boys were the guides? I was blown away by that. And then the fact that he becomes a spy inside the German High Command, and he does it all at seventeen and eighteen? It's just incredible.

How did you meet Pino?

I call him in Italy and I talk to him. He asked me why I wanted to do this, and I tell him he's a hero. He says, "No, I'm more of a coward," and that only intrigues me more. So I go to Milan, and Pino picks me up in this beat-up Citroën that he drives like a Ferrari. I'm petrified. We go on this three-week odyssey together, where he tells me a version of the story and I start digging, and deeper and more disturbing parts of it keep coming out. It was really an emotional journey for both of us.

Meanwhile, you're writing other books and you have a family. What did they think of this long-gestating mission?

My wife was fascinated by it. Pino ended up coming to our house. My sons had met him. They listened to him describe the story for years. They were as fascinated with it as I was. I think they thought I was never going to get it done. But now they are thrilled.

What was the most rewarding scene to write?

The thing I loved writing the most was the scene where Pino carries Mrs. Napolitano on his back and skis them down the mountain. I just loved that scene. I loved writing it. I loved everything about it. The way Pino described it was, "Yeah, I put people on my back and skied them down the mountain. It was no big deal." And I'm going, "OK, buddy. I'm a great skier, and probably couldn't have done that at seventeen."

Wait, that was real?

Yeah! He skied down a mountain with a woman on his back! Definitely. That was one of the original things we talked about. And there was an avalanche. And somebody blew up a stove with a grenade. All of that happened.

No wonder this thing is being adapted into a movie starring Tom Holland. Are you freaking out?

Yes. In one sense I am, and then the other sense is, of course it's being turned into a movie. This whole story has been one serendipitous event after another.

What do you hope happens to readers after they finish the last page?

I hope they realize that the human spirit is infinite. That it has remarkable reserves. To paraphrase Pino toward the end of the book, no matter how flawed, we have to be thankful for the miracle of every moment. Because it is a miracle.

What's next, Mark Sullivan?

I have no idea. I really don't. I've got some basic ideas, but I haven't been seized by them yet. At this point in my life—I'll be sixty in 2018—I'm writing stories from the heart. I love every single one of the thrillers and mystery stories that I wrote, but I've seen what a story like this can do, and that's the kind of story I want to write. I want stories that move and uplift. And I'll find one. I know I will.

Alynda Wheat is a senior writer for Amazon. She has previously written for People, Entertainment Weekly, *and* Fortune. Beneath a Scarlet Sky *is published by Lake Union Publishing, an imprint of Amazon Publishing. This interview has been edited for length and clarity.*

ABOUT THE AUTHOR

Mark Sullivan is the acclaimed author of eighteen novels, including the #1 *New York Times* bestselling Private series, which he writes with James Patterson. Mark has received numerous awards for his writing, including the WHSmith Fresh Talent Award, and his works have been named a *New York Times* Notable Book and a *Los Angeles Times* Best Book of the Year. He grew up in Medfield, Massachusetts, and graduated from Hamilton College with a BA in English before working as a volunteer in the Peace Corps in Niger, West Africa. Upon his return to the United States, he earned a graduate degree from the Medill School of Journalism at Northwestern University and began a career in investigative reporting. An avid skier and adventurer, he lives with his wife in Bozeman, Montana, where he remains grateful for the miracle of every moment.